The Spymistress

The Spymistress

a novel

JENNIFER CHIAVERINI

**Doubleday Large Print
Home Library Edition**

DUTTON

DUTTON
Published by the Penguin Group
Penguin Group (USA) LLC
375 Hudson Street
New York, New York 10014

USA | Canada | UK | Ireland | Australia | New Zealand |
India | South Africa | China
A Penguin Random House Company

REGISTERED TRADEMARK—MARCA REGISTRADA

ISBN 978-1-62490-844-6

Printed in the United States of America

To Marty, Nick, and Michael,
with love and gratitude

The Spymistress

Confidential. Hd. Qrs. 18th
Army Corps,
Dept. Of Va., and N. C.,
Fortress Monroe, Dec. 19, 1863
Commander Boutelle, U. S. Coast
Survey Office,
Washington, D. C.

My dear Boutelle:

You will find enclosed a letter from a dear friend of yours in Richmond. I am informed by the bearer that Miss Van Lieu is a true Union woman as true as steel. She sent me a bouquet, so says the letter carrier.

Now, I much want a correspondent in Richmond, one who will write me of course without name or description of the writer, and she need only incur the risk of dropping an ordinary letter by flag of truce in the Post Office at Richmond, directed to a name at the North. Her messenger thinks Miss Van Lieu will be glad to do it.

I can place my first and only letter in her hands for her directions, but I also place the man's life in her hands who delivers the letter. Is it safe so to do? Will Miss Van Lieu be willing to either correspond herself or find me such a correspondent? I could pay large rewards, but from what I hear of her I should prefer not to do it, as I think she would be actuated to do what she does by patriotic motives only.

I wish therefore you would write me, confidentially—and as so much is depending, in the strictest secrecy, what you think of the matter. Of course you will readily see that I can furnish means by which a very commonplace letter on family affairs will read very differently when I see it.

Truly yours,
Benj. F. Butler

Chapter One

APRIL 1861

The Van Lew mansion in Richmond's fashionable Church Hill neighborhood had not hosted a wedding gala in many a year, and if the bride-to-be did not emerge from her attic bedroom soon, Lizzie feared it might not that day either.

Turning away from the staircase, Lizzie resisted the urge to check her engraved pocket watch for the fifth time in as many minutes and instead stepped outside onto the side portico, abandoning the mansion to her family, servants, and the apparently bashful bridal party ensconced in the servants' quarters. Surely Mary Jane wasn't having second thoughts. She adored Wilson Bowser, and just that morning she had declared him the most excellent man of her acquaintance. A young woman in love would not leave such a man standing at the altar.

Perhaps Mary Jane was merely nervous, or a button had come off her gown, or her flowers were not quite perfect. As hostess, Lizzie ought to go and see, but a strange reluctance held her back. Earlier that morning, when Mary Jane's friends had arrived—young women of color like Mary Jane herself, some enslaved, some free—Lizzie had felt awkward and unwanted among them, a sensation unfamiliar and particularly unsettling to experience in her own home. None of the girls had spoken impudently to her, but after greeting her politely they had encircled Mary Jane and led her off to her attic bedroom, turning their backs upon Lizzie as if they had quite forgotten she was there. And so she was left to wait, alone and increasingly curious.

Grasping the smooth, whitewashed railing, Lizzie gazed out upon the sun-splashed gardens, where the alluring fragrance of magnolia drifted on the balmy air above the neatly pruned hedgerows. Across the street, a shaft of sunlight bathed the steeple of Saint John's Church in a rosy glow like a benediction from heaven, blessing the bride and groom, blessing the vows they would soon take. It was a perfect spring day in Richmond, the sort of April morning that inspired bad poetry and impulsive declarations of affection best kept to oneself. Lizzie could almost forget that not far away, in the heart of the city, a furious debate was raging, a searing prelude to the vote that would determine whether her beloved Virginia would follow the Southern cotton states out of the fragmenting nation.

Despite the clamor and frenzy that had surged in Richmond in the weeks leading up to the secession convention, Lizzie staunchly believed that reason, pragmatism, and loyalty would triumph in the end. Unionist delegates outnumbered secessionist fire-eaters two to one, and Virginians were too proud of their heritage as the birthplace of Washington, Jefferson, and Madison to leave the nation their honored forebears had founded.

Still, she had to admit that John Lewis's increasing pessimism troubled her. Mr. Lewis, a longtime family friend serving as a delegate from Rockingham County, had been the Van Lews' guest throughout the convention, and his ominous reports of shouting matches erupting in closed sessions made her uneasy. So too did the gathering of a splinter group of adamant secessionists only a block and a half away from the Capitol, although outwardly she made light of the so-called Spontaneous People's Convention. "How can a convention be both spontaneous and arranged well in advance, with time for the sending and accepting of invitations?" she had mocked, but the tentative, worried smiles her mother and brother had given her in reply were but a small reward.

Although Lizzie managed such shows of levity from time to time, she could not ignore the disquieting signs that the people of Richmond were declaring themselves for the Confederacy in ever greater numbers. Less than a week before, when word reached the city of the Union garrison's surrender at Fort Sumter in Charleston, neighbors and strangers alike had thronged into the streets, shouting and crying and flinging their hats into the air. Impromptu parades had formed and bands had played spirited renditions of "Dixie" and "The Marseillaise." Down by the riverside at the Tredegar Iron Works, thousands had cheered as a newly cast cannon fired off a thunderous salute to the victors. Lizzie had been dismayed to see, waving here and there above the heads of the crowd, home-sewn flags boasting the South Carolina palmetto or the three stripes and seven stars of the Confederacy. But when the crowd marched to the governor's mansion, instead of giving them the speech they demanded, John Letcher urged them to all go home.

Lizzie had been heartened by the governor's refusal to cower before the mob, and she prayed that his example would help other wavering Unionists find their courage and remember their duty. But two days later, word came to Richmond that President Lincoln had called for seventy-five thousand militia to put down the rebellion—and Virginia would be required to provide her share. Many Virginians who had been ambivalent about secession until then had become outraged by the president's demand that they go to war against their fellow Southerners, and they defiantly joined the clamor of voices shouting for Virginia to leave the Union. John Minor Botts, a Whig and perhaps the most outspoken and steadfast Unionist in Richmond politics, had called the mobilization proclamation "the most unfortunate state paper that ever issued from any executive since the establishment of the government."

But would it prove to be the straw that broke the camel's back? Lizzie could not allow herself to believe it.

"Rational men will not cave in to the demands of the mob," Lizzie had argued to Mr. Lewis that very morning. Like herself, he was a Virginia native, born in 1818, and a Whig. Unlike her, he was married, had children, and could vote. "They will heed the demands of their consciences and the law."

A few crumbs of Hannah's light, buttery biscuits fell free from Mr. Lewis's dark beard as he shook his head. "A man who fears for his life may be willing to consider a different interpretation of the law."

At that, a shadow of worry had passed

over Mother's face. "You don't mean there have been threats of violence?"

"It pains me to distress you, but indeed, yes, and almost daily," Mr. Lewis had replied. "Those of us known to be faithful to the Union run a gauntlet of insults, abuse, and worse whenever we enter or depart the Capitol."

"Goodness." Mother had shuddered and hunched her thin shoulders as if warding off an icy wind. Petite and elegant, with gray eyes and an enviably fair complexion even at almost sixty-three years of age, she was ever the thoughtful hostess. "You must allow us to send Peter and William along with you from now on. They will see to your safety."

"Thank you, Madam, but I must decline. I won't allow my enemies to believe they've intimidated me."

"When the vote is called, wiser heads will prevail," Lizzie had insisted, as much to reassure herself and Mother as to persuade Mr. Lewis. "Virginians are too proud a people to let bullies rule the day."

"As you say, Miss Van Lew. Nothing would please me more than to be proven wrong."

Remembering his somber words, Lizzie gazed off to the west toward the political heart of the city, scarcely seeing the historic church, the gracious homes, and the well-tended gardens arrayed so beautifully before her. Instead she imagined the view from the Capitol gallery, where she had often sat and observed the machinery of government, and she wished she could be there to witness the contentious debate for herself. Of course, that was not possible. The gallery had been shut to visitors for the closed session, and Lizzie could not miss Mary Jane's wedding. She could only wait for news and hope that her faith in the men of Virginia had not been misplaced.

The scrape of the door over stone warned her that she was no longer alone. "Your mother has come down," announced her sister-in-law, Mary, in a peevish tone Lizzie found particularly grating.

"Very good," she said briskly, turning around. "And the bride?"

"I haven't seen her, and I haven't inquired." Mary spoke airily and tossed her wheat-brown hair, but her frown betrayed her annoyance. "I don't understand why the family is obliged to make such a fuss over a colored servant. A wedding service at Saint John's and a luncheon on our own piazza! Why shouldn't they exchange vows at the African Baptist Church or whatever it's called, you know the one I mean—"

"I do know the one you mean." Lizzie fixed her with a level gaze and a sweet smile. "It's a charming church, but Mary Jane is family—"

"Oh, Lizzie, don't be sentimental. She's not, not really."

"Mary Jane is family," Lizzie repeated, coolly emphatic. "And as a member of the Van Lew family, she has every right and expectation to be married at Saint John's."

Mary shook her head, exasperated. "You have the oddest notions." Mary was sixteen years younger than Lizzie and a good two inches taller, with delicate features, wide brown eyes, and a petulant pout gentlemen seemed to find adorable. Lizzie's brother certainly had, until he had discovered that her pout heralded spats and tantrums, after which he had learned to dread its appearance.

Lizzie managed a tight smile. "Yes, I do. I am, after all, the resident eccentric. Please don't feel obliged to join in our celebration if it offends your sense of propriety. I'd be delighted to ask Caroline to send up a plate to your room, a safe distance away from our fuss and frivolity."

If Caroline included a tumbler of whiskey on the tray, Lizzie thought witheringly, Mary would be happier still.

"I'll ask Caroline myself," Mary retorted, and flounced back inside. "It would be just like you to forget and allow me to go hungry."

Through the open door, Lizzie watched Mary storm past Mother, who stood in the foyer clad in her shawl and bonnet. Mother's gaze followed her daughter-in-law until Mary disappeared down the hall, and then she turned to Lizzie, eyebrows raised. Lizzie smiled weakly and shrugged, but Mother was not fooled, and lingering on the portico would only delay the well-deserved reprimand.

"Lizzie, dear," Mother chided gently when Lizzie joined her inside. "What did you do this time?"

"I merely pointed out that Mary needn't attend the wedding feast if she finds it so terribly inappropriate."

"You spoke without thinking."

"Yes, I realize that now. I should have added that my nieces are still very much welcome."

"That's not what I meant and you know it." Mother shook her head, her expression both fond and regretful. "I believe sometimes you go out of your way to provoke her. For your brother's sake, won't you try harder to practice forbearance? You know how much it pains John to see the women he loves at odds."

Lizzie did know. She drew herself up, inhaling deeply and quashing the pangs of guilt that pricked her whenever she earned her mother's disapproval. She wished she could be as good and gracious as Mother, but what seemed to come naturally to Mother required constant effort for Lizzie. "For John's sake and for yours, I will try harder. I will even apologize to Mary when I next see her."

"Apologize?" A smile quirked in the corners of Mother's mouth. "She may faint from shock."

"Then I'll be sure to guide her to the sofa before I speak."

A sudden burst of laughter from above drew their attention, and in unison they glanced to the top of the stairs, where they discovered Mary Jane surrounded by her attendants.

"At last, the bride descends," Lizzie remarked.

"And none too soon," said Mother, sighing with delight. "Oh, isn't she lovely?"

She was indeed, but Lizzie found herself suddenly too moved to say so. Mary Jane's smile was radiant, her coffee-and-cream complexion luminous as she descended the grand staircase in a gown of ivory linen trimmed with flounces of eyelet lace at the hem, throat, and wrists. One of Mary Jane's friends must have lent her the amber necklace and earbobs adorning her graceful head and neck, for Lizzie did not recognize them. Her cheeks were flushed with excitement, but her gaze was calm and steady, preternaturally wise for a young woman of scarcely twenty-five.

By the time the bridal party reached the foot of the stairs, Lizzie had found her voice. "My dear Mary Jane." She hurried to embrace her. "You are a vision. You look exactly as a bride should."

"Thank you, Miss Lizzie." Mary Jane's voice was low and mellifluous, but her smile, as ever, hinted at sardonic mischief. She was well practiced at using that smile to her benefit—and at concealing it where it might bring her unwanted attention. "I hope Wilson thinks so."

"He's a fool if he don't," one of her friends declared, provoking laughter from the others.

Wilson Bowser was no fool, Lizzie reflected as her brother John appeared to escort the bride across the street to the church. Wilson was freeborn, tall, and dark-skinned, with a broad chest and strong shoulders earned from years of working on the railroad. He loved Mary Jane, and better yet, he seemed to respect her. He was not the man Lizzie would have chosen for Mary Jane, but he was a good, decent man, and as likely to be faithful as any other. Lizzie's greatest concern about the match was that Mary Jane, who had been educated in the North and had worked as a missionary in Liberia, might eventually become disenchanted with Wilson, who had no education to speak of and had never traveled more than ten miles from Richmond. But who could say whether such disparities doomed a marriage to failure?

After all, on the day her brother and Mary had wed, they had seemed an ideal match despite the difference in their ages. Regrettably, a mere seven years later, anyone could see that their marriage was utterly joyless, except for the two delightful daughters their union had produced.

If a match that had once seemed so promising could take such a dismal turn, who could predict whether Mary Jane and Wilson would end up content or miserable? Certainly not a spinster of forty-three who had last enjoyed the heady flush of romance more than two decades before.

Absently, Lizzie touched the silver locket at her throat, then slipped her hand into her pocket, finding reassurance in the familiar weight and coolness and patterns of delicate engraving of her pocket watch, another gift. They were her most cherished possessions—mementos of her youth, treasures from a faded age.

Perhaps Mary was right to call her sentimental.

Beckoned from their tasks by the sound of voices, the servants had joined the family and the wedding party in the foyer—Caroline, the cook, who assured Mother that all was ready for the luncheon; Hannah Roane, the nurse, who had brought her two young charges clad in their Sunday best, although their mother was nowhere in sight; Hannah's grown sons, William the butler and Peter the groom; Judy, who was officially Mother's maid, though she assisted all the Van Lew women with their dresses and hair; and old Uncle Nelson, proud of his title of gardener although in recent months his rheumatism had kept him from all but the lightest work. The Van Lews employed other servants, of course, kitchen assistants and laundresses and housecleaners, but they lived out, and since the bride knew them only in passing, it had not seemed appropriate to invite them.

Together the cheerful party left the mansion and strolled down the block and across the street to Saint John's Episcopal Church. The front doors had been adorned with magnolia blossoms, and inside the vestibule, more friends and family of the happy couple waited to greet the bride and her retinue. Others had seated themselves in the rows of wooden pews, and as Lizzie escorted her mother to their places, she glanced down the aisle and suppressed a smile at the sight of Wilson standing up front between the minister and his best man, rocking back and forth on his heels, his hands clasped behind his back—and, if Lizzie was not mistaken, a sheen of nervous perspiration on his brow. Searching for his bride, he happened to look Lizzie's way, and when she gave him an encouraging smile, he managed a perfunctory nod and a weak grin of his own.

Within moments his anxious demeanor gave way to elation as the organist struck up a triumphant march and Mary Jane came down the aisle on Uncle Nelson's arm. Lizzie and Mother exchanged a look of surprise—the wedding had begun, and John and the girls had not joined them in their family pew. Perhaps Annie and Eliza had gotten out of hand and he was sorting it out, or perhaps he had been called to the hardware store on urgent business, or perhaps—Lizzie's heart thumped—perhaps Mr. Lewis had sent unfortunate news from the Capitol. But peering over her shoulder, she glimpsed John seated in the back pew between Annie and Hannah, who held little Eliza on her lap.

Suddenly Mother rested her hand upon Lizzie's, so Lizzie quickly turned around to face front again, but her mother's apprehensive frown immediately told her that some other worry troubled her, not her daughter's fidgeting in church.

"Perhaps they should have married another day," Mother whispered, something she never did after the minister stood at the pulpit.

"Why not today?" Lizzie whispered back, and with a teasing smile, added, "'Marry on Monday for health, Tuesday for wealth, Wednesday the best day of all—'"

"No, that's not what I meant." Mother's gaze was fixed on the bride and groom, who were gazing at one another with shining eyes, their hands clasped, fingers intertwined. "Should they marry today, in such troubled times, with the vote for secession coming any moment? It seems an inauspicious day, bearing ill omens for their future happiness."

"No, Mother," Lizzie said, her voice low and gentle. "You have it quite in reverse. Think instead of what this wedding portends for the vote. Today, in this sacred place, where Patrick Henry declared 'Give me liberty or give me death,' we celebrate **union**."

A warm smile lit up Mother's soft, lined face, and she thanked Lizzie with a gentle squeeze of her hand.

The ceremony was lovely—simple, reverent, and heartfelt—and as the congregation's voices joined in the final hymn, Lizzie felt her spirits rising. The wedding party, friends, and family showered the newlyweds with rice and laughter as they departed the church, and then all made their way to the Van Lew mansion, the bells of Saint John's ringing out the happy news for all of Richmond to hear.

Caroline had never before produced a more delicious feast, or so the guests declared—asparagus soup, halibut cutlets, roasted ham, stewed spinach, French peas, brandy peaches, and plum wedding cake with raisins and sugar icing—all savored in the pleasant shade of the Van Lews' grand, two-story piazza, with its imposing columns and commanding views of the James River. Thanks to Mother's tender care and Uncle Nelson's diligent assistance, the gardens were in their full springtime glory, fragrant and bursting with color as they cascaded in graceful terraces down the hill toward the river in the distance far below. The conversation was merry, the happy couple was appropriately feted and teased, and no one dwelt too long on the subject of politics, deferring worry for another day. Mary did not put in an appearance, but six-year-old Annie danced and frolicked on the grass like a little bird, and sweet Eliza, Mother's namesake, claimed Lizzie's lap before soup was served and refused to relinquish it until after the cake.

"She never wanders far from her favorite auntie," Mother remarked when Eliza wriggled down from Lizzie's lap to inspect a butterfly that had alighted upon the nearest tall white column.

"Someday she will," Lizzie replied, as the butterfly flitted away, sending the young girl scampering back to her. "She'll marry and move away, as Anna did."

Her younger sister had wanted to attend the wedding, but she and her husband, a physician in Philadelphia, had decided that it was too far to travel for a brief visit, especially considering that political turmoil might disrupt train schedules and delay her return indefinitely. As soon as Virginia voted to remain in the Union, once its allegiance was confirmed, Anna could visit again, and perhaps bring her children. Lizzie had not seen them in ages and she missed them terribly.

"Forgive me, Lizzie, but I can't help but wonder if, for you, occasions such as this inspire more desolation than joy."

"For me?" Lizzie echoed, surprised. "Do I seem unhappy? I know I tend to scowl when I'm lost in thought. Mary Jane and John tease me about it, which does nothing to help me break the habit, more shame on them."

"You make no outward sign of melancholy," Mother replied, "but it would be only natural if a wedding celebrated in our own home might turn your thoughts to . . . what might have been."

Of course. Lizzie resisted the urge to touch the locket, the pocket watch. More than twenty years before, her beloved had given her the locket upon the occasion of their betrothal, and after a swift, devastating fever had claimed his life, his heartbroken parents had given her the watch, elegantly engraved with their intertwined initials. He had intended it as a wedding gift, but he had gone to his grave before they could enjoy a single day of nuptial bliss. After her time of mourning had ended and she had put off her garments of black crepe, Lizzie had known that she would never meet his equal, and thus that she would never marry.

"Don't worry on my account, Mother," Lizzie assured her, fighting to keep the tremor from her voice. "I am content, living here with you and my brother and nieces. I've witnessed far too many happy women become quiet, lonely wives to yearn for their state simply to escape the dreaded honorific of spinster. I'm happy to have known one true marriage—yours and Father's—an egalitarian union based on love, loyalty, and respect. It's enough for me to know that such a thing exists."

Tears filled her mother's gray eyes. "If I could truly believe that, if I could know that you are happy—"

"I **am** happy, Mother. I'm surrounded by family and friends, I reside comfortably in a beautiful home, and I need give no account of how I spend my hours to any man. That is reason enough to rejoice in my spinsterhood." Smiling, Lizzie rose, took her mother's hands, and lifted her to her feet. "And as Miss Austen wrote, 'It is poverty only which makes celibacy contemptible to a generous public! A single woman, with a very narrow income, must be a ridiculous, disagreeable, old maid! The proper sport of boys and girls; but a single woman, of good fortune, is always respectable, and may be as sensible and pleasant as anybody else.'"

"Oh, daughter, no one could ever consider you contemptible." Then Mother caught herself. "If you must emulate one of Miss Austen's heroines, could you not choose one more admirable than flighty, meddling Emma? Elizabeth Bennet, perhaps? Jane Fairfax?"

Because it was Mother who asked, Lizzie laughed and agreed.

As the afternoon waned, the party drew to a close and the guests departed, although some, Lizzie suspected, would surely reappear, uninvited, at the newlyweds' home later that evening to give them a raucous sendoff to the bridal chamber. When a light rain began to fall, Lizzie offered Mary Jane and Wilson the use of her carriage, and she insisted upon accompanying them home. She had already begun to feel Mary Jane's absence in the household, and she wanted to postpone their farewells as long as possible.

"You don't need to come out in this storm, Miss," Wilson said as Peter brought the carriage around.

"Careful, Wilson," Lizzie said archly, "or I'll think you don't want my company. This is hardly a storm. It would be generous to call it a drizzle."

Resigned, Wilson assisted her into the carriage, and then helped his bride, and soon they were off, rumbling over the rain-slicked cobblestone streets northwest through the heart of the city to the colored neighborhood, about a mile from the Capitol. Mother had sent Mary Jane's belongings ahead, and as they rode along, Lizzie queried the newlyweds about their arrangements and offered last-minute advice at an increasingly rapid pace the closer they came to Mary Jane's new home. There was so much more she urgently wanted to teach the young woman, so many lessons she had overlooked in the frenzy of wedding preparations and political debate, but when the horses halted in front of a charming row house on Leigh Street, Lizzie reluctantly accepted that the time for guidance and instruction had passed.

"You're going to be fine," she said as Wilson helped his bride down from the carriage, more to reassure herself than anyone else. "You are both going to be just fine."

Mary Jane reached through the window to press her hand. "Thank you, Miss Lizzie. Thank you for a perfectly beautiful day."

"The pleasure was all mine, Mary Jane. Oh, my goodness," she said with a start. "You're Mary Jane Bowser now. Mrs. Bowser. Well, how nice. A new name to help you keep one step ahead of the authorities."

Rainwater trickled from Mary Jane's bonnet and fell upon the carriage seat as she leaned closer. "That was my plan all along, you know," she murmured conspiratorially. "This may prove to be my cleverest ruse yet." Then her merriment faded. "I think the authorities will soon be too preoccupied with other concerns to worry about

one incorrigibly willful colored girl who refuses to leave Virginia."

Lizzie felt the heavy weight of responsibility anew. She had sent the clever, intelligent girl to Philadelphia, knowing full well
that free colored people who traveled north
to be educated were forbidden by law to
return to Virginia. She had assumed that
Mary Jane would not want to come back
to the land of slavery after enjoying Northern liberty. She should have realized that
the pull of home and family and friends
would prove too strong to resist. "You were
born here. You're a free woman, and you
shouldn't be banished from the land of
your birth. It's a ridiculous law."

"But go she must—out of this rain, though
no farther," Wilson broke in, drawing the
collar of his coat closed and offering Mary
Jane his arm. "Would you like to come in,
Miss Lizzie?"

As much as Lizzie wanted to inspect
their new residence and reassure herself
that Mary Jane would be safe and comfortable there, she suspected the newlyweds
would prefer to cross the threshold alone.
So she thanked Wilson but declined.

The couple bade her good-bye and darted indoors. "Straight home, Miss Lizzie?" Peter called from the driver's seat, rain dripping off his hat and long oilskin coat.

"No, Peter, let's take the long way, around the Capitol."

He nodded and chirruped to the horses. The wedding had provided a few hours of welcome distraction from political turmoil, but it had also left Lizzie craving news, and she could not wait for Mr. Lewis to return to the mansion later that evening after the closed session concluded—or early the next morning, if debate ran overlong. A quick tour of the blocks surrounding the Capitol would allow Lizzie to take her measure of the city's temper, even if she only observed her fellow citizens through the window of a passing carriage.

The rain had lessened, and as they approached the city center, Lizzie observed men gathered on street corners and hurrying down the sidewalks in a state of distracted agitation. The closer they drew to the Capitol, the thicker the crowds became, and a chilly uneasiness settled upon her when she realized that an electric air of celebration filled the air. She heard shouts of "Virginia!" and "Hail the Old Dominion!" but that told her nothing; the most ardent secessionist could proclaim his loyalty to their fair state as loudly as she herself could, with an entirely different meaning. But then she saw them again, the flags of rebellion—the palmetto of South Carolina, the dreadful three stripes and seven stars of the Confederacy. And then the Capitol came into view, and atop its flagpole, where the Stars and Stripes had once boldly waved, flew the flag of the Confederate States of America.

"Oh, no, no," she murmured. It could not be. The delegates could not have voted already, and they could not have voted in favor of secession. It was impossible, unthinkable—and yet all around the carriage, men were flinging their hats into the air, women wept for joy at the sight of Confederate flags being hoisted on high, boys whooped and marched and played at soldier with sticks for rifles. Somewhere unseen, a band struck up "Dixie," and a more euphoric and vengeful rendition she had never heard.

Richmond had gone mad. All around,

her fellow citizens, neighbors, acquaintances were celebrating their disloyal repudiation of their country. What were they thinking? How would secession bring them anything but sorrow and death?

Balling her trembling hands into fists, she knocked on the carriage wall for Peter's attention. "Let's go home," she called to him, her voice shaking, her vision blurring with tears. "I've seen enough."

Chapter Two

APRIL 1861

Peter swiftly turned the carriage toward Church Hill, and when they reached home and he helped her descend, he looked as shocked and apprehensive as she felt. When he offered to get his brother and return to the central district to gather what news they could, she did not want to let him go for fear of his safety, but his assurances that they would be careful and her own urgent desire for news overcame her objections.

"Be careful," she told the brothers as they headed out—William, the elder of the two, slim, bespectacled, with a quiet manner and impeccable courtesy that ignorant people mistook for deference, and Peter, tall and strong, his elder brother's greatest admirer, unfailingly gentle yet unyielding with the animals in his care. "The crowds are in a frenzy, and they could turn on you without the slightest provocation. Do you have your passes?"

"Yes, Miss Lizzie," said Peter. "Don't you worry about us."

"We'll learn all we can," William promised.

"Don't be gone long," Lizzie urged. "Find out the results of the vote and hurry back." When they nodded, she waved them off before she changed her mind. As she hurried inside, she prayed they would return safely before Hannah realized her sons had left. If only Mary Jane could have gone with them. With her prodigious memory, she could scan the records of the closed session and recite them verbatim later, but if venturing out into a secessionist mob was unsafe for the Roane brothers, it was doubly unsafe for a woman.

Fortunately, Hannah was busy settling little Eliza and Annie down for their naps when her sons departed, and after that, she went to the kitchen to sew and gossip with Caroline. Since the mansion was so grand, three stories tall and fourteen rooms, the absence even of one's own sons could easily go unnoticed for an hour or two. They were grown men, perfectly capable of looking out for themselves, and they should have been free men too, but Lizzie's father had thwarted Mother's plans to give them liberty. As Father's illness had progressed, he must have suspected that Mother and Lizzie intended to free the family's slaves upon his death, for he had secretly added a codicil to his will allowing Mother the use of the slaves for the duration of her life but forbidding her to free or to sell them. Obeying the law if not the spirit of his decree, Mother, Lizzie, and John paid their servants wages and allowed them to come and go as they pleased, as any paid servant would. Some of the Van Lews' slaves lived elsewhere in the city, and months might pass between occasions when Lizzie saw them, when they were obliged to return to the Van Lew residence for updated passes so they would not be thrown into the Negro jail for vagrancy. They were slaves in name only, but the indignity of it, the profound unfairness, grated at Lizzie. She could only imagine how it made Peter, William, and the others feel.

Scarcely more than an hour after they departed, the brothers returned, grim-faced and breathless, as if they had been pursued. Taking her mother's arm, Lizzie ushered them into the library, glancing over her shoulder to be sure that Mary would not observe them. She would no doubt welcome the bitter news, and if she clapped her little hands and cheered, Lizzie could not trust herself to hold her tongue.

"They gone and done it," Peter reported after Lizzie shut the door behind them. "They voted, and Virginia's out of the Union."

"Oh, my word," said Mother, sinking into a chair by the fireplace.

Lizzie patted her mother's shoulder absently, her gaze fixed on the brothers. Perhaps there was yet hope. Whatever measure the secession convention had passed that day would still need to be ratified, and if enough reasonable men voted against it— "The ordinance must have passed by a very narrow margin to have passed at all."

William shook his head. "Not even close. Eighty-eight to fifty-five."

"How can this be?" Lizzie exclaimed. "There were more Unionists than secessionists among the delegates. For all his grave predictions, even Mr. Lewis acknowledged that."

"Dozens of 'em must've had a change of heart," said Peter. "They say the old governor Mr. Wise made a fiery speech right before the vote. Maybe that's what did it."

"But there have been countless speeches already." Dizzy, heartsick, Lizzie grasped the tall back of her mother's chair to steady herself. "Mr. Wise is a fine orator, I grant you, but how could one more bit of rhetoric cause men to abandon all reason?"

"It wasn't just powerful speechifying," said William, "or the old horse pistol some say Mr. Wise was waving around while he spoke. There's more to it, something we couldn't quite figure out. So many rumors flying around, it's hard to tell what's real. Something about captured federal fortresses."

"You mean Fort Sumter, of course," said Mother.

"No, not Sumter, not anything in South

Carolina," said Peter. "Here, right here in Virginia."

Lizzie went cold. Mother gasped and pressed her fingertips to her lips. "That's all you know?" Lizzie's voice sounded distant to her own ears. "You heard no mention of any specific cities, fortresses, anything?"

"I'm sorry, Miss Lizzie," said William. "That's all we got. Maybe if we went back out—"

"No, absolutely not. Your mother would never forgive me." Night had fallen, and it was simply too dangerous to send the Roane brothers out again past curfew, passes or no passes. "You've done well. We're better informed now than we were before, but—" She steeled herself, suddenly glimpsing a dark and uncertain future that had been awaiting her all along, though she had stubbornly refused to see it. "But in the days to come, we must all endeavor to sharpen our ears and our memories."

When the brothers nodded, Lizzie forced a smile, thanked them, and sent them off to the kitchen for their supper. Then she began to pace from the fireplace to the door to the window. A glance outside revealed only the faint glow of lights to the west, where bonfires and torches and effigies were surely burning. "Mr. Lewis will know more," she said, letting the lace curtain fall, obscuring the glass. "When he returns, he'll tell us what happened within the Capitol today, and perhaps things will not look so bleak."

"Or perhaps they'll look much worse." Two deep creases of worry had formed between Mother's brows. "He's late. I pray he hasn't come to any harm."

Lizzie glanced at the clock on the mantelpiece, and her heart skipped a beat when she discovered that Mr. Lewis was an hour overdue. "I'll ask Caroline to keep dinner warm," she said, as calmly as if a ruined meal were the greatest of her concerns. "I'm sure he's fine, merely delayed, and that's certainly understandable given all this—this nonsense." She waved a hand toward the west, to the Capitol, where madness apparently ruled the day.

Another hour passed in anxious waiting. When Caroline protested that the chicken would only grow drier and the salad more wilted as the evening wore on,

Mother agreed that the family should sit down at the table. They hoped Mr. Lewis would join them belatedly, but the meal was finished and the dishes cleared away, and still he did not return.

Long after Lizzie's nieces were tucked into bed and Mother too had bade her good night, Lizzie sat alone in the library with an unopened book of poetry on her lap and a cup of tea cooling on the table by her side, brooding. At the sound of the front door opening, she tossed the book aside, leaped to her feet, and reached the foyer just as William was helping Mr. Lewis out of his coat. "Thank heavens you're safe," she greeted him.

"My sincere apologies for worrying you," said Mr. Lewis, removing his hat and handing it to William. "I would have sent a message, but there wasn't a messenger to be had."

Lizzie took his arm and led him to the dining room, where Caroline quickly appeared with a remarkably appetizing plate considering how long Mr. Lewis's dinner had been kept for him. Lizzie held back her questions as long as she could to allow her ravenous guest to eat, but when his pace slowed a trifle, she said, "How did this happen?"

"I warned you that it might."

"Yes, and I thought you were being ridiculously pessimistic, and for that I apologize." She reached across the table and lay her hand on his arm. "Mr. Lewis, don't mince words out of concern that you will worry me. I'm not easily frightened, and nothing you say could be worse than what I imagine."

Mr. Lewis sat in quiet contemplation, placed his hand over hers for a moment, then took up his knife and began to butter a slice of bread. "In the hours leading up to the vote, I was told that if I failed to vote for secession, I would never leave Richmond alive."

Lizzie's heart thumped, but she held on to her composure. "And yet here you are, safe and sound. I assume you intend to leave the city soon, before they can make good on their threats."

He regarded her with an expression of surprise and gratitude. "You didn't ask me how I voted."

"I don't need to." She managed a smile. "You of all people would never allow the

Intimidation Convention to sway your vote. I can only assume that a great many other delegates lacked your courage."

"At the crucial moment, their fear for their own safety outweighed their love of country." Mr. Lewis's gloom deepened, and he pushed his plate aside. "Any man who dared profess love for the United States was jeered and stoned whenever he set foot outside the Capitol. We were told we must vote for secession or the streets of Richmond would run with blood."

Lizzie sighed and sat back in her chair. If only John Minor Botts had not been excluded from the convention. He would have rallied the Unionists. He would not have allowed them to falter. "I heard a rumor that federal arms have been captured in Virginia."

"It grieves me to tell you that's no mere rumor. And because of it, the vote was lost." Mr. Lewis rested his arms on the table, his shoulders slumped in exhaustion, all formality momentarily forgotten. "For weeks, perhaps longer, our erstwhile governor and his fellow radicals have been demanding that Governor Letcher seize all federal posts in Virginia before the secession vote. He refused, again and again."

"More credit to him," said Lizzie staunchly, remembering how he had sent the celebrating crowds home after the Confederates captured Fort Sumter.

"Don't praise him just yet. Mr. Wise must have grown impatient with Governor Letcher's delays, because he took matters into his own hands."

"What? But how? What do you mean?"

"Wise ordered the Virginia militia to seize the federal arsenal at Harpers Ferry and the navy yard at Gosport across the river from Norfolk. When it was all said and done, Governor Letcher had no choice but to endorse the actions after the fact."

"He certainly did have a choice," Lizzie protested, stunned. So much of her hopes for Richmond's future depended upon Governor Letcher's faithfulness to the Union, which seemed to have crumbled. "He could have denounced Mr. Wise's treasonous actions. He could have had him arrested."

"I don't know that he could have. All was bedlam in the Capitol, Miss Van Lew—anger surging, tempers flaring, voices rising. If

Letcher had given the order, I don't know who would have dared to carry it out." He inhaled deeply, straightening in his chair, interlacing his long, bony fingers on the tabletop. "Near the end of the session, Mr. Wise took the floor and made the most astonishing, the most supernaturally excited speech I've ever witnessed."

"We heard something of it," said Lizzie. "I understand he brandished a horse pistol."

Mr. Lewis nodded. "Brandished it, then placed it on the desk before him, then lashed out at us Unionists with supernatural fury. When he announced what the militia had done, the chamber rang with wild applause. He seemed charged with electricity, the hair standing straight up from his head. I've never witnessed anything like it."

He fell silent, his gaze far away. "All around me I could feel my friends' courage wavering, but I could not hope to rally their spirits against such a powerful display. The vote followed only moments after Wise finished, but I knew then that we had lost, before a single ballot had been cast."

Lizzie clenched her hands together in her lap, aching from the effort to hold herself perfectly still. She wanted to bolt to her feet, overturn the table, raise her face to the skies, and let out a ferocious howl of rage and betrayal. But she could do nothing. She could not vote. She had no husband whose vote she could influence. There was nothing she could have done to prevent her city from hurtling itself toward disaster, and yet she must suffer the consequences of actions she had not chosen.

They would surely be swift and terrible in coming.

Early the next morning, after a hasty breakfast, Mr. Lewis departed, but not before confiding to Lizzie and John another startling revelation—he and other Unionist convention delegates from western counties were planning to meet at the Powhatan Hotel to discuss their next step. "We may not secede from the Union with the rest of Virginia," he said, lowering his voice. He could not be too cautious, even within the home of longtime friends; Mary, bustling and cheerful, could scarcely contain her delight at the result of the vote that had left the rest of the household stunned and outraged, and the makings of a Confederate banner were draped over her sewing basket in the parlor. "It's been suggested that we break off into our own separate state and remain within the Union."

"Is that possible?" queried John. "Is it legal? Constitutional?" Then he shook his head, exasperated with himself. "Foolish question. If Virginia can secede from the United States, western counties can secede from Virginia."

"If only Richmond could go with you," said Lizzie, impassioned. But she knew that was not possible, nor was it what she truly wanted. The breaking apart of her beloved Virginia was almost as terrible as leaving the Union, and it was all too clear that most of her fellow citizens were clamoring to join the Confederacy. Already rumors were circulating that the Confederate capital might move from Montgomery, Alabama, to Richmond, although some newspapers had brazenly proposed Washington instead, as if it were dangling unprotected from a low bough, ripe for the picking.

Lizzie knew the Union would not relinquish its capital city without a fight.

"What should we do now?" she asked her brother after Mr. Lewis left. Even as she spoke, she realized that circumstances had stampeded furiously past her, uncontrolled and uncontrollable, while she had stood by watching in disbelief. Now she wanted desperately, irrationally, to shut the corral gate even though she knew it would not bring the wild herd back.

John thought for a moment. "I'm going to open the hardware store." He placed a hand on her shoulder and kissed her forehead. "And you, dear sister, should keep to the house unless you can better conceal your feelings. Loyal Unionists like us are outnumbered and surrounded, and until we know who our friends are, you cannot afford to antagonize the rebels—including my wife."

"In that case, it might be more prudent for me to go out," Lizzie retorted, but his words unsettled her. Until that fateful vote, she had believed herself a part of the political majority, but everything had shifted around her. The Van Lews—except for her sister-in-law—now resided in enemy territory.

Lizzie followed her younger brother's advice for the rest of that day, but the next, impatient and determined to see this strange new Richmond for herself, she decided to call on her friend Eliza Carrington and propose a stroll downtown. Eliza lived on "Carrington Row," across the street from the Van Lew mansion, and although she was nine years younger than Lizzie, she was her most intimate friend. With Eliza, a proud Virginian and loyal Unionist like herself, Lizzie could speak her mind freely, if only in whispers.

Eliza greeted her at the door, her soft, wide brown eyes shining with unshed tears. "Oh, Lizzie, it's too terrible to be believed," she lamented, flinging herself into her friend's embrace. Lizzie had to stand on tiptoe and Eliza had to stoop to meet her.

For a moment, Lizzie clung to her friend, as slender and gentle as a doe, but then she remembered herself. "We mustn't look too unhappy," she warned, glancing over her shoulder to see if they had been observed. "Too many of our neighbors are rejoicing."

Quickly Eliza released her, straightened, and wiped tears from the corners of her eyes. "Yes, of course you're right. We must be cautious. But surely we aren't the only citizens of Richmond who are mourning today?"

"Surely not the only," Lizzie conceded, "but I suspect our numbers are few. Why don't we see for ourselves?"

Eliza darted back inside to inform her family and returned moments later in her dove-gray shawl and a new bonnet trimmed in dark purple—the colors of half mourning, although the choice was probably unintentional. They linked arms and strolled off toward the heart of the city, stifling gasps at the sight of Confederate banners hanging from windows of people they liked and had thought they knew well. Instinctively, they drew closer together whenever they passed a cockerel of a politician standing on a soapbox on a street corner, denouncing the "criminal abolition president," urging the young men of Richmond to take up arms in defense of their state, and calling for swift measures to join the Confederacy. "We shall have war now," Lizzie heard a young woman call from her window joyfully, waving her handkerchief at passersby. "We shall have war, if Lincoln is not a coward!"

Lizzie felt a chill raise the hairs on the back of her neck, and beside her, Eliza moaned and froze in her tracks. War. Of course war was inevitable now. "Come along," Lizzie murmured, propelling her friend forward. Eliza took a few stumbling steps until she steadied herself, her grip upon Lizzie's arm tightening.

Then they turned a corner and through the trees caught their first glimpse of the Capitol building, and they halted, insensible to the crowds milling about them. The flag of the Confederate States of America that Lizzie had glimpsed through the carriage window on Mary Jane's wedding night was no longer flying atop the dome, replaced by the state flag of Virginia. Lizzie gazed up at the state seal upon the field of bold blue, the Roman goddess Virtus standing with spear and sword above a defeated enemy. The flag was too far away for her to read the motto emblazoned beneath the figures, but Lizzie knew it by heart. **"Sic semper tyrannis,"** she said quietly, watching the flag of her beloved Virginia snap and wave in the breeze. It was a small comfort that the flag of treason had been taken down, but Lizzie did not doubt that it would fly there again soon.

"Oh, what will become of our city?" Eliza

whispered, her voice breaking. "What will become of us?"

"Don't lose heart." Perhaps it was the sight of the flag of Virginia, but suddenly Lizzie was filled with a sense of calm determination and resolve, stronger than she had ever felt. "We will endure. Whether it takes weeks or months, whatever comes, we will endure."

Eliza choked out a nervous laugh. "I wish I could be as brave as you. The sight of that flag makes me want to scurry home and draw the curtains."

"Well, then, that is precisely what we must **not** do." Lizzie led her friend on at a brisker pace, head held high. "We cannot cower at home. Let us see what we're up against."

Eliza nodded, assumed an air of confidence, and strode along beside her. As they approached the Capitol, the crowds swelled, the air shifted, and voices rose in jubilation. Young ladies and their beaux linked arms and sang "The Marseillaise" while cheerful, whistling clerks adorned shop windows with bunting and banners. People thronged around the bulletin boards posted outside the newspaper offices, jostling one another as they pressed forward, some exclaiming aloud at whatever it was they read there. On street corners and in front of hotels, officious gentlemen took down the names of younger fellows in small leather books, calling out for other volunteers to enlist, warning them that now was the time to choose their company rather than await a possible draft later and risk being stuck in an undesirable post. Lizzie shuddered and said a silent prayer of thanksgiving that John would surely be too old for a draft, if the rebel government decided to implement one. Elsewhere, she spotted other men, pale and silent, walking alone with their hands in their pockets and shoulders hunched, while others gathered in small groups, speaking quietly and exchanging furtive glances. She recognized a few—the red-haired, stocky Scottish baker; a tall, black-bearded man in a railroad engineer's suit and cap—but most were strangers to her. The guarded anger in their eyes reminded her of John's warning to conceal her feelings, and with great effort she relaxed her strained features and put on a vaguely pleasant smile.

A block away from the Capitol, newsboys hawked extra editions of the **Examiner,** the **Dispatch,** and the **Enquirer,** and as eager customers flocked around them, Lizzie hesitated before joining the queue for the **Examiner**. She was reluctant to give a single penny to any of them, the **Dispatch** and the **Enquirer** least of all because of their annoying habit of referring to President Lincoln as a baboon or "the Illinois Ape." Just as she was taking a coin from her pocket, a bright-eyed, beaming girl of about fourteen dashed their way, her long, brown locks slipping free from a pink ribbon. "Maria, oh, Maria," she cried out to someone behind them, waving her hand. "The New York Seventh Regiment is all cut to pieces!"

Something in her accent reminded Lizzie of her Philadelphia relations, and without thinking, she spun away from the newsboy and caught the girl by the elbow. "Little girl, where were you born?"

"In the North," she replied, surprised, "but I can't help that." She wrenched herself free and ran off.

"Cut to pieces," Eliza echoed faintly. "She said they were cut to pieces."

Quickly Lizzie bought a paper, nearly

tearing it in her haste to unfold it. With Eliza reading over her shoulder, she went as cold and rigid as stone as she learned that federal troops traveling from Northern states to Washington City had been attacked as they passed through Baltimore. The first train cars carrying several companies of the Sixth Massachusetts had been towed through the city without incident, but word of the soldiers' presence had spread quickly, and soon a hostile crowd had massed in the streets, shouting insults and threats. They had torn up the train tracks, forcing the last four companies of the Sixth to abandon their railcars and march through the city. Almost immediately, several thousand men and boys had swarmed them, hurling bricks and paving stones and bottles. The companies had pushed onward at quick time, but when the furious mob blocked the streets ahead, the soldiers opened fire. The crowd had fallen back and the soldiers had managed to fight their way to the Camden Street station, and after other sabotaged tracks were repaired, the train and its battered and bloodied passengers sped off to Washington. Four soldiers and at least nine civilians had been killed and scores more injured in the melee, railway lines had been destroyed, bridges burned, and telegraph lines severed. Worst of all, Washington City had been cut off from the North.

Beside her, Eliza muffled a low moan and began to tremble uncontrollably. As word swiftly spread through the crowd, exultant cheers rang out, pistols were fired into the air, and bands scrambled together and struck up the merry notes of "Dixie." Numbly, Lizzie folded the paper and held it out to the newsboy, who stared up at her uncomprehendingly and made no move to take it. A man whooped and snatched it from her hand; relieved of her burden, she tucked her arm through Eliza's again and they resumed their tour of the block. Certain voices cut through the din and the fog of Lizzie's thoughts: A shriveled, silver-haired gentleman brandished his cane and declared that any single Southern man could whip five Yankees single-handedly. "One Southern man could whip five **hundred** Yankees," a portly fellow with flushed cheeks joined in, raising a silver flask into the air, "a race whose extermination, even of women and children, would be a blessing." The crowd roared its approval with such vehemence that it left Lizzie breathless and light-headed.

"I feel ill," said Eliza, swaying in her tracks. "I need to sit down."

"Not here," said Lizzie, looking about her for a sheltered nook and finding none. "We'll go to the hardware store and wait there with my brother until the crowd disperses."

Eliza nodded, gulped air, and resumed walking.

"I am neither a prophet nor the son of a prophet," a man Lizzie recognized as a member of the Virginia legislature shouted from the high portico of the Capitol as they passed. "Yet I predict that in less than sixty days, the flag of the Confederacy will be waving over the White House!"

"In less than **thirty** days," someone shouted back, and the crowd broke into raucous cheers. The pale, solemn men Lizzie had glimpsed before had vanished, and the air fairly crackled with the electricity of celebration.

"Let's go home," Eliza begged. "This is getting quite out of hand."

Lizzie agreed. They hardly spoke as

they fled the downtown for Church Hill, but although the commotion diminished behind them, Lizzie suspected it would not be long before their peaceful serenity was disrupted as news of the bloodshed in Baltimore swept through the city.

After parting with Eliza at her doorstep, Lizzie hurried home, where she found her mother and sister-in-law sewing in the parlor. When she told them all she had learned, Mother sat in grave silence, but Mary beamed and laughed aloud. "This is all for the best. You will see," she proclaimed. "Oh, it's regrettable that people were hurt, of course, but their noble sacrifice will drive Virginia into the welcoming arms of the Confederacy, and that is for the greater good."

"I strongly disagree," said Lizzie flatly.

"That's only because you're stubborn," Mary replied lightly, too cheerful to take offense. "Mr. Lincoln will let the South go willingly now that he's seen we'll put up a fight if he tries to prevent it. He's no general, just a country lawyer turned politician. He doesn't want a war."

"I hope you're right," said Mother, with a warning look for Lizzie, "but I fear that you are terribly, terribly wrong."

Mary, habitually reluctant to contradict her gentle mother-in-law, offered a little shrug and thrust out her lower lip as if she were willing to consider that possibility, but she soon resumed sewing with a new liveliness and a secret smile toying with the corners of her mouth. Lizzie held back a sharp rebuke and stiffly announced that she meant to find her nieces and distract herself with a bit of play and a fairy tale. She managed not to add that when it came to fanciful stories, she preferred Hans Christian Andersen's to Mary Carter West Van Lew's.

But escaping the Confederate jubilation was not as easy as that. The celebration that had begun at the Capitol grew as the hours passed, grew and spread, so that by dusk it had invaded even the sanctuary of Church Hill. Tin-pan music and flickering lights drew Lizzie and John outdoors and to the foot of the garden, where they watched in apprehensive silence as a torchlit parade marched by with the joyful fierceness of a surging, swelling revolution. Men's faces, reddened and shadowed by the fiery torches, turned monstrous and ugly as they shouted traitorous slogans. Women, hand in hand, marched and sang and threw flower petals into the air.

"My country," Lizzie murmured, her eyes filling with bitter, blinding tears. "Oh, my country!"

She felt her brother's hand on her shoulder, but she took no comfort from his steadfast presence. All around her, the people of Richmond were rushing headlong and heedless into the gaping maw of war. Did they not understand that only carnage would meet them? Had they forgotten their fathers' harrowing tales of the Mexican War, their grandfathers' of the War of 1812?

The procession seemed endless, the flags of rebellion without number, the painted slogans on their banners increasingly shocking and defiant. Lizzie thought of France, and of the bloodshed on the streets of Paris, and suddenly felt herself staggered by the nearly tangible power of the thousands of people united in anger. She dropped to her knees in the soft earth beneath the magnolia tree, clasped her hands in prayer, and called out, "Father, forgive them, for they know not what they do!"

Several heads turned her way, a few men scowled darkly, a little boy pointed and jeered. Mostly the mob ignored her and marched on by, but one man paused long enough to shake a fist at her and shout, "Hold your tongue, Madam! That fine house of yours can burn!"

John seized her by the elbow and hauled her to her feet. Heartsick, Lizzie prayed on silently until the last spectral figure disappeared down the street and around the corner. As the harsh torchlight and dizzying cacophony faded into the distance, she clung to her brother's arm, gathered her long skirts in one hand, and unsteadily climbed the path through the garden terraces back to the house, the only sanctuary that remained.

Chapter Three

Lizzie slept restlessly the night of the torch-light parade, but she woke in the morning preternaturally calm and resolute.

"It is strange to think that Virginia is a sovereign state, separate from both Union and Confederacy," she mused to her mother as they played with the girls in the garden after breakfast.

"Only for the moment," said Mother, plucking an errant dandelion and tickling Annie beneath the chin with the butter-yellow blossom. "Virginia will join the Confederacy, and Richmond will become its capital. I foresee no other course for us now."

Lizzie folded her thin arms over her chest and shivered, chilled by her mother's quiet fatalism. "I still cannot believe it, though I've seen it with my own eyes—our city, our friends and neighbors, hurtling themselves gladly, unrestrainedly, eagerly, into a bloody civil war."

Mother sighed and regarded her with fond compassion, but before she could speak, they caught sight of William descending the back stairs of the grand piazza and crossing the dew-damp lawn toward them. For the first time in the many years Lizzie had known him, his straight back and proud carriage struck her as an almost military bearing. "Ma'am," he said to Mother when he reached them, "you have a visitor."

Mother picked up Eliza and made her way back to the house. "I wasn't expecting any callers today."

"The lady gave her name as Mrs. Matthew Lodge." William fell in step beside Mother and Lizzie followed along behind. "She said she knows you through the Bible Society, so I showed her to the parlor."

"Oh, yes, of course. Mrs. Lodge." When Mother passed Mary dozing in her chair on the piazza, she placed Eliza on her lap, startling her awake. "Take Eliza, dear. I have a caller."

"A caller?" Eager for distraction, Mary scrambled to her feet, but she sighed and acquiesced when Eliza held up her arms and asked to be carried. Perhaps sensing that she might be left behind, Annie seized Lizzie's hand, so it was a curious quintet of three generations of Van Lews who met the unexpected visitor in the parlor.

Mrs. Lodge sat in the best chair near the window, gazing outside at a pair of robins twittering in the low branches of an olive tree. Her dress was of sprigged lavender calico, her face mousy and pinched, her brown hair thinning along the center part and pulled back tightly into a broad bun at the nape of her neck. She seemed both plain and fussy, and, muffling a sigh, Lizzie promptly abandoned all hope of interesting conversation.

"Why, Mrs. Lodge," Mother greeted her pleasantly. "What an unexpected pleasure. Would you care for some tea?"

"That's very kind, but no, thank you."

Mrs. Lodge's voice was sweet but her gaze was sharp. "I have to visit all the ladies on both sides of the street before luncheon."

"Whatever for?" Lizzie inquired, spreading her skirts and seating herself on the sofa. "Are you taking a political poll?"

Mother smiled, but Mrs. Lodge looked affronted. "Certainly not," she said crisply. "I do not aspire to dabble in politics like some mannish, giddy bluestocking."

"Of course not," said Lizzie brightly, happily revising her original opinion. Perhaps the visit was about to take a more interesting turn. "Why dabble when one can fling oneself into something wholeheartedly? Don't you agree?"

"Well—I suppose, in proper circumstances, but that's not quite what I—" Mrs. Lodge frowned quizzically at Lizzie before turning her attention to Mother. "I've come in the spirit of patriotism to ask for your help with a very important cause."

"Certainly," said Mother. "I confess I've allowed my membership in the Bible Society to lapse, but I'm always willing to lend a hand—"

"Oh, no, Mrs. Van Lew, this isn't for the

Bible Society," Mrs. Lodge interrupted. "Although my cause is equally worthy. With so many young men of Richmond enlisting, several ladies of Church Hill have decided to form a sewing circle to make shirts for our valiant soldiers. We would be glad to have you join us."

Incredulous, Lizzie said, "You're asking **us** to make uniforms for Confederate soldiers?"

Mrs. Lodge nodded. "We all must do our part for our noble cause."

Lizzie imagined herself sewing buttons on a gray wool jacket some neighbor's son would wear as he aimed his rifle at a Northern boy, and she recoiled. "Indeed we must."

"Then may I tell my friends that you will join us?"

"Indeed you may not."

Mrs. Lodge's smile faltered as she gazed at Lizzie, uncomprehending. "Do you mean you would prefer to meet here? I suppose that could be arranged, and in fact it would be a pleasure. You have such a lovely home."

"What my daughter means," Mother

broke in before Lizzie could reply, "is that sadly, we cannot join your sewing circle. It's very kind of you to think of us, but it is quite impossible." She gestured vaguely around the room, as if her reasons were known to all and yet too delicate to be spoken aloud.

"It's not impossible for me," protested Mary. "I'd be delighted to help. It would be my great honor to sew shirts for our brave defenders. If only I were not so busy caring for my daughters . . ."

"I'm sure between the two of them, Lizzie and Hannah could manage to look after the girls in your absence," said Mother. Lizzie shot her a look of utter astonishment, which she ignored. Beaming, Mary promised Mrs. Lodge to attend every meeting faithfully, and after exchanging all the details of where and when, they sent Mrs. Lodge on her way, thoroughly satisfied with the result of her visit.

As Mary hurried off to make certain her sewing basket was well supplied with thread and needles, Lizzie whirled upon her mother. "You would have her help the rebel cause?"

"Better her than you or I," Mother replied serenely, "and one of us must. Don't you see? We must make an outward show of support, despite how we feel in our hearts."

"I'm not ashamed of my loyalty to the Union."

"Of course not, my dear, and neither am I." Mother held her by the shoulders and fixed her with an imploring gaze. "But you must not let anyone outside this home know it. Let Mary be our decoy. Let her make a hundred rebel uniforms if she must. It will keep her busy, and it will divert suspicion from the rest of us."

Later that afternoon, John returned home from Van Lew & Taylor to report, ruefully, that secession was proving to be very good for the hardware business. Knives, axes, hatchets, rope, pocket cutlery, and other tools were fairly flying off the shelves, and he was racing to reorder ample stock before all ties with the North were severed. "Be forewarned," he said. "When next you visit the store, you'll find Confederate banners and bunting in the window."

"Of course," said Lizzie, though she felt

a pang of disappointment. "It's a necessary pretense. Better to don a disguise
than sweep up glass after some fool hurls
a brick through the window."

"For some members of our family, such
accoutrements are no disguise." John grimaced as if he hated the news he was
obliged to deliver. "Cousin Jack has joined
the Richmond Howitzers."

"What?" Lizzie exclaimed.

Mother blanched. "Good heavens."

"It was either choose now or be drafted
later, Jack told me, and he didn't want to
miss his chance for glory and be stuck
peeling potatoes or driving wagons at the
rear while other fellows marched off to
battle."

Mother shook her head, her lips pursed
in a tight, worried line.

"Jack's regiment may be assigned to
guard the city," Lizzie said, taking Mother's
hand. "Someone surely will be. Why not
the Richmond Howitzers?"

Mother patted her hand to thank her
for the kindness, but her sad smile revealed
that she would not be soothed into a false
sense of reassurance. "He's made his

choice," she said. "Now all we can do is pray for his safety."

Two days later, on a bright, balmy Sunday morning, Lizzie sat in the family pew at Saint John's and prayed fervently for her cousin, for her misguided neighbors, and for her fractured nation, but eventually her thoughts began to wander and she sank into a brood. The Scripture for the service had come from the second chapter of Joel: "Then will the Lord be jealous for his land, and pity his people. Yea, the Lord will answer, and say unto his people, Behold, I will send you corn, and wine, and oil, and ye shall be satisfied therewith; and I will no more make you a reproach among the heathen. But I will remove far off from you the Northern army, and will drive him into a land barren and desolate . . ." From the nods and stirrings of the congregation, Lizzie knew that many of her fellow worshipers heard in the verses a prophecy for their own age, and their self-righteousness left a bitter taste in her mouth. The Lord of justice and mercy could not be on the side of the slaveholder. Her bitterness sharpened with outrage when the minister made his own opinions known by omitting the customary prayer for the president of the United States. A faint murmur followed the omission, but Lizzie thought, despairingly, that it indicated surprise rather than protest.

None too soon the service ended, and with a sigh Lizzie put away her missal, rose, and stretched discreetly. She took Annie's hand as the family joined the other worshipers filing from the church, pausing every now and then so that Mother could exchange greetings with friends and neighbors. They had not yet left the churchyard when Lizzie heard the distant clanging of a bell—two long peals, a pause, and then a third—coming from the direction of the Capitol. With a sudden chill, she recognized the source of the solemn timbre—the old iron bell in the truncated brick tower with the wooden belfry on the southwest corner of the Capitol Square. In peacetime the tocsin struck the hours or warned of fire, but on rare occasions it summoned the militia to arms.

The alarm sounded again, resonating ever louder as church bells near the Capitol joined the iron clamor. Lizzie jumped as, behind her and very near, the bell in the steeple of Saint John's began to toll.

"What is it?" Annie cried, squeezing Lizzie's hand tighter as all around them, ladies gasped and men shouted questions. Neighbors hurried from their homes into the street, glancing wildly about and querying one another in various degrees of fright and confusion.

"Lizzie!" Suddenly Eliza was beside her, breathless. "What's happened? Why are they sounding the alarm?"

"I don't know." From what she had overheard, the consensus of the anxious people milling about them was that the city was under attack, but Lizzie would not repeat the rumor with young Annie so close and so frightened.

"Could it be the Union army?" Eliza's face lit up with hope. "Are we going to be delivered? Praise God!"

"Hush," cautioned Lizzie, glancing over her shoulder. To her dismay, Mary stood nearby watching them, lips pursed in disapproval, but had she overheard? "Such sentiments are best expressed among friends, not in a crowd."

Suddenly a young man clad in the uniform of the F Company raced up on horseback. "Union warship coming up the James!" he bellowed, wheeling his horse about in the middle of the street. "All militiamen report for duty!"

A woman shrieked. Several men broke away from the throng and raced into their homes, reappearing moments later pulling on their uniforms and grasping their weapons and kits. Lizzie gathered her family and ushered them swiftly home, but she paused on the front portico to watch in astonishment as civilians of all ages raced after the militiamen, toting weapons that seemed better suited to display nostalgically above the hearth—rusted fowling pieces, long-bored duck guns, antique blunderbusses, swords gone so dull that they had probably last inspired fear in Cornwallis's men at Yorktown, pistols of every caliber and description.

"Those decrepit weapons won't leave so much as a mark on a warship," said John, who had remained with her on the doorstep after seeing the others safely inside. "I bet only half of them are loaded, and the other half look like they'd be more dangerous for the wielder than his target."

Lizzie laughed shakily, alternately excited and terrified. If a Union gunship fired upon Richmond, it would rain down destruction on loyalists and rebels alike. "I knew the Union would deliver us eventually, but even in my wildest hopes, I didn't think they would come so soon." Gathering up her skirts, she turned to go inside. "I'm going up to the roof to watch."

Lizzie darted up the stairs to the attic and then out a back window to the rooftop, where she found most of the servants already gazing out upon the James low in the distance. At first glance she beheld nothing but the broad curving ribbon of the river sparkling silver beneath a cloudless sky—no warship, no smoky flash of cannon, nothing.

"What have you seen?" she queried, glancing down the row from Peter and William to Caroline, Judy, and old Uncle Nelson.

"Nothing," said William. "Nothing except the great multitude of Richmond, who apparently got the same idea we did."

When he gestured, Lizzie turned her gaze closer to home and discovered figures crowding other rooftops, peering out from church steeples, climbing Church Hill on foot, all for a better view. After nearly an hour had passed with no change in the lovely, familiar landscape, she spied John on horseback, making his way up Grace Street.

Quickly Lizzie went back inside and downstairs to meet him, but by the time she reached the foyer, Mary had already led her husband off to the parlor. There Lizzie found her sister-in-law reclining on the sofa, pale and silent, while John paced and Mother knitted, unperturbed.

"What's the news?" she demanded, taking John's hands in hers.

"Governor Letcher received official intelligence that a Union sloop of war called the **Pawnee** has passed City Point and is steaming hard to Richmond." John's face was a tight mask of agitation. "Its mission is to shell the city and burn it to the ground."

Mary let out a low moan. "That coward," she shrilled. "That cowardly baboon Lincoln! Sneaking down the James to attack an undefended city on a Sunday. On a Sunday!"

"I'm sure President Lincoln is not on board," snapped Lizzie. "It's unfair to accuse him of sneaking."

"If we're setting the facts straight, I don't believe he's a baboon either." Mother set her knitting aside. "John, dear, tell us what we should do. Evacuate to the farm?"

"I'm not leaving," Lizzie promptly declared.

"No, nor do I think that's necessary at this point." John frowned and went to the window, though there was nothing to see but the throng milling outside. "The militia have taken up positions at Rocketts Wharf, but they're armed only with rifles and bayonets. Some fellows hauled the cannons out of the armory—"

"Not those magnificent bronze cannons France gave to the state of Virginia," Lizzie broke in.

"The very same."

"But those were ceremonial gifts from one government to another. They were never meant to be used in war."

"And they likely won't be. The mob managed to hoist the cannons onto a wagon and hitch it up to a team of horses and mules, but as they were hauling the heavy load through the city, one of the cannons broke free, rolled down the hill toward the Custom House, and tumbled into the gutter, where as far as I know it remains."

Lizzie laughed, and Mary glared at her. "You would enjoy this," she said brittlely. "You're Union to the core. Mrs. Lodge says—"

They all watched her, waiting for her to continue, but she fell abruptly silent.

"Mary," said John levelly, "I will not have you carrying tales about Lizzie through the neighborhood."

Balling her hands in her lap, Mary glared up at him. "I have nothing to say to my friends about **her** that they haven't already heard elsewhere or observed for themselves."

"Nevertheless"—John's voice carried an edge—"I will not have my wife gossiping about my sister. Do not embarrass me."

"That's all that matters, isn't it? That your sister is thought well of." Mary bolted to her feet, tears in her eyes. "My parents warned me that I was marrying down when I agreed to be your wife, but they couldn't have known how very low I would fall, that I would always come second to your precious spinster sister."

"I'll be in the garden," Lizzie said, cutting short the painful exchange, and hurried out back for a better view of the James. Shading her eyes from the sun, she walked to the foot of the garden, where she had watched the torchlight parade march past a few nights before, but the only boats she observed on the winding, silvery river were those docked at Rocketts Wharf and a rowboat carrying several especially fool-hardy sightseers.

"That Yankee gunboat ain't comin', Miss Lizzie."

Startled, Lizzie whirled about to find Nelson sitting on his heels tending the olean-der, and despite everything, it occurred to her that she ought to chide him for working on his day off. "How can you be so sure?"

"I got a nephew works on one of them pole barges." Stiffly, Nelson straightened with a grunt, brushed soil from his palms, and joined Lizzie at the edge of the ter-race. "Spoke with him after worship, soon as we all heard the warning. I'll tell you what he told me and you make up your own mind. City Point's about twenty miles away, where the Appomattox meets the James. The river's narrow and twisting, and some places the channel's so narrow all you got to do is fell a single tree to block any ship that might want to come further. Set a few fieldpieces up on them high ridges, and hide a few marksmen on those steep bluffs, and that gunboat wouldn't stand a chance."

Lizzie felt faint. "Have the rebels placed any soldiers there?"

"I surely don't know, but the Yankees don't either." Nelson squinted at the distant river, shaking his head. "My nephew says with them odds, no gunboat captain would risk his ship and his crew just for the chance to shell a small city like ours, not even if he was drunk or insane."

As evening fell and the bewildered, disappointed, relieved citizens of Richmond abandoned their lookout posts, descended Church Hill, and returned to their homes, Lizzie stepped out onto the rooftop again and looked to the east until the sun set. She saw flickering campfires along the riverbanks down by Rocketts Wharf, where the city's defenders had bivouacked for the night, but the **Pawnee** never appeared.

A quiet night passed, and in the morning, William went out after breakfast for the papers and brought the **Dispatch** to Lizzie on the back piazza. A bold headline caught her eye: "The Excitement Yesterday."

"Shall I read to you how the **Dispatch** accounts for the invasion that wasn't?" she called to Mother, who was cutting flowers in the garden and laying them carefully in a basket.

"No need, dear," she called back. "I was there."

Lizzie smiled and read on silently. "In times like these we must be prepared for any emergency, and every rumor deserves careful and considerate attention," the article declared, but to Lizzie the affirmation read like an embarrassed apology on behalf of a city that had flown into a panic at the first sign of real danger. The city of Richmond—and perhaps the entire state of Virginia—was woefully unprepared for war. And so would she be if she relied upon the papers and the gossip of the streets for information, never knowing for certain what events were unfolding in her own city. She must see for herself.

As soon as she could get away, Lizzie crossed the street to the Carrington residence and rapped upon the door. When Eliza appeared, she smiled brightly and inquired, "Shall we see if any new gunboats or vice-presidents have come to town?"

Soon the pair were strolling around Capitol Square, market baskets dangling from the crooks of their elbows. Watching and listening intently to the conversation and activity flowing around them, they soon learned that Vice President Stephens had arrived in Richmond before dawn that morning, that he was staying at the Exchange Hotel, and that he was at that very hour in conference with the governor and his most important advisers. They also discovered to their consternation that the **Pawnee** had never even set out upon the James the previous day, but had been steaming up the Chesapeake between Norfolk and Washington all the while Richmond was scrambling to prepare for its arrival. Meanwhile, residents of outlying villages had experienced their own version of the previous day's panic, having heard that the Pawnee Indians had invaded the city and were viciously scalping and toma-hawking its citizens.

"Rumors," Lizzie murmured in disgust. "They will be the death of me."

"How do such tales get started?" Eliza wondered, setting down a bunch of leeks after barely glancing at them.

"Usually with some small grain of truth, but to discern that grain from all the others . . ." Lizzie lowered her voice. "We should purchase something, you know, so that people don't begin to wonder why we're wandering about with empty baskets."

Eliza purchased the leeks, while Lizzie selected a bunch of radishes, delectably red and shiny, with lush greens. They left the market and strolled around the Capitol, where there might be more to learn. They had just decided to turn toward home when a carriage pulled up in front of the elegant new Spotswood Hotel at the corner of Eighth and Main, a jubilant crowd of men and boys and even a few ladies following close behind. When a gentleman in his midfifties clad in a tall silk hat and fine suit stepped from the carriage, a smattering of applause broke out, which he politely acknowledged with a modest bow, his expression bemused. Although his hair was turning gray, his thick, full mustache was nearly black, his figure trim and strong, his bearing dignified.

As three other gentlemen escorted the newcomer into the Spotswood, Eliza gasped and seized Lizzie's arm. "I know him," she exclaimed. "He's acquainted with my uncle, and we met at the White Springs Resort last summer. That's Mr. Lee."

"The colonel? Robert E. Lee?"

"I don't suppose he's a colonel anymore. He resigned his commission after Virginia voted to secede. He said—oh, what was it? It was in all the papers—that despite his devotion to the United States, he could not bring himself to raise his hand against his family and the people of Virginia. He said that he would never again draw his sword except in defense of his native state, and then he retired to his home in Alexandria."

That would explain the adulation and the civilian attire. "He has come out of retirement, it seems," Lizzie said, watching as Mr. Lee and his entourage disappeared inside.

Chapter Four

Soon thereafter, all of Richmond would learn that on the afternoon Lizzie and Eliza witnessed Robert E. Lee checking into the Spotswood Hotel, Governor Letcher bestowed upon him the rank of major general and offered him command of the whole of Virginia's military and naval forces. Mr. Lee readily accepted, the state convention swiftly approved the appointment, and on the morning of April 23, he was formally inducted at the Capitol. The newspapers reported the day's momentous events in rapturous language, and even Lizzie, dismayed though she was by his choice of allegiance, could not fail to be impressed and moved by his solemn humility: "I accept the position assigned me by your partiality," he had said. "I would have much preferred had the choice fallen upon an abler man. Trusting in Almighty God, an approving conscience, and the aid of my fellow citizens, I devote myself to the service of my native State, in whose behalf alone will I ever again draw my sword."

At last Lizzie and Mary found a rare subject on which they could agree: Robert E. Lee was a brilliant choice to lead Virginia's armed forces, his love of Virginia and his nobility of spirit were inspiring, and he would pose a formidable challenge to any Union opponent who dared face him. "I wish he were on our side," Lizzie grumbled to John, who heartily agreed.

Things were moving too quickly, one heart-stopping event following another like boulders tumbling down a hillside. The day after General Lee was put in charge of Virginia's military, Confederate vice-president Stephens and a convention committee led by the aged former United States president John Tyler signed a treaty proclaiming that Virginia would adopt the Confederate constitution and place all its military resources under Confederate control.

Lizzie was badly shaken when it was all said and done. She blinked back tears when the papers reported that John Minor Botts, a Unionist Whig she had long admired, had declared the signing of the treaty illegal under state law, a courageous act with so many powerful enemies arrayed against him. When his protests were summarily dismissed, Mr. Botts had withdrawn to his rural home two miles northwest of the Capitol.

Indignant, Lizzie and her mother called on him at Elba Park to express their sympathy and enduring admiration, and they were heartened to find that despite the sudden and dramatic downturn in his political fortunes, he remained stubbornly Unionist. They spent a pleasant afternoon doing their best to raise the spirits of Mr. Botts and his wife, but as they departed, Mr. Botts kindly but firmly discouraged them from calling on him again. "I am carefully observed, day and night," he said, nodding across the street to a placid, round-faced man in a gray suit who stood watching them over the top of a newspaper.

"Was he there when we arrived?" Mother asked, watching the man from the corner of her eye.

"Yes, and he'll be there long after you depart, and around six o'clock, a skinny fellow with a scraggly, tobacco-stained beard will replace him." Mr. Botts's thick, unruly brows knitted and his stern features softened with regret. "I'm grateful for your friendship, good ladies, but your kindness imperils you. You must not seem too fond of me, or of my unpopular opinions."

Lizzie and her mother bade him a sad farewell, uncertain when they might meet again. They departed for Church Hill without a single glance for the man in the gray suit studying them from across the street.

President Jefferson Davis must have ordered troops into Virginia the moment it joined the Confederacy, for it seemed that the ink on the treaty had scarcely dried before troops from South Carolina began to arrive in great numbers, setting up encampments at strategic points throughout the city and providing entertaining distraction to its residents. The press hailed the heroes of Fort Sumter as "an invincible

and heroic race of men" and "perfect gentlemen in every respect," and indeed all
who beheld them were impressed by their
smart, dashing uniforms, their military ardor, and their bold, sun-browned, manly
countenances. To Lizzie's disgust, the
ladies of Richmond became thoroughly
smitten, and in pairs and in crowds, they
met the troops at the train station, eagerly
attended every evening dress parade, and
visited the camps to deliver the shirts, uniforms, and tents they had sewn, as well as
tasty delicacies from their kitchens and
gardens. The **Dispatch** praised the ladies
as ministering angels who "have demonstrated their faith by their works. All honor
to them," and singled out the women of
Church Hill for not only providing necessary supplies, but also for nursing soldiers
who had fallen ill.

Mary, recognizing herself, proudly clipped
the article from the paper and pasted it in
her scrapbook. "You could join us," she
reminded Lizzie and Mother. "We could use
your help. The other Church Hill ladies
wonder why you refuse."

"What do you tell them?" Mother inquired.

"That you're indisposed." Mary shrugged

helplessly. "What else could I say? Would you have them believe you're lazy or disloyal? Forgive me, but your disinterest reflects badly upon all of us."

Lizzie wanted to retort that she **was** loyal, and keenly interested, but she managed a tight smile and said, "Thank you for making our excuses."

"I do what I can for the sake of the family," said Mary, returning her attention to her scrapbook, "but people are beginning to talk."

Militia companies and untrained recruits from throughout Virginia followed quickly after the South Carolinians. The first regiments set up tents and training fields at the old fairgrounds on West Broad Street, a rough settlement dubbed Camp Lee. Soon thereafter, one hundred and eighty-five cadets from the Virginia Military Institute arrived from Lexington fully armed, equipped, and prepared for war, bringing along a battery of nine field pieces, including a rifled cannon. After setting up quarters at the fairgrounds and undergoing a laudatory review by the governor on Capitol Square, the cadets began training the volunteers, many of whom were old enough to be their fathers. Leading the young drill-masters was a tall, dark-bearded major named Thomas J. Jackson, who was reputed to be somewhat awkward and peculiar, but also a brilliant strategist and a particular favorite of Governor Letcher as well as General Lee, with whom he had served in Mexico. Rumors of the gentlemen's admiration were quickly proven true, for soon after his arrival, Thomas Jackson was promoted to colonel and placed in command of Harpers Ferry, a crucial outpost General Lee was determined to defend.

Richmond already seemed full to bursting, but the population continued to swell as Virginians who had been visiting or working in the North fled south, seeking sanctuary in their native state. Before long, the strain of welcoming so many strangers began to wear on the residents of Richmond. Even the newspapers, which generally regarded the city's transformation into an armed camp with euphoric approval, began to draw attention to the potential danger. The **Examiner** warned that "Richmond contains at present a large number of secret enemies of the South, in petticoats as well as pantaloons" who must be watched closely lest they pass useful information to their cronies in the North.

The Richmond city council evidently shared their concerns, for they passed an "Ordinance Concerning Suspicious Persons" decreeing that any citizen who suspected another of entertaining or expressing dangerous sentiments must inform the mayor. Lizzie could not help but think of the numerous letters she had written to her sister Anna in Philadelphia describing the changes secession had wrought within their beloved city. If her letters were intercepted, a malicious person could twist an ordinary conversation between sisters into something sinister and treasonous. Henceforth she would have to censor herself, and warn Anna to choose her words carefully too.

The city council's halfhearted attempt to prevent overzealous Southern patriots from forming anti-Unionist vigilante mobs by obliging the mayor to suppress the creation of vigilance committees did nothing to ease Lizzie's anxieties. Under the new ordinance, any neighbor with a grudge could inform on any other, since believing that the accused "entertained dangerous sentiments" was sufficient grounds for arrest.

"If I am to be prosecuted," Lizzie said defiantly, pacing the length of the parlor while her mother knitted in her chair by the window, "may it be for something I do—some bold, brave action in defense of the Union—and not merely for what I **feel**."

"I would prefer that you not be prosecuted at all," said Mother, shuddering. "Remember Mr. Botts's wise council and be cautious."

"How could I forget?" Lizzie went to the window and peered outside, glowering at the bunting and banners proudly adorning nearly every window and door frame and flagpole up and down the street. A sudden movement caught her eye, and she turned just in time to glimpse a tall figure disappearing behind the broad trunk of an oak tree in a neighbor's garden. She waited for him to emerge on the other side, but he did not reappear. Unsettled, she watched awhile longer before concluding that her anxious mind was playing tricks on her, and as she turned away from the window, she silently berated herself for imagining phantoms and villains where none existed.

She must be strong, clear-eyed, and skeptical, and must never allow her nerves to get the better of her. She would need every scrap of her wits about her in the days to come.

Lizzie wondered if General Lee and Colonel Jackson, men who had seen battle, were half as bloodthirsty as the ladies of Richmond had become. Young women spent their days sewing and knitting, and when they delivered the gifts of socks and shirts to the camps, they exacted promises from the soldiers to kill as many Yankees as they could for them, or to bring back Mr. Lincoln's head in a box, or at least a piece of his ear.

No man wanted to seem a coward, and no woman wanted to seem indifferent, which made the Van Lews' absence from sewing bees and dress parades all the more conspicuous. Lizzie could not mistake the sidelong glances and whispers that followed her whenever she strolled around Church Hill.

One morning, Lizzie was crossing the street to call on Eliza Carrington when she spotted a thin man halfway down the block, leaning up against a lamppost and carving a stub of wood. He did not so much as glance her way, but when he spat a long stream of tobacco juice into the street, she noticed that his scruffy blond beard was stained brown around the mouth. Her heart thumped, and without thinking that she might arouse his suspicions, she quickly turned and hurried back inside.

She watched him from the parlor window through the lace curtain, gnawing on the inside of her lower lip, wondering what to do. The man fit Mr. Botts's description of one of his observers too perfectly for him to be anyone else, and she knew he was no resident of Church Hill, nor did he seem to have any proper business there. When he seemed perfectly content to remain there all day, idly carving and utterly unconcerned that he did not belong, Lizzie found Mother in the gardens and invited her to the parlor on the pretext of discussing poetry, a subject that did not interest Mary in the least and would ensure she stayed away. Drawing the curtain aside, Mother studied the man gravely for a long moment, then sighed. "I suppose we must make some token gesture to dispel suspicions."

"I cannot sit and sew with Mary and her

insipid friends," Lizzie declared. "I could not bear it. Not for a single day, nor a single hour, not even to save my life."

"I suspect that if it were indeed to save your life, you would find the strength to sew a shirt or two," Mother replied, amused. "We don't have to join in Mary's efforts, dear. We can contrive some innocent service of our own."

After pondering their options, they decided that gifts of books, fresh flowers, and paper and pencils to write letters home would do no harm, so Lizzie perused the family's substantial library for volumes she could bear to part with while Mother took cuttings from the garden. They pretended not to notice the man with the tobacco-stained beard as they left the house, and rather than take the carriage, they walked to the soldiers' encampment to better display their feigned devotion to the cause. There they found rows upon rows of perfectly aligned small white tents, most with small fire circles at the entrance, a few with stovepipes poking up rakishly out back. Small wooden buildings, so new the pine boards were still yellow, were clustered along one end of the field, and Lizzie observed officers and their aides bustling in and out, delivering messages and carrying out orders. The First South Carolina Regiment drilled on the parade grounds while a flock of admiring ladies watched from behind a fence a few dozen yards away. Other ladies strolled among the neat rows of tents, pausing to offer a blanket to one soldier, a meat pie to another.

Lizzie and her mother followed their example and walked through the encampment chatting with soldiers, distributing writing materials and helping compose letters, offering flowers and sincere good wishes. Lizzie truly did not want any harm to come to those young men, enemy soldiers though they were. Each cordial greeting to a young rebel placed another weight upon her heart, for they seemed not to realize what lay ahead. Blinking back tears, she resisted the urge to warn them not to be driven like cattle but to resist the call to arms, but she said nothing, not only because they would be shot as deserters if they heeded her, but because she knew they would not listen. The newspapers had described the soldiers as gallant gentlemen, but the young recruits Lizzie and her mother met were of a different class entirely—uneducated, rough boys whose fathers toiled in trades in the cities or eked out a living on tiny plots of land. When Lizzie offered them **Chambers's Miscellany** and poetry chapbooks and collections of instructive essays, some politely declined, explaining that they could not read, while one asked if she had any "ballard books" instead—hymnals, or so she eventually puzzled out.

"Why have you come to Virginia?" she asked one young fellow, inspired by the eagerness with which he thanked her for a well-read copy of Emerson's **The Conduct of Life**. "Why leave home and come so far?"

The young fellow exchanged a look of surprise with his partner before answering, "Why, we come to protect Virginia, Ma'am."

"Why?" Lizzie was genuinely curious. "Protect Virginia from what?"

"From them Yankees, Ma'am," the other soldier replied. Freckled and dark-haired, he seemed little older than the young volunteer drummer boys, and for a moment Lizzie wondered if he had wandered into the wrong part of the camp.

"Mr. Lincoln said he's coming down to take all our Negroes and set them free," the first soldier explained, tucking the book beneath his arm. "If they dare to do so, we'll be here to protect you women."

"If this should come to pass, we'll be grateful for your protection, of course." Lizzie ignored her mother's warning look, the subtle shake of her head. "But why do you believe it will?"

They regarded her with twin expressions of bewilderment. "Because the papers said so, Ma'am," said the freckled soldier.

"Lizzie, dear," her mother murmured, "let it be."

But Lizzie couldn't. Looking around the tent the two young men shared, she quickly surmised that they would benefit greatly from a visit by Mary and her sewing circle. "Do you have sufficient warm clothing and blankets?"

"We got uniforms," said the first soldier proudly, tugging on the brim of his cap and drawing himself up to show off his jacket. "Finest suit I ever had."

"And we don't need blankets so much anyway," said the second. "The nights are warm enough with a good fire, and they're bound to get warmer with summer comin' on."

But autumn would follow soon enough, and then winter—but with God's mercy, the war would be over by then. "What about arms?" Lizzie queried, mindful of the approach of a group of smiling, gracious young ladies who might find her questions strange. "Have you brought rifles from home, and have you been trained to use them?"

"Oh, no, Ma'am, we don't got any rifles yet," the freckled soldier said. "You're givin' 'em to us."

"We are?" said Mother, startled into participating in the conversation.

"Not you in particular, Ma'am," the first soldier said, grinning shyly. "The state of Virginia's gonna furnish our arms. That's what the sergeant told us."

"If that is what Virginia has promised, then that is what you should expect." Mother linked her arm through Lizzie's. "Come, dear, we've monopolized these soldiers' time long enough. Let's allow other ladies a chance to meet them." She nodded graciously to them both, and their eyes lit up with admiration as they tugged their caps and bowed. Mother was the very ideal of the Southern lady—kind, gracious, polite, well spoken, pious, and charitable. She strolled through the muddy fairgrounds with as much grace and ease as if she were welcoming the soldiers into her own parlor.

"That was an afternoon well spent," said Mother as they walked home. "We provided only the most innocent aid and comfort, but I believe it will add much to our own comfort to have our neighbors believe us sympathetic to their cause."

"I hope so," said Lizzie fervently. "Anything to spare me Mary's sewing circle."

A few blocks from home, they passed the Lodge residence on Twenty-Third Street, where they spotted Mrs. Lodge and her two eldest girls on the front porch knitting gray wool socks. Mary had mentioned a son too, who had enlisted in the first heady days of secession. Lizzie smiled brightly and waved, but Mrs. Lodge merely regarded her through narrowed eyes before nodding politely to Mother. Evidently, Lizzie would have to deliver a thousand books and blossoms before she redeemed herself in Mrs. Lodge's esteem.

When she and her mother arrived home,

the man with the tobacco-stained beard was gone.

On April 27, the Virginia convention formally invited the Confederate States of America to make Richmond its capital. Nearly seven hundred miles to the southwest in Montgomery, Alabama, the Confederate Congress debated the proposal for nearly a month, and on May 20, they voted in favor of the move. The next day the government adjourned with plans to reconvene in Richmond two months hence.

As soon as Richmond was officially named the new capital of the Confederacy, politicians, public servants, and opportunists joined the flood of newcomers, arriving in astonishing numbers to seek patronage from the fledgling government. The city buzzed with anticipation for the arrival of President Jefferson Davis, his wife Varina, and their brood of three young children. With nary a vacant hotel room or boardinghouse to be found, government officials scrambled to find a suitable residence.

On May 23, Mr. Davis's impending arrival was the popular subject of conversation at the polls as eligible voters turned out for Virginia's secession referendum. Virginia's course was so rigidly fixed that the referendum seemed almost an afterthought, and since the vote was by viva voce rather than secret ballot, Lizzie never doubted that intimidation would rule the day. Faced with death threats, Mr. Lewis had not returned to Richmond to cast his ballot against ratification, but instead remained in Rockingham County, where he presumably continued rallying the western counties to break away from the rebellious portion of the state. Mr. Botts, who did not dare show up at the polls, nevertheless continued to protest from Elba Park, calling the entire process a contemptible farce and arguing that although the vote might ratify secession, it did not validate the measure to join the Confederacy, a move he adamantly insisted was illegal. Lizzie feared for him, especially after Peter brought word from his friends serving in other households that the few brave Unionists who had voted nay were pursued from the Capitol Square by jeering, stone-throwing mobs.

The day after the vote, word that Union general-in-chief Winfield Scott had sent troops from Washington City across the Potomac into Virginia did nothing to dispel the prevailing euphoria. President Jefferson Davis was on his way, greeted as a conquering hero by cheering crowds that lined the railroad tracks and packed the stations at every stop along his route. Though suffering from a bout of poor health, he nevertheless acquiesced to demands for speeches along the way, and at one town after another, he promised his ardent listeners that the Northern invaders would suffer terrible consequences for their aggression. His words, transcribed in the newspapers by approving editors, preceded him to Richmond, so he had already become a great favorite with the people by the time his train approached the city on the morning of May 29, more than two days overdue.

When word came that Jefferson Davis's train was crossing the bridge from Manchester, cannon thundered a fifteen-gun salute to herald his arrival. As he and his entourage of friends and dignitaries emerged from the train, eager civilians and soldiers crowded the platform and the grounds all around, cheering and applauding. A band struck up a rousing serenade as Governor Letcher and Mayor Joseph Mayo escorted the visibly exhausted president to an open carriage pulled by four magnificent bay horses. Thousands of cheering onlookers lined the four-block uphill route to the Spotswood Hotel, the men shouting and throwing their hats in the air, the women waving handkerchiefs and tossing flowers. Visibly moved, Mr. Davis set aside his weariness and rewarded the citizens for their patience by smiling, waving, and offering firm handshakes as he graciously accepted their ebullient welcome.

Lizzie stood silently among them, her arm linked through Eliza's. Rather than wait for the next day's papers and rely upon what were certain to be absurdly rapturous descriptions of Mr. Davis's arrival, she had been determined to see him for herself and take her own measure of him. She knew that he was fifty-two, and that he had been a soldier and a planter, that he had served in the United States House and Senate, and that he had been secretary of war to President Franklin Pierce. What she saw as he stepped down from the carriage at Eighth and Main was a tall, thin, dignified gentleman with a prominent nose and brow, high cheekbones above sunken cheeks, a thin mouth, and neatly trimmed chin whiskers. He was pale, and his left eye looked filmed over with some infection, and he seemed less eager for the office to which he had been chosen than resigned and determined to do his duty.

After one last wave to the adoring crowd, Mr. Davis disappeared inside the Spotswood, but when the people's cries for a speech did not diminish, he appeared at a flag-draped window. "This is not the time for talk, but for action," he began, and continued to address them for ten minutes more, praising the Old Dominion as the cradle that had rocked Washington, Jefferson, Madison, Monroe, and a whole host of other noble patriots. These great statesmen had bequeathed to them a perfect model of government that had become twisted and perverted by an administration determined to deprive them of their constitutional rights, but the new heroes of the South would not let that stand. When at last Mr. Davis bade his avid listeners good morning and withdrew to sit down to breakfast, the throng roared its approval.

"They adore him," Eliza said, bending close to Lizzie's ear and nearly shouting to be heard over the din.

"They adore him today," Lizzie retorted grimly, and having had quite enough, she linked arms with Eliza and together they pushed their way through the crowd, glad to leave the jubilation behind.

Lizzie did not turn out to observe the president's wife when she arrived three days later, but Mary, by virtue of her exemplary and prolific service to the cause, had been invited along with several other prominent Church Hill ladies to a special reception welcoming Varina Davis to Richmond. It was truly the most exciting spectacle she had ever witnessed, Mary enthused that evening at supper, fairly glowing as she recounted all she had witnessed. "Mrs. Davis arrived by train with her three children and servants," she told them as the soup was served. "A host of other dignitaries accompanied them, as well as the president's favorite horse. Do you know Mr. Davis has a special military saddle with a compass set in its pommel?"

"I didn't know that," said Lizzie shortly. "Nor, I think, should that come as any surprise."

Mary's eyes widened in feigned innocence. "Why, Lizzie, on the contrary, your ignorance on any subject always comes as a great surprise." Her rapturous smile returned as she resumed her tale. "They say that Mr. Davis's saddle signifies that whenever he rides to battle, he will always point north toward the enemy."

"I don't expect he will ride to battle very often," John remarked.

Mary frowned thoughtfully. "No, perhaps not. Even so, the thought of it alone rallies the spirits."

Lizzie blew on her soup to cool it, but the delectable aromas of cream and celery offered no balm to her annoyance. "Perhaps the compass is meant to help him find his way from the Spotswood to the Capitol."

"Oh, the Davis family will not remain at the Spotswood for long," Mary said. "That lovely gray stucco residence at Twelfth and Clay is being prepared for them. And

Mr. Davis's office is to be in the Custom House, not the Capitol. But you make me leap ahead. Let me tell it from the beginning."

Lizzie supposed there would be no dissuading her, so she remained silent.

"Mr. Davis had gone to the train station to welcome his family and escort them the rest of the way," Mary continued. "Crowds lined the streets, and they cheered and threw flowers in their path. One sweet young girl threw a bouquet that fell short, so the president ordered the carriage to halt, sent a servant for the bouquet, and presented it to his lady. Oh, it was so gallant! The crowd was absolutely enchanted, the ladies especially."

"What were your impressions of Mrs. Davis?" Mother inquired. "Were you introduced?"

"Oh, yes, of course. The reception was held in the Spotswood's finest parlor, gloriously decorated in Confederate colors." Mary paused, thoughtful. "Mrs. Davis is quite a bit younger than her husband, but the difference cannot be any greater than that which separates John and me. She looked to be no more than thirty-five, and I would say in all kindness that she is handsome rather than beautiful. Her eyes are dark and intelligent, her complexion olive, her lips full and curving. She is as soft and round as her husband is thin and angular, but although she has lost her girlish slimness, I think it gives her a more regal bearing." She lowered her voice confidentially. "It is rumored that she is in a delicate condition, but I detected no such sign."

"It could be very early yet," said Mother.

"I suppose. She wore the most beautiful gown of blue silk, with a lovely neckline, a flattering bodice, and an elegant train that draped into a perfect cascade. When I complimented her, Mrs. Davis's expression grew wistful, and she told me that the gown had been made for her by an extraordinarily gifted dressmaker in Washington City." Mary put her head to one side, considering. "I do believe she misses her former home very much, for all that it is now overrun with Yankees."

"Perhaps it's her dressmaker she misses," Lizzie remarked.

Mary dismissed that with a wave of her hand. "She'll have her choice of excellent dressmakers right here in Richmond. Every lady of quality will put forward her favorite in an attempt to win her friendship."

"Will you do the same?" Mother asked.

"Perhaps I shall," Mary said, lifting her chin and smiling. "I would consider it a great honor to call Varina Davis my friend, and it can only be to our benefit if our families become acquainted."

Lizzie managed a nod and a tight smile, although she could imagine great harm coming from knowing the Davises—or rather, from the Davises knowing the Van Lews too well.

Little more than a week later, all thoughts of dressmakers and befriending the Davises fled as the Van Lews were suddenly, sharply reminded why the Confederate president had come to Richmond.

It was well known—and a source of considerable outrage throughout the new Confederate capital—that Union troops from Fort Monroe had crossed the Potomac and were venturing up the Peninsula. On June 10, Union major general Benjamin F. Butler led an attack on a Confederate outpost at Bethel Church in Hampton. In a fierce skirmish, the Richmond

Howitzers along with fourteen hundred infantrymen led by Confederate colonel John Magruder threw back the Union incursion, inflicting seventy-nine casualties and seizing victory in the first land battle of the war.

Richmond fairly burst with jubilation. Newspapers published thrilling accounts of the battle, and downtown businesses flaunted captured Union regimental banners in their front windows. Spectators turned out to watch as the first Union prisoners were marched to the Custom House, where they were to be held until room could be found for them in the city's overcrowded jails. The Confederacy's first casualty, a private with the First North Carolina Infantry named Henry L. Wyatt, was lauded as a noble martyr to the cause.

The constant deafening clamor of speechmaking and parading and drilling made Lizzie's head throb and her clenched jaw ache. When word of the battle reached the city, her first thought had been of Cousin Jack, who had fought with the Richmond Howitzers, but once she was assured of his safety, her relief quickly gave way to dismay. Troops returning from the battlefield, flush with the red-hot pride of the newly triumphant, boasted of tossing dead Yankees into pits, as suited creatures too disgusting to touch and undeserving of a proper Christian burial.

How the conflict would end, and when, God alone knew.

Chapter Five

JULY 1861

From the Capitol to the soldiers' encampments, from lofty Church Hill to downtrodden Penitentiary Bottom, longtime residents and newcomers alike celebrated the Confederate victory at Bethel Church. To Lizzie's surprise, Mary, the last person she would have expected to minimize the significance of the rout, cautioned restraint. "Some of the most patriotic officers do not believe the popular notion that a single Confederate soldier could whip a dozen Yankees," she confided one evening in mid-June after returning home from a soiree the Church Hill ladies had hosted for

General Beauregard and his officers in Springfield Hall. "President Davis believes that the Yankees will fight with courage, and he predicts a long war, with many a bitter experience."

"How do you know what Mr. Davis believes?" Lizzie countered mildly, tempering her tone for the sake of little Eliza, who was fussing drowsily on her lap. It was past her bedtime, but she had insisted upon waiting up to kiss her mother good night, and Annie refused to go to bed earlier than her younger sister. Lizzie never would have given in to their pleas had she known Mary would return home an hour late.

"My friend Mrs. Chesnut told me, and Mr. Davis himself told her."

John's brow furrowed. "I've never heard you mention a Mrs. Chesnut."

"Of course I've mentioned her. You must not have been listening," Mary replied crisply. "Her husband is James Chesnut, who once was a senator in the Yankee government but is now a member of our Congress. Her father was a senator too, and a former governor of South Carolina."

"My goodness," said Mother, setting aside the book she had been reading to

Annie and helping the girl down from her lap. Annie ran to her mother and flung her arms around her waist as if Mary had been gone for days. "Such important gentlemen."

"Mrs. Chesnut is important in her own right," said Mary as she absently accepted Annie's embrace. "She's already become one of Mrs. Davis's dearest friends, and mine too. She kindly recommended a tincture that she assures me will bring me some comfort from my headaches."

Lizzie had long suspected that Mary's headaches were an excuse to escape her maternal duties for a few hours every other afternoon, and that she nipped from the bottle of whiskey hidden poorly in the top drawer of her bureau to ease herself to sleep. A witty retort came to mind, but she held her tongue. Lizzie would have included Mr. Davis and his officers among the worst offenders in exaggerating the rebel army's prowess, so it was intriguing to learn that behind closed doors, the men who had seen battle were far more realistic.

As the Fourth of July approached, Lizzie was surprised to discover that the rebellious citizens of Richmond seemed to anticipate the holiday with newly ardent patriotism. The Declaration of Independence represented the views of the secessionist South more than it ever had for the Union, or so the argument went, and the recent capture of a Union steamer and several other vessels on the Chesapeake Bay made a Confederate victory and its recognition as a sovereign nation seem ever more imminent. And so a celebration was planned, one that Lizzie studiously avoided with a day of letter writing, quiet reflection, and prayer.

Her peace was interrupted by the distant sounds of pipes and drums playing spirited martial tunes and the low booming of an eleven-gun salute fired by the Thomas Artillery from its camp at the Baptist college, one round for each of the Confederate states. Shortly before noon, the State Guard fired another eleven-gun salute from Capitol Square, and in between, Lizzie knew, there had been lively parades and fiery speeches.

She was relieved to have avoided the scene. The rebellious speeches would have outraged her, the Confederate flags would have made her mourn anew for her beloved United States, and the guns would have reminded her of the hundreds of soldiers still fighting around Bethel Church, still fighting and still dying.

Each morning came the newspapers. Daily Lizzie was amazed anew at the reporters' lack of censorship, which amounted to their fighting for both sides. In the first weeks of July, all of Richmond was aware that Union general Irvin McDowell intended to advance deeper into Virginia by midmonth. Alerted to the danger, the Confederate general Beauregard dug in and waited for reinforcements to arrive from the Shenandoah Valley. Word came from the front that General Beauregard's men had won a skirmish along a creek called Bull Run. Immediately ambulance wagons were dispatched, swiftly carrying doctors, bandages, and medicines to the battlefield.

The next day, July 20, came the long-awaited reconvening of the Confederate Congress in its new home. Legislators entered the historic building Thomas Jefferson had designed, passing Houdon's magnificent statue of George Washington in the rotunda on their way to the chamber, but the momentous occasion was overshadowed by the victory at Blackburn's Ford one hundred miles to the north and expectations of more fighting to come. Newspapers later reported that President Davis had left his sickbed that morning intending to hurry to the field, but could not leave because he had been obliged to carry out an important duty of his office—the delivering of the State of the Confederacy address to the newly reconvened Congress. He rushed through his speech, and the next morning, he left his office in the care of General Lee's son, Captain George Washington Custis Lee, and took the first train north.

In Richmond, churchgoers turned out for Sunday services, slaves went about their thankless toil, and everyone waited anxiously for news. People milled about the streets, gathering in hotel lobbies and outside telegraph offices and in front of newspaper offices' bulletin boards, but no one knew much of anything except that fierce fighting had begun at Manassas around six o'clock that morning. By midday the first train carrying wounded from the battle arrived at the depot, and their reports of Confederate regiments torn to pieces and the desperate need for more medical supplies sent waves of apprehension and fear rippling through the city. The warm, sunny day wore on, and nerves frayed and rumors spread and the women left behind paced and waited and tended children and tried to reassure one another that no harm would come to their loved ones.

As night fell and the bells in Richmond's steeples remained silent, Lizzie allowed herself to hope that the Union would triumph. Good news, if the rebels had any, would have been sent with all haste to the capital and trumpeted to the anxious populace and the press. Bad news would be delayed, on the chance that it might improve. "The longer General Beauregard waits to send a messenger," she told her mother and brother as they lingered in the library after the rest of the household had gone to bed, "the better it goes for the Union. You shall see."

They nodded, hopeful, and together they waited for word, but the night wore on, and Mother fell asleep in her chair, and John gave in to the temptation to rest his head on the desk and was soon snoring away softly. Lizzie started awake in her armchair shortly after midnight with a crick in her neck, and as she rubbed it away, she took the silence outside as a promising sign. Gently she woke Mother and John and urged them off to bed before retiring herself. Sunrise would bring welcome news, she told herself as she put out the lamp and drew up the sheet. She lay on her side watching the linen curtains stir in the breeze until she drifted off to a sleep unbroken by the tolling of bells.

She woke Monday morning to silence but for the music of songbirds and the steady clip-clop of a horse pulling a carriage sedately down Grace Street. "No alarm," she murmured, scrambling out of bed, her heart pounding with excitement. Surely the lack of celebration meant a Union victory.

But when she dressed and went downstairs to breakfast, she found John and Mother drawn and grave, and Mary irritatingly cheerful. "What's the news?" she asked as she seated herself, dreading the reply.

"The rebels won the battle," said John quietly. "News is still trickling in, but by all accounts, it was a very costly victory."

"They say Mr. Davis himself led the troops in the field," said Mary, her eyes bright with awe. "Now, **that** is a proper commander in chief. You won't see the Illinois ape doing anything half as brave."

"Don't speak of Mr. Lincoln in that manner," said John brusquely. "Show some respect to the office if you cannot think well of the man."

"He's not **our** president any longer," Mary snapped.

"He is mine," said Lizzie angrily. She should not lose her temper, but news of another Union loss, Mary's crowing—it was too much at once so early in the morning.

Mary scowled, but she looked more worried than angry. "You're a fool to say that aloud."

"Not within my own home, I'm not. Who here would betray me?" She fixed Mary with a challenging stare, and when Mary looked away, she steeled herself and turned to John. "You say it was a costly victory. Dare I hope the Union did not suffer as many casualties in defeat?"

It was a vain hope, and she knew the answer even before John shook his head. "There were heavy losses on both sides. It may prove to be the bloodiest battle ever fought on American soil."

"Hundreds of women were made widows yesterday," said Mother softly. "Hundreds of children lost fathers. Hundreds of parents lost sons."

Suddenly Lizzie felt heartsick and ashamed for bickering so pettily while young men were dying, and one glance at Mary convinced her that her sister-in-law felt the same.

After so many parades and bonfires and artillery salutes, the day was strangely still as an expectant hush shrouded the city. The Confederates had won, but at what cost? Later, when John came home from Van Lew & Taylor, he reported that Mayor Mayo had presided over a citizens' meeting at City Hall, where they had organized three committees: one to establish hospitals and care for the wounded, another to raise funds, and a third, led by the mayor himself, to travel to the battlefield and help tend to the casualties. A storm rolled in that afternoon and a heavy downpour fell throughout the night, but thousands of citizens waited anxiously in the rain at the depot for the trains from Manassas, hoping for some word of their loved ones.

President Davis returned to the capital on Tuesday, and he offered a speech on the train platform and another, later, from the Spotswood Hotel. In the days to come, Lizzie would learn that he had described how the Confederate heroes had repulsed the Yankee invaders, sending them scurrying back to Washington City. She would hear that Mr. Davis had not led troops into battle after all but had kept well behind the advancing lines, rallying stragglers, reassuring the wounded, and congratulating the victors. She would hear tales of how Colonel Thomas Jackson had spotted a gap in the defensive line and had driven his troops forward to protect it against a Union attack, inspiring one impressed general to exclaim, "There is Jackson standing like a stone wall!" He earned a promotion to major general for his courage and quick thinking on the battlefield—and a new nickname.

The number of Southern men killed, wounded, and captured was still being tallied as the press lauded the fallen as heroes and declared that the victory proved that neither raw Yankee volunteers nor the regular army could withstand the charge of the Confederate bayonet. "It would be difficult to overestimate the effect of the victory that has been gained for the Southern cause," proclaimed the **Examiner**, reveling in the great number and value of Union men and artillery captured and predicting dire consequences for Yankee recruitment efforts, as well as the United States stock market. "By the work of Sunday, we have broken the backbone of invasion and utterly broken the spirit of the North."

Lizzie fumed at the suggestion that the Union would abandon hope so readily, and even Mary fretted at the newspaper's boast that "the sentiment of invincibility will take possession of every man of the South," and its extraordinary prediction that the worst of the war was behind them. "Mrs. Chesnut says that Mr. William Trescot says that these easy, early victories will lull the South into a fool's paradise of conceit, and in the meantime, the shameful losses will light a fire beneath the men of the North."

"Mrs. Chesnut said Mr. Trescot said that?" Mother asked lightly. "Goodness.

I've never met the gentlemen, but he talks like a Yankee. Did anyone ask where he was born?"

"South Carolina." Mary shook her head. "I don't mean to say that I asked him. Mrs. Chesnut told me. I never would have embarrassed him by making him admit he was not born in Virginia."

"Well, we can't all be," said Mother, the only one among them who had not been.

"We've discovered another common cause, you and I," Lizzie told her sister-in-law with a levity she did not feel. "We agree that the Confederates may become overconfident, and we're united in our displeasure with the press."

"These are strange times indeed," Mary replied. Lizzie burst out laughing, but only after Mary shot her a sour glare did she realize that her sister-in-law had spoken in all seriousness.

There was little enough to laugh about in the days following the Battle of Manassas. Soon hundreds of wounded came streaming into Richmond, quickly filling the hospitals and overflowing into schools, hotels, and warehouses that had been hastily turned into makeshift infirmaries.

Many citizens welcomed ill and wounded soldiers into their own homes, tending their injuries and nursing them back to health as best they could. Dozens more soldiers were brought back to the city in plain pine boxes, to be buried in Richmond or to be shipped farther South to their grieving families. Across the street from the Van Lew mansion, Saint John's Church hosted an almost continuous succession of memorial services, and from her window Lizzie observed so many military funerals for slain Confederate officers, with black-clad bands in procession with marching soldiers and warhorses bearing empty saddles that she could not keep track of their numbers. The scenes of mourning wrenched Lizzie's heart, not only because she knew many of the deceased and had considered them friends before secession had driven a wedge between their families, but because their deaths were so needless. The cotton states never should have seceded, Virginia never should have cast her lot with the South, and war never should have broken out.

Soon, into this strange, volatile brew of

triumph and mourning spilled nearly a thousand Union prisoners, bedraggled, demoralized, and hungry, many bearing untended wounds. With county jails already full beyond capacity, the captives were marched from Richmond's Central Depot to Liggon's Tobacco Factory, mere blocks from the Van Lew residence. When Lizzie read the terse newspaper accounts of hundreds of men being squeezed into a three-story brick structure that could not possibly accommodate them all, she became almost breathless from dismay. There were no beds, no sanitary facilities, no kitchens in the factory, only tobacco presses and perhaps a few offices. Reports that Brigadier General John H. Winder, the inspector general of military camps for Richmond, intended to commandeer a few other factories and warehouses to convert to military prisons did nothing to alleviate her worries.

She wasted not a moment worrying what the neighbors might think, nor did she pause to invite her mother or Eliza to accompany her. Instead she left her house alone, nodded to the man with the tobacco-stained beard sitting on a fence across from Saint John's—he nodded sheepishly back—and strode purposefully downhill toward the river, pausing at Twenty-Fifth and Main to study the prison and steel her nerves. From the street, the building seemed unchanged except for the uniformed military guards posted at the main entrance and others patrolling the block, rifles in hand.

Lizzie took a deep breath, squared her shoulders, and approached the nearest guard. "Good afternoon," she said pleasantly, fixing the plump young fellow with a winning smile. "I'm here to see your commandant."

"You mean Lieutenant Todd, Ma'am?" The soldier frowned at her quizzically. "Is he expecting you?"

She took her watch from her pocket, glanced at the time, and feigned surprise. "My goodness, no. It's not yet half past one." Taken separately, both statements were true. "Would you be so kind as to escort me nonetheless?"

He hesitated, but then he nodded and showed her inside, where the smells of tobacco and sweat mingled unpleasantly above something else, something rotten and fetid that she dared not allow herself to think too much about. Floorboards creaked overhead as if trod upon by hundreds of aching, poorly shod feet, and in the distance she heard a long moan of pain, which cut off abruptly just as her guide halted at a closed door. "Wait here, if you please, Ma'am," he said, and ducked inside, only to return a moment later looking somewhat shamefaced. "The lieutenant will see you, Ma'am. You can go on in."

She thanked him graciously and swept into the small office, which boasted a worn pine desk with a pair of low-backed wooden chairs arranged before it. Along the walls, bookcases were stuffed with hundreds of papers and files. Behind the desk, a man who looked to be not yet thirty rose and gave her a stiff bow. His dark hair was parted on the right and combed back, and his visage boasted a long, tapered mustache that curved upward and thick, short chin whiskers. "Good afternoon, Madam," he greeted her, gesturing to one of the low-backed chairs. "You must forgive me for not offering you a more solicitous welcome, but I was not informed of our appointment, nor did my aide think to introduce us. I am Lieutenant Todd, the commander here."

Lizzie's heart thumped as she seated herself. The prison commandant was none other than David Humphreys Todd, half brother to Mary Todd Lincoln and brother-in-law to President Abraham Lincoln. How did a man with such relations end up a rebel? "I am Elizabeth Van Lew, of Church Hill. Thank you for seeing me."

"It's my pleasure," he said perfunctorily, but as he returned to his chair behind the desk, a glimmer of recognition appeared in his eye. "Van Lew of Church Hill. Are you not the widow of John Van Lew, who made his fortune in hardware?"

"That would be my mother, Eliza Baker Van Lew," said Lizzie. "I am their eldest child. My brother, John Newton, runs the store now."

"Ah, yes, of course." The lieutenant's brow furrowed. "And to what do I owe the honor of your visit?"

"I come on a mission of Christian charity," she said. "I would like to serve as hospital nurse for the Union prisoners."

He had taken up a pen, but at her words his hand froze in the air, suspending the nib above the ink. "You are the first and only lady to make any such application."

"Why, then, the need is even greater than I anticipated."

Lieutenant Todd set down his pen emphatically, steepled his fingers, and rested them upon the desk. "If charity is what compels you, why not offer to nurse our own suffering soldiers?"

Lizzie smiled knowingly. "The young belles of Richmond nearly ran me over in their haste to volunteer for that noble duty. Since our gallant soldiers have an abundance of nurses, I thought I would be more useful caring for those who might otherwise be neglected."

"Our soldiers don't have an abundance of anything," said the lieutenant sharply. "And neglect is better than the Yankee scum deserve."

"Lieutenant Todd," said Lizzie, shocked. "Wounded men suffer whether they hail from the South or the North. Where is your compassion?"

"I'll reserve my compassion for the innocent and the just." He shook his head and leaned back in his chair, folding his arms over his chest. "Altogether I find this a very odd and disquieting request. A prison, even a prison hospital, is no place for a lady. I cannot believe you would volunteer for such work if you knew what it's like in here."

"I would like to know," said Lizzie. "May I meet some of the prisoners?"

"Absolutely not. I would be remiss in my duties to expose you to such filth."

"Only the officers, then," Lizzie quickly countered. "Surely they are gentlemen despite being Yankees, and they would behave as gentlemen ought."

"I'm not willing to give them a chance to disappoint you." He rose and came around the desk to assist her to her feet, and her heart sank as she realized the interview was over. "If you want to serve the Confederacy, then look to our own suffering men. Your good works would be wasted upon these wretches."

She pressed her lips together tightly and nodded as he showed her to the door, unable to trust herself to speak. The same guard was waiting in the hallway, and he escorted her outside, where she thanked him graciously, as if the meeting had gone exactly as she had wanted. Then she turned and walked briskly away, her anger smoldering. How dare Lieutenant Todd turn her away! It would cost him nothing in time, money, or inconvenience to let her nurse the poor injured men, and yet he would prefer to let them suffer.

She would have to go over his head—but to whom?

She pondered her options as she walked the mile between the prison and the Custom House on the corner of Tenth and Main, where the Confederate government kept its offices. Gazing up at the five round arches that formed the arcade marking the entrance to the grand Italianate structure, she quickly ran through a mental list of the men who toiled within its granite and limestone walls. To whom could she appeal? She knew no one in the president's innermost circle; there were no Virginians in the Cabinet, as the Confederate government had formed before Virginia seceded. Who, among these people who did not know her, would listen?

And then she remembered Mr. Memminger.

Christopher G. Memminger, the secretary of the treasury, was a native of Germany but had immigrated to the United States with his mother when he was a very young child. He was a South Carolinian to the core—and also a devout Christian. Although he had no direct authority over the prisons, he had influence with those who did.

Lizzie gathered up her skirts and climbed the stairs, passing beneath an enormous Confederate flag as she entered the stronghold of the rebel government.

Perhaps curiosity inspired Secretary Memminger to make time to speak with her, because she waited in his outer office scarcely a quarter of an hour before an aide ushered her inside. The room was about the size of Lieutenant Todd's, but much tidier and brighter, with a window that looked out upon Bank Street and the pleasant smell of lemon oil and fresh sawdust in the air, the latter a remnant of the partitions hastily constructed to divide a large room into several smaller, private chambers.

Secretary Memminger rose and bowed when she entered. "Miss Van Lew, welcome," he greeted her, offering her a comfortable chair by the window, though he remained standing. He was a gentlemen not yet sixty years of age, with fair hair, dark-blue eyes, and chiseled features. "What request would you make of the Department of the Treasury?"

"My request is not for your department, Mr. Secretary, but for you."

His eyebrows rose, and he clasped his hands behind his back as he regarded her from above. "How may I be of service, Madam?"

"I realize that you are an exceptionally busy man, and I believe I can express my gratitude best by getting right to the point." Lizzie paused to take a breath and smile up at him, hopeful. "I would like to nurse the sick and wounded Union prisoners being held in the tobacco factories. They're only a few blocks away from my own neighborhood, so you can understand why I would feel a special responsibility to extend the hand of charity to them."

"Are you a trained nurse?"

"No, no more than any other woman who has cared for ailing members of her own family."

He allowed a rueful smile. "In other words, as qualified as most of the ladies serving as nurses throughout Richmond at this very moment."

"Yes, Mr. Secretary. We women are well practiced in caring for the sick, and we all want to be useful."

Suddenly his smile disappeared. "Your good intentions are woefully misdirected," he said sternly. "The prisoners are a very different class of men than a lady such as yourself is accustomed to, and they are wholly undeserving of your ministrations."

"Deserving or not, they need care, and no one else seems eager to take on the task." She clasped her hands together in her lap and tried not to show how desperately she wanted him to agree. "I beg you, sir, please consider my offer. I am a woman of independent means, and I assure you I will bear every expense myself."

"That does not change the nature of the men you seek to nurse," he pointed out. "They are a very low, rough, violent sort, not worthy or fit for a lady to visit."

"Oh, yes, of course. I see." Lizzie paused, thinking. "But you cannot fault me for wanting to help them. As a lady—as a Christian lady—it is my duty to dispense charity to the less fortunate."

"I do not fault you at all," he assured her. "In fact, I commend you."

"I knew you would understand." Lizzie fixed him with an admiring smile. "You are the very model of the Christian gentleman, as I knew you would be. I heard you speak once, in peacetime, at a religious convention, and I must say you spoke beautifully on the subject of Christian duty. I was quite moved."

"Thank you, Miss Van Lew," he said, visibly pleased. "It is a subject that has occupied my thoughts quite a lot during these challenging times."

"What was it our Lord said?" Lizzie mused, gazing thoughtfully at the bookshelf to the secretary's left, where a thick, well-read, leather-bound Bible was given pride of place on its own shelf. "'Naked, and ye clothed me: I was sick, and ye visited me: I was in prison, and ye came unto me.' Matthew 25:40, is it not?"

"I believe it is Matthew 25:36."

"Really? Then what is Matthew 25:40?"

Secretary Memminger appeared somewhat chagrined as he recited, "'And the King shall answer and say unto them, Verily I say unto you, Inasmuch as ye have done it unto one of the least of these my brethren, ye have done it unto me.'"

"Mr. Secretary," said Lizzie earnestly. "Surely these Union prisoners **are** the least of our brethren. My obligation as a Christian woman is to help them as I would help our Lord Himself."

He frowned and shifted his weight uncomfortably, but he did not ask her to be silent.

"If we want our cause to succeed," she continued, emboldened, "we must begin with charity to the thankless. We should also be mindful that the Yankees took many prisoners too, and for their sakes as well as the sake of our own souls, we should show by our example how enemy captives ought to be treated."

For a long moment, the secretary regarded her in silence, but then he nodded. "Of course you're right," he said. "It is not always pleasant to be reminded of our duty, but the Lord Jesus Christ could not have been more clear on this subject. We must care for these prisoners, though they are our sworn enemies, because they are also our brothers."

"However much we might wish to disavow them."

He let out a short laugh. "Yes. **Especially** then, I warrant." He sat down at his desk, took a sheet of paper from a basket, dipped a pen in ink, and began to write. Lizzie watched, holding herself perfectly still and scarcely breathing rather than disturb him, until he set down the pen and looked up. "Take this letter of introduction to General Winder and tell him I trust he will offer you his complete cooperation." He waited for the ink to dry before folding the page and sealing it. "He keeps an office on Bank Street—a bit shabby, but it's only temporary until something better can be found."

"Yes, I know the place." When he held out the letter, she quickly rose and took it before he could change his mind. "Mr. Secretary, I cannot thank you enough."

He accepted her thanks graciously and rose to show her to the door. He was a true gentleman, she thought as she left the Custom House by the Bank Street exit, the precious letter in hand. She could not help thinking, as she had of Mr. Lee, that it was a pity such a man was a rebel.

In no time at all she arrived at General Winder's shanty office, where she found him seated at a table where two clerks were busily writing. The general—a stout, stern, silver-haired man of about sixty years—received her most politely and kindly, but when his frown deepened as he read Secretary Memminger's letter, she knew he would require more persuasion.

As to that, the sunlight had faded from her golden ringlets, her youthful softness had given way to angularity, but she had not forgotten how to charm a gentleman.

His silvery white hair waved in handsome locks, and as he reached the end of the letter, she suddenly exclaimed, "Dear me, General Winder, my friends told me you were handsome, but their compliments scarcely do you justice. What noble physiognomy! Your hair would better adorn the temple of Janus. It seems out of place in such surroundings."

The general glanced up from the letter, surprised. "Thank you, Madam," he said. "You are very kind."

"Oh, not at all." Lizzie smiled and waved

a hand breezily. "I'm sure you've heard it before. You must know how much the ladies of Richmond admire you."

He smiled, flattered. "From the moment I arrived, the ladies of Richmond have impressed me with their grace and kindness. I'm very pleased to know I've made a favorable impression upon them."

"Indeed you have. In fact, that's why I was not the least bit nervous approaching you with my little petition, because your reputation for wisdom precedes you." She gave him her most winning smile. "As an act of Christian charity, I should like to visit the Union prisoners, and nurse them if they are ill or wounded, and bring them little delicacies from my kitchen, and such books as will distract them and keep them from causing any disturbances. I will, of course, bear all expenses myself, as part of my service to the cause."

Two clerks exchanged a look of surprise as General Winder mulled it over. "I have no objection," he said. "I would prefer for you not to go alone, however. Soldiers can be a rough breed."

Lizzie's smile deepened. "Perhaps, but I have also discovered—quite recently, in fact—that among them one may also find the most charming of gentlemen."

The general chuckled and his cheeks took on an ever so slightly rosier hue as he asked the clerks for paper and pen. "I am writing you a pass," he declared as he wrote, "granting you permission to visit the prisoners, and to bring them books, food, whatever you may please."

"That is most kind, General."

He stood and reached across the desk to hand her the pass, and she quickly rose and took it. "This should suffice, but if any-one refuses you, send word to me right away and we'll sort it out."

She thanked him profusely and swept from the office, throwing him one last smile over her shoulder in parting. Back on the street, she closed her eyes, clutched the precious paper to her bosom, and inhaled deeply, wishing she could shout for joy. At last she could fulfill the sacred duty of caring for the Union prisoners in their distress—and no one, not even the es-tranged brother-in-law of the president of her beloved United States, could stop her.

Chapter Six

The next day, Lizzie instructed Caroline to cook up a pot of rich chicken soup and a simple cornmeal gruel, and to spoon them into covered dishes. Lizzie's favorite was a clever contrivance with a double bottom into which boiling water could be poured to keep the food warm. At the last moment, she asked Caroline to make a ginger cake, the same delicacy Mr. Botts was so fond of, and to fill a bottle with buttermilk. "We must take a gift for Lieutenant Todd," she explained to little Annie, who was too small to be useful but insisted upon helping her auntie load the basket.

"He won't be pleased to learn that I went to his superiors," she told her mother as they strolled down the hill to the Liggon prison complex, heavy baskets in their arms. In addition to the food, Mother had wisely packed bandages, lint, and a bottle of brandy, mostly full.

"Caroline's ginger cake will sweeten him," said Mother confidently, puffing a bit from exertion. "And even if it doesn't, Lieutenant Todd dare not ignore General Winder's command."

Lizzie certainly hoped so.

When they arrived at the main gate, the plump young guard who had escorted Lizzie before was absent, and a tall, lank-haired soldier with a pockmarked face stood at his post. Mother explained their errand, and when the guard disappeared inside and returned with the news that Lieutenant Todd could not see them, Lizzie sighed disconsolately. "Oh, what a pity," she exclaimed, lifting the cloth over the basket holding the ginger cake so that the delicious aroma wafted out. "We had so hoped to deliver our gifts while they're fresh and warm. I suppose we could return tomorrow, but they will not taste half as good."

"I did not think I would have to carry these heavy burdens uphill on our way home," said Mother, sounding much distressed. "We had expected to empty our baskets here."

The guard eyed their baskets longingly as if he wished he could accept them on the lieutenant's behalf. "Let me ask again. Maybe he can spare a few minutes."

They smiled and thanked him, and soon enough he returned and ushered them through the gate and down the long hallway. Lieutenant Todd was writing in a ledger of sorts when they arrived at his office, but he set his pen aside and rose when they entered. "We come bearing gifts," said Mother, setting the bottle of buttermilk on his desk while Lizzie placed the ginger cake in his hands, still warm, wrapped in a cheesecloth.

"This smells delicious," he said, admiring the ginger cake, but when he glanced up, the gaze he fixed on Lizzie was curious. "I confess I don't know what I did to earn such a delicacy. My impression was that you left our first meeting rather displeased with me."

"I know you were thinking only of my

welfare," Lizzie assured him, taking General Winder's letter from her pocket. "I confess I was disappointed, but not undaunted, and I'm happy to say that General Winder agrees that I should care for the Union prisoners—at my own expense, of course. My work will free up the more qualified nurses to care for our own suffering soldiers."

The lieutenant straightened, and his mouth hardened into a line. Pretending not to notice his annoyance, Lizzie smiled and held out the letter to him with both hands. He set the ginger cake on the desk next to the buttermilk, took the page, and read it slowly. "I see," he said when he had finished, folding the letter and returning it to her. "If General Winder says you may visit the soldiers, I cannot refuse. I do hope you ladies are prepared for what you will see."

"I'm sure that we are **not** prepared," said Mother frankly. "We have read about the violence of war, and we have had occasion to tend to the ailing and broken bodies of loved ones, but I am quite sure that nothing we have experienced in our fortunate lives could adequately prepare us for the task we want to undertake. And yet we must set aside our fears and squeamishness, and do what we are afraid to do, because those men are suffering and we can help."

Lieutenant Todd studied her in silence, and Lizzie could tell that he was impressed. "I won't delay you any longer," he said, and beckoned to the guard. "Take these ladies to the infirmary. Give them anything they need."

They followed the guard down a long corridor, silent, steeling themselves. The smell told them that they had arrived even before their escort halted at a door. He opened it and gestured for them to proceed him inside, but when she crossed the threshold, Lizzie drew back, gagging from the smell of defecation and urine and rot. Mother shifted her basket to the crook of her elbow, pressed a rosemary-scented handkerchief to her mouth and nose, and pushed past Lizzie into the room. Swallowing hard, her eyes tearing up, Lizzie followed.

It was, not unexpectedly, a hospital ward in name only. Nearly six dozen men were crammed into a room that could not have held a third that number in any comfort. They had no beds, but lay on straw scattered upon the rough, uneven wooden floor. Only half of the men had blankets, which they had wadded up into pillows or spread upon the straw for comfort, needing no coverings in the stifling summer heat. Lingering near the door, where the air was not so thick and foul, Lizzie saw men with open, oozing wounds; amputees with stumps wrapped in strips of fabric torn from the uniforms of many different regiments; haphazardly tended injuries with blood and pus seeping through the bandages. One man groaned, another called out weakly for water.

And suddenly Lizzie knew where to begin. Quickly she set down the baskets of gruel and soup and whirled upon the guard. "Water," she said tersely. "Clean, fresh water. A pail with a dipper for drinking, a bucketful for washing."

The guard gave her a wary, appraising look and seemed as if he might speak, but he hurried off without a word, and Lizzie and her mother set themselves to their grim duty.

All morning and well into the afternoon

they cleansed and bandaged wounds, offered the men water, dispensed small doses of brandy, and spooned soup or gruel into the mouths of prisoners who were well enough to eat. They badgered the guards to summon a doctor to examine the most seriously afflicted men, but although they were assured a doctor would come as soon as possible, one had not yet appeared by the time the exhausted women withdrew from the infirmary. They stopped by Lieutenant Todd's office, assured him they would return the next day, and left the prison, their footsteps quickening as they approached the exit. Outside, Lizzie gasped as the breeze swept over her; never before had the sultry July air by the river felt so refreshing and tasted so sweet. She thought she heard someone call out from above, but when she glanced upward, she saw no one at any of the small, tightly shut windows.

"At the very least," she muttered, "the prisoners should be permitted to raise the sashes and allow a breath of air to stir inside."

"They might climb out and make their escape," her mother replied.

"The sick and injured wouldn't, and neither would those on the third floor." Lizzie sighed as they trudged wearily up the hill toward home, the empty dishes rattling in their baskets. "Oh, Mother, their suffering was even worse than I expected—and we saw only one room!"

"But in all likelihood, it was the worst room." Mother paused to catch her breath in the shade of a walnut tree growing close to the street. "Tomorrow, we'll ask to be introduced to the officers. We'll bring books and bread and writing materials."

"And another pair of hands," said Lizzie as they continued on their way. "Eliza will help us, I'm sure."

The next morning, when they stopped by the Carrington residence on their way to the prison with their refilled baskets, Eliza grew pale as they described the conditions within the infirmary and how desperately more help was needed. "I believe we have some fresh bread I could bring," Eliza said faintly when they finished. "And some preserves. And a bottle of cherry cordial."

"Thank you, my dear," said Mother. "We can offer that to the lieutenant."

He accepted it most appreciatively, and upon their arrival in the infirmary, they discovered a handful of new patients, one who had broken his arm in a scuffle with a guard and three suffering from the flux. Mother kept the latter as far away from the others as she could in such close quarters, and while she and Eliza began changing dressings and feeding soup, cornmeal gruel, and bread to those who could eat, Lizzie returned to the lieutenant's office and presented him with a list of requests for the prisoners that she had worked out the night before—cots, of course, and sheets and blankets to dress them. Bandages, as many rolls as they could get. The liberty to open the windows. Permission for the walking wounded to take their exercise in the courtyard. Ample supplies of fresh, clean water. Chamber pots and necessaries. Regular visits from qualified physicians.

"Doctors' visits will be few and far between," Lieutenant Todd said, scanning the list. "There are hundreds of patients throughout the city requiring their attention. Water and exercise will be granted. As to the rest of it—" He tossed the list on his desk, folded his arms, and shrugged. "I have no objection if you wish to provide such supplies as you believe the Yankees require. I only hope you are giving as generously to our side."

"Of course," she said, hiding her surprise. She had not expected him to agree to half of her requests, so she had asked for twice as much as she thought she could squeeze out of him. "When we've finished tending to the men in the infirmary, we'd like to visit some of the other prisoners and inquire as to their needs."

She held her breath, waiting for him to object. She had General Winder's letter in her pocket, but she hoped Lieutenant Todd would not force her to produce it. To her relief, he frowned, but nodded.

At midday, Eliza remained behind in the infirmary while a guard escorted Lizzie and her mother to the officers' quarters on the first floor. Upon entering the room, Lizzie's first impression was of a dark, cramped, and dusty space, oppressive with the smells of old tobacco and unwashed bodies and the sounds of low voices rumbling and throats clearing. As her eyes adjusted to the dim light, she saw that the room was more than twice as long as it was wide, about thirty feet by seventy-five, although half that space was taken up by tobacco presses. At least forty men sat or stood or walked aimlessly about, glancing curiously at the visitors, but they had no beds or blankets that Lizzie could discern.

As Lizzie and her mother stepped into the room, gazing about and nodding politely to the prisoners, one man in a civilian suit broke away from the crowd and approached. "Welcome to our humble abode, ladies," he said, inclining his head solicitously. "I'm Congressman Alfred Ely, the senior prisoner here. How may I be of service?"

"We rather hope that we could be of service to you." Lizzie opened her basket to reveal two dozen round buns, their golden tops crisp and marked with crosses. "I fear that we underestimated your numbers."

"Thank you very much. The men will be happy to share." Turning, he beckoned two men, a lieutenant and a captain, and instructed them to distribute the bread to the others, who seemed to be exercising great restraint in not rushing forward to snatch the food from the baskets. "Half a loaf is better than none, especially here."

"**Congressman** Ely, you say?" queried Mother. "Then you are not a soldier?"

He smiled ruefully, but even then his dark eyes, piercing gaze, and strong, intelligent features gave him an air of command. "No, Madam, merely an unfortunate politician, punished for his curiosity. When the fighting began at Bull Run, I rode out from Washington City like thousands of others to witness the glorious spectacle. But I drove my carriage too far, and in the chaos of McDowell's retreat, I was captured."

"Oh, how dreadful," Mother exclaimed, shaking her head.

"We have it better here than the poor enlisted men on the third floor. We're treated to three meals a day, though the portions are small and not particularly appetizing." He glanced at the guard, who had taken up a position just inside the doorway, and lowered his voice. "Those of us who managed to smuggle in a bit of coin can usually convince the guards to purchase additional food for us. The enlisted men—" He shook his head. "They usually get but one meal, on a good day, two. But we keep our spirits up." A few disheveled soldiers who overheard chimed in their agreement stoutly.

As the prisoners eagerly dug into their half portions of bread, Lizzie introduced herself and her mother to Mr. Ely, the usual formalities having been forgotten in their grim surroundings. As Mother strolled through the room, greeting each soldier kindly, offering gentle words, and distributing books, Lizzie chatted with the congressman, who seemed remarkably sanguine given his circumstances. The civilian officers had not expected to be shut up in a prison at all, he explained, shaking his head at their naïveté. They had assumed they would surrender their swords and then be paroled, with the freedom to mingle with their captors and go about the city as they pleased until they could be transported to the North. "We learned quite early on that this will be a very different sort of war," Mr. Ely said matter-of-factly. "We're not certain if Washington even knows where we are and who are among us."

"Your families must be frantic," said Lizzie. "Have you written to them?"

"We would have, if we'd had pen and paper, and if Lieutenant Todd had not expressly forbidden it."

"But simple human decency obliges him to permit it."

"Miss Van Lew," he said steadily, "make no mistake, this is not a place where the rules of human decency are in force."

Indignant, Lizzie thought for a moment, then strode across the room to take one of the last volumes from her mother's basket. "This book is a favorite of mine," she said as she placed it into Mr. Ely's hands, though she had not even glanced at the spine for the title. "I think you will find it quite illuminating."

A slight furrow appeared on his brow. "Thank you, Madam."

"I adore it so much that I can allow you to borrow it only until my next visit." Mindful of the guard observing them from the doorway, she wagged a finger playfully at the congressman and added, "I trust you will take excellent care of it. I'll notice if you leave a single smudge or mark, no matter how small."

"I understand perfectly," he said, inclining his head and tucking the book beneath his arm. "I am grateful to you."

"Tomorrow we'll bring more bread," Mother promised as she joined them, her empty baskets hanging from the crook of her arm. "You must let us know what else we can do for you."

He promised to do so.

After bidding the officers good-bye, Lizzie and her mother asked the guard to escort them back to the infirmary, where they found Eliza bathing the brow of a feverish soldier. He had suffered a blow to the head on the battlefield, a fellow captive from his brigade had told them, and he had not awakened since falling unconscious on the train to Richmond.

"Tomorrow I will bring a mustard plaster," she said, her voice faint from exhaustion. "And the boy in the bed by the corner needs a poultice for that dreadful cough, and they all need fresh bandages. I have some old sheets I can tear up, and—" She broke off, her eyes wide and tearful. "Oh, there is so much to do, and the war has only just begun."

Without a word, Lizzie folded Eliza in

her arms and held her while she trembled and fought back tears. "Be brave," Mother murmured. "The men will see you and think you weep because they're going to die. You must be cheerful and calm so they believe they're going to be perfectly fine."

Eliza nodded, took a deep breath, and offered a tremulous smile.

"That's a good girl," said Mother quietly. "Today was the worst day because it is so new. Tomorrow will be better."

The next morning when they called for Eliza at home, they found her pale but determined, with two heaping baskets full of bandages, remedies, and nutritious broths and porridges. Lizzie and her mother had packed rich custards for the officers and several loaves of bread for the enlisted men, whom Lizzie was determined to visit. She had also brought a satchel full of more books, to supplement the few she had left the previous day and to exchange for the one she had given to Mr. Ely.

The young soldier with the head injury had died during the night, but two new prisoners were stretched out upon the straw where he had lain, and two more had been left on the bare floor across the room. The ladies set themselves to work, but as soon as Lizzie could tear herself away, she carried the basketful of bread upstairs—under careful watch of the ubiquitous guards—where she was appalled to discover hundreds of disheveled, filthy, ravenous men crammed into a room the same size as the one below shared by forty officers and civilians. They too had no beds, nor straw, and their fervent thanks as they devoured their bread convinced her they had next to nothing to eat as well. It was the most heart-wrenching scene she had ever witnessed, and she grew indignant as she thought of the fine residence being refurbished for the Jefferson Davis family while the poor prisoners were kept in squalor.

She had scarcely finished distributing the last of the bread when the guard brusquely ordered her from the room. Rather than raise his ire by brandishing General Winder's pass, she bowed graciously and asked him to take her to the officers' quarters. There Congressman Ely greeted her as courteously as before, though he looked wan and tired behind his good cheer.

"Is it my imagination," she asked, looking about the room, which seemed smaller than the day before, "or have your numbers increased?"

"Yes, we've welcomed more good fellows into our company," he said. "The rumor is that the commandant is going to throw together a few more prisons and distribute us among them, but although this place is quite as miserable as it could be, we don't know whether to hope for a transfer or pray to remain."

"You don't know whether you're in the frying pan or the fire."

He managed a laugh. "Yes, Miss Van Lew. You understand perfectly."

"I hope the book I lent you yesterday offered you some distraction." She studied his face, where exhaustion and determination were plainly written. "I hope you didn't stay up late to finish it. I could have waited another day."

"I would have been awake anyway." He winced and rubbed his shoulder. "Our generous guards overstuffed my featherbed, so it was impossible to get comfortable. I was also determined to return the book to you today, knowing how it is your favorite."

He limped slightly as he made his way through the crowd of prisoners to an orderly pile of belongings placed against the wall—a jacket, a newspaper, a tin cup, and Lizzie's book. Stooping, he picked it up and brought it to her.

"What did you think of it?" Lizzie asked, aware of the guard's eyes upon them.

"It was a pleasant enough diversion, but I found the underlying message . . ." He paused to consider. "Somewhat odd."

"Yes, I thought the same." Lizzie placed the book in her satchel and took out another. "Would you prefer a collection of Shakespeare's comedies?"

"That sounds like just the thing." Mr. Ely managed a smile. "I must thank you again, Miss Van Lew, for your gifts and for your visits. The men and I think of you as a ministering angel."

"Thank you, Congressman," she replied, "but if you had spent any time in Richmond at all, you'd realize that is not an opinion commonly held."

For the rest of the afternoon, the book remained tucked away in the satchel on the floor of the infirmary, where Lizzie needed all her strength of will to refrain from glancing at it. She was eager to see if Mr. Ely had hidden a letter within its pages, but she dared not check while under the watchful eye of the guard. Instead she waited until she was safely home and Mary had retired for the night before hurrying off to the library with the satchel, John and Mother at her heels.

Once there, she shut the door and quickly flipped through the book for a scrap of folded paper, but found nothing. She turned the pages more slowly, but there no letter to be found, nor had Mr. Ely written anything faintly in the margins or between the lines. She held the book by the spine, the pages facing downward, and gave it a few vigorous shakes, but nothing fluttered to the floor. Perplexed, she handed the book to her mother and sat down. "Apparently he misunderstood me," she said. "Or I misunderstood him."

Mother sat in her own chair, examining the book and running her fingertips over the printed lines. "Or Mr. Ely is more clever than you thought."

"An encoded message?" asked John, leaning over the back of her chair for a better look.

"I believe so, or something like it. Here." Mother held up the open book to him. "Touch the paper, gently."

John ran his fingers lightly over the page. "I feel bumps of some sort—no, indentations."

Suddenly Lizzie remembered Mr. Ely's words. "Is that an odd-numbered page?"

John glanced to the upper right corner and held the book out to her. "Page fifteen, as it happens."

"He said he found the book's underlying message **odd**." Lizzie bounded out of her chair, took the book from her brother, and traced the printed lines slowly with a fingertip. "He has indented particular letters by pressing upon them with a pin, or perhaps a sliver of wood." Quickly she ran a hand over page seventeen, and then nineteen, and twenty-one—each exhibited an invisible pattern of bumps and indentations.

"John," she said breathlessly, opening the book to page one, "get pen and paper."

Quickly he seated himself at their father's desk, procured pen and ink and paper, and as Lizzie ran her finger over the lines and called out the indented letters, he wrote them down. Before long, they realized that they were compiling a list of names, ranks, and regiments.

Congressman Ely had concealed a roster of all the Union prisoners at the Liggon complex within the book. But that was not all. After the names—forty officers and nine hundred enlisted men—followed a letter to President Abraham Lincoln briefly describing the harsh conditions within the prison and imploring him to do all he could to seek the men's release.

"I'll write it over in a better hand," John vowed, "and send it off to Washington City without delay."

"Peter can take the letter in the wagon past the pickets to the farm and give it to Mr. and Mrs. Whitehall," said Mother. "Our kind neighbors will see it safely on its way." She turned to Lizzie. "That was very dangerous, daughter. If you had been caught, Mr. Ely would have been severely punished, I'm sure. As for you, at the very least, you would have been banned from visiting the prison."

"Yes, Mother," said Lizzie. "Of course you're right."

"Mind you, I'm not asking you to stop."

Mother managed a small, anxious smile. "But I will ask you to be as careful as you can."

Soberly, Lizzie nodded. They all knew there would be more messages, and they could not refuse to deliver them.

Lizzie, her mother, and Eliza could not visit the prison every day, but they went as often as they could. Despite their sweet words and delicious gifts, Lieutenant Todd seemed to grow more suspicious day by day. He insisted upon inspecting the baskets they carried to and from the prison, often helping himself to the delicacies they carried, and he restricted the duration of their visits arbitrarily and without warning. As the days passed, Lizzie smuggled out several other coded notes from Congressman Ely, transcribed the letters, and sped them along, but although the lieutenant flipped through the books, he never detected their hidden messages.

But Lieutenant Todd watched them carefully, and he was not alone. The skinny fellow with the tobacco-stained beard often followed them to and from the prison, hanging back a block and strolling on the opposite side of the street. Mary complained that the ladies of the Church Hill sewing circle often called upon her to explain her mother- and sister-in-law's strange behavior, which Mary could not do, because she did not understand their compulsion to nurse Yankees either. And then, one morning, Lizzie learned from an acerbic reporter for the **Examiner** that their infamy had spread beyond their own neighborhood:

SOUTHERN WOMEN WITH NORTHERN SYMPATHIES

Two ladies, mother and daughter, living on Church Hill, have lately attracted public notice by their assiduous attentions to the Yankee prisoners confined in this city. Whilst every true woman in this community has been busy making articles of comfort or necessity for our troops, or administering to the wants of the many hundreds of sick, who, far from their homes, which they left to defend our soil, are fit subjects for our sympathy, these two women have been expending their opulent means in aiding and giving comfort to the miscreants who have invaded our sacred soil, bent on rapine and murder, the desolation of our homes and sacred places, and the ruin and dishonour of our families.

Out upon all pretexts of humanity! The largest human charity can find ample scope in kindness and attention to our own poor fellows who have been stricken down while battling for our country and our rights. The Yankee wounded have been put under charge of competent surgeons and provided with good nurses. This is more than they deserve and have any right to expect, and the course of these two females, in providing them with delicacies, buying them books, stationery and papers, cannot but be regarded as an evidence of sympathy amounting to an endorsation of the cause and conduct of these Northern Vandals.

"At least they didn't mention us by name," Lizzie remarked as she set the paper aside. Seated beside her on the back piazza, Mother made no reply but only gazed out upon the gardens, silent and pale.

"They didn't need to," said John, visibly shaken. He rose and began to pace along the piazza.

"Eliza escaped their notice entirely," Lizzie added.

John was not pacified by her attempt to point out the bright side. "Sister, you know I would never find fault with anything your conscience compels you to do, but you must be more discreet."

"I know." Lizzie knotted her fingers together in her lap. "I know." She inhaled deeply. "Please don't ask me to stop helping the Union prisoners, because I won't. I can't."

John strangled out a laugh. "I know you too well to even suggest it."

"Of course we won't abandon our sacred duty," said Mother. "I dislike being scolded in the newspaper, but I won't let it frighten me into cowering at home when those poor, suffering men need us so desperately. What would Aunt Letitia have done in our place?"

Letitia Smith—the sister of Hilary Baker, Mother's father—was revered in family lore as a true heroine of the Revolutionary War, having devoted herself to the welfare of prisoners held by the British when they occupied New York.

"She would be working right alongside us," said Lizzie stoutly. "Or more likely, she would be leading the way."

"Your work is noble, as was hers," said John. "But it is dangerous, and it puts this entire household in peril."

Lizzie nodded, acknowledging the truth of his words, but she could not apologize, nor could she promise to visit the prisoners less frequently.

Two days later, as the family was finishing supper, John reached for Mary's hand, held her gaze for a moment, and waited for her to smile before clearing his throat and saying, "Mary and I have news."

Fond gestures between the two were so rare that Lizzie, startled, set down her fork with a clatter. "News?" she echoed weakly.

"Oh, my gracious," said Mother. "Mary, my dear, are you expecting a child?"

Mary's eyebrows rose. "No," she said so emphatically that Lizzie understood that a third child was extremely unlikely, and perhaps a practical impossibility. "John, you explain."

"I've taken a house west of the Capitol," said John, his smile fixed, his gaze begging for Mother and Lizzie to understand. "It's on Canal Street between Second and Third."

"What?" Lizzie exclaimed, as Mother gasped. "John, you and the girls, you're . . . leaving?"

"We thought it was time we had a home of our own."

"Long past time," Mary chimed in.

"But, John," Mother said, "to go to such expense and trouble, when we have so many rooms—"

"How were you even able to find a place?" asked Lizzie, puzzled and hurt. "Everyone says there aren't any homes to be had."

John's smile turned into a grimace. "There aren't any **reasonably priced** homes to be had."

"An important distinction to be sure," said Lizzie tightly. She couldn't look at Mary. She was to blame for this disruption of the household. Lizzie's heart constricted as she imagined waving good-bye to her dear little nieces as a carriage took them away, their empty chairs at the breakfast table, her own empty arms.

"There's a nice garden for the girls to play in," John said, "and it's a far more convenient walk to the hardware store."

"We have a lovely garden here," said Lizzie, "and your walk is not so bad now."

"It's done, so there's no use trying to talk us out of it," said Mary cheerfully. "The papers are signed, and we can move in on Thursday."

"Why did you not say anything earlier," said Mother, stricken, "so that we could have tried to dissuade you before it was too late?"

When John made no reply, Lizzie realized that was precisely why he had not mentioned it earlier.

Though close to tears, she kept her composure as best she could, unwilling to spoil one of her last precious evenings with Annie and little Eliza. It was only later, after she had tucked them in and kissed them good night, that she caught John alone. "Why?" she choked out, trying not to weep.

He offered a wan smile. "I would have thought you'd be glad to be rid of my wife's company."

"That's not funny, and it's not fair." Her

voice broke, and she reached out and clutched his arm beseechingly. "You know how much I adore those little girls. They're the daughters I'll never have. This is the only home they've ever known. How can you take them away?"

"Lizzie, I must." He held her by the shoulders, and she recognized the pain in his eyes. "I admire what you're doing for the prisoners, but you have only yourself to think about. You chose to put yourself in danger, but you can't make that choice on behalf of my daughters."

"I never meant to."

"I know that, but it's happened, and now it falls to me to protect the girls from the consequences." John released her, sighed, and raked a hand through his hair. "I also want to protect you and Mother. You think Mary is a simple, foolish girl, but she's shrewd and observant, and despite my warnings, she gossips. You and Mother will be safer if she doesn't have any new stories to share about your . . . activities."

Lizzie wanted to protest that she could avert Mary's suspicions and that the safest place for her nieces was their home on Church Hill, but a seed of doubt had been planted in the back of her mind, and it quickly took root. What if, God forbid, something should happen to the girls because of her? Suddenly she remembered the torchlight parade after fighting had broken out in Baltimore; she remembered the red-faced man who had stopped to shake his fist at her and shout, "That fine house of yours can burn!"

Her protests deserted her. Heartsick and afraid, she nodded, clung to her brother, and wept.

Chapter Seven

AUGUST–SEPTEMBER 1861

Mary, cheerful and bustling, had her little family ready to move out of the Church Hill mansion within three days. Numbly, Lizzie offered to help her pack, but her heart was not in the work, and Mary often chided her for mixing up the girls' clothes or not wrapping delicate items carefully enough before tucking them into boxes. When Mother suggested that Lizzie help by playing with her nieces instead, she was all too grateful to accept. Annie was downcast but did not complain or lament, and little Eliza seemed to think that she and her Mama and Papa were going away for only a little while—an afternoon, perhaps, or a day. Lizzie's throat constricted whenever a chance arose to correct Eliza's innocent misunderstanding. She finally gave up and decided to leave it to John and Mary to explain. Although Lizzie understood her brother's good intentions, she was not convinced that the children would be safer away from Church Hill.

"Perhaps this move will be good for John and Mary," Mother said to Lizzie when they were alone. "Perhaps when she is no longer standing in your shadow, Mary will blossom as a wife."

Lizzie was so astonished she laughed. "I, a bookish spinster of almost forty-three, cast a shadow over Mary Carter West Van Lew of the prosperous Virginia Carters, married to a successful businessman and devoted mother of two beautiful daughters?"

Mother regarded her curiously, her brow slightly furrowed. "Yes, Lizzie, you. John defers to you, and you know it."

"He defers to you too, because he knows we offer him sensible advice."

"Perhaps Mary wishes he would seek her counsel instead. Perhaps when we aren't around, he will."

Lizzie supposed Mother made a fair point, but Mary's insecurity and jealousy seemed to her an irrational impetus to take up residence elsewhere.

It was Mother's idea for Hannah to accompany them. "It will be easier for the girls to settle into an unfamiliar place if they have their beloved nurse there," she explained, first to Lizzie, and then to Hannah, who thought it over for a moment before thanking them for offering her the choice.

"Of course you have a choice," said Lizzie, surprised. "We would never send you off somewhere you didn't want to go."

Hannah regarded her skeptically. "Miss Lizzie, you forget I'm a slave."

"You apparently forget that's only because a legal technicality renders us powerless to free you. You know the restrictions imposed upon Mother by my father's will."

"That's all fine and good," Hannah said, letting her exasperation show, "but in the end it's the same. I'm a slave, and if I go with Miss Mary, she'll treat me like a slave."

"Yes," said Mother. "She probably will, more so than she does here. I truly regret that."

"I'll miss my sons too."

"Peter and William can visit you," Lizzie quickly promised, "and you're welcome here whenever you like."

"Whenever Miss Mary let me go, you mean, and that ain't likely to be often." Hannah turned a level look on both of them in turn. "If she ever raise a hand to me, I am done there, and you'll bring me home."

"Of course," Mother assured her. "John would not permit her to strike you, but if she does, you need not stay an hour longer."

Hannah promised to think it over, and before long her affection for the girls and her concern for their well-being won out. Only after she agreed did they propose the plan to John and Mary. John thought it was an excellent idea, but Mary resisted. "One mammy is the same as any other," she said. "We could easily find someone younger, more biddable. I don't care for the way Hannah scowls at me."

"Our daughters have a particular attachment to Hannah," John pointed out. "They've known her all their lives."

"Finding and training a new nurse is a difficult and expensive undertaking," Lizzie remarked. "I admire you, Mary, for taking on such an arduous task. I certainly wouldn't have enough hours in my day for it."

Mary frowned slightly, and said she would think it over, and in the end she decided that it would be to everyone's advantage if Hannah continued on as the girls' nurse.

A day later, John, Mary, Annie, and little Eliza moved out of the Church Hill mansion. Mother accompanied them in the carriage, while William and Nelson followed, driving the wagon full of their belongings. Lizzie was invited to go along too, but she couldn't bear it, so instead she spent the day on the piazza with Eliza Carrington, knitting socks for the prisoners.

"We need more help," Lizzie said to Eliza as they packed up their workbaskets for the day. "The load is heavy, and more hands will bear it more easily."

"I cannot think of anyone I would feel safe inviting to join us," said Eliza. "Most ladies of my acquaintance, and yours, don't want to help the Union prisoners, and those few that do are too afraid."

"We must find braver friends," Lizzie said, escorting Eliza to the garden gate.

"Trustworthy friends who won't be frightened off by a few scornful paragraphs in the newspaper. Friends who can keep secrets, and who will be discreet."

Eliza uttered a helpless laugh. "I don't know of anyone but you and your mother who fit that description."

"I know of one other," said Lizzie thoughtfully. "Someone who should have a particular interest in helping us help the Union."

The next morning, Lizzie packed a basket full of preserves and fresh bread and had Peter drive her to the charming row house on Leigh Street where newlyweds Mary Jane and Wilson resided. She rapped upon the door and waited, but although she thought she heard stirring within, no one answered. Puzzled, she knocked again, louder, but again there was no response. Disappointed, she had just made up her mind to return to the carriage when the door swung open, quickly, but only wide enough to reveal Mary Jane, and nothing of the room behind her.

"Miss Lizzie," she exclaimed, breathless. She was clad in a dark-blue dress with thin, vertical stripes of tan and white and a collar of fine white lace trimming the round neckline. "What a pleasant surprise."

"My dear Mrs. Bowser," Lizzie cried, planting a kiss on Mary Jane's cheek. "I'm so glad to find you at home. I hope I didn't choose an inopportune time to call."

"Well, as it happens—" Mary Jane glanced over her shoulder. "I'm delighted to see you, but the—my parlor isn't tidy enough for visitors, and I have nothing to offer you for refreshment—"

"Nonsense! You've always kept a neat room, and even if you didn't, we know each other too well to deny ourselves the pleasure of a visit over such a small thing. As for refreshments—" Smiling, she drew back the cloth covering the basket. "I have come prepared."

"Miss Lizzie . . ." Mary Jane hesitated, glanced over her shoulder again, then sighed and held open the door wider. "You may come in, but please, say nothing of what you see here."

Taken aback, Lizzie nodded and followed Mary Jane across the threshold. Inside, the curtains were drawn against the lovely morning sunshine and the lamps were lit, but even as Lizzie puzzled over this oddity, her eyes adjusted to the light and she discovered the reason for it. Eight mismatched desks were arranged in four neat rows in Mary Jane's front room, and at them sat ten small Negro children, books and slates before them, their wide eyes fixed solemnly on the unexpected visitor.

"Mary Jane," she said in wonder. "You've set up a school."

"One needs something to do besides sweep and cook all day." Mary Jane clapped her hands for attention. "Pupils, I'd like you to meet a friend of mine, Miss Elizabeth Van Lew."

"Good morning, Miss Van Lew," the children chorused.

"Good morning to you," replied Lizzie, thoroughly charmed. "You are all very fortunate children indeed to have such a good teacher. I trust you work diligently for her."

They nodded, some vigorously, others shyly.

"Continue with your readers," Mary Jane instructed. "When I come back, we'll begin recitations." She took Lizzie's arm and led her through a doorway into a small dining room outfitted with a square table and four chairs, a modest china closet with a few pieces proudly displayed behind glass doors, and an old sideboard that had been polished to a high sheen. The room smelled pleasantly of peaches and fried chicken, and at the far end, Lizzie glimpsed a doorway, which she presumed led to a coal shed or the kitchen.

"A school, Mary Jane," Lizzie exclaimed, setting the basket on the sideboard. "What a marvelous idea."

"But also very dangerous," Mary Jane reminded her, interlacing her fingers and twisting them, an old nervous habit. "The Black Code prohibits gatherings of five or more Negroes except at church."

"I can't imagine that law was written with little children in mind."

"Perhaps not, but I have no doubt that an unscrupulous person would use it against me if they wanted to shut down my school." Mary spread her hands, then let them fall to her sides. "Now you under-stand why I haven't invited you to call."

"I assumed you and Wilson were too

preoccupied with newlywed bliss to entertain guests," said Lizzie dryly. "Also, Wilson doesn't like me."

"He does too like you."

"Oh, indeed?"

"He doesn't **dislike** you," Mary Jane amended, "and he respects you."

"That's good enough for me," said Lizzie, amused. "I wish you had invited me sooner nonetheless. I could have helped tutor your pupils."

Mary Jane gave her a knowing look. "From what I hear, you've found other ways to keep busy. 'Two ladies, mother and daughter, living on Church Hill,' defying local custom and propriety by tending to Union prisoners—who else could they mean?"

Lizzie pulled out a chair and waved a hand airily as she sat down at the table. "Oh, don't believe everything you read in the papers."

"I don't. I know better." Mary Jane regarded her skeptically. "Are you saying that you and Mrs. Van Lew aren't the Church Hill ladies in question?"

"I'm not saying that at all. That's one part of the story they got right." Lizzie smiled and patted the table to encourage Mary Jane to sit. "That's actually why I called today. I hope to enlist you for our cause."

Warily Mary Jane sat down. "How could I help? I'm busy with my students almost every day. Although my heart goes out to those poor prisoners, I can't cancel school to visit them. These children's education is too important."

Lizzie could hardly disagree. "If you cannot visit the prisons yourself, perhaps you would introduce me to friends who could."

"You mean colored friends."

"Yes, I do mean your colored friends, Mary Jane." Lizzie sighed. "I am going to speak plainly, and please know, before I do, that I mean no offense."

"I am duly forewarned," said Mary Jane, looking amused. "Please proceed."

"I need men and women who will be ignored, passed over, taken for granted." Lizzie folded her hands and rested them on the table. "An eccentric Church Hill spinster and her sweet elderly mother carrying baskets to and from the prisons day after day draw too many curious eyes.

We need to spread the work among more people to dilute the scrutiny, and colored servants, whether free or slave, can go about their masters' business unquestioned."

"As long as the servant has an unexpired pass," Mary Jane said. "And does not break curfew, and does not block a sidewalk, and does not speak insolently to a white person—"

"I have lived in Richmond since before you were born," Lizzie reminded her. "I know the Black Code very well."

"Not as well as we do."

"No, I imagine not, you whose lives depend upon obeying it." Lizzie sighed and sat back in her chair. "Mary Jane, dear, surely you want the Union to triumph. If the North wins this war, slavery will be finished. If the South wins, everything will go on as it always has. You can't want that."

"No, of course I don't want that, but not every Northerner is an abolitionist. I learned that well during my time in Philadelphia. A Union victory does not necessarily mean the end of slavery."

"But it's far more likely, and slavery will never end under Confederate rule." Once

Lizzie had believed that emancipation would come to Virginia gradually, as time and reflection and a greater understanding of slavery's horrors brought about enlightenment, but the outbreak of war had sharpened her perspective.

"On that point, we agree." At a sudden sound of a chair scraping against the floor, Mary Jane glanced toward the front room. "I should get back to my students."

"Do consider who among your most trustworthy friends would be willing to help us," Lizzie urged. "We need people to take money for bribes and food and other goods to the prisoners, but we also need friends among the workers already in place. Many people of color are employed as janitors, laborers, laundresses, and cooks at the prisons, the Capitol, the Custom House—everywhere. White people pay little attention to them as they go about their work. They are perfectly situated to assist the prisoners and to gather information that will help speed the end of the war."

"You want them to be spies," said Mary Jane.

"I don't think **spy** is an appropriate

word," protested Lizzie. "The word **spy** conjures up visions of nefarious characters who work in the shadows and sneak into forbidden places to steal secrets from a legitimate government. That is not the case here. The Confederacy is an occupying force, not a sovereign state. Your friends and mine would simply observe the activities and conversations all around them as they go about their duties precisely where they are expected to be. It's not their fault if a careless clerk leaves important papers on his desk where anyone could see them, or if a general discusses secret military plans in front of his colored valet, forgetting that his valet is a man, with ears and brains and a conscience."

A high, shrill laugh came from the front room, and Mary Jane sighed and gazed heavenward. "I must get back to the children before all bedlam breaks loose." When Lizzie began to speak, Mary Jane held up a palm. "I have friends who may be interested in helping you. I'll inquire, and I'll send you a note."

"Or call on us at Church Hill," Lizzie implored, rising. "Mother would love to see you, and with John and the children gone, we could use a pleasant diversion."

"Oh, yes," said Mary, sympathetic. "I heard about that." Lizzie didn't need to ask how. Servants talked, and although Mary was no longer a servant, she was still included in their broad social circle and knew what they knew. "I have no doubt you would gladly suffer Miss Mary at her worst if it meant keeping those precious girls near."

Lizzie felt tears gathering. "You understand perfectly." She drew in a breath and forced a smile. "You've just provided an excellent demonstration of the value of the grapevine telegraph. Now you see why I'm so eager for your help."

"And here I thought you just missed me." Mary Jane smiled and led her to the door. "I promise to do what I can."

Lizzie thanked her and left, greatly heartened. She knew Mary Jane's capabilities well, and if she did all she could, that would be considerable.

"You have an abundance of sympathy for these Yankees," General Winder remarked, studying Lizzie on the late summer day she had come on behalf of Congressman Ely, Colonel Michael Corcoran of the Sixty-Ninth New York, and another civilian prisoner, a lawyer named Calvin Huson Jr., to the general's Bank Street office to lodge the prisoners' substantial list of grievances with Lieutenant Todd. "It's a pity you cannot do as much for our own poor soldiers languishing in Northern prisons."

Lizzie's heart thumped, but she smiled brightly and kept her voice steady. "Oh, General Winder, I knew you would be wise enough to discern my true motives—the true sentiments of my heart—even when all about me unkind people grumble and make the most horrid accusations."

"Thank you, Madam." His expression did not change. "Every man likes to think himself wise."

"Yes, but far too many do so without cause. Unlike you." Lizzie fixed him with an admiring gaze. "I'm sure few among them understand what you figured out so quickly—that what I do, I do not only out of Christian duty, but also out of concern for our own poor, brave Confederate prisoners."

"And if they inquired, these unkind people—how would you explain yourself to them?"

"I would tell them that when we commit atrocities upon the Yankees under our control, we give those Northern commandants license to inflict the same or worse upon the Southern men they hold." Quickly Lizzie told him of Lieutenant Todd's insistence on entering the prison with his sword drawn, and for using the flat of the blade to strike captives who did not fall in for roll call quickly enough. Guards were instructed to shoot—and kill—prisoners who leaned out of the windows for a breath of fresh air. "As the morally superior party in this dreadful conflict, we must show by our example how prisoners must be treated. What do you suppose those Yankee prison guards would do to our brave, suffering men if they knew Lieutenant Todd believes the punishment for glancing out a window is death?"

The general thought silently for a moment, but eventually he agreed to investigate. "The Yankees have a formidable advocate in you," he said as he rose and showed her to the door.

"They may think they do, but they do not," Lizzie replied lightly. "You and I both know that the spirit of Christian charity and concern for our own prisoners are all that compel me."

True to his word, General Winder reviewed the formal protest and made inquiries, but ultimately accepted Lieutenant Todd's explanation that the prisoners had been shot attempting to escape. "Even the Yankee wardens would agree that shooting a prisoner in the midst of an escape attempt is perfectly justified," he told Lizzie.

"Yes, I'm quite sure they would," said Lizzie, knowing that she was beaten. It was a rare defeat in her ongoing battle of wits with General Winder.

On the first day of August, President Davis and his family moved into the refurbished gray stucco mansion at Twelfth and Clay Streets. Even before they settled in, some proud citizens began calling the residence the White House of the Confederacy, but others rejected the homage to President Lincoln's mansion in Washington City. The Gray House was a popular alternative, although most residents referred to it simply as the President's House or the Executive Mansion.

By any name, it was an impressive home, three and a half stories tall, with a small stoop in the front as befitting the elevation facing the busy, unattractive street, and a glorious columned portico to the rear, which offered sweeping vistas of Shockoe Valley beyond a steep, terraced garden and orchard. Lizzie heard others tell of the airy, elaborately decorated rooms and halls, with their high ceilings and beautifully adorned fireplaces and winding staircases, but of course she did not see them herself, because she had not been invited to any of Mrs. Davis's receptions. John and Mary, however, were invited to a dinner by virtue of John's considerable status in the business community. When Lizzie and her mother visited John, Mary, and the girls at their new home the following Sunday afternoon, Mary described in rapturous detail the twin statues of the goddesses of comedy and tragedy bearing gas lamps in the entrance hall, the heavy green-and-gold brocatelle draperies in the dining room, the elegant crimson flocked wallpaper in the parlor and drawing room, and the many fine pieces of rosewood furniture and china. As Mary chattered on about the ladies' dresses, their fascinating conversations, and her friend Mrs. Chesnut's witty observations of it all, John's expression became so gloomy that Lizzie realized that he was miserably reliving an evening he had suffered through unwillingly the first time. She could not resist teasing him a little, and so whenever Mary paused to take a breath, she feigned innocence and asked her brother for his impressions of the evening. All that John would allow was that the food was delicious, the president treated everyone courteously but looked as if he found formal social gatherings akin to torture, his wife seemed very clever, and the Davis children were undisciplined little terrors.

"Oh, John." Mary laughed. "It was nothing like that. I could almost believe we had not attended the same party."

Lizzie thought that John looked as if he wished they had not.

As the evening approached and Lizzie and her mother called for the carriage, Eliza, who had been sweet and cheerful all afternoon, suddenly planted herself between her grandmother and aunt and the door. "No," she said firmly, stamping her foot. "Don't go."

"Eliza," exclaimed Mary, as Annie stood nearby, tears filling her eyes as she looked from her sister to her mother to Lizzie. "Behave yourself."

Lizzie knelt in front of her youngest niece, who thrust out her lower lip and valiantly fought off tears. "Eliza, dearest," she soothed, embracing her. "I'll miss you too, but it's all right. We'll come back next week, or perhaps you and your mama and papa and big sister shall come to us."

Eliza peered up at her. "To stay?"

Lizzie felt her heart wrench. "No, my sweet little lamb. You live here now."

"I hate it here," she shouted. "I want to go home."

"Eliza, that is quite enough," snapped Mary. She glanced about for Hannah, but the nurse was already hurrying over to whisk the unhappy children from the room. She moved stiffly as she crossed the floor, which told Lizzie that Mary had neglected to purchase the liniment Hannah relied upon to ease the pain in her knees. Furious, Lizzie could only murmur a few soothing words to Eliza before Hannah took the girls by the hand and led them off, hobbling slightly.

"You could move back, you know," Mother said gently, her eyes on John's. "It might be better for the children."

"In these times, it's better for us to live apart," John said in an undertone. "You know I'm right."

"Of course he's right," Mary chimed in, having easily overheard. "Your Union sentiments mark everyone close to you with the taint of disloyalty. It's bad enough that we all share the last name. I can't imagine how much worse it would be for us if we lived beneath the same roof again."

"My word, yes," Lizzie retorted. "You might not receive any more invitations to the Gray House, and your dear friend Mrs. Chesnut might pretend not to know you. How dreadful! I can imagine nothing worse. Oh, except, perhaps, for starving in a crowded prison that stinks of piss and vomit and is rife with vermin and disease. Perhaps that!"

"See?" Mary looked to John and gestured toward Lizzie. "This—this vile language is what I must shelter the girls from.

In her words, her deeds, and her very ideas, she is a terrible influence."

"**I'm** a terrible influence?" echoed Lizzie, astonished. "Which of us sips whiskey from a hidden flask when no one is watching? Which of us takes laudanum when the days are too dull and the children too lively?"

Mary's mouth fell open in shock. "John," she spluttered, "husband, are you just going to stand there and—"

"I agree it is bad that we all share the same last name, Mary," Lizzie said tightly, "but not for the reasons you do."

"That is quite enough," said John firmly. He took Lizzie by the arm, offered his other elbow to Mother, and steered them toward the front door. "Sister, if you want to persuade her to never let you see your nieces again, keep behaving as you are right now."

The bright, swift flare of her anger had burned out, leaving a fading residue of remorse. "I'm sorry," she said as they stepped onto the small front porch. Peter, waiting with the carriage on the street, was watching them, his brow furrowed in concern. "When she said that about the Van Lew name—"

"I am no less offended, and I will speak to her about it." John's voice was grim, and his grasp on her arm eased. "I—I suspected about the whiskey, but I knew nothing of the laudanum."

"Neither did I, until she did not deny it," Lizzie admitted. "The remedy Mrs. Chesnut recommended for headaches—do you recall Mary mentioning it a few months ago? Her behavior changed for the worse shortly thereafter."

He stood with head bowed for a long moment, then straightened and escorted them to the carriage. Lizzie could not be certain, but she thought his eyes glistened with tears.

"The longer this war endures, the harder it will be for Unionists to remain undetected," he said, leaning into the carriage while they settled into their seats. "You've heard about the arrests."

"Men of the lower classes only," said Lizzie, feigning nonchalance. "Drunkards, criminals, the insane. Undesirables the war excused the new government to clear off the streets."

"They will not stop with the undesirables," John said. "They will not stop with men."

"They would not arrest a lady from a good family," protested Mother.

"Not today they wouldn't," said John. "But someday soon. Enemies wear petticoats as well as pantaloons, or so the papers warn us, remember?" He shut the carriage door and regarded them through the window. "I will speak with Mary."

"And in the meantime, Lizzie will write her a sincere letter of apology," said Mother.

Lizzie knew better than to argue. "I won't sleep tonight until it is finished and perfect. I will be as humble and ingratiating as I can possibly be."

"Be sure to have Mother read it over before you send it," said John. "I don't want to worry you, but all of Richmond is going to suffer in the months ahead, even Church Hill. The time may come when all we will have is one another, and you may be grateful for Mary's friendship then."

It was difficult to be grateful for something she'd never had, Lizzie almost said, but instead she merely pressed her lips together and nodded as the carriage pulled away.

It occurred to Lizzie, later, that perhaps something John had overheard at the

Davises' levee accounted for his uncanny prescience.

Soon after the unfortunate dinner at John and Mary's home, the newspapers buzzed with the story of a Mrs. Curtis from Rochester, New York, the sister of a soldier with the Rochester Regiment, who had been captured at Falls Church dressed in military attire. The **Dispatch** called her a "Female Hessian," the **Whig** described her as "quite young, but by no means prepossessing," and all agreed that she did not disguise her animosity toward the South, and that she was certainly a spy.

Lizzie's nerves frayed as she followed the story through newspapers and the rumor mill, wondering what terrible fate awaited the accused spy. Although she was somewhat comforted to learn that Mrs. Curtis was being detained in a private home rather than some dark corner of the prison complex, Lizzie was plagued by nightmares and waking dread until the middle of the month, when Mrs. Curtis was unconditionally discharged and returned to the North.

If Lizzie were arrested for spying, and thereafter convicted, would she be banished to the North? It might not be so terrible to wait out the war in Philadelphia with her sister, Anna, who would surely take her in. Or instead, since she was Richmond born and bred, would the authorities imprison her with murderesses and women of the streets, or execute her for treason as an example to others?

The very thought of it made her dizzy and sick, but as the days passed, one unerring truth emerged from the fog of her apprehension: She must protect her mother—not only her health and security, but also her reputation. If accusations of treason fell upon the household with the full force of the Confederate government, Mother must be blameless.

Throughout August, while Lizzie brought food and money and goods into the prisons and smuggled incriminating letters out, the Confederate Congress took aggressive measures to thwart Union sympathizers. First they passed the Alien Enemies Act, which compelled men over fourteen who were not citizens of Southern states to swear an oath of allegiance to the Confederate government. If they refused, after a forty-day grace period, they would be deported. John was a citizen of Virginia, so he was not obliged to take the oath, and as women, Lizzie and her mother were exempt, but the law's foreboding overtones filled Lizzie with apprehension for what might come next. She did not have to wait long to find out. At the end of the month, Congress passed the Sequestration Act, which authorized the seizure of property belonging to Unionists—men and women alike.

The dreadful law strengthened Lizzie's resolve to disentangle her mother from her clandestine activities. The Church Hill mansion and the rest of Father's estate were in Mother's name, so even if Lizzie were caught and convicted, the Confederacy could confiscate only her personal fortune of nearly ten thousand dollars. Mother would not lose her home, nor could their servants be taken away and sold.

Mother would be protected, Lizzie reassured herself when she woke at night in a sweat, her heart pounding from fear-induced nightmares. Mother would be protected, but only as long as she could not be implicated in her daughter's deeds.

Perhaps Lizzie should have moved out, she thought miserably, and left the home to her family, for their own good. But it was too late for that now—and where would she have gone?

The harrowing month ended with the revelation of a cautionary tale that, under other circumstances, would have over-joyed Lizzie—the arrest and imprisonment of a Confederate spy in Washington City. Born in Maryland, Rose O'Neal Greenhow had been orphaned at age sixteen after her father was killed by his own slaves, and she had moved to the nation's capital to live with an aunt. Later she married a prominent doctor and became a popular hostess among the city's social elite, and when secession fever broke out, the newly widowed Washingtonian pledged her fe-alty to the rebels. Since the beautiful, wealthy, and vivacious Mrs. Greenhow had an utterly unimpeachable history of enter-taining distinguished politicians of all party affiliations at her mansion on Sixteenth Street, Confederate General Beauregard's adjutant recruited her to gather information about Union military operations from her unsuspecting guests. Some admirers credited her with gathering and smuggling out crucial secrets that led to the Confederate victory at Manassas, but the praise brought her to the attention of the famous detective Allan Pinkerton, who placed her home under surveillance and arrested her a few weeks later. Mr. Pinkerton's detectives tore apart her home searching for evidence, recklessly knocking down shelves and strewing the family's possessions upon the floors, with utter disregard for precious mementos, including the belongings of Mrs. Greenhow's recently deceased child, which had become cherished relics.

As August drew to a close, Mrs. Greenhow, her young daughter, and a few other women accused of corresponding with the enemy remained under house arrest in her Washington mansion, which soon became known as The House of Detention for Female Rebels or Fort Greenhow. There they awaited their unknown fate.

While newspapers across the South lauded their loyal daughter of the Confederacy for her courageous devotion and denounced the Yankees for treating a woman so harshly, Lizzie knew that, woman though she was, she herself could expect no gentler treatment if the Confederates discovered the Union sympathizer in their own midst.

Chapter Eight

SEPTEMBER–OCTOBER 1861

September brought no relief from the torrid summer, nor from threats against Unionists. Throughout the South, but especially in the mountains of western Virginia and eastern Tennessee, men who refused to disavow their loyalty to Mr. Lincoln's government were arrested for treason and sent to Richmond to be incarcerated. Lizzie expected one day to discover Mr. Lewis among a new shipment of prisoners, but until then, she liked to think of him still free and unharmed, still urging his fellow Western Virginians to break away from the Confederacy and return to the Union as a new state.

By the first week of September, there were nearly fourteen hundred Union men confined within the four prisons on Main Street, and three hundred fifty more, the most desperately sick and wounded, at the hospital. The prisoners included about sixty officers and a handful of civilians like Congressman Ely and the lawyer Mr. Huson, who, Lizzie was surprised to discover, had run against Mr. Ely in the election for his seat in the House, and like his former opponent had been captured in the chaos after the Union rout at Manassas.

Not long into September, Mr. Huson came down with a terrible fever. Mr. Ely campaigned for his friend's release—not only was he gravely ill, but he was also a civilian—but Lieutenant Todd flatly refused. Lizzie resolved to plead Mr. Huson's case to the lieutenant herself, so she instructed Caroline to pack a basket with his favorites, ginger cake and buttermilk, and added a bouquet of autumn blossoms for good measure.

When she asked the guard to take her to see the lieutenant, he gave her a curious look and said, "You must mean the captain, Ma'am."

"I suppose I do," said Lizzie, surprised. In her opinion, nothing about Lieutenant Todd's service merited a promotion. Perhaps the guard, whom she did not recognize and was likely new at his post, was mistaken.

But when she arrived at the commandant's office, she stopped short in the doorway. A tall, dark-haired man with a full, untidy beard stood behind the desk, which was cluttered and disorganized to a degree Lieutenant Todd never would have tolerated, sorting through stacks of papers and muttering to himself. He looked to be about five years younger than herself, and he wore the uniform and insignia of a captain.

"Captain Gibbs, sir," said the guard. "Miss Van Lew to see you."

The captain glanced up, his gaze traveling from her face to the basket on his arm. "Miss Van Lew," he greeted her, wiping his palms on his trousers before gesturing to a chair and seating himself. "Lieutenant Todd told me much about you. I was expecting you to call eventually."

"Why, the lieutenant never mentioned you at all," said Lizzie, concealing her surprise behind a show of disappointment and mild affront. "I do hope you like ginger cakes and buttermilk. They were his favorites."

"I like them very much indeed," he replied, his eyes lighting up eagerly. She had scarcely set the basket on his desk before he was digging into it, and by the time she had arranged her skirts gracefully and sat down, he already had ginger cake crumbs in his beard.

"I shall have to learn your favorites too." She paused to allow him time to finish eating, but the noisy smacking of lips and licking of fingers was so off-putting that she had to look away. "I gather that you have taken over as commandant?"

"Yes. Quite an honor. Quite a responsibility." Vigorously he wiped his palms over the desk, scattering crumbs on the papers. "Of course, I would prefer to be on the battlefield, but one must serve where one's duty requires."

"I wholeheartedly agree." Lizzie paused, preparing herself. "Duty is, in fact, what brings me to you today, Captain: my duty as a Christian and as a lady to dispense charity with mercy upon the sinner as well as the just. You have in your care a desperately ill gentleman, a civilian, who will likely perish if he is not returned to his family, whose tender ministrations may yet restore him to health."

"You refer to Calvin Huson, the lawyer from New York."

"Yes, Captain, I do."

"I could paper the walls of this entire room with the notes his friend Mr. Ely has consumed in writing to me about him," the captain remarked, and Lizzie smiled obligingly. "Of course, I must refuse."

Lizzie kept her expression serene. "And why **must** you refuse, Captain?"

"I'm reluctant to criticize my predecessor, but regrettably, his discipline was wanting." Captain Gibbs shook his head, frowning. "The prisoners are unaccustomed to a firm hand. They must learn, and quickly, that I will not indulge them as he did."

"Releasing a gravely ill civilian to his family is not a sign of indulgence but of mercy."

"I would not expect a lady like you to understand." Captain Gibbs's smile was patiently condescending. "I cannot free every prisoner who falls ill."

"I am not asking you to release every ill prisoner—"

"Not yet, but this is how it begins." He rose and came around to the front of the desk. "Fruit pies."

She blinked up at him. "I beg your pardon?"

"You asked for my favorites. Your ginger cake is delicious, but I prefer fruit pies." He shrugged apologetically. "I confess I don't care for buttermilk."

"I won't forget." She rose, extended her hand gracefully, and managed to put some warmth into her smile as he shook her hand and bade her farewell.

Rebuffed but undaunted, Lizzie went over his head to General Winder, just as she had done when Lieutenant Todd would not cooperate. There she ran into another immovable obstacle. General Winder would not release Mr. Huson without receiving an equally valuable Confederate prisoner in exchange, but President Lincoln and Secretary of State Seward refused to exchange prisoners, because to do so would be tantamount to official recognition of the Confederate government.

Outraged and increasingly alarmed by his friend's worsening condition, Mr. Ely flooded the prison mail with letters to officials both North and South, imploring them to initiate a system of prisoner exchanges to alleviate suffering on all sides. Even the Richmond press seemed to support the idea of prisoner exchanges, not only to benefit Southern soldiers held captive in the North, but also to relieve the Confederacy of the great expense of keeping so many Yankees under lock and key. "Within the past ten days, $700 has been expended for bread for their consumption, and $2,000 for meat," the **Enquirer** complained in mid-September, going on to estimate that the Yankee prisoners cost the Confederacy around eleven thousand dollars each week. "It has been found necessary, within a few days past," the reporter continued, with an irritating air of satisfaction, "to discontinue the rations of coffee and sugar hitherto allowed the prisoners, and the deprivation is said to have told more upon the spirits of the Yankees than any other circumstance connected with their captivity."

Disgusted, Lizzie concluded that only someone who had never set foot inside the prisons could believe that.

As the senior prisoner, the energetic

Congressman Ely did what he could to boost morale. Not long after Manassas, he and the other officers formed the Richmond Prison Association "for mutual improvement and amusement." Mr. Ely was elected president, and the association's first order of business after choosing a vice-president, secretary, and treasurer and toasting themselves with tepid water from a wooden pail was to design an official seal—a swarm of lice arranged in a circle with the motto, "Bite or Be Damned." Their meetings featured recitations, debates, card games, or music, with "Home Sweet Home" a particularly favorite song.

Neither the entertainments offered by the Richmond Prison Association nor the comforts provided by Lizzie, Eliza, and an increasing number of colored servants—their own, or those employed by other anonymous Unionists, or acquaintances of Mary Jane who came of their own accord—could make the prison tolerable, and occasionally prisoners would attempt to escape. On September 5, Colonel de Villiers, a surgeon with the Eleventh Ohio Regiment, stole a Confederate officer's coat and hat, hid behind the prison gate until he heard the guards offer the challenge and countersign, and used the password to make his exit through the front gates. The following night, two enlisted men stole out a first-floor window and fled all the way to the foot of Libby Hill before they were shot by members of the Louisiana Battalion stationed nearby. Ten days later, four men escaped from the prison depot but were pursued by guards to Rocketts Wharf, where one of the fugitives was shot and killed, a second was mortally wounded, and the two others were compelled to surrender. Three nights later, six more prisoners, undeterred by the deaths and recaptures of their comrades, fled the prison and disappeared into the city, eluding their frustrated pursuers, who eventually gave up after a vigorous but fruitless search.

"We have heard it alleged," the Richmond **Whig** opined tartly, "in explanation of the escape of so many federal prisoners from the factories in this city, that the sentinels are more vigilant in keeping outsiders out, than in preventing the egress of insiders. There is some plausibility in this allegation, as it is a fact that if a citizen projects his big toe half an inch over the 'line,' on the sidewalk in front of either factory, he will be requested to make a retrograde movement of the offending foot; whilst those who are passed in are suffered to depart, without much, if any, questioning. The officers in command should reform this practice, if it be still continued, as it is far more important to keep strangers in than to prevent them from entering."

Lizzie knew Captain Gibbs had read the report, for she overheard him in the yard the next day, berating the guards for their inattention and negligence. They must have taken the criticism to heart, for not quite a week later, she learned from the **Enquirer** that it was no longer necessary for a prisoner to lean out a window to be shot by guards patrolling outside:

A YANKEE PRISONER KILLED BY A SENTINEL.

—A Yankee prisoner, named N. C. Buck, a member of the 79th New York Regiment, confined in the lower prison, near Rockett's, was shot and instantly killed, about 1 o'clock Saturday morning, by one of the sentinels who kept watch over the building.—The latter observing the Yankee to approach the window in a suspicious manner, as if contemplating an escape, ordered him away several times. To these repeated commands the prisoner returned an insolent and defiant refusal, and the sentinel finally leveled his musket and fired. The ball struck the luckless Lincolnite in the stomach, inflicting a terrible wound, which terminated his life in a very few moments. The sentinel has not only been exonerated from all blame in the matter, but has received the applause of the proper military authorities for his prompt and decisive conduct in carrying out his instructions. The unfortunate Yankee was buried during the evening, in the burial ground at the foot of Third street, set apart for the interment of the Federals who may shuffle off their mortal coils in this locality.

It came as a dizzying shock to learn about such a terrible event from the newspaper considering that Lizzie spent so much time at the prison, but it happened that she had not visited the prison in several days. She had reluctantly sent servants instead, because for most of the week the man with the tobacco-stained beard had planted himself directly across the street, as bold as brass, and had taken to following her at a distance just beyond arm's reach. His interest in shadowing her seemed to wax and wane, but with no predictable pattern. She might find him observing her for several days on end but then see him not at all for several more. The unsettling thought occurred to her that perhaps even on the days she thought herself rid of him, he might still be watching her from someplace unseen. Sometimes she eluded him by taking the carriage in the opposite direction, but other times she would lead him on a dull, lengthy, aimless walking tour of Church Hill or Capitol Square or the markets, hoping to bore him into leaving her alone.

By late September, Mr. Huson's condition had drastically deteriorated. Desperately worried for his friend, Mr. Ely arranged for him to be moved to the infirmary, where despite Lizzie and Eliza's ministrations, fever continued to wrack his body and steadily drain his vitality. Dr. Edward Higginbotham, the medical director and surgeon in charge of prison hospitals, who had seen Mr. Huson a few weeks before during one of his routine calls on the prison, gave him a more thorough examination and determined that he was suffering from typhoid fever.

"I will take him in," said Lizzie. "This place is too foul, too wretched. He will never get better here."

"Lizzie," Eliza whispered, turning her head away from Mr. Huson, though he was in too wretched a state to overhear. "It's too dangerous. Everyone will hear of this. All that you've done to dispel suspicions will be undone in an instant."

"I cannot leave him here to die," Lizzie protested. "He wasn't even engaged in battle when they captured him. He was a spectator. He should have been freed long ago, or sentenced to house arrest somewhere in the city. If Mrs. Greenhow was entitled to such comforts, Mr. Huson certainly should have been."

On October 9, with General Winder's reluctant consent, Mr. Huson was wrapped in blankets and brought on a litter borne by several of his fellow prisoners to the Van Lew mansion, where he was soon settled into a bright, warm, airy room Mother and Judy, Mother's maid, had prepared for him. To Lizzie his countenance seemed brighter, and he weakly spoke of feeling, on average, a little better, but his tongue remained very much swollen and white with deep ridges. Later that day, Francis Clark, a private who had tended Mr. Huson in the prison hospital, was paroled and sent to the Van Lew residence with instructions to assist them however he could.

"I would give one hundred dollars if Mr. Huson's family could see for one moment how comfortably situated he is here," prison commissary Captain Jackson Warner confided to Lizzie when he paid an unannounced visit to the sickroom the next morning. "They would be deeply touched and relieved if they knew what tender care you and your mother offer him."

"Perhaps when he is recovered enough to travel, you could appeal to your superiors," Lizzie suggested. "He will surely recuperate much faster in his own home, looked after by his own devoted wife." To her relief, Captain Warner agreed.

The following day, Mr. Huson, though still feverish and pale, professed to feel much improved, and spoke hopefully of returning home. Lizzie sat by his bedside as he told her, in a thin, quavering voice, of his loving wife and energetic young children; of Rochester, New York, his dear old hometown; of his pride at being appointed by President Lincoln to be the United States' commissioner to Costa Rica; and of his regret at being prevented from undertaking his duties. "When you are well, you surely will," Lizzie encouraged him, smiling. His recovery seemed a hundredfold more likely than when he had been brought to Church Hill.

Yet on the morning of October 12, Lizzie met Captain Warner at the door gravely, wringing her hands, and as she led him to the sickroom, she explained that Mr. Huson had relapsed overnight. Dr. Higginbotham had administered medicines, shaken his head, and said that it was perhaps time to notify his wife.

"Can you get a message to her?" Lizzie

implored, laying her hand on Captain Warner's sleeve. Postal service between the North and South had been severed earlier in the summer, but diplomatic channels still existed, as well as enterprising private couriers who had managed to talk their way into receiving passes from both sides. "If not a telegram, then a letter?"

"I will certainly try."

Lizzie nodded, deflated. A few other wives had been permitted to come to Richmond from the North to care for their wounded husbands in prison hospitals, earning themselves grudging praise for their womanly devotion from the people and the press. But even if a message reached Mrs. Huson, and even if she were granted entry into the city, it seemed unlikely that she would arrive in time. "Mr. Ely is his devoted friend," she said. "Could you arrange for him to call? Even a brief visit might raise Mr. Huson's spirits and encourage him to rally once more."

"I am sure I can do that much," Captain Warner replied in a choked voice. "He is a gentleman and I wish him well, though we have chosen opposite sides in the war."

Although he abruptly turned away and strode into the sickroom, Lizzie was certain she saw tears glistening in his eyes.

She did not sleep that night but dozed in a chair by Mr. Huson's bedside. His breathing had become so labored that any moment she expected the rasping sounds to fall silent and be heard no more. She held his hand, dry and burning hot, and spoke to him gently of his home and family, echoing back all that he had told her mere days before. When dawn broke, unable to bear it any longer, she shook Private Clark awake so he could attend the ailing man and sent Peter to prepare the carriage. Before long they sped off to the prison complex, where Lizzie hurried to Captain Gibbs's office and begged to speak with Mr. Ely at once.

She found him at breakfast. "Mr. Ely," she began, "I—I regret that I have very bad news."

He shook his head slowly, his eyes never leaving hers. "Mr. Huson cannot be dead."

"No, no, he is not." Lizzie took a deep, shaky breath. "But I do not think it is possible for him to live much longer. Will you come to see him?"

"Of course. I will come at once, if I am permitted."

Lizzie rushed home and dashed upstairs, where she found her mother at Mr. Huson's bedside, holding his hand and murmuring prayers while Private Clark bathed his brow. Mother looked up and caught Lizzie's eye, and slowly shook her head.

Her heart plummeting, Lizzie hurried over and took Mr. Huson's other hand. "You will be pleased to know that Mr. Ely is on his way," she said with gentle good cheer, uncertain whether he could even hear her. "He will owe you a favor for arranging this brief parole for him. I think you should ask for his seat in Congress."

She wanted to believe she saw the faint curve of a smile upon his lips, but she knew it was only wishful thinking.

She sat beside him as the moments slipped away, listening for the sound of the front door, heralding Mr. Ely's arrival. Mr. Huson's breaths came in shallow gasps, fainter and further apart, until suddenly Lizzie realized that a full minute had passed in silence. Her throat constricting, she pressed her ear to Mr. Huson's chest and listened for his heartbeat, motionless and silent, listening, straining her ears, waiting, until she felt Mother's hands on her shoulders. "He's gone," Mother said, pulling her upright. "He suffers no more."

Lizzie nodded and stepped away from the bedside to allow Private Clark to confirm what they all already knew to be true. Not twenty minutes had passed since she had left the prison.

Moments later, Mr. Ely arrived accompanied by Captain Gibbs, who held Lizzie back while Mother led Mr. Ely to the sickroom. "We would have been here earlier," he said, agitated. "Mr. Ely was ready to go, but I had some business to attend to, and—the delay is my fault, is what I mean to say."

With an effort, Lizzie forced an understanding smile and patted him on the arm. "There is no need to explain, captain. Truly, you need say no more."

Mother invited the visitors to accompany her to the parlor, where Caroline soon appeared with coffee and sandwiches. Captain Gibbs had no appetite, and indeed, crumbs from his breakfast toast yet remained in his beard, but the hollow-eyed Mr. Ely ate and drank everything placed before him. Mother suggested that they summon a photographist to come and take a likeness of Mr. Huson to present to his family, but by the time the artist arrived, the body had become so changed that Mr. Ely decided it would be better not to attempt it in his present condition, as the image could afford no satisfaction to his family and friends.

The undertaker was summoned, and Mr. Ely took the lead in arranging the details of the funeral and burial, which they decided should take place at four o'clock the following afternoon. When Mr. Ely pressed him, Captain Gibbs agreed that the most prominent officers and close friends among the prisoners should be permitted to attend. The congressman also requested a metallic coffin in the event that Mr. Huson's family might someday wish to exhume and rebury the remains in his native country, and again the captain consented, but queried, "Who will bear these expenses?"

Before Lizzie could declare that she would be honored to pay every bill, Mr. Ely said, "I will, of course. Did you think I would submit a bill to the prison? What a question. It is beneath you, sir." Captain Gibbs glowered guiltily but said nothing.

The following day, the Reverend John F. Mines, a prisoner from Maine, presided at the funeral service held in the Van Lews' parlor, with Lizzie, John, their mother, Mr. Ely, Eliza Carrington, Captain Warner, and the undertaker in attendance. Afterward, the hearse and four carriages headed out to the Church Hill Cemetery, where Mr. Huson was laid to rest.

"Patrick Henry is also interred here," Lizzie told Mr. Ely when none of the Confederate officers could overhear, hoping to comfort him. "Thus even though Mr. Huson's grave is far from home, in a hostile land, he is yet among patriots."

Two days later, the sun rose upon a beautifully crisp autumn day. The loveliness of the morning lifted Lizzie's spirits somewhat, and so after breakfast, she spent time in the garden, weeding and pruning, accepting the warmth of the sunshine like a benediction from above, lost in thought. When she knelt on the ground and felt the cool dewy grass through her skirt, she almost felt as if she were praying.

"You," came a harsh shout from behind her. "Miss Van Lew!"

Startled, she craned her neck to discover a man in his middle years on the other side of the fence, glaring at her. Instinctively, she began to rise, but a cramp in her calf forced her to fall back upon her hip, holding herself up with her arm.

"I hardly know how to respond to such a summons," she managed to say. "Are you accustomed to shouting at ladies over fences? Because I assure you, we are un-used to such forms of address on Church Hill."

"You Yankee filth should all be hanged," he shouted, his face an ugly, red mask of antipathy. "You should be driven into the streets and slaughtered!"

Stunned, Lizzie could only stare at him as he yelled and shook his fist, white spit-tle flying from the corners of his mouth. After a while, she pushed herself to her feet, took up her basket and pruning shears, turned her back to him, and walked mechanically back to the house, his angry tirade a stream of nonsense syllables burn-ing in her ears.

Chapter Nine

OCTOBER–NOVEMBER 1861

After too many fearful, sleepless nights, Lizzie decided to seek protection from the one person every secessionist would surely obey—President Jefferson Davis himself. By all accounts he was a gentleman, Lizzie reasoned, and as a gentleman he would be compelled by the rules of honor and chivalry to respond if an unmarried lady and her widowed mother appealed to him to keep them safe from harm.

Informing only Eliza of her intentions, Lizzie set off. When she arrived at the president's office, his private secretary,

Mr. Josselyn, informed her that Mr. Davis could not see her.

"Oh, what a shame," said Lizzie. "I trust he is not ill."

"No more than the usual," replied Mr. Josselyn, but then he caught himself. "The president is well, thank you. He is in a cabinet session."

Smiling hopefully, Lizzie gestured to a nearby chair. "I would be content to wait."

"They may not be finished until after midnight."

Somewhat deflated, Lizzie nonetheless seated herself. "I'll wait as long as I can, and with any luck, they'll finish early."

He seemed torn between wanting to ignore her and wanting to speed her on her way. Apparently the latter won out, because after a moment, he said hesitantly, "May I be of assistance instead?"

"Perhaps you can." Earnestly, she explained how her acts of benevolence for the Union prisoners of war had turned the citizens of Richmond against her, and that she and mother suffered terrifying threats of violence, and that fear for their safety compelled them to appeal to President Davis for protection.

When she finished, Mr. Josselyn scratched his head, bemused, and folded his arms over his chest. "Could you not appease the people's anger by dispensing your Christian charity to Confederate soldiers instead?"

"It would hardly be Christian charity if I dispensed it only to the popular and the deserving. Did not our Lord go among the lepers and tax collectors?"

"Yes, he did," the secretary admitted, and heaved a sigh of resignation. "Very well. I'll pass along your concerns and your request to the president."

Relieved, Lizzie stood, and offered him her first genuine smile of the interview. "That would be most gallant of you."

"I cannot promise that he will help," Mr. Josselyn cautioned. "I think you would be better off appealing to the mayor in the meantime."

Lizzie promised to follow his advice, and she did so promptly, with much the same result. Mayor Mayo was out, or so his secretary claimed, but he would be informed of her concerns.

. . .

Later that day, Eliza Carrington burst into the parlor, outrunning William in her haste. Lizzie broke off from explaining to her mother why they ought to give the servants a larger raise than usual at Christmas—prices for everything money could buy had been increasing steadily throughout Richmond ever since the war began—and regarded her friend with mild surprise. "My goodness, Eliza. Whatever is the matter?"

"I'm glad to see you," she exclaimed, breathless. "I thought for certain I would next visit you in prison. Did you see the president?"

"What?" asked Mother. "You told me you were going to visit your brother at the store."

"I may have ridden past and waved." Lizzie beckoned Eliza to join her on the sofa. "I did not see the **president**. The president is Mr. Abraham Lincoln and he is, as far as I know, more than one hundred miles north of here, toiling away in the White House to bring a swift end to this dreadful war. I did, however, speak with **Mr. Davis**. Well, not with Mr. Davis but with his secretary, and with Mayor Mayo's secretary after that."

"And?"

"And I was assured of their sympathy."

Eliza put her head to one side, skeptical. "Their sympathy is welcome, I'm sure, but are they going to do anything to protect you?"

"That remains to be seen." Abruptly Lizzie rose and went to the narrow desk by the window, where she found paper and pen and ink. "I should write to Mr. Davis immediately."

"Whatever would you say to him?" wondered Mother.

"Don't tell him he isn't the president," Eliza begged.

"I concur," said Mother. "He thinks he is, and he will not take it well if you deny it."

"Listen to you two. You think I have no common sense at all." Lizzie pretended not to notice the guilty look they exchanged. "I am going to thank him for his time," she said as she wrote, "and for turning his attention to our plight. I am also going to wish him good luck in the upcoming election, and assure him that if I were permitted to vote, I would vote for him."

Mother's eyebrows rose. "Would you?"

"Of course. He is frail and sickly, and he

does not relish the job, although no one could say that he is not utterly faithful to his duty. Mr. Stephens, on the other hand—though he is vice-president now, he was a reluctant secessionist. If one of Mr. Davis's frequent illnesses should claim his life, or if a stray bullet should strike him down on one of his many excursions to cheer the soldiers—"

"Lizzie," Mother exclaimed, and Eliza too looked shocked. "It is unbecoming of a lady to wish for a man's death."

"I don't wish for it," Lizzie protested. "Honestly, what do you think of me? But death comes to us all, and if it should come to Mr. Davis while he is in office, it would be a blessing for everyone, North and South alike, if a reluctant secessionist succeeds him."

Mother and Eliza exchanged another look. "She makes a fair point," Mother admitted, and after a moment to consider, Eliza nodded.

"And so I **do** wish for Mr. Davis's reelection," Lizzie declared, signing her name with a flourish. "But I cannot say I hope he completes his term."

"The war will be over long before then,"

Eliza said stoutly. "It cannot last six years more."

This time, it was Lizzie and her mother who exchanged a look—one full of doubt, and worry, and wistful hope.

Lizzie was disappointed but not surprised when neither gentleman acknowledged her visit, or her letter, or her plight. Glares and accusations followed her wherever she went, and so she spent more and more time indoors, telling herself she was simply accommodating the change of seasons, but knowing the truth—she was anxious and afraid.

She resolved to find another way to convince the people of Richmond that the Van Lews were loyal to the rebel cause—and soon, she was inspired by a solution that would divert suspicion and raise their own downcast spirits.

With Mother's blessing, she wrote to Cousin Jack's commander with the Richmond Howitzers and invited them to a grand dinner and reception in their honor at the Church Hill mansion. When he gladly accepted, Lizzie sent out invitations in her mother's name to the most prominent families of Church Hill, including the Lodges; the other ladies of Mary's sewing circle, their husbands, and their daughters; Mary herself and John; and, for good measure, General Winder, Captain Gibbs, and Captain Warner, the prison commissary who had been so kind to Mr. Huson in his final days. A few neighbors coldly declined, but nonetheless, on the appointed evening the mansion was filled with happy guests, eager for a pleasant diversion and an opportunity to honor one of Richmond's most respected regiments. Cousin Jack enjoyed himself thoroughly, and when he was not at the side of one charming young lady or another, he could almost always be found courteously attending Mother, his aunt and hostess. "My aunt has always been a friend to the Confederate soldier," Lizzie overheard him proudly tell General Winder. She felt a pang of guilt for not correcting his misapprehension; the Van Lews' love, concern, and affection for Cousin Jack did not extend to every Confederate soldier except in the broadest humanitarian sense.

It was a regrettable but necessary deception, and it seemed to work. In the aftermath of the party, the threats came less frequently, the hostility at church services diminished, and several neighbors who had rejected their invitations seemed heartily sorry when they heard the glowing accounts of the delicious food, beautiful music, spirited dancing, and fine company. Captain Gibbs was especially effusive in his thanks, for his wife, Julia, had longed for an evening away from the cramped hotel rooms they shared with their four children. He was especially solicitous to Lizzie in the days following the party, which granted her the unexpected boon of more time with the prisoners and more leeway in what she brought them.

Lizzie wished that Captain Gibbs's leniency would set an example for his underlings to follow, but often, the guards and sergeants proved more cruel than their officers. When she queried enlisted men about fresh scrapes and new bruises, they reluctantly admitted that they had been beaten by their guards for offenses both real and invented. Lizzie knew too well that some guards enjoyed trying to intimidate her, leisurely examining her baskets and boldly helping themselves to the choicest delicacies. One guard in particular, a corporal by the name of Mickey Cook—a short, pale, thin-haired blond, with flat lips and a faint smudge of a mustache—took particular pleasure in cornering her against the wall, forcing her to stand and hold the basket while he pawed through it, and then standing boldly in her way while he leisurely munched whatever foodstuffs he had confiscated, his impertinent gaze never leaving her face. Corporal Cook was also the most persistently annoying of the guards who inspected her baskets and dishes upon her departure. Most guards simply peered inside and, finding nothing, nodded and sent her on her way, but the corporal made her stand and wait, barely concealing her impatience—or terror, if she carried a secret message—as he painstakingly examined every nook and cranny.

More frustrating than Corporal Cook's insolence was the loss of the secret crevice between the two sections of her favorite serving dish. For weeks the guards had unwittingly allowed her to smuggle papers back and forth, unaware that the dish she used to carry soup and gruel had a double bottom, but one day Corporal Cook discovered it as he used his fingers to wipe up the last delicious drops of a custard. "What have we here?" he drawled, separating the double bowls.

"The bottom piece is filled with boiling water," Lizzie explained, "to keep the food hot during transport."

"There's no water in it now."

"There's no food to keep warm any longer, so I poured out the water. Why should I carry the extra weight home?"

"Right," he said skeptically, handing her the pieces and grinning as he watched her fumble to reassemble them.

From that day forward, he made a special point of examining the dish, rendering it useless as a hiding place. Lizzie silently fumed whenever she arrived at the prison to find Corporal Cook on duty, knowing that she could not dare to accept any papers to carry out for Mr. Ely. Every day her frustration grew until she could not bear Corporal Cook's insolent smirks any longer, and she resolved to win back the use of her favorite smuggling place.

One day, after spending many long hours caring for the sick and injured in the makeshift infirmary, Lizzie emptied the cooled water from the double bottom into a pot, stoked the fire, and put the pot on to boil. When the water roiled and steamed, she refilled the double bottom of the serving dish, fitted the top piece securely in place, and carefully returned the dish to her basket.

She immediately made to leave the prison, and as she expected, Corporal Cook detained her at the door. "Awful heavy for an empty bowl," he remarked, lifting the dish from the basket.

"Careful," Lizzie warned. "It isn't empty. The bottom is full of water."

"Yeah, water and what else?"

"Nothing else. Simply water." As he made to separate the dishes, she quickly added, "I wouldn't do that if I were you. It's very hot."

He silenced her with a glare, staring her down as he pulled the sections apart— and then he bellowed in pain as scalding water cascaded from the dish.

"Oh, corporal," Lizzie exclaimed as the pieces of the dish clattered to the floor. She bent over him as he collapsed to his knees, moaning. "Your uniform!"

"My uniform?" he yelped. "Good Christ, woman, my hands. My hands!"

A quick glance revealed red and blistering flesh. The corporal's shouts had brought another guard running, and Lizzie quickly sent him to fetch a doctor while she helped the corporal to his feet and eased him into a chair. The guard soon returned not with the prison doctor, for none had called that day, but one of the imprisoned officers, an assistant surgeon with the First Maine Cavalry. "I warned him the water was hot," Lizzie told the Yankee surgeon as he tended the corporal's burns. There was no need to feign distress, for the corporal's moans and the sight of his raw, scalded skin made her queasy. She had seen far worse in the infirmary, but she had not caused any of it.

She had warned him, she reminded herself as she made her way home. She had warned him, and he had ignored her, and he had burned himself. He had only himself to blame, and far better men had suffered far worse in that war, some of them at Corporal Cook's behest.

But the satisfaction she felt at teaching him a lesson and having the full use of the dish's hidden chamber restored to her was diminished whenever the memory of his blistered skin and shrieks of pain sprang unbidden to her mind.

Shame kept her away from the prison for the rest of the week, but duty soon called her back. Corporal Cook was nowhere to be found, and when she inquired with Captain Gibbs, he told her that the guard was on medical leave.

Lizzie felt a pang of guilt, but then she remembered his insolent stares and the many times he had stood too close and had backed her up against a wall, and anger drove away any sympathy she might have felt for him. "Thank you, Captain," she said, leaving him to the plum tart Caroline had made for him.

"No, thank **you**," he said, breaking off a piece of crust and savoring it. "If I were a better man, I would save this to take back to the hotel for my family, but the temptation will prove too great, I'm sure."

"Next time I'll bring two," Lizzie said. "One for you, and one for your wife and children." She had met Mrs. Gibbs at the party for the Richmond Howitzers and had rather liked her. Some of her comments and candid expressions had made Lizzie wonder if she were not something of a secret Union sympathizer too.

"They would be most grateful to you." The captain shook his head, frowning. "They are so tired of eating at the hotel. Home-cooked food has become a luxury. Mrs. Gibbs can't wait until she is mistress of her own kitchen again."

"Is there any chance she may have that pleasure soon?"

"Thankfully, yes. I've found a dwelling for us, but it won't be ours until the officer currently residing there moves out. His transfer won't come for another month." Captain Gibbs sighed, rueful. "We'll make do until then."

Lizzie thought quickly. "Since you find the Spotswood so odious, why don't you board with my family in the meantime?"

His eyebrows shot up. "Dare I hope you are in earnest?"

"I'll have to check with my mother first, of course, but I'm certain she'd be delighted to welcome you into our home."

"My wife would be so very pleased," he said fervently. "If you only knew how she has praised your beautiful home since the evening of your party, and your cook—

why, she is a marvel." Suddenly he looked pained. "You do recall that we have four young and very lively children?"

"Of course I remember," Lizzie assured him, smiling. "I insist that you bring them too. We've missed having children around the house. They will be a most charming distraction."

Captain Gibbs rubbed his hands together, beaming. "As soon as your mother agrees, I'll ask my wife, but I'm certain she'll accept your invitation as gratefully as I do."

Lizzie inclined her head graciously, but as soon as she turned away, her thoughts began to race. Inviting the Gibbs family into their home would surely convince their suspicious neighbors that the Van Lews were not Union sympathizers, but first she would have to convince her mother that this was an inspired plan and not a disaster in the making.

Mother listened soberly as Lizzie explained her scheme, and after taking several hours to consider, she agreed that they should take in Captain Gibbs's family. "If this does not dispel suspicion, I can think of nothing else that will," she said. "But, Daughter, you must be vigilant. Neither he nor his wife nor even his little children can ever overhear you speak a single word against the Confederacy. You have never excelled at keeping your opinions to yourself. Are you certain you can now?"

"I must," Lizzie said, spreading her hands. "Everything depends upon it. I didn't burst into 'Hail, Columbia' when our house was full of Confederates at the party, and I'm sure I can demonstrate the same restraint after the Gibbs family moves in."

A few days later, Captain Gibbs, his wife, and their four children moved into the Van Lew mansion. At first it was all a friendly bustle of settling in and unpacking and getting to know one another, but before long, Lizzie began counting the days until their departure. Yet the angry glares and whispers of the citizens of Richmond declined considerably after word of the Van Lews' new boarders spread, and threats of violence ceased altogether. Moreover, Captain Gibbs was so pleased with his comfortable quarters and fine meals that he promised Lizzie liberal access to the prisoners at her discretion, although sometimes his subordinates imposed their own restrictions in his absence.

And, not insignificantly, Captain Gibbs's presence in the house also compelled Lizzie to practice her role of devoted Confederate lady, day and night, until she knew the part perfectly. She did not doubt that someday, those intense rehearsals might save her life.

Warfare and politics dominated the Richmond gossip mills throughout autumn. On October 24, the counties of western Virginia voted to split off from the rest of the state and join the Union. Privately Lizzie applauded their courage and loyalty, but she also mourned the fracturing of her beloved Virginia, and felt the pain and grief of secession anew. By private courier, she sent Mr. Lewis a letter of congratulations, but she did not entertain hopes of a reply.

On November 6, eligible voters across the South turned out to elect Jefferson Davis as president and Alexander Stephens as vice-president, confirming their approval of the provisional appointments made by the Confederate Congress shortly after secession. Both men ran unopposed, so even though nearly fifteen hundred citizens wrote in the names of other candidates for president on their ballots, afterward Lizzie concluded that it had been the least suspenseful election in the history of democracy.

Four days later, Lizzie was at the prison distributing hot rolls and fresh apple cider to the officers when General Winder suddenly appeared at the door, a stiff piece of paper in his hand, his military staff as escort. Instinctively Lizzie stepped back into the shadows of one of the tobacco presses, but her movements only brought her to the general's attention. He held her gaze for a moment, his face grim but otherwise unreadable. He had not come for her, Lizzie realized when he tore his gaze away, but her relief soon gave way to apprehension.

"Gentlemen, your attention," he began, frowning as he turned a look of warning upon the men. Some of them drew closer; all fell silent. "I have been ordered to read to you a proclamation from Secretary of War Judah P. Benjamin." A murmur of surprise went up from the men as the general held up the paper and began to read. "'To Brigadier General John Winder, Richmond, Virginia. Sir: You are hereby instructed to choose, by lot, from among the prisoners of war of highest rank, one who is to be confined in a cell appropriated to convicted felons, and who is to be treated in all respects as if such convict, and to be held for execution in the same manner as may be adopted by the enemy for the execution of the prisoner of war Smith, recently condemned to death in Philadelphia.'"

The murmur surged and turned ugly, and Lizzie heard a scattering of muttered curses and echoes of the word **execution**. She did not know who the prisoner of war Smith was, or why Mr. Benjamin would decree that a Union hostage should be held on his account. She stepped out from the shadows to peer questioningly at the general, but he did not glance her way.

"'You will also select thirteen other prisoners of war—'" A roar of discontent drowned him out, so he raised his voice and began again. "'You will also select thirteen other prisoners of war, the highest in rank of those captured by our forces, to be confined in the cells reserved for prisoners accused of infamous crimes, and will treat them as such so long as the enemy shall continue so to treat the like number of prisoners of war captured by them at sea, and now held for trial in New York as pirates.'"

The roar of discontent swelled, joined by a chorus of shrill whistles and jeers. This reference Lizzie did understand; in June and July, the Union navy had seized two rebel privateers, the **Savannah** and the **Jefferson Davis**, but since the Lincoln administration did not recognize the Confederacy as a sovereign nation, the captured officers and seamen had not been treated as prisoners of war but as civilian criminals. They had been charged with piracy, a capital offense, and confined within civilian jails. They were tried in New York in October, but when the jury deadlocked, a retrial was set for Philadelphia. There the jury found the men guilty and sentenced them to death.

"'As these measures are intended to repress the infamous attempt now made by the enemy to commit judicial murder on prisoners of war,'" the general continued, almost shouting to be heard above the din, "'you will execute them strictly, as the mode best calculated to prevent the commission of so heinous a crime.'" His arms fell to his sides and he recited the rest from memory. "'Your obedient servant, J. P. Benjamin, Acting Secretary of War.'"

"This is an outrage," a captain from Michigan shouted, shaking his fist.

"You cannot choose who will live or die by drawing names from a hat," another yelled.

"Would you prefer that I chose the men myself based upon who most provokes me?" countered General Winder, glaring in the direction of the voice. The din subsided a trifle, but the room crackled with ugly, violent energy, and Lizzie felt herself shrinking back until her hip banged painfully against a tobacco press. "Did you not hear what I just read? Those who are chosen will not be executed unless your Old Abe decides to murder one of the sailors. In other words, you should save your complaints for your letters home, and pray that your friends and families will have some influence over your president's decision." Scowling, General Winder looked challengingly around the room. "Now. Colonel Lee, front and center."

After a pause, the white-haired commander of the Twentieth Massachusetts Infantry, a distant relation of Robert E., stepped forward. General Winder beckoned to one of his staff, who handed Colonel Lee six slips of paper. "The names of six federal colonels now held as prisoners of war are written upon these papers," he said. "Open each one and verify that this is true."

Colonel Lee held on to the papers, but he kept his arms by his side. "I decline to participate in this atrocity."

A murmur of approval rippled through the crowd. "If you do not," General Winder barked, "then instead of one colonel, you choose all six by default."

Colonel Lee glared back, but after a moment, he unfolded each slip of paper and read the names of the six Union colonels. Then, following instructions, he folded them again and placed them in a tin case about a foot deep. General Winder closed the lid, gave the case a vigorous shake, and said, "Mr. Ely, if you please."

The congressman, who had been standing at the front of the crowd, stepped forward, crossing his arms over his chest and glowering. The general acknowledged him with a nod and lifted the lid. "You shall draw the name of the officer who will stand as a hostage for the Confederate prisoner of war Smith."

Mr. Ely studied him darkly, a muscle working in his jaw. "I will not," he said through clenched teeth. "I will not send one of our brave and gallant officers to a felon's dungeon to suffer and stand as a pledge to die in case of the execution of a condemned pirate."

"Then you send all six plus thirteen more."

"Go ahead, Ely," said one of the colonels, and other prisoners quietly chimed in their consent.

Pained, Ely nodded, thrust his hand into the tin, and withdrew a slip of paper. "Colonel Michael Corcoran," he read aloud, and to the general, he added bitterly, "First you transfer him to Castle Pinckney in South Carolina, and now you force me to add to his misery."

Lizzie's breath caught in her throat. The Irish-born Colonel Corcoran had been one of Mr. Ely's messmates and his intimate friend. She could only imagine the congressman's anguish at having drawn his name.

More slips of paper were produced, the names of the remaining officers were placed into the tin, and Mr. Ely was again called upon to draw lots for the thirteen officers who would stand as hostages for the **Savannah** privateers. "J. W. Rockwood," he read flatly, and withdrew a second slip of paper. "J. B. Ricketts."

Without thinking, Lizzie called out, "Captain Ricketts presently resides at the general hospital. He was very badly wounded at Manassas." Months before, his devoted wife, Fanny, had traveled from the North to nurse him and had remained with him faithfully ever since. Lizzie had befriended her and found her to be a most interesting and amiable lady, and she could not bear the thought that Fanny would be bereft of her husband again, or that his recovery would be cast into jeopardy.

General Winder shot Lizzie a dark look, silencing her, and he gestured for Mr. Ely to draw another lot. "Major Paul Joseph Revere."

Lizzie's heart sank. Major Revere of the Twentieth Massachusetts was not only the grandson of the famous midnight rider, the patriot Paul Revere, but was also an intelligent and agreeable man, one of her particular favorites among the prisoners.

Two more names were called, each

greeted with a murmur of regret, and then H. W. McQuade was selected.

Lizzie pressed her lips together to restrain her protests. Captain McQuade too was languishing in a hospital cot, recovering from the amputation of his leg. Suddenly another soldier pushed to the front of the crowd and presented himself to General Winder. "Captain Thomas Cox, Ohio. General Winder, put my name upon your list in the place of Captain McQuade."

"I have no authority to do so."

A chorus of disapproval for the general's response soon gave way to applause for Captain Cox, who stepped back into the crowd of prisoners, scowling in disappointment.

The remaining lots were drawn, the names called out, and when it was done, the general announced that the chosen officers would be removed to the Henrico County Jail as soon as possible.

Silently fuming, Lizzie resolved to provide the best possible welcome she could for them.

Chapter Ten

NOVEMBER 1861–APRIL 1862

The next day, General Winder returned to the officers' quarters to announce that Secretary Benjamin had exempted wounded officers from acting as hostages, and so two more names were drawn to replace Captains Ricketts and McQuade. When, hours later, the unlucky men were scheduled to be transferred to the Henrico County Jail, Lizzie and Eliza went ahead of them, employing General Winder's old pass to gain access to the hostages' quarters. They were appalled to discover that the men would be held in a cramped cell about twelve-by-sixteen feet, with thick walls and a double-barred window through which only a sad, dim light penetrated. Sobered by her powerlessness to improve the conditions, Lizzie left behind a basket full of hot rolls and a stack of books, as well as a note promising more.

Jefferson Davis declared November 15 a day of fasting, humiliation, and prayer for the success of Confederate arms, and in order to maintain their façade of loyalty for the Gibbs family, the Van Lews were obliged to perform the perfunctory duties of the occasion. Ignoring her own annoying hunger pangs, Lizzie secretly gave the servants permission to eat as much as they usually did as long as they kept out of sight, and she encouraged them to pray for the Union instead, as she herself did, silently, with head bowed.

On December 6, all of Richmond celebrated the news that Varina Davis had given birth to a son, William. Although the child was reported to be perfectly healthy and robust, Mrs. Davis was confined to her sickbed for weeks thereafter, and so her sister Margaret temporarily took over her role as official hostess.

A few days later, Captain Gibbs and his

family—who had underestimated the duration of their stay by two weeks—at last moved into their own dwelling a few blocks from the Capitol. "I will miss the children," Mother admitted. "It is almost too quiet without them."

Lizzie would too, but the sweet, piping voices she most longed to hear ringing through the halls again were those of her nieces, and no one else.

On December 18, Captain J. B. Ricketts was released from the prison hospital and sent north on the **Norfolk** in the company of his devoted wife, Fanny. "Captain and Mrs. Ricketts have been the recipients of kind attentions from our most distinguished citizens, during their stay in Richmond," the **Enquirer** noted. "It is supposed they leave the Confederacy with a better opinion than seems to be entertained of us among their people. If so, we trust they will enlighten the ignorance of their friends in the North." A Confederate captain detained in Washington was returned to Richmond in exchange, and Lizzie dared to hope it would be the first of many such trades.

Christmas came to Richmond, the first Christmas of the war. Warfare, blockades, and disorder sent prices soaring—coffee sold for a dollar fifty a pound, salt at a dollar forty a sack, apples twenty dollars a barrel, ice cream nine dollars a quart, turkeys for the astonishing price of four dollars each, and French candy at one dollar a pound. Thanks to Caroline's genius in the kitchen, Mother managed to put together a splendid Christmas feast nonetheless, and Lizzie and Mary set aside their discord so the family could celebrate together at the Church Hill mansion. By the raucous sounds outside their windows—rockets bursting, firecrackers snapping, drums resounding, horns tootling, voices caroling—the people of Richmond enjoyed the holiday as much as any Christmas past, despite the absence of loved ones and the deprivations of wartime.

On Christmas Day, Mr. Ely received a welcome gift: He was released and sent north, exchanged for a Southern civilian, the former United States minister to France, a secessionist Virginian who had been detained at Fort Warren since the outbreak of war. Although negotiations for Mr. Ely's release had been ongoing for weeks, when the decision was finally made, the exchange happened so swiftly that Lizzie had no opportunity to bid him farewell. He left behind a kind letter expressing his gratitude, but although she was elated for him and thought his release long overdue, she felt strangely bereft after he was gone.

New Year's Day dawned blessedly springlike and sunny, but the soft breezes whispered forebodingly that fair weather would herald the resumption of furious battle, which had fallen into a lull with the onset of winter. President Davis and his sister-in-law hosted a New Year's Day levee modeled after those that Jefferson and Varina Davis had attended at the White House when Mr. Davis served as a senator and secretary of war. For more than three hours, Mr. Davis cordially welcomed hundreds of visitors to the Executive Mansion, shaking hands and chatting amiably. Former president John Tyler was in attendance, as were John and Mary.

The very next day, Lizzie discovered that her own prayers for the new year would be answered to some extent. Two hundred and forty Union prisoners were exchanged, sent north to Fort Monroe for an equal number of Confederate soldiers held at Fort Warren on Georges Island in Boston Harbor. A week later, 160 more captives were exchanged under flag of truce. Only two days later, Captain Gibbs was promoted to major and transferred to Salisbury, North Carolina. Lizzie would not miss him, but she was dismayed all the same, for she would have to cultivate a relationship with his replacement, and the devil she knew was in many ways preferable to the one she had not met.

First, she would have to match wits with a familiar adversary, the War Department. Acting assistant surgeon in charge of prisons, Dr. Owen B. Hill, had informed Lizzie of Dr. Higginbotham's latest orders: no food or drink could be brought into the prisons except what was furnished by the commissary of the post. "I have not forgotten the taste of your delicious custard, which you were so kind to offer me," Dr. Hill closed his note, "and I know it to be very good and beneficial to the prisoners. Acting as his assistant, however, I cannot violate any order he may give or I would cheerfully oblige you."

Lizzie refused to accept the decree without a fight. As soon as Caroline made another custard, she and Eliza rode downtown to the office of Colonel Albert T. Bledsoe, the assistant secretary of war. "When you taste it, you will wonder how Dr. Higginbotham could possibly forbid it," Lizzie promised as she and Eliza were shown into his office still wearing their wraps. "What harm could an innocent custard possibly do?"

"It is difficult to see why anyone would object to custard," he acknowledged, looking as if he were making a great effort not to laugh. "Especially an innocent one."

His amusement irritated Lizzie. "Colonel Bledsoe," she said, sharply imperious, "I do hope you take our petition seriously."

"I do, Madam," he replied. "In fact, I confess that I am on your side. This is quite an assumption of power on Dr. Higginbotham's part. I assure you I will take the matter up with Secretary Benjamin as soon as possible."

The next day, in hopes of prompting a quick reply from the colonel, Lizzie sent a servant back to the War Department to retrieve her favorite serving dish. It was returned to her safely, along with a disappointing note:

Richmond, Jany. 24, 1862

My dear Miss Van Lew,
The Secretary of War declined to act on your application and referred it to Genl. Winder. If I can see Genl. Winder, I will try to get him to grant your request.
The custard was very nice, and many thanks to you. I borrowed some cups from an eating house nearby, and brought some crackers. So it was eaten in fine style.
Truly Yours,
T. Bledsoe

"What a waste of custard," Lizzie fumed, crumpling the letter and pacing the length of the parlor while Mother wound a skein of yarn with the help of her maid, Judy. "It has all circled around to General Winder."

"Is that not in your favor?" Mother inquired. "He likes you. He grants every request you make whenever it is in his power to do so."

"That is why I must appeal to him sparingly." She knew too that the general was frequently criticized in the press for his clemency to the Yankee prisoners—an accusation she could easily refute—and that someday he would feel compelled to prove just how strict a warden he could be.

"Miss Lizzie," said Judy, but then she hesitated.

"Go on, Judy," Mother encouraged. "Do you know something that could help?"

"I might and I might not." Judy's lined face furrowed even more in her uncertainty. "My niece is courting with that doctor's valet. She says that her fellow says that the doctor and your General Winder hate each other."

Lizzie and her mother exchanged a look. "Is that so?" mused Lizzie.

Judy nodded. "I don't know why, exactly, but my niece says they got some feud going."

"In that case, Lizzie, you could play them against each other," said Mother.

Lizzie thought of the times the general had been reluctant to follow the doctor's recommendations, and she vowed to trust her own powers of observation—and to act on them. "Judy, you are wonderful," she said, and startled the older woman by kissing her on the cheek, as she had done when she was a small child. "This knowledge will help tremendously."

And so when she called upon General Winder the following day, she brought him a generous portion of the custard and asked him if he could please explain Dr. Higginbotham's decision to her.

The general's expression grew stonier with every word she spoke. "Such insubordination will not stand."

"You don't mean—" Lizzie furrowed her brow and feigned bewilderment. "Surely he didn't issue this decree without consulting you."

"Unthinkable, isn't it?" Abruptly he pushed back his chair and rose from his desk. "Do you still retain the pass I issued you?"

"Yes," Lizzie said, rising. It was creased and smudged, and her most valuable possession.

"Don't be afraid to brandish it. Consider your privileges restored, although truly they were never rescinded." He scowled as he escorted her to the door. "I will see to Dr. Higginbotham."

True to his word, General Winder ordered Dr. Higginbotham arrested for taking precedence in rank. Although the doctor was soon released with no lasting harm done except to his pride, Lizzie did not doubt that she had made a powerful enemy.

On the dreary, rainy Saturday morning of February 22, Jefferson Davis was inaugurated as president of the Confederate States of America. The downpour did not discourage the people of Richmond from attending the grand event; ladies filled the galleries, which were reserved exclusively for them, while gentlemen packed the rotunda. Shortly before noon, Mr. Davis—pale, tense, and dressed in black—and his vice-president, Alexander Stephens, were conducted into the hall to be received by the assembly, who gave them a standing ovation.

At half past noon, the procession moved outside, where Mr. Davis ascended a bunting-draped platform at the base of the

Washington Monument on the Capitol Square before a crowd of two thousand citizens, who huddled beneath umbrellas on the muddy grounds and nearby streets. Standing in the rain, Mr. Davis waited several minutes for the cheering to subside before he took the oath of office, lifted and kissed the Bible, and addressed his ardent listeners. He reminded them that it was the birthday of the man most linked in memory with the foundation of American independence, George Washington, and likened their own revolution to his and his compatriots'. He denounced Union aggression and, especially, what he called Mr. Lincoln's blatant disregard for the Constitution and "all the time-honored bulwarks of civil and religious liberty"—the suspension of the writ of habeas corpus, the unlawful arrests, the abandonment of the right to due process. Although he acknowledged recent setbacks on the field of war, he predicted that the tide would soon turn their way again, and that the Union would soon collapse under the mountain of debt it had incurred to fund its unlawful invasion of the South. In a closing prayer, he thanked the Almighty for His divine protection and invoked His blessing upon their country and its cause.

Two days before his inauguration, Mr. Davis had declared Friday, February 28, another day of fasting, humiliation, and prayer to appeal to the Lord for His protection and favor, that they might be saved from their enemies and from the hands of all who hated them. Official fast days were observed more scrupulously than the Sabbath because they were considered a test of loyalty, and when the Gibbs family had resided with them, the Van Lews had diligently done what was expected. This time when the appointed day came, Lizzie and Mother refrained from joining the public prayers and instead invited Eliza's family over, drew the curtains, and enjoyed the most sumptuous meal Caroline could put together with the markets closed. "We should always resolve to have a better meal than usual on Mr. Davis's fast days," Lizzie declared, and the merry company raised their glasses and chimed in their agreement. It was a rare comfort to be able to speak freely with sympathetic friends.

It was the last lighthearted moment they would know for quite some time.

At midnight on March 1, one week after condemning the suppression of civil liberties in the North, President Davis placed Richmond and the surrounding countryside within a ten-mile radius under martial law.

The measure had not been announced beforehand, but Lizzie and her mother learned of it early, and discovered just how swiftly, suddenly, and mercilessly it would be implemented. They had just sat down to breakfast when they heard a distant pounding on the back door, and moments later, Mary Jane Bowser dashed into the room. They scarcely had time to greet her before she blurted, "Mr. Botts has been arrested."

Lizzie bolted to her feet. "What? Why? On what grounds?"

A friend who knew of their mutual ties had witnessed everything, Mary Jane explained breathlessly, slipping out of her wraps and dropping into a chair. Shortly before dawn, one hundred armed deputies had surrounded the Botts residence at Elba Park while others burst into the home and dragged Mr. Botts from bed. While he fumed and protested in his nightclothes, the assistant provost marshal read the charges and placed him under arrest as other detectives collected his private papers and letters. His wife and children were frantic; one son fainted dead away from fear. Mr. Botts was allowed to dress before he was taken away in a buggy to the filthy McDaniel's Negro Jail, a holding pen for slave dealers on Lumpkin's Alley off Franklin Street.

"What are the charges?" asked Lizzie shakily, pacing.

"I don't know," Mary Jane said, "but I can find out."

Lizzie stopped short, instinctively shrinking away from the window, half expecting to see a stranger's ugly visage glaring menacingly back at her. "Who else?"

"Who else has been arrested?" Mary Jane shook her head and shrugged. "No one that I know of."

"We must learn if Mr. Botts has been singled out because of his prominence or if they're rounding up all suspected Unionists." Her heart pounded with dread and fear, knowing it was likely the latter. There was no need to declare martial law to arrest a single man, but if the authorities wanted to cast a net and drag in many—

Lizzie took a deep, shaky breath, forced herself to draw back the curtain, and peered outside. It was a lovely morning, cool and dewy, fresh with the promise of the coming spring. She saw no one lurking outside, watching the house—no armed deputies, no soldiers, not even the lanky man with the tobacco-stained beard, who had been absent for many weeks.

"Do you suppose—" Mother hesitated. "I wonder if they are coming for us."

Shuddering, Lizzie wrapped her arms around herself as if caught in a sudden chill wind. "Not for you, Mother." She had done what she could to ensure that.

With the aid of Mary Jane's grapevine telegraph, by the end of the day, they had assembled a rough picture of the morning's alarming events. The prosperous distiller Franklin Stearns, who had never made a secret of his Union sympathies and was said to have done more with his whiskey to contribute to illness and absenteeism within the army camps than any weapon the enemy had yet produced, was arrested at his Tree Hill estate southeast of Richmond shortly after dawn. A butcher named Valentine Heckler and a grocer named John M. Higgins were also arrested on charges of uttering incendiary sentiments. A slave named Allen was arrested too, charged with treasonous language for allegedly declaring, "Jeff Davis is a rebel," and "I acknowledge no man as my master." Also caught up in the sweep were an ice dealer, a city night watchman, a lieutenant in the Wise Legion, and many others, but except for a carpenter who did business with the Van Lews' hardware store, Lizzie knew none of them. They were tradesmen and laborers, outside her usual social circle.

In the days that followed, the roundups continued and more arrests were made, men snatched from every neighborhood in Richmond and each outlying district. A shipbuilder, a merchant, a barkeeper, a Maine-born Universalist pastor who had refused to open his church on an official day of thanksgiving marking the Confederate victory at Manassas—the newspapers printed every name, every accusation. Lizzie and her mother and their entire household waited in terror for a pounding upon their own door. They slept little and went out not at all, sending Peter and

William to collect whatever news they could, awaiting messages from Mary Jane. Once, Lizzie sent Peter to carry a letter to Mr. Botts to encourage him in his confinement, but just as he was leaving, she frantically called him back, realizing almost too late that the letter would lead the authorities right back to her.

Days passed, but the dreaded knock on their door never came.

A week after martial law was imposed, Lizzie became too restless and agitated to skulk behind closed curtains any longer. She packed a basket with two dozen rolls and half as many ginger cakes for bribes and ventured out into the streets, which seemed strange in their ordinariness. The city she knew in her heart and mind had been shaken so violently that she had expected to find it reduced to rubble. But with every unimpeded step her courage returned to her, so that by the time she was within a few blocks of the prison complex, she was striding along as briskly as ever, head held high, a cordial smile upon her face should anyone dare to greet her.

But a block away from the prison entrance, she stopped short at the sight of a double cordon of sentinels stationed around the tobacco warehouses. She held perfectly still for a moment, pondering her next step, but then she took a deep breath to steel herself and approached the nearest guard with a smile.

"I beg your pardon," she greeted him pleasantly, taking care to remain a respectful distance away, "but I couldn't help noticing how the guard has been increased lately. Was there an escape attempt?"

"There's always one or two Yankees tryin' to run off," the guard replied. "But General Winder ordered the double guard on account of the recent mischief of the Unionists. Nothin' and no one goes in or out. No visitors, no letters, no newspapers. Them Yankees are none too happy about it."

"Nor would any reasonable person be in their place." Smiling, Lizzie took a ginger cake from the basket and gave it to him. "This is for your time and your charming conversation. I do hope you're allowed to eat on duty."

He grinned and thanked her, and as she went down the row of sentinels handing out the ginger cakes and the rolls she had intended to give the prisoners, she made pleasant small talk, though her thoughts were churning. She dared not use General Winder's pass to bluster her way into the prison, not in defiance of the extraordinary restrictions he himself had set in place. The pace of the Unionist roundups had already slowed. When the crisis passed, if the new rules were not lifted, she would call on the general and ask him if she might continue her work.

When the basket was empty, she apologized to the remaining guards for not having enough for everyone, for she had not expected so many. With the empty basket on her arm, she walked next to the Henrico County Jail, where the fourteen Union hostages were confined, and there too she found that the guard had been doubled. Disheartened, she turned toward home.

By the middle of March, the former slave pen on Lumpkin's Alley, which had acquired the nickname "Castle Godwin" after its commander, held twenty-eight men accused of disloyalty, including Mr. Botts. The suspects denied that they were involved in any conspiracy, and those who could afford decent lawyers petitioned the government for their immediate release. Through Mary Jane's channels, Lizzie managed to get a letter to Mr. Botts expressing her profound sympathies and offering to help him any way she could, and when he managed to smuggle out a reply, she learned that since his arrest, he had been kept in solitary confinement, forbidden visits from his family and his lawyers. "Can any true Virginian witness such scenes as these," he wrote, "men detained without benefit of hearing or counsel, and not feel the blood curdle in his veins?" He added that General Winder was pressuring the men, whose numbers increased daily, to betray one another, but although he and Mr. Stearns were very good friends, most of the accused had never met before their arrests, so they had nothing to confess.

Lizzie's heart sank at the mention of General Winder. Even as the widespread seizure of Unionists had earned him accolades in the press and on the streets, he had grown hard and brittle, and his responsibilities had only increased. At the end of March, so that fewer guards would

be needed to prevent escapes, the prison
complex at Twenty-Fifth and Main was
closed down and all five hundred or so
prisoners were marched to the large, connected structure of Libby & Sons' old warehouses on Cary Street, below Twentieth
near the dock. Lizzie dared not approach
him across such uncertain ground as this
new venture. But perhaps if she were patient, and allowed time for his inexplicable,
sudden fury to pass, she might find a way
to persuade him to parole Mr. Botts.

Every morning when Lizzie read the papers, she took note of the arrests and
learned by heart the names of those who
were accused of harboring Union sympathies.

Without ever meaning to do so, the Confederate government had introduced Lizzie
to her allies.

Chapter Eleven

Richmond's Unionists were not the only enemies of the Confederacy swept up in the arrests that followed the imposition of martial law. A handful of agents from Mr. Pinkerton's detective bureau in Washington had infiltrated some of the most sensitive departments in the Southern capital, but even in a city full of strangers, they had stood out enough to raise suspicions. Most were brought to the attention of the authorities by alert citizens, but one was turned in by his fellow spies.

Timothy Webster, a Pinkerton with years of undercover experience, had managed to earn the confidence of important officials in the War Department, including General Winder and Secretary of War Benjamin, who trusted him enough to employ him as a dispatch courier. He carried many secrets from Richmond to Washington City, but he was undone when two other Union agents, John Scully and Pryce Lewis, were sent to check on him after illness kept him bedridden and unable to contact Mr. Pinkerton for two weeks. Soon after their arrival in Richmond, Mr. Scully and Mr. Lewis were recognized on the street by a civilian whose family home in Washington they had once searched for evidence of Southern collusion, and they unwittingly led Confederate agents to the boardinghouse rooms Mr. Webster shared with his wife and colored servant. Mr. Scully and Mr. Lewis were arrested, convicted, and sent to Castle Godwin, where, under orders from General Winder, they were alternately threatened with death and offered mercy if they cooperated. Eventually they were broken, and they confessed not only their own missions as spies but also Timothy Webster's. He and his wife were immediately arrested and sent to join the others at Castle Godwin, where Mr. Botts and all the men taken in the early days of martial law still languished. Mr. Scully and Mr. Lewis were scheduled to hang within a week, and Mr. Webster, gravely ill from rheumatism, was sentenced to die at the end of the month.

Lizzie hung on every word the papers offered about the captured spies, sickened by the thought of their impending executions. "Why did Mr. Pinkerton send Northern agents south?" she asked her mother. "Why did they not recruit among Richmond's loyalists, people who are known here, who don't have to explain their presence in the city?"

"Perhaps these were men he knew well and trusted. Perhaps he couldn't send anyone here to do the recruiting."

"If he could send agents to spy, he could send agents to recruit." Lizzie wondered what would become of Mrs. Webster, who had not yet been sentenced, but remained in prison. Surely they would not hang a woman. Surely the same government and press who had condemned the Union's imprisonment of Rose O'Neal Greenhow would not be so hypocritical and cruel as to execute a woman.

On the day John Scully and Pryce Lewis were scheduled to hang, the road from Castle Godwin to Camp Lee, where the gibbet had been erected, was thronged with curious onlookers. No one had been hanged for spying on American soil since Nathan Hale was executed by the British in 1776, and many people couldn't quite believe it would happen that day either. Lizzie could not bear to be a spectator at such a horrifying event, so she stayed well away. Only later did she learn that the crowds seeking a novel entertainment were disappointed. At the last moment, Mr. Scully and Mr. Lewis were granted a reprieve and returned to prison.

Perhaps the Confederate government did not want to hang **anyone** for spying, not only women—but although Lizzie searched the papers every day for an announcement that Mr. Webster's death sentence had been commuted, she never found one.

The first few months of 1862 brought reports of Union victories in Missouri,

Kentucky, Tennessee, and North Carolina, and of Union troops massing and preparing to march under their new young leader, General George McClellan. At Yorktown, General Magruder's Confederate line was stretched thinly, but holding, as they awaited reinforcements. General Joseph Johnston was determined to bring them swift support, and so he decided to march his troops through Richmond and down the Peninsula. It was almost noon on a Sunday when word of the first arriving regiments swept through the city, passing from church to church: Three trainloads of soldiers had come from Fredericksburg, famished and weary, having had nothing to eat for twenty-four hours. While the ministers preached on, young wives and elderly matrons alike began stealing quietly from the pews, determined to share their family's dinners with the passing soldiers.

Soon Broad and Ninth Streets were lined with women, children, and servants carrying baskets of food—loaves of bread and hams and apples and hunks of cheese, anything they had been able to seize in a hurry. As the regiments marched past, the citizens of Richmond passed out food to the ravenous soldiers, until it seemed that every man among them was eating and stuffing his haversack. As soon as a woman emptied her basket, another stepped forward with more foodstuffs to take her place.

Beckoned from Saint John's by the distant commotion, Lizzie stood in the churchyard amid a crowd of curious worshipers and looked down upon the scene from atop Church Hill. While some of her fellow parishioners promptly raced off to carry more provisions to the troops, Lizzie could only stand and watch, shocked by the contrast between these ragged, hungry, sunburnt, filthy soldiers and the bright, grinning, untested young recruits in spotless uniforms who had marched through those streets less than a year before. "Poor fellows," Lizzie murmured. "What they have seen, and what they have suffered these past months."

"God bless and protect them," said Mother, beside her. "Come, Lizzie. We should do our part."

Lizzie tore her gaze away. "Mother," she protested in an undertone, mindful of the people around them, any one of whom could be an informant. "Are you really suggesting that we aid and abet the enemy army? Do we want them well fed and strong?"

"Lizzie," Mother chided her gently. "What if Cousin Jack were marching off to battle through a town full of strangers? What if John were?"

Not for the first time, Lizzie thanked God that John was not enlisted in either army, but she knew her mother was right. She was ashamed that she had considered even for a moment to refuse to feed hungry men.

"Let's make a good impression on the neighbors," she said, linking her arm through her mother's. "We'll burden the rebels with so much food that the suspicious citizens of Richmond will never doubt us again."

That was not her only reason, but she did not need to explain that to her mother.

Soldiers from all corners of the South had filled the capital in the early months of the war—so many that some of them had been sent home, to be called upon if needed later. So Lizzie was startled by new rumors that the troops were spread too thin, and that recruitment must be drastically and swiftly increased. In mid-April, the Confederate Congress passed a conscription act requiring all healthy white men between the ages of eighteen and thirty-five to join the military for three years, and all soldiers currently serving one-year terms to have their enlistments extended to three years. Men engaged in certain essential occupations—ironworkers, railroad laborers, telegraph operators, civil officials, miners, nurses, and teachers, among them—were exempt, for they were considered more valuable on the home front than on the battlefield.

Lizzie clutched the arms of her chair, dizzy with relief—the Confederate ranks were thinning, but John, at thirty-eight, would not be conscripted.

"I don't believe a draft will make any difference," said Mother. "All Southern men of that age are already harassed and coerced into the service by friends and neighbors and lovely young ladies they want to impress. Where are these enormous throngs of idle, healthy young men they hope to drive into the army?"

"Not every man craves battlefield glory," said Lizzie. "The men who have refused to be intimidated into enlisting will be outraged if they're forced to by law, and I don't mean only the secret Unionists among them. Perhaps they'll mount a second rebellion against their own Confederacy."

Mother looked dubious. "It seems unlikely that men who aren't disposed to fight would mount a rebellion."

"I am going to hope for it all the same."

"As long as it is not a false hope."

"Hope is never false. One's hopes may not be fulfilled, but that does not mean it was wrong to hope."

Sometimes hope was all that kept Lizzie from sinking into despair and abandoning her mission to help the imprisoned Union soldiers. Hope was what drove her to gather information about troop movements and Confederate defenses from recently captured prisoners and send it to the North. Hope compelled her to smuggle money into the prisons so the captives could bribe their way out and escape to Union lines. If she allowed herself to consider that perhaps she harbored nothing more than **false** hope, she might give up altogether.

Around the same time that the conscription act was announced, Mr. Botts was finally brought under guard from Castle Godwin to the court house to appear before a military tribunal. Though he had hired three lawyers, he represented himself in the trial, and over the course of several days he argued that although his objections to secession were well known, he had never been part of any conspiracy against the Confederate government; that he had been falsely accused; and that he was being wrongly prosecuted for his beliefs rather than any crime he had committed or intended to commit.

At first the tribunal seemed not to know what to do with him, but eventually they released a general order stating that it seemed compatible with the public safety to release him on parole, but it was not practicable to allow him to return to his home at Elba Park. Instead, until the Department of War declared otherwise, he would retire to the interior of the state at a place approved by the department; he would proceed to the approved destination "without unnecessary delay"; he would not leave that place or travel more than five miles from his residence; he would do nothing to injure the Confederate government while on parole; and—a requirement Lizzie thought would be impossible for him to obey—he would not "express any opinion tending to impair the confidence of the people in the capacity of the Confederate States to achieve their independence." The tribunal would have better luck, Lizzie thought, asking the wind not to blow or water not to be wet. Almost as an afterthought, the tribunal had added, "Mr. Botts's family will receive passports to join him, if desired."

So Mr. Botts was to be banished to the interior of Virginia, but at least he would not face exile alone.

He had not been sentenced to death, Lizzie reminded herself when she grew melancholy thinking of Richmond without its most outspoken Unionist, the last great Whig in the city, the man she most admired in politics. He had not been sentenced to spend the duration of the war locked in the gloom of Castle Godwin, subjected to the cruel whims of the odious Captain George W. Alexander. He would not even have to leave Virginia.

Within a few days, she was reminded anew that it was never false to hope.

Mr. Botts had agreed to the terms of his parole, but moments before he was going to be released, he requested an interview with the secretary of war. When the meeting was granted the following morning, he strongly remonstrated against being sent from his home and asked to read a formal protest for the official record. Secretary Randolph was either persuaded by his lengthy argument or simply wanted to be done with the matter, for he agreed that Mr. Botts could spend his parole confined to a family farm in Hanover County, a mere ten miles northeast of the center of Richmond.

There was always reason to hope, Lizzie thought with satisfaction as she read Mr. Botts's letter informing her of his parole, the first he had written to her from the farm. "I know you will be tempted to visit," he warned, "and I do have much to tell you, but I beg you to choose the hour carefully. I am still closely watched, and I would not have you deemed guilty by association. If you seek interesting conversation in my absence, I encourage you to make the acquaintance of Lieutenant

Erastus Ross, the nephew of my good friend Franklin Stearns. He is a clerk in the War Department under Captain Godwin, and you should feel welcome to call on him there."

Mr. Botts's strange turn of phrase told her that he suspected that his letter might be intercepted before it reached her. Lizzie knew of Franklin Stearns, the prosperous whiskey distiller and staunch Unionist who had been arrested the same day as Mr. Botts, but she knew nothing about the nephew. Surely Mr. Botts was trying to tell her that Lieutenant Ross was a Unionist too, and a potential friend, despite his place of employment.

Lizzie visited the prisoners at the Henrico County Jail as often as she was allowed, bringing them food, books, money for bribes, and, she hoped, encouragement, but she had not yet been allowed to set foot in the new prison, Libby, named after the tobacco merchant who had once owned the warehouse, and whose sign yet remained above the door.

The rule was not devised specifically for her, General Winder explained when she protested that the impertinent sentinels would not permit her through the gates. No civilian ladies were allowed.

"My visits did no harm at the old prison," Lizzie reminded him. "In fact, I recall you yourself saying that I did quite a lot of good."

"If I make an exception for you, I will have to permit everyone," General Winder replied, coolly rational and utterly unlike him. He had become strangely vengeful, obdurate. She hardly knew how to bargain with him anymore.

A few days after receiving Mr. Botts's letter, Lizzie invented an errand with Captain Godwin's office at the War Department in order to take the measure of Franklin Stearns's nephew, Erastus Ross. "We have a mutual acquaintance, I believe," he said as he welcomed her into his office. He was tall and likely no older than twenty-two, with pleasant features, neatly parted fair hair, and a long mustache that followed the curve of his mouth and cheeks and tapered at the ends. "Mr. Botts has spoken highly of you."

"He speaks well of you also," said Lizzie, and then, mindful of other clerks and officers passing in the hallway, she turned the conversation to her errand, a small matter of a servant found at large with an expired pass. Although she was obliged to choose her phrases carefully to avoid entrapping herself, Lieutenant Ross's remarks and responses convinced her that he was no ardent rebel. Thus satisfied, after concluding her business, she invited him to take tea with her and her mother the following afternoon.

He arrived five minutes early, smartly attired in civilian clothes and looking wary as she escorted him to the library. He fidgeted through tea and cakes and a bit of chat about the weather until Lizzie decided to have mercy on him and get to the point.

She began by showing him numerous fond letters from Mr. Botts to prove herself worthy of his trust, and then she confided what he surely already suspected—she was as loyal to the Union as Mr. Botts, as loyal as President Lincoln. After that, Mr. Ross confessed his own Unionist sentiments in a flood of words constrained too long behind a dam of prudent reticence.

"I trust that Captain Godwin is convinced of your loyalty, despite your uncle's arrest?"

Lizzie queried, pouring her guest another cup of tea.

"Yes, he is," replied Mr. Ross. "General Winder's own son is a captain in the Union army, so how can anyone condemn me for my uncle's misplaced loyalties?"

Lizzie set down the teapot and offered him sugar and cream. "But he is not so satisfied with the quality of your work that he would refuse to let you go if you requested a transfer?"

Mr. Ross stirred his tea slowly—to buy himself time to think of a response, Lizzie suspected. "I'm a good clerk to him, but not exemplary. I lack the impetus to be any more productive than absolutely necessary to keep my job. Where would you have me go?"

Lizzie drew herself up, interlaced her fingers, and rested her hands in her lap. "Libby Prison has a vacancy for a clerk."

He laughed abruptly and set down his teacup. "Miss Van Lew, I'm trying to stay **out** of prison."

"We need a man on the inside," Lizzie explained. "As clerk, you would be privy to all manner of valuable secrets, which you could pass on to me. You can tell me what the prisoners need and help me get necessities to them. You could smuggle in money so they can bribe the guards for better treatment. I'm sure you know they're beaten if they cannot pay."

Mr. Ross nodded, pained. "I've heard the rumors. If . . . I suppose if I were made clerk there, I could put a stop to it, or at least try—"

"No, you could not," Lizzie interrupted. "You must seem as indifferent to the prisoners' suffering as every other guard or you'll raise their suspicions."

He winced. "So I must work at the prison, and observe the guards' cruelty, and witness the prisoners' suffering, and keep silent and ignore those I most want to help."

Lizzie nodded.

He inhaled deeply, set his jaw, and gazed out the window in silence, brooding. Lizzie and her mother exchanged an anxious look, but just when Lizzie could not bear the tense silence a moment longer, he said, "I'll apply for the transfer. I'll invent some excuse about how it's always been my ambition to become a warden, and this job at Libby Prison would be—I don't know. A promising first step. I'll think of something."

"Be sure to figure out your story before you approach Captain Godwin," Lizzie cautioned. Mr. Ross managed a wry smile and assured her he would.

Very soon, Lizzie hoped, she would have an important contact well placed within the prison. Until General Winder relented and permitted civilian volunteers to visit the prisoners, Erastus Ross would be her eyes and ears.

Lizzie's stubborn hopes also allowed her to believe until the very last hour that the condemned spy Timothy Webster would somehow escape execution.

At the end of April, as reports of Union advances upon New Orleans began trickling into the capital, Mr. Webster waited out his last days in Castle Godwin—and Lizzie waited, increasingly anxious, for the announcement that his sentence had been commuted.

On the appointed day, Lizzie rose before dawn, forced herself to choke down some tea and toast, and waited for Peter to return with the early editions. Every paper noted that the gibbet had been erected at Camp Lee, and that Captain Alexander was expected to escort the condemned man there shortly after dawn.

Lizzie was torn. If Mr. Webster was to die, she ought to bear witness to his final moments, to pray for him, to let him know he was not alone. However, they had never met, so he would receive no comfort from the presence of a friend but would assume she was just another voyeur. She also did not know, despite the grim scenes she had grown accustomed to within the prisons, whether she could bear the ghastly spectacle of a hanging.

"I'll go," Peter said, after she had paced and wrung her hands and pondered her options until time had almost run out. "You shouldn't. People will take notice of a lady like you, but I'll be just another colored man in the crowd."

With a pang of relief and pain, Lizzie gratefully agreed, and Peter set out.

When he returned, hours later, she knew from his expression that Mr. Webster was no more.

From what Peter was able to learn, at a

quarter past five o'clock, Captain Alexander had come to Mr. Webster's cell and ordered him to prepare himself. Mr. Webster asked for more time but was refused, so he bade farewell to his wife, who had been permitted to spend his final hours with him. Then the captain took the condemned man by carriage from Castle Godwin to Camp Lee, but no crowds lined the roads, as if everyone had assumed this execution too would be halted at the last minute. They stopped along the way to pick up a minister, whom Mr. Webster asked to read the Psalm of David, invoking vengeance on his enemies. When the minister indignantly rejected his choice, Mr. Webster angrily rebuffed him, so the offended minister refused to offer him any comfort whatsoever.

When he arrived at Camp Lee, Mr. Webster might yet have entertained hopes that he would not be put to death, thinking, perhaps, that it was all a sham meant to intimidate him into betraying his country's secrets. But when he was taken from a holding pen and beheld the gallows, and the gathered soldiers, and about two hundred civilians who had taken to trees and rooftops to obtain a better view of his death, the truth dealt him a staggering blow. He began to shake, and asked for a chaplain, and pleaded to be shot like a soldier instead of hanged like a common criminal. He was granted the chaplain—a different man than had accompanied him in the carriage—but was refused the bullet.

Captain Alexander led Mr. Webster to the foot of the gallows, but he climbed the stairs alone, slowly, calmly, and erect, clad in a black suit and silk hat. As he stood on the platform, his jailers bound his hands and legs, the minister spoke a solemn prayer, a black hood was drawn over his head, the noose slipped around his neck, the trapdoor sprung—and Mr. Webster plummeted straight through the platform, hitting the bare earth below with a sickening thud.

The hangman's knot had come undone. Stunned from the fall, bound hand and foot, Mr. Webster lay limp and motionless before the gathered throng. Quickly, Captain Alexander ordered his men to lift him up and carried him back up to the scaffold.

"I suffer a double death," Mr. Webster was heard to say as his jailers hastened to adjust the trap and again placed him upon it. The noose was again slipped around his neck, this time so tight as to be excruciatingly painful. "You will choke me to death this time," Mr. Webster rebuked them hoarsely, his voice muffled by the rope and the enveloping hood.

A moment later, the trap was sprung a second time, and within a minute, Mr. Webster was dead.

Blinded by tears, Lizzie groped for a chair and sat heavily as Peter reached the end of his grisly tale. "We must do something for his poor widow," she said.

"Surely she will be released now," said Mother, pale and shaken. "Surely, now that they have killed her husband, they will allow her to return to the North."

"We shall take her in until they do," said Lizzie decisively. "We will persuade them to parole her into our care. If they can parole an outspoken Unionist like Mr. Botts, they can certainly free a grieving widow whose only crime was to faithfully attend her husband."

Mother agreed, but she begged Lizzie

not to visit the prison alone out of a super-
stitious fear that she would not be allowed
out again. Lizzie soon enlisted Eliza as
her companion, and together they ventured to Lumpkin's Alley and Castle Godwin, where Captain Alexander had already
returned from Camp Lee. He looked a
perfect villain, Lizzie thought as they were
introduced, large, dark-haired, and thick-
bearded, with a belligerent set to his jaw.
As a lieutenant in the Confederate army,
he had been captured on the Eastern
Shore and imprisoned in Baltimore for
three weeks, but while awaiting execution
he had escaped by leaping from the fort,
badly injuring his ankle. As his injury prevented him from returning to the battlefield, he had been assigned to prison duty,
and—both strangely and sadly, Lizzie
thought—his brief experience as a prisoner of war had rendered him less rather
than more empathetic to the captives under
his control.

Something about his manner made
Lizzie instinctively adopt a respectful, def-
erential tone when she asked him to release Mrs. Webster into her care. "She is
a poor, agonized widow, and powerless to

harm anyone," Lizzie implored. "Let her remain with us until she can be transported to the North."

"No," Captain Alexander flatly replied. "She's going to be sent off soon enough, and until then she can enjoy the finest hospitality a spy deserves."

"She is no spy," protested Lizzie. "Her only crime, if such it can be called, was to be a dutiful and obedient wife. Please don't punish her for her husband's deeds."

The captain barked out a laugh. "Even if I were inclined to release her, which I am not, I would never let her stay with you." He fixed Lizzie with a steely gaze. "You introduced yourself simply as Miss Van Lew. Are you not Miss Elizabeth Van Lew of Church Hill?"

Her stomach turned queasily. "Yes, I am. As the only Miss Van Lew in Richmond, I saw no need to elaborate."

An insolent smile crept over his face. "It may interest you to know that you have already been reported several times."

Lizzie's heart thudded, but before she could speak, Eliza said, "What an outrage! Reported for what?"

His gazed drifted laconically to Eliza.

"For improper attention to the Union prisoners."

"Nonsense! Anyone who would spout such ridiculous accusations is either ignorant or lying. Did those same informants mention that Miss Van Lew welcomed Captain Gibbs and his family into her own home for nearly two months when they had nowhere else to go? Did they describe the many entertainments she has hosted for the Richmond Howitzers and other regiments? Why, just last week she hosted a dinner for a whole contingent of Texas cavalry officers commanded by Colonel Trinidad Martinez. They have not yet left Richmond, I believe. You can ask the colonel what he thinks of these spurious reports about the Van Lew family."

"I can ask him and I will," Captain Alexander said, a lazy threat in his voice. "Your eagerness to defend your friend is commendable, but don't get carried away."

Eliza pressed her lips together indignantly and bowed her head. Lizzie suddenly, desperately, wanted to get away. She murmured pardons and farewells, took Eliza by the elbow, and steered her back out to the street, jumping when the heavy doors clanged shut behind them.

"I don't know what came over me," said Eliza faintly as they hurried off toward Church Hill. "Thinking of that poor widow, and the threats against you—"

"You did well. I just stood there dumbfounded, too frightened to speak." Lizzie quickened her pace, eager to put the prison behind her. "I wouldn't have thrown that dinner party for just anyone. Colonel Martinez is a longtime friend of the family, the son of a prosperous and influential rancher. We don't agree on politics, obviously, but he is otherwise an intelligent man of sound judgment and integrity. He will have nothing but sincere praise for my family to offer if Captain Alexander does question him."

"Perhaps you should host another party for the Richmond Howitzers soon," Eliza said, anxious.

"Yes, I shall, the very day they next return to the city." People's memories were short except when it came to scandal, and Lizzie would be wise to bring out the façade of Confederate loyalty for a good polish more often. "In the meantime, I'll see if Captain Alexander wants to board with us as Captain Gibbs once did."

"Lizzie," Eliza gasped, halting abruptly. "You cannot be serious!"

Lizzie laughed, a trace of hysteria in her voice. "Evidently I can't. Eliza, forgive me. That was my poor attempt at a joke."

"Very poor," Eliza spluttered, shaking her head as she resumed walking. "Very poor, and not at all funny, because that's exactly the sort of dangerous, foolhardy thing you would do, if you did not have wiser, more prudent friends to advise you against it."

"If only I listened to you more often," said Lizzie ruefully, slipping her arm through Eliza's.

"Yes, if only you did."

"You must admit, though, taking in Captain Alexander as a boarder would convince even my most suspicious neighbors that I have nothing to hide."

"Yes," Eliza grumbled reluctantly. "It probably would. But promise me you won't do it. My nerves are frazzled and frayed enough without bringing him to the neighborhood."

Lizzie fervently vowed that she would not. It would be an easy promise to keep. The very thought of seeing Captain Alexander again repulsed her, and her heart sank as she realized she dared not approach him a second time about paroling Mrs. Webster. She only hoped he was telling the truth when he said that the grieving widow would be returned to the North soon, for Lizzie was powerless to help her.

Chapter Twelve

APRIL–JUNE 1862

It was curious, Lizzie thought, how the most exciting news of the war always seemed to come to Richmond on a Sunday.

It was the last Sunday in April when word came that Union gunboats steaming upriver from the Gulf of Mexico had captured New Orleans, the largest city in the South and the gateway to the mighty Mississippi. It was a tremendous blow to the Confederacy, the worst loss the South had yet suffered.

As Union general Benjamin Butler invaded New Orleans a thousand miles to the south, the people of Richmond were distracted by a much closer threat. General George McClellan had moved his troops from the outskirts of Washington City down the Potomac and the Chesapeake Bay to Fort Monroe, and from there north along the Peninsula toward Richmond. Now, about sixty miles to the southeast, he assembled his massive army at Yorktown, where, six days after the fall of New Orleans, General Johnston withdrew and pulled his troops back toward the Confederate capital, abandoning Yorktown, Norfolk, and the Lower Peninsula—and leaving the entryway to the James River vulnerable. On May 6, Union troops took Williamsburg, and three days later, the rebels were forced to evacuate their naval base at Norfolk.

The next day, John arrived at the Church Hill mansion just as Lizzie and her mother were sitting down to lunch. Delighted by the unexpected visit, they cajoled him into joining them, but even as he sat down, it was evident that he had brought urgent news.

"Last night, Mary and I attended a reception at the Executive Mansion," he began, accepting a cup of coffee from Caroline with a nod of thanks.

"Again?" Lizzie felt a sharp sting of jealousy. "You spend more time with the Jefferson Davis family than with us anymore."

John's wry look told Lizzie that he did not relish those social engagements, as she ought to know. "Mary's friendship with Mrs. Chesnut ensures that we're invited to far more gatherings than I wish to attend. Yesterday evening I couldn't come up with an excuse good enough to satisfy my wife, so attend we did. At one point Mr. Davis was called away by a messenger, and when he returned, his expression was grave."

"Did he share the bad news with the party?" asked Mother.

"No, but I managed to be nearby when he took his wife aside and told her."

"What did he say?" Lizzie prompted, impatient, wishing she too could befriend Mrs. Chesnut and be included on the Davises' guest lists.

"Union gunboats are heading up the James."

Mother gasped, and Lizzie clasped her hands to her heart. "Praise God," she exclaimed. "When are they expected to reach Richmond?"

"That, I don't know. Mr. Davis told his wife that he hoped the gun batteries along the riverbank and the torpedoes and vessels they sank in the channel would prevent the Union boats from coming too close, but just in case, he commanded her to take their children and valuables and flee the city."

"The president's family, evacuating the capital," Lizzie said in wonder. "Our deliverance is at hand."

"Unless this proves to be another 'Pawnee Sunday,'" cautioned Mother, but her eyes shone with hope.

"Mr. Davis apparently doesn't think it is," said John. "This morning, Mrs. Davis and the children were seen boarding the train to Raleigh."

Many other citizens soon followed their example. The Confederate Congress had already decamped from the capital—abruptly, and immediately after voting themselves a pay raise—citing vague fears of potential accidents on the railroad. In their absence, their clerks hurriedly stacked packing cases full of essential documents outside government offices, preparing them for shipment to Danville or

Columbia. Businessmen boarded up their windows and locked their doors. Many residents fled into the countryside, fearing that if Richmond were taken by the Yankees, they would be subjected to the same harsh treatment General Butler had inflicted upon the defiant citizens of New Orleans. Houses were deserted, while every wagon and canal boat heading west or south was packed full of frightened people and their suitcases and trunks. At the same time, streams of rural dwellers flooded Richmond from the Peninsula ahead of General McClellan's advancing army, believing they would be safe if only they could reach the city.

General Robert E. Lee, who had been summoned back to Richmond to serve as Mr. Davis's military adviser a few weeks before, reportedly vowed that Richmond would never be surrendered, but others planned for it nonetheless. Some of the richest men in town declared that they would set fire to their homes rather than allow them to be desecrated by the Yankees, while others made the same promise regarding the Capitol. The **Dispatch** urged that Mr. Houdon's magnificent statue of George Washington be removed from the "rickety old State House" for safekeeping, and rumors circulated that the president's cabinet had issued orders for all tobacco warehouses to be burned rather than allow such a valuable resource to fall into enemy hands.

Lizzie observed the frantic activity with increasing alarm, wondering if her family should move to the farm until the invasion was over, though it was impossible to know whether they would be any safer on the outskirts of the city, and she was reluctant to abandon their home to the vengeful citizens of Richmond. Nor did Lizzie want to leave the Union prisoners, now that Erastus Ross had been appointed clerk of Libby prison and she could do more good there. Though she was still forbidden to enter, Lieutenant Ross had persuaded the more lenient guards to carry her gifts of food and books to the prisoners on her behalf, and news had a way of finding its way out when her baskets were returned to her. From the prison's upper floors, the inmates had an excellent view of the bridges over the James connecting Richmond and Manchester, and they took careful note of train movements and any other activity that could be of interest in Washington.

Lizzie had also forged a bond with a particularly useful inmate—Robert Ford, a Northern free man of color who had been employed by the quartermasters' department of the Union Army as a teamster. Upon his capture at the end of May, he was sent to Libby and assigned to work as a hostler, tending the horses of the prison keeper and second in command, Richard Turner. Since he was often outside, Mr. Ford was able to pass messages between Lizzie and the inmates, whom she could only glimpse at a distance through the windows. Lizzie arranged with Mr. Ford to quietly point her out to the prisoners, tell them where she lived, and instruct them to seek sanctuary at her home if they should ever find occasion to escape. After Mary Jane Bowser and the Roane brothers vouched for her integrity, other colored workers employed in the prison also agreed to help, at no small risk to themselves. Nearly every Sunday, Lizzie would stroll down from Church Hill at a leisurely pace and pass along the street in front of Libby Prison, never glancing toward it for fear that a look in that direction might betray her keen interest in its inhabitants. At that very moment, a colored worker might set down his mop, look over his shoulder to be sure no guards were near, and point out the window, whispering, "That is Miss Van Lew. She will be a friend to you if you can escape."

If any fugitives did make their way to Church Hill, Lizzie was determined to have a safe hiding place ready for them. She had William and Nelson cut a hole in an attic wall and build a small chamber in the eaves above the front portico, which she furnished with bedding, blankets, a lamp, and other small comforts. It was not luxurious by any means, but it was tidy and snug, and since the panel over the entrance could be completely concealed by a large box, it was all but undetectable unless one knew precisely where to look. It would serve well as a fugitive's temporary quarters until he could be smuggled from the city to the farm and onto Union lines.

· · ·

The days passed, and tensions grew, and as General McClellan's army pushed forward and Johnston's fell back, all of Richmond seemed to hold its breath, waiting for the colossal battle that would surely determine the outcome of the war. Mr. Davis rode out into the field daily to observe the defenses, and some wags remarked that his stony expression suggested that he was annoyed with General Johnston and was considering taking command of the army himself. Women like those of Mary's sewing circle, who had been stitching sandbags for fortifications, switched to rolling bandages. Governor Letcher and Mayor Mayo recruited boys sixteen to eighteen and men over forty-five to form a Home Guard, and the sixty-six-year-old mayor evoked cheers when he declared that if needed he would take up arms himself. Overnight, painted slogans appeared on the walls of shops and warehouses—"Now is the time to rally around Old Glory!" "Hail, Columbia!"—but proud, affronted Confederates scrubbed them away before noon.

In the Van Lew mansion, apprehension and fear and excitement built to such heights that Lizzie thought the pressure might shatter the windows and burst through the roof. She wished she possessed her mother's inherent serenity rather than dull spirits and raw nerves. She needed to do something bold, something to restore her optimism, something to give her hope for liberation the way creating the secret chamber had given her hope that eventually prisoners would escape from Libby and use it—

And suddenly the answer came to her.

"Mother," she said, slowly turning as the vision unfolded in her mind's eye. "General McClellan is coming."

"Yes, dear," her mother replied. "That is what we all pray for."

"Yes, we do, but Mother, I don't mean I **hope** he is coming. I mean he **is** coming, and he will be here soon."

Mother paused and rested her knitting in her lap. "You seem . . . very certain."

"I **am** certain, but there's a problem." Lizzie spread her hands. "He has no place to stay."

"Well . . ." Mother studied her curiously. "The Spotswood Hotel comes very highly recommended."

"And it's been packed full for nearly a year, not that we would dream of allowing such an illustrious personage to stay in a hotel when we can accommodate him far more comfortably here." Lizzie clasped her hands together, beaming. "We must prepare a room for him."

After a moment, a slow smile appeared on Mother's soft, lined face. "Why, yes," she declared. "That is the very ideal. How better to thank our liberator than to welcome him into our home."

"After so many days eating camp food, and so many nights sleeping on the hard earth—or a cot, perhaps, he **is** a general—think what a pleasure it would be for him to enjoy Caroline's cooking and a soft featherbed."

"The very best we could offer would be no more than he deserves."

"My thinking exactly." Beaming, Lizzie crossed the room, took her mother's hands, and pulled her to her feet, letting her knitting tumble to the floor. "We must start right away. He could be here any day."

"Any hour," Mother corrected, eyes shining.

And so they set about preparing a chamber for General McClellan, choosing a room with a beautiful view of the gardens to the rear and the James River below, a landscape sure to be of keen interest to him. They put up new wallpaper, the best they could find from the days before blockades prevented drapers and shopkeepers from replenishing their inventory with the latest fashions. Judy, Caroline, and the other servants helped from time to time, but although they never said so, the glances they exchanged suggested that they considered the project an impractical waste of time.

John showed no such restraint. "How will General McClellan even know to come to you?" he asked when Lizzie stopped by the hardware store for a jar of paste.

"When he enters the city, I'll have Peter deliver an invitation." She sighed at her brother's dubious look. "Oh, John, indulge me. It's my time to waste, if that's what I'm doing, but I must believe that the general's arrival is imminent if I am to endure the wait."

John nodded and dropped the matter, and he did not discourage her again.

On the afternoon of May 31, Lizzie and her mother were on the piazza sewing pillowcases for the general's bed when a distant dull roar shook the house and rattled the windows.

"Thunder?" asked Mother, glancing up at the overcast skies.

Another boom sounded, and Lizzie shook her head.

"Cannon," called Nelson from the garden.

Lizzie and her mother exchanged a look, apprehensive and hopeful. "He's coming," Lizzie said determinedly, setting herself back to work. Before long, the wind carried the sharp, rapid cracking of musket fire to them. Distracted, Lizzie kept glancing up from sewing to gaze out upon the river, impatient for her first glimpse of Union gunboats, until she was picking out one stitch for every two she made.

"Oh, Lizzie," said her mother, shaking her head and smiling, although the strain showed around her eyes. "You fidget as if your chair were made of hot iron. Why don't you go see what's happening, if you can?"

She needed no further inducement.

Quickly she set aside the pillowcase and hurried upstairs to the rooftop, where she found William, Peter, and Caroline studying the southeastern horizon. Lizzie shaded her eyes with her hands, but all she could see was gun smoke drifting in the distance, and in between, the hills and rooftops of Richmond crowded with curious, anxious onlookers. When the rumble of artillery fire built to a crescendo, loud cheers rose from the crowds, and when the sounds diminished, their voices sank into an unintelligible murmur as they debated whether an important tactical advantage had been won.

"President Davis is out there," Peter remarked, nodding toward the gun smoke clouds. "So they say."

"What else do they say?" Lizzie queried.

"Rumors and more rumors," scoffed Caroline. "It's a waste of time to try to sort it out before it's over."

"You can only believe what you see with your own eyes and not what you hear," said William. "That's why we're up here, watching and waiting."

Lizzie stayed and watched with them a

while longer, but when nothing about the scene changed—no Union gunboats suddenly appeared from around a bend in the river, no strong wind blew away the smoke clouds to reveal the Confederate army in hasty retreat—she returned to the back piazza, her mother, and her sewing.

General McClellan was coming, and his room must be ready.

That evening, a seemingly endless procession of ambulances, ox carts, and wagons brought the dead and wounded into Richmond. The hospitals filled and then overflowed. Hundreds of suffering soldiers—battered, bleeding, groaning in anguish, or silently slipping away—were carried to warehouses or into abandoned homes. Hundreds more were unloaded from wagons and train cars onto the sidewalks until it seemed that the entire city had become an open-air hospital. The women of Richmond rushed to their aid, offering food and comfort and whatever nursing skills they possessed. Young mill girls and seamstresses toiled alongside elegant society matrons, the war having made colleagues of women who otherwise never would have met. Lizzie's mother went out once, to distribute bread with a group of ladies from Saint John's, but otherwise she and Lizzie stayed home, redoubling their efforts to prepare the general's room, which seemed ever more likely to welcome its honored occupant soon.

The fighting resumed in the morning about five miles outside Richmond, but by noon it was over, ending in a tactical draw—a vicious, bloody stalemate. Over the next few days, rumors coalesced into truth, and Lizzie learned that the intractable, thin-skinned General Johnston had been seriously wounded, and that President Davis had placed Robert E. Lee in command of his army. General Lee promptly renamed his forces the Army of Northern Virginia and set his men to work fortifying Richmond's sparsely defended earthworks and gathering his brigades for a counterattack.

The Richmond papers praised General Lee's appointment and declared the Battle of Seven Pines a glorious victory, but General McClellan's army, some one hundred thousand troops strong, remained encamped on the outskirts of Richmond.

From the rooftop Lizzie could easily see their observation balloons floating above the earth, and the deep booms of their heavy artillery reverberated throughout the city. If McClellan's army advanced any further, the city would be in range of the big guns, and it would surely fall.

Deliberately, Lizzie and her mother finished their preparations, hanging curtains, laying new matting on the floor, and arranging cut flowers in elegant vases.

"He will come," they assured one another from time to time. The flowers wilted and were replaced with fresh blooms, and still they waited.

On June 25, General Lee launched his attack, crossing the Chickahominy River to engage Union troops at Oak Grove. Wounded men brought from the battlefield to Richmond reported that the Confederates had inflicted much higher casualties than they had suffered, and that General Lee intended to augment his tactical victory by confronting Union forces at Mechanicsville. Lizzie inhaled sharply when she heard the familiar name; Mechanicsville was a crossroads village about six miles northeast of Richmond, not far from the farm where Mr. Botts lived in exile.

The next morning dawned hot and humid, and all of Richmond buzzed with anticipation for the climactic battle expected to begin at any moment. Eager to witness the momentous clash, hundreds of citizens—some with children in tow, others hauling picnic hampers and opera glasses—ventured out into the heights around the city to behold the spectacle.

Anyone traveling north could disappear into that crowd, thought Lizzie, suddenly inspired. At last, the distraction she had longed for ever since Mr. Botts was paroled had come.

Mother tried to discourage her, and when that failed, she implored Lizzie not to travel alone. "I'll ask Eliza to accompany me," she promised. Eliza already had a passport signed by Provost Marshal Godwin, a longtime friend of her father's, and she could get one quickly for Lizzie too.

"Two women, traveling alone, with war almost on our doorstep?" said Mother, distressed. "Lizzie, I should not have to tell a young lady as intelligent as yourself that the sensible thing to do under these

circumstances is to ride **away** from a raging battle, not toward it."

"I cannot help where Mr. Botts put his
farm," said Lizzie, strangely lighthearted.
"We will ask one of Eliza's cousins to escort us if that will reassure you."

"Which cousin?"

Lizzie pondered the options as she tied
on her bonnet. "Theodore, I suppose. He's
a fine horseman and would likely enjoy a
jaunt out to the countryside."

"Is he the one they call the commodore?"

"Yes."

"Why is he home instead of serving in
the navy?"

"They call him the commodore because
he was president of his yacht club at college." Quickly Lizzie kissed her mother's
cheek. "I'll be home tonight. Don't worry,
and don't wait up."

"You know very well that I shall do both."

Eliza blanched and rested her head
against the doorjamb when Lizzie proposed riding out to see Mr. Botts, but she
swallowed hard, nodded, and squeaked
out her agreement. With admirable efficiency she acquired a pass for Lizzie,

signed by Provost Marshal Godwin and good for thirty days. After making a valiant attempt to dissuade them, Eliza's cousin Theodore eventually agreed to escort them, but only after they made it clear they intended to go with or without his protection.

By the time they set forth, the hot morning had turned into a blistering afternoon. Lizzie's heart pounded with excitement as they rode northeast out of the city. The route to the Botts family farm took them along the Mechanicsville Turnpike directly toward the fighting, and as the sounds of distant gunfire grew louder, Lizzie found herself urging her horse toward them ever faster. They passed soldiers watering horses and cavalrymen riding at a flat-out run; Lizzie eagerly looked for Colonel Martinez's Texas regiment but did not spot them from the road. All was a frenzy of noise and barely constrained chaos, played to the tune of rattling gear and canteens and arms, of the whinnying and splashing of warhorses as they rushed in and out of the watering pond. The smell of dust and gun smoke and horses filled her senses as they galloped along, past the cannons aligned on crop roads and fields, the ambulances preparing for their grisly duty, the long lines of infantry awaiting orders. Somewhere unseen but none too distant, artillery boomed and rifles cracked.

They passed through a thickly wooded region, glancing warily into the shade of the trees as they hurried their horses on, and from a distance Lizzie glimpsed a dilapidated farmhouse slumping dejectedly in the middle of an untended tobacco field. Before they reached it they came to a crossroads, where, arms at the ready, Confederate pickets moved to block their way and ordered them to halt. Breathless and wary, they pulled up a few paces away from the soldiers.

"What're you folks doing out this way?" demanded a corporal, incredulous. "Turn around and hightail it back to Richmond before you get yourselves shot."

"We're on our way to Mechanicsville," said Lizzie. "We have passes from the provost marshal."

The corporal gestured. "Let's see 'em."

As they took out their papers, a private removed his hat, scratched his head, and spat into the dirt. "What kind of muddle-headed fool brings ladies into the middle of a battle?"

"That's unkind," Lizzie protested without thinking. "The truth is, **we** brought **him**."

"I'm doing my best to see my cousins safely home," said Theodore. "They were visiting my mother, but when the battle began, they became too frightened to remain in the city any longer."

Frowning, the corporal squinted dubiously at Lizzie and Eliza. "It's safer in the city than out here."

"That's what I told them," said Theodore, "but they insisted that we return to the farm immediately, and they said they were resolved to go with or without me. What was a devoted elder cousin to do?"

"You coulda tried locking them in their rooms," the private drawled, tugging his cap back over his matted brown hair.

"That was my first thought, but my mother wouldn't allow it. She feared they would climb out the window and create a scandal with the neighbors."

The private grinned, but the corporal glanced up from inspecting their papers and shook his head, his brow furrowing. "Your passes are in order, but you'd be better off going back to the city until to-morrow."

"No," said Eliza, trembling with un-feigned fear. "It must be today."

"Tell us, corporal," said Lizzie, leaning forward eagerly. "How goes the fighting?"

His worried expression relaxed a trifle. "It's going our way so far, Ma'am."

"We're whippin' the federals left, right, and center," the private declared. "We've taken scores of prisoners, maybe hun-dreds. General Lee's gonna win the day."

As they were speaking, the roar of the guns had grown louder, and Eliza anx-iously turned her head this way and that, wheeling her horse about for a better view of the surrounding countryside as if she expected an attack to come from all direc-tions at once.

"We don't have much farther to go," said Lizzie. "Please, may we press on?"

The corporal hesitated, but then he nodded. "Anywhere's safer than out in the open, I guess." He returned their passes and waved them on through.

Exultation surged through Lizzie as they galloped away.

"You didn't need to make us sound so foolish and flighty," Eliza admonished Theodore as soon as they were out of earshot.

"All part of the ruse, my dear cousin," he called back, speeding his mare onward.

Before long the farm came into view, green and verdant and untouched by war, with a lovely white house nestled in a grove of elm and walnut trees and several sturdy outbuildings nearby. Only the distant sounds of battle disturbed the perfect bucolic loveliness of the scene. A young boy of about twelve came running from the stable to tend to their horses, and as they approached the house—hot, breathless, perspiring, and terribly thirsty—Lizzie saw Mr. Botts step out onto the front veranda, fanning himself with a straw hat and regarding them with amazement.

"You braved the gauntlet today," he declared, meeting them at the bottom of the stairs and shaking their hands heartily. "Whatever possessed you to ride out in this?"

"Do you mean, in this excessive heat?" teased Lizzie, smiling.

"I mean in this excessive danger," he

scolded, but then he smiled. "Come in, come in. Mrs. Botts is preparing refreshments, and after that ride I daresay you need them."

Shade and a steady breeze through the open windows cooled the house, and after Mrs. Botts alternately welcomed them and admonished them for risking the journey, she served them lemonade, blessedly cold, and sponge cake with blueberry compote, with promises of a hearty dinner later.

Mr. Botts pressed them for all the news from the capital, and they wanted every detail of his sojourn in Castle Godwin, and so they passed the afternoon talking and listening to the roar of the artillery. Sometimes the sudden, violent rattling of the windows or the flash of a bursting shell brought their conversation to an abrupt halt, but after a breath, they plunged back into it, refusing to allow the battle to silence them when so much more remained to be said.

Later, as they dined, the rapid succession of guns seemed to slow, and gradually the din of warfare diminished until it ceased entirely around nine o'clock. Mrs. Botts urged them to spend the night, but they decided to venture out while all was quiet since the fighting would likely resume at dawn.

They bade their hosts farewell, but before they departed, Mr. Botts took Lizzie aside. "I always considered you a woman of rare courage, but in these past few months you have proven it."

Lizzie smiled fondly. "Most people would call it stubborn foolhardiness rather than courage, but I thank you all the same."

"Call it what you will, Miss Van Lew, as long as you know that it is the very quality that makes you essential to the Union cause." He hesitated. "I am in exile, and I come perilously close to breaking the terms of my parole even to speak of this, but in my absence, it would please me to know that you will do what I cannot."

Lizzie studied him, puzzled. "And what is that, sir?"

"Unify Richmond's loyalists."

"Unify—" Lizzie broke off and stared at him, shaking her head. "I don't understand. I'm no politician. I am not even, strictly speaking, what anyone would consider popular."

"You are smart, and brave, and witty,

and you can think on your feet. You're not easily intimidated by powerful men, and you have lost none of your youthful charm."

"Oh, my dear Mr. Botts," Lizzie gasped through her laughter, "now I know you're teasing me."

"Miss Van Lew, listen to me. Richmond will not fall unless loyal Unionists chip away at its defenses from within." He placed his hands on her shoulders and regarded her levelly. "You said yourself that the spate of arrests gave you the identities of many Union men and even a few women throughout the city. I know you've befriended Erastus Ross—his uncle told me it was your idea for him to become clerk of Libby Prison, and what a stroke of genius that was—but there are other loyalists you do not yet know. Are you acquainted with William Rowley?"

She shook her head. "I don't know anyone by that name."

"He's a native of New York, but he's kept a farm on the outskirts of Richmond for several years. During the secession crisis, he impressed me with his loyalty to the United States government. You should know him. Have you ever had occasion to visit McNiven's Bakery on North Fifth Street?" This time he paused only long enough for Lizzie to shake her head. "You must make a point of it. The proprietor is a red-haired Scotsman with British papers, which, coupled with his accent, somehow renders him above suspicion though he's as fierce a Unionist as any you'll find. You'll like him, and I daresay you'll enjoy the specialities—shortbreads, tea cookies, scones, and information."

A sudden rush of light-headedness swept over her, and she pressed a hand to her heart. In her isolation and loneliness, she had been surrounded by sympathetic friends all the while, never knowing it. "You're right. We loyalists must come to-gether. We'll be far more effective if we work in unison." She looked up at him, uncertain. "But we'll become more vulnerable too. As we are now, our separate contributions to the Union cause may be modest, but if we're noticed at all we're dismissed as harmless, and none of us can betray any other. If we join forces, we may accomplish greater things, but at extreme peril."

"That's true," Mr. Botts replied. "I won't deny the danger, which is why I cannot ask you to assume the burden of command, but only suggest it. Since it will be your life at stake, only you can decide whether the good you could accomplish justifies the risk."

"I want to serve the Union, and I'm deeply touched by your confidence in me." Lizzie placed a hand on his forearm. "I promise to consider very carefully everything you've said."

He closed his hand around hers. "Miss Van Lew, I've been to Castle Godwin. I know the horrors awaiting enemies of the Confederacy there. I would not inflict them upon anyone, least of all a loyal friend like you. Please know that I would not encourage you in this if I were not absolutely certain you were up to the task."

Her heart filled with such warmth and gratitude that she was struck speechless. She managed a smile, squeezed his hand in farewell, and hurried into the yard, where she mounted her horse and rode off into the hushed, expectant twilight with Eliza and Theodore.

It was nearly ten o'clock by the time she reached the Church Hill mansion, where she found the entire household in a state of great excitement, as they had expected her home hours before. When she explained that they had been delayed by the ongoing battle, her mother and the servants interrupted and talked over themselves in their eagerness to describe how close the fighting had come to them too, how the bursting of shells had been distinctly seen from the windows, and how the walls had shaken with every artillery roar.

Lizzie listened and agreed that they had indeed known a harrowing afternoon, but her thoughts were far away, racing on a swift horse past the blighted fields of war-torn Virginia lit by the pale summer moon. She had never known such excitement—the bright rush of life, the hurry of death—and she realized then that valor took many forms, and she did not have to don Union blue and take up arms to help her beloved country.

The garb of a Southern lady would be her uniform, her cleverness her weapon, her battlefield the prisons and markets and dining rooms of Richmond, or wherever else duty beckoned her.

Chapter Thirteen

JULY–AUGUST 1862

Lizzie and her mother waited anxiously for General McClellan's forces to take Richmond, listening in dismay as the sounds of battle grew fainter day by day after the Union army was thrown back from Mechanicsville. To prevent General McClellan from marching upon the capital, General Lee led a furious assault on his right, while on his left, General Magruder paraded his meager forces back and forth, stirring up dust and raising such a commotion that General McClellan was apparently deceived into believing that he was vastly outnumbered. Then, at Gaines's

Mill, eight miles northeast of the city, General Lee's troops severed the Union lines and drove the federals south of the Chickahominy, forcing General McClellan to pull back toward the James, away from Richmond.

In the end, the week of fighting that soon became known as the Seven Days Battles concluded with the capital securely in Confederate control and General Lee proclaimed a hero. In the meantime, General McClellan regrouped his forces at Harrison's Landing, nineteen miles from Richmond, as the crow flew, but a much longer and more hazardous journey along the crooked country roads and winding rivers he would be obliged to follow if he dared mount another assault.

While Richmond rejoiced, Lizzie and her mother dejectedly swept up the fallen flower petals from the floor of the bedchamber they had prepared for General McClellan, and when they threw out the withered stems and emptied the murky green water from the vase, they did not replace it with a fresh bouquet.

It was a decisive Confederate triumph, but even as pride and relief surged through

Richmond, the people's jubilation swiftly diminished as they learned the terrible price of victory. The more than twenty thousand Confederate casualties included thirty-three hundred dead and sixteen thousand wounded, while the Union suffered seventeen hundred deaths, eight thousand wounded, and six thousand taken captive and crammed into Richmond's already overflowing prisons.

Again trains and wagons and carts hauled the dead and wounded into Richmond, and again hospitals and private homes strained to accommodate the injured and sick and dying. Venturing downtown to observe the scene, Lizzie discovered the largest and finest shops on Main Street filled with rows and rows of cots, each bearing a groaning, coughing, suffering man. The doors and windows were left open to collect the faint breezes that barely stirred the air within, and no curtains shielded the suffering from the curious glances of passersby, or protected horrified residents from witnessing their anguish, gruesome and heartrending to look upon. Tents were erected in the streets and on the hillsides to accommodate the most hopeless cases, patients afflicted with gangrene and injuries considered likely to prove fatal. In the heat of the day, a sickening, fetid odor permeated the city, so that even high atop Church Hill, the air was so foul that Lizzie and her mother could not sit on the piazza for long before choking, clutching handkerchiefs to their faces, and fleeing back inside.

Lizzie might have remained behind the safe walls of home if not for her memory of Mr. Botts's urgent appeal—and her own longing to shake off her oppressive loneliness by meeting other Unionists. She went first to McNiven's Bakery at 811 North Fifth Street, where she introduced herself to the proprietor only to learn that the stocky, red-haired Scotsman knew her on sight and had been monitoring her activities in and about the prisons for months, debating whether to contact her. Mr. McNiven was well practiced in smuggling and subterfuge, he told her with gruff, modest pride, for even before the war, he had been active in the Underground Railroad, concealing fugitive slaves in a secret compartment in his bakery wagon and transporting them north out of Richmond.

His bakery served some of the most important households in the Confederacy, including Jefferson Davis's, where Mr. McNiven often picked up useful information from the slaves and servants employed therein.

In a similar fashion, Lizzie wrote a cheery note to Mr. William Rowley, thanking him for lending her the book that their mutual friend had recommended so highly and inviting him to call on her at home whenever he wished to retrieve it. She assumed he would be clever enough to figure out who their mutual friend was and that she had invented the borrowed book to divert suspicion should the letter fall into the wrong hands—and if he was not clever enough, she did not want to speak to him. But he understood what she could not risk writing down, and he visited her the day after receiving her letter—a tall, lean man with short, neatly trimmed reddish-brown hair atop his head and a remarkably long, bushy beard that more than made up for it. They quickly fell into an easy, earnest conversation in which they discovered their opinions matched perfectly on all the most important subjects. Mr. Rowley owned no slaves, and commiserated with her that she could not free her mother's. He was perhaps only a year or two older than she, married, with three sons aged ten to sixteen whom he was determined to keep out of the Confederate army. He confided that a friend, one he trusted with his life, had become a private courier, and that any secrets Lizzie could bring to him would be swiftly and safely carried across Union lines, all the way to Washington City if needed.

"We will keep your friend busy," Lizzie promised, and they soon arranged that Lizzie would send a servant to Mr. Rowley's farm once a week so they could exchange information, more often if an urgent matter compelled them.

Mr. Rowley also advised Lizzie to choose an ingenious hiding place for her letters and papers, something the pickets had not encountered dozens of times before, yet something so ordinary they would not bother to inspect it. "No false bottoms in suitcases," he said firmly. "They search every valise, every trunk, every satchel. No hollows carved out of the pages of books; they know that one too."

"I used to smuggle many secrets in books, although not in that fashion," Lizzie remarked, thinking of Mr. Ely. His ingenious method of concealing messages on the printed page could be useful in a pinch, but her serving dish, adequate enough for the prisons, would not fool an average Confederate private on picket duty. She would have to contrive another hiding place, and soon. Already Lieutenant Ross had brought out from Libby prison sketches of the interior, prisoner rosters, and copies of confidential letters from General Winder and Secretary Benjamin to the prison commandant, Major Thomas Pratt Turner. Lizzie handed these papers to Mr. Rowley herself, but there would be more from Lieutenant Ross, and from Robert Ford, who occasionally slipped her letters from newly arrived prisoners describing troop movements and enemy fortifications they had witnessed on the battlefield and during transport to Richmond. Mr. Ford also unwittingly confirmed that Lieutenant Ross was thoroughly convincing in the role of cruel overseer, for the prisoners hated him bitterly and complained about his nasty temper and arbitrary punishments.

"When all this is over, Mr. Ross should take to the stage," Lizzie remarked to her mother one afternoon as they gathered up the scraps of papers and hid them in a sconce above the fireplace until they could be delivered to Mr. Rowley's farm. "He would give Mr. John Booth some competition for the admiration of Richmond's theatergoers."

"You condemn Mr. Ross with faint praise," Mother scoffed, smiling. "In my opinion, likening him to John Booth is to label him a fair to middling actor. John Booth's elder brother Edwin is the far superior performer. Your father and I saw him in **Richard III** in Boston in 1849, and he was marvelous. And—don't you remember?—you yourself saw them share the stage in **Hamlet** at the Richmond Theatre. You must agree that Edwin's Hamlet was far better than John's Horatio."

"I suppose so, but **you** must admit that John made a very convincing Brutus a few years back." Lizzie smiled wistfully. It felt like ages since she had last enjoyed a night at the theater, although several were still open in the city, drawing tremendous crowds from among the soldiers, politicians, and opportunists who had flooded the capital since secession. "Even so, you're absolutely right. Mr. Ross is no John Wilkes Booth. He must be an Edwin, or the prisoners would not loathe him as they do."

Lieutenant Ross was obliged to perform not only for the prisoners, but also for Major Turner, the junior officers, and the guards. So convinced were they of his commitment to the cause and his antipathy for Yankees that he was permitted to move about the prison as he pleased, and at the end of his shift, he carried out copies of important documents in his pockets, unbeknownst to all.

Lizzie knew that **she** could not rely on a hiding place as obvious as pockets, and eventually a box of old Easter decorations inspired an ingenious solution—a hollowed eggshell, with a hole just large enough to contain a narrow scroll of paper. Nestled into a basket of real eggs, with the opening buried in straw, the false egg was indistinguishable from the others and would go undetected unless a particularly scrupulous guard examined each egg by touch.

Every Thursday, Lizzie would send Peter and Caroline out to Mr. Rowley's farm, precious secrets hidden within the basket of eggs on Caroline's lap. Mr. Rowley would send back news of the war from the North and money that Lieutenant Ross and Mr. Ford smuggled in to the prisoners, who could then purchase extra food, a blanket, a few minutes to stand in the outside doorway and savor the wind and the sun, or a respite from beatings.

With every battle, more Confederate wounded and more Union prisoners packed into the capital. Even with a prisoner exchange system finally in place, Richmond's prisons filled, overflowed, and spilled into neighboring buildings. To help ease the overcrowding, General Winder ordered a temporary holding facility established on Belle Isle, an island in the middle of the James River at the fall line, fifty-four acres of rocky earth surrounded by swift rapids, a serendipitous deterrent against escape attempts. Since it was meant to be used only until more adequate quarters could be arranged, no barracks were built, although a makeshift hospital was hastily constructed. Earthworks about three feet high encircled the perimeter of the island, and roughly three hundred conical pole tents, each sleeping ten men, provided the prisoners' only shelter. The need for the prison camp never diminished, however, so by midsummer it was decreed that captured Union officers would remain at Libby Prison, but all noncommissioned officers and privates would be held on Belle Isle.

Belle Isle was "a very pleasant spot," the Richmond **Enquirer** remarked soon after the open-air stockade was established, "much more agreeable than any locality which has been given to our wounded soldiers . . . Their friends in the North may be perfectly satisfied that they will pass a pleasant summer at Richmond."

A pleasant summer, perhaps, Lizzie thought worriedly, but summer would not last forever. It was true that the cool breezes off the river would provide welcome relief from the hot, stifling warehouses during the sultry days of summer, but as Lizzie eyed the tents from the riverbank and watched the flaps flutter and the poles bend, she pictured the scene in autumn, and then in winter, and she could not imagine how the prisoners would survive until spring.

Upon returning home from one of her walks along the riverbank, where the wind and swift current brought blessed escape from the foul miasma of gangrene and rot that hung like an invisible fog over every street in the city, Lizzie was pleasantly surprised to discover an invitation from Mary Jane Bowser to call the following afternoon. The next day, Lizzie spent the morning browsing the shops on Main Street for suitable books, slates, pencils, and other necessary items for Mary Jane's school, and in the afternoon, she took the carriage to the Bowser residence and happily delivered the gifts.

"Thank you very much, Miss Lizzie," said Mary Jane, delighted. "The children will be so pleased."

"Let's arrange everything on their desks so it's the first thing they see when they enter the classroom tomorrow morning," Lizzie suggested, wishing she could see the children's sweet faces when they discovered the surprise.

Mary Jane agreed, and as they worked,

they chatted like old times, catching up on all the family news. Afterward, Mary Jane invited her into the dining room, and over tea and shortbread—from McNiven's Bakery, if Lizzie was not mistaken—the conversation turned to the war and the horrific, heartbreaking changes it had wrought upon their city.

"We all must do our part to bring about a Union victory, no matter what the danger," said Mary Jane, "and as swiftly and decisively as possible, so this terrible carnage will come to an end."

Something in her tone—fear, anxiety, determination, pride—told Lizzie she had not reached that conclusion easily. "Are you worried about me and all that my ardent patriotism compels me to do, or are you concerned for yourself?"

Mary Jane picked at a piece of shortbread on her plate, crumbling the edge into coarse, buttery crumbs. "Neither." She glanced up from her plate to give Lizzie a small, anxious grimace. "I'm afraid for my husband. And now we come to the reason for my invitation."

"There's a reason?" Lizzie asked lightly. "I assumed you simply missed me."

"I did miss you, of course, but Wilson wanted to speak with you too. He . . . discovered something at work that he thought might be useful to you."

"At work—you mean, on the RF&P Railroad?"

Mary Jane nodded. "That's right."

Lizzie drew in a slow breath, her thoughts racing. The Richmond, Fredericksburg, and Potomac Railroad ran north from Richmond through Henrico, Hanover, and Caroline counties to a terminus five miles south of Fredericksburg. It had once run all the way to Aquia Creek on the Potomac River, but in April, Union troops had forced the Confederates to retreat fourteen miles to the Rappahannock, and in an attempt to delay the federals' advance, the rebels had destroyed the Aquia Creek wharf and warehouses, several bridges, and three miles of track. Even so, the RF&P remained a crucial supply line for General Lee's army. "What does Wilson know?" Lizzie asked.

"He should tell you himself. I'll go fetch him."

Mary Jane slipped into the kitchen and returned holding Wilson's hand. He nodded politely, his expression solemn and wary.

"Good afternoon, Wilson," Lizzie said, folding her hands in her lap and regarding him expectantly.

He gave her a brusque nod. "Afternoon, Miss Lizzie."

He didn't like her very much, Lizzie knew, and he didn't entirely trust her. He found her imperious and disliked the way she ordered Mary Jane about—as if Mary Jane were a slave, or so Wilson assumed. What he didn't understand was that Lizzie bossed Mary Jane around not because she had been born a slave but because she was younger, because Lizzie liked to have her own way, and because she always bossed around younger women if they let her get away with it. Eliza Carrington didn't like it either, but she complained far less than Mary Jane did.

"I understand you have something to tell me," Lizzie prompted.

Mary Jane pulled out a chair for her husband and inclined her head ever so slightly to ask him to sit. After a moment's hesitation, Wilson seated himself, folded his arms on the table, and said, "Do you know the superintendent of the RF&P, Samuel Ruth?"

"No," she replied, concealing her excitement. The superintendent of the RF&P had enormous influence over the railway line, and thus over General Lee's supplies. "I have not had the pleasure of making his acquaintance."

"Well, you should. I think he'd be a friend to you."

When he said no more, Lizzie turned an inquiring look upon Mary Jane, who explained, "Wilson thinks he's one of us. A Unionist."

Lizzie returned her questioning gaze to Wilson. "Why do you suspect that?"

Wilson frowned, his dark eyes grim. "I might be wrong. I don't want to see him thrown into Castle Godwin on my account. He's a good man."

"You're not wrong," Mary Jane told him, placing a hand on his arm. "Everything you've noticed—he's been very careful, but the pattern is there."

"I promise, whatever you tell me, I won't divulge it to anyone," said Lizzie. "You have my word."

Wilson heaved a sigh of resignation and fixed Lizzie with a steely look that told her he still did not think it was wise to confide in her, and she would regret it if she betrayed him. "Mr. Ruth's been meddling with rebel troop movements for months. Somehow the trains always run much more slowly than they need to when Lee's brigades are aboard."

"Is that so?"

"Yes, that's so, or I wouldn't say it," Wilson replied brusquely. "He's good, I'll give him that. His schemes are subtle, just small changes here and there to make everything less efficient. His interference has been practically undetectable."

"Undetectable by everyone but my husband," said Mary Jane proudly.

"Mr. Ruth takes his sweet time about repairing key bridges," Wilson said. "He cuts back on the number of workers, and he always has a perfectly logical reason for doing it. He regularly gives private freight shipments priority over military supplies. Why would he do that if he wasn't on the side of the Union? He's not a stupid man. He puts on a convincing show of being a fire-breathing rebel, but he's got to know he's hindering the entire rebel army."

"It seems an unlikely collection of coincidences," Lizzie acknowledged. A man in

Mr. Ruth's position would make an invaluable ally. He could help smuggle information and escaped prisoners out of Richmond,
and of course he would know every detail
about every shipment of men, arms, and
supplies on the RF&P lines. "If you're certain of his loyalties—"

"I am."

"Then we must recruit him to our cause."

Wilson nodded. "I can introduce you if
you like. He likes me, and I think he trusts
me."

"No, I think not," Lizzie mused. "We
would make a curious pair if anyone observed us together. You, on the other hand,
have every reason to speak with him often,
to be seen with him at work every day. You
should be the one to approach him."

Wilson's mouth twisted in a skeptical
grimace. "That way, if I'm wrong about him,
he'll report me to the authorities rather
than you."

"That's true," said Lizzie evenly. "That's
not why I've suggested that you act as our
intermediary, but you're right. I suppose
the question is, how much do you trust
your own judgment? You want me to accept your observations, your conclusions,

as accurate. Are you willing to rely upon them yourself?"

"I know what I've seen," Wilson retorted. "I can put the pieces together. I know he's a Unionist."

"If you're right, then you shouldn't have to worry that he'll report you."

Wilson glowered at her, and by his side, Mary Jane sat perfectly still, almost seeming to hold her breath.

"All right," he eventually said. "I'll do it. I can't ask you to take a risk I'm unwilling to take myself."

Lizzie felt a rush of elation. "Thank you, Wilson," she said. "I don't know what else to say except thank you."

"I know what else. Promise you'll look after Mary Jane if I'm whipped to death or sold into slavery for helping you."

"Wilson," Mary Jane protested. "Don't say such things. That won't happen."

He regarded her levelly until she had to look away. They all knew it could happen, and likely would, if he was caught.

Within days, Mr. Ruth confirmed Wilson's suspicions, and although he was disconcerted to learn that he had been found out, he accepted Wilson's offer to assist him in his clandestine efforts. In turn he agreed to collaborate with Lizzie.

And so the reach of her intelligence network grew, an invisible railroad with lines extending throughout the Confederate capital and the surrounding countryside and herself at the central hub.

"Miss Lizzie."

Someone was shaking her awake, and through the fog of half sleep, Lizzie thought she heard the soft rumble of men's voices somewhere below.

She bolted upright in bed, heart pounding. For more than a year she had dreaded a knock on the door in the middle of the night, and now it had come.

"Miss Lizzie," Judy whispered again, urgent. "Mr. Van Lew's come with the children. He needs you."

"John?" Lizzie threw back the covers and slipped into the dressing gown Judy offered her. "What time is it?"

"Not quite ten o'clock. I put them in the parlor."

"What's wrong?" Something dreadful must have happened for John to bring the girls out at that hour.

"Your brother didn't say, but Eliza's sick and Annie's crying, and there's two men I don't know with them."

Lizzie's heart pounded as she hurried from the room. "And Mary?"

"I don't know," Judy said, racing to keep up with her. "She's not here."

Bewildered, alarmed, Lizzie raced down the stairs and into the parlor, where she found Eliza dozing listlessly on the sofa and John holding a sobbing Annie, walking her back and forth and patting her back in an attempt to soothe away her tears. Two men stood by the window, holding their hats and conversing in hushed, serious tones, and after a second look she recognized them as friends of John's, lawyers who shared a practice on Main Street, if she was not mistaken.

Mindful of her state of undress, she nevertheless flew to Eliza's side, stroking Annie's head in passing. "What is going on?" she asked John, touching the back of her hand to Eliza's burning forehead and flushed cheeks. "Where's Mary?"

"She's at home, under Hannah's watchful eye." John's voice was like stone, and his evident anger filled Lizzie with relief—

she had feared he would tell her that Mary was dead. "I returned home from a late meeting to discover that she had forsaken her children to go out for a night of dreadful sin."

"What?" Lizzie exclaimed. "She left the children alone? But where was Hannah? What—what sort of sin do you mean? Where did you find her?"

"Never mind that now," John snapped, and the two men exchanged quick, embarrassed glances. "I'd like to leave the girls here with you and Mother, if you don't mind."

"Of course not. They're always welcome. You know I love them as if they were my own."

"Better than that, I think, judging by their own mother's neglect." John's mouth was hard, bitter line, and his eyes sparked with fury. "I'll return in the morning with their things, and with Hannah."

As he turned to go, Lizzie caught him by the arm. "John." She glanced over her shoulder at the two men, who were putting on their hats, and she lowered her voice. "Is it the laudanum? Whiskey?"

"Both, and more," he replied in a whisper, his voice trembling with outrage. He kissed her swiftly on the cheek and departed, his friends following after, nodding to her in polite apology as they passed.

With Judy's help, Lizzie soon had the girls tucked into bed, Eliza with a cool, damp cloth on her brow. Lizzie remained at her bedside through the night, dozing now and then, until Mother came in shortly after dawn to relieve her. "You should have woken me last night," she scolded in an undertone as she sent Lizzie off to her own bed, but mercifully, she saved her questions for later.

Lizzie was still asleep when John returned with Hannah and his daughters' clothing, books, and toys, so it was Mother to whom he confessed the shameful story. The previous evening, when he had come home to find Mary absent, Hannah missing, Eliza ill, and Annie crying, he interrogated Mary's diffident maid until she reluctantly admitted that Mary had hired Hannah out to a neighbor for the night, and then she had gone out alone, as she apparently always did whenever business detained John late into the evening.

"Mary hired Hannah out to strangers?"

asked Lizzie, disbelieving. "John allowed this?"

"Of course not," said Mother. "He knew nothing of it, although evidently Mary has done it before."

"Why didn't Hannah tell him? Why didn't did she tell us? She must have known we wouldn't stand for it."

Mother shook her head helplessly. "She was afraid that Mary would sell her off Down South before we could stop her. She also worried that we would bring her home but leave Eliza and Annie with their mother, helpless, with no one to look after them."

After John had gotten the story out of Mary's maid, he fetched Hannah back from the indignant neighbors who had hired her for the night, apologizing profusely for the mistake and smoothing things over by assuring them they owed him nothing for the hours Hannah had worked. He then stormed from one tavern and hotel to the next, searching up and down Main Street, and eventually he found his wife teetering on a stool in the bar of a third-rate hotel accompanied by a gentleman of uncertain origin and questionable morals, her mind addled by laudanum and drink. Mary had screeched and clawed and fought as John wrested her away from the bar and outside, but as he struggled to lead her down the street toward home, his two acquaintances had spotted him through the window of their law office and had come to his aid.

"What will he do?" Lizzie asked, appalled, when her mother had finished.

"He wants to leave the girls with us, for now," Mother said. "Of course I said that would be fine."

"Not only fine but necessary. Mary is clearly in no state to care for them." Lizzie took a deep breath. "Mother, do you think they will . . . divorce?"

"Oh, Lizzie, I don't know." Mother's voice broke, and she wrung her hands. "John found Mary in the bar of the hotel, not emerging from a rented room or even descending the stairs, so I'm not sure he can have her charged with adultery."

"But she was with another man."

"Who doubtless has disappeared into the crowd of strangers Richmond has become, never to be found again. Without his testimony, Mary could claim their meeting was perfectly innocent, which it very well could have been."

Incredulous, Lizzie said, "A married woman leaves her children home alone at night so she can dose herself with laudanum and meet a strange man for drinks in a hotel bar. You could not fit the word **innocent** into that description with a shoehorn and a crowbar."

Mother acknowledged the truth of Lizzie's words with a nod. "Even if John could divorce Mary for adultery, think of the scandal. Think of what it would mean to those poor little girls."

"I **am** thinking of those poor little girls," said Lizzie. "They would be better off removed from their mother's influence."

"And they shall be, for a while. They will remain here with us until Mary is capable of caring for them herself."

Lizzie imagined Hannah would have quite a lot to say about Mary's capabilities. "And John? Will he come home?"

"I believe he intends to stay with Mary. He won't abandon her, but he will insist that she stop drinking and taking laudanum. If she refuses, or if she cannot . . ."

When her mother fell silent, Lizzie hesitantly filled in the rest. "The sanitarium?"

Mother's eyes filled with tears as she nodded. "What else can he do?"

"I don't know," Lizzie said. As much as she disliked Mary, she would not have wished this fate on her, nor on anyone. And John—her poor brother, to have been so publicly humiliated, and now, likely to become the subject of ugly gossip.

She longed to help him, to help them both, but in her bewildered uncertainty, all she could think of to do was to resolve to care for their daughters with all the devotion a loving aunt could offer.

Annie and little Eliza were overjoyed to be home, as they had never stopped referring to the Church Hill mansion, and they settled into their familiar rooms so easily it was almost as if they had never moved away. John visited at least every other day, and the girls were showered with so much attention from their grandmother, auntie, and nurse that they did not seem to miss their mother, judging by how infrequently they asked about her. When the girls could not overhear, Lizzie and her mother asked John about Mary, but he said very little other than to assure them that she was on the mend, and that she was meeting regularly with her minister and a nurse, and that as far as he knew, she had not touched a drop of alcohol or laudanum since that dreadful night. "She was terribly sick at first," John said, "but every day, she seems a little stronger, although she is furious with me."

"Does she ask about the girls?" Lizzie asked, almost afraid to hear the answer.

"No," John said flatly. "That is, she asked once, after the worst of her illness passed. I told her they were here, and that you were looking after them. She nodded, turned away from me, and hasn't asked about them since."

She will, Lizzie thought. Mary was too overwhelmed by her own troubles to think about her children at present, but a time would come when she would want them back—and Lizzie would have a terrible time letting them go.

She was reading the girls a bedtime story one evening when William appeared in the doorway. "Miss Lizzie," he said urgently, "You have a visitor, in the kitchen."

Guests were customarily escorted to the library or parlor depending upon the time of day, although they might be left standing in the foyer if they were strangers or if the Van Lews did not like them. Only one sort of visitor was taken to the kitchen instead. Quickly Lizzie finished the book, helped the girls say their prayers, tucked them in, and kissed them good night, and after turning down the lamp, she hurried to the kitchen, which smelled of freshly baked bread and pickling spices. A pale, dark-haired young man with full cheeks, a prominent nose, and a short, thick, bushy beard sat at the table devouring a plate of cold ham, cheese and leek pie, stewed greens, and bread left over from the Van Lews' supper. He wore the gray uniform of a Confederate major, but it was too snug, and the sleeves scarcely reached his wrists.

He started when she appeared in the doorway, jostling the table and setting the dishes clattering as he half-rose out of his seat. "Please, don't get up," Lizzie said easily, covering for his alarm. "I'm Elizabeth Van Lew, and this is my home. How is your supper?"

"It's the most wonderful meal I've ever

tasted," he said reverently, running the heel of the loaf over his plate to collect every last crumb. A moment later, Caroline was at his side to offer him seconds, which he gratefully accepted. Then he remembered his manners, rose, and offered Lizzie a slight bow. "I'm Captain William Lounsbury, Seventy-Fourth New York Infantry." He sat down again, looking dazed. "And I can't believe I'm here. An hour ago I was in Libby Prison."

Lizzie smiled. "I'm very glad you made your escape."

"I didn't do it alone." The captain shook his head, still disbelieving. "I was standing with the rest of the men in quarters when Ross entered—Ross is the clerk who calls the rolls and superintends the prison under Major Turner."

"Yes, I know," Lizzie remarked. "I've met him."

"He never calls the rolls without swearing at us and abusing us and calling us Yankees, and other vile names not suited for your ears, begging your pardon, Ma'am. We all hate him, and many a man has said that if given a chance, he would get even with the little scamp."

"Oh, dear," said Lizzie, unsettled. Perhaps she should warn Mr. Ross that he was playing his role too convincingly. "Are you aware of any plans to do him harm?"

"No, and if I were, I'd tell you so you could warn him." Captain Lounsbury paused to polish off another piece of ham. "This evening, we were lining up for roll call when Ross struck me in the stomach and said, 'You blue-bellied Yankee, come down to my office. I have a matter to settle with you.' I had no idea what he was talking about. I couldn't think of anything I had done wrong, any rule I had broken."

Sighing, Lizzie seated herself at the table. "I'm told prisoners are often punished even if they've done nothing wrong."

"Well, that's true enough. All the men had noticed that Ross would from time to time take officers away for punishment, but they would never return to quarters. We had no knowledge of what became of them, whether they were transferred to another prison or exchanged or killed. So when Ross ordered me to come with him, some of the other men whispered to me, 'Don't go. You don't have to.'"

"But of course, you did."

The captain nodded. "I followed Ross down to his office in the corner of the prison, an old counting room on the first floor, right by the exit. There was no one inside the office, but through the window I saw a sentry standing outside in front of the door on the sidewalk. Ross motioned for me to go behind a counter, and when I did, found a Confederate uniform there."

Lizzie rested her elbow on the table and cupped her chin in her palm. "Imagine that."

"I lost no time in getting into it, although—" He gestured wryly to his straining buttons. "It was too small for me."

"So I see."

"Ross put a finger to his lips to warn me to be silent, then he jerked his head to show that I was to follow him. He left the office, and I waited a bit before following after. He had exited the prison, and when I peered outside, I saw him strolling off with the sentry down the sidewalk. So I just walked out the door."

"I would have done the same."

"It was just after dark, so I ran across the street to a vacant lot thinking to hide in a patch of overgrown brush until I could decide what to do. As I was catching my breath, a colored man stepped out and said, 'Come with me, sir. I know who you are.' And then he led me here, to you."

Lizzie reached across the table and clasped his hand. "And we are so very glad to have you. That was Nelson who brought you here, and in a day or two, when you're rested, he'll guide you to the next safe haven along your route." She rose, smiling. "When you've eaten your fill, William will show you to your room. It's a bit small and there's no view whatsoever, but it's snug and no one will find you there." She turned to go, but she paused in the doorway and added, "Please don't think unkindly of Lieutenant Ross. He is a great friend of mine, and of the Union, although he has been obliged not to let it show."

"I know that now," the captain declared. "Believe me, Miss Van Lew, I take back every unkind word I ever said about the man. As soon as I get back to the North, I'm going to send him a box of cigars."

"Send it to me rather than the prison," Lizzie advised. "I'll see that he gets it. You wouldn't want your gift to betray him."

"Never." Suddenly the light of understanding appeared in Captain Lounsbury's eyes. "So all those missing officers, taken aside for punishment—Ross freed them all, and they sought refuge here."

"Not always here," said Lizzie. "We have other friends throughout the city, but you will forgive me if I divulge no more than that."

With a parting smile, she left him to finish his supper.

Captain Lounsbury remained with them two days to rest and regain his strength, and to allow the furor of pursuit to diminish before embarking upon the most dangerous part of his journey. They used that time to study maps, and with Lizzie's help he learned which roads to follow and which to avoid, where to take to the woods to elude the Confederate pickets, and where he was most likely to be able to cross over into Union lines safely. On the third evening after his escape, Lizzie provided him with a civilian suit, packed some food in a haversack, and had Nelson escort him under the cover of darkness to McNiven's Bakery, where he would hide in the delivery wagon, travel beyond the city limits, and continue on foot to Mr. Rowley's farm.

For several days following his departure, Lizzie and her mother anxiously searched the Richmond papers for an announcement that Captain Lounsbury had been recaptured, but with each day he remained free, their hopes that he would safely reach the Union army rose. Then, two weeks later, they were rewarded with an unexpected, terse announcement in the Richmond **Dispatch**: "We have heard from the Yankee press that Captain W. H. LOUNSBURY, 74th NY Infantry, late of Libby Prison, has arrived in New York City, where he will be feted before returning to his brigade. It does not seem possible that his escape could have happened without the aid of Yankee-lovers in our own city and perhaps within the prison itself. We trust that General Winder will roust the traitors from their dens and fling them into the darkest corner of Castle Thunder."

Lizzie felt a chill. Earlier in August, General Winder had commandeered three adjacent tobacco factories and warehouses on a single block of Cary Street to establish a new prison for Confederate deserters, political prisoners, and Union sympathizers. The stark name was meant to evoke the storm and fury that would be brought down upon the treasonous men—and, increasingly, women—who were imprisoned there.

That was where she would be sent if she were found out. Lizzie could not walk past the new prison or glimpse its name in the newspaper without brooding over that grim truth. Sometimes Lizzie imagined that her lurking enemies had already prepared a dark, gloomy, lonely cell for her, and that they were watching and waiting, burning with eager malice, determined to catch her in a mistake.

If she were discovered with escaped prisoners in her home or secret papers on her person, if the evidence against her were irrefutable, she knew not even General Winder's pass would grant her liberty from Castle Thunder.

It was far more likely that General Winder would himself shove her into a cell and lock the cold iron bars behind her. She would find no mercy there.

Chapter Fourteen

SEPTEMBER 1862–JANUARY 1863

August ended with all of Richmond—and indeed, all the South—celebrating Robert E. Lee's triumph at the Second Battle of Manassas, and September began with General Lee pressing his advantage. After trouncing Union major general John Pope's army on the familiar fields where so much blood had already been spilled, General Lee led his army across the Potomac River at White's Ford near Leesburg and into Union territory. As terrified Pennsylvanians evacuated government archives, treasure, and personnel from offices in Harrisburg and Philadelphia, the Confederate army captured food and horses, and searched with less success for recruits among sympathetic Marylanders.

By September 7, General Lee's forces were marching into Fredericksburg, with General McClellan in pursuit. The people of Richmond waited anxiously for news, hearing only frustratingly vague rumors about fighting around South Mountain and Harpers Ferry. Then, in the middle of the month, word came of fierce and terrible fighting that had broken out the misty morning of September 17, of an enormous clash of armies on the ridges above the village of Sharpsburg and along Antietam Creek. Both sides consolidated their forces overnight and resumed the bloody battle in the morning, but ultimately General Lee was forced to withdraw his troops back across the Potomac, his brief invasion of the North thwarted.

In the days that followed, as the Union claimed victory and the Confederacy declared the battle a draw, rumors about a curious incident preceding the Battle of Sharpsburg began to circulate throughout the capital. It was said that a Union soldier crossing a campground recently vacated by the rebels had discovered three cigars wrapped in a piece of paper lying forgotten on the ground. Astoundingly, the document turned out to be a copy of General Lee's battle plan for Maryland, which the soldier promptly turned over to his commanding officers. Already possessing superior numbers, General McClellan—informed of Lee's plan to divide the Army of Northern Virginia and armed with foreknowledge of the Confederate troop movements—had been handed the opportunity to soundly defeat General Lee's divided army.

Arguments about what might have been if not for that crucial mistake quickly fell silent as wounded soldiers returning to Richmond described in stark, horrifying detail what they had witnessed along the banks of the Antietam. Their stories of carnage left Lizzie dazed and shocked and sickened—thousands upon thousands killed and maimed, hillsides dotted with prostrate corpses clad in blue, sunken roads filled with bodies in butternut and gray mowed down like grain before the scythe. Men frozen in the final acts of their brief lives—a hand gripping a sword hilt as a lieutenant rallied his men, teeth clenched in a last grimace around the bitten end of a cartridge as a corporal reloaded his weapon, brains and blood splattered on broken green leaves of corn. Bodies bloated in death, fallen alone, in pairs, behind fallen logs and tangled in thickets, eyes staring blankly up at the sky or down into the thick mud.

Lizzie could scarcely comprehend the estimates in the papers of the numbers of dead and wounded. It had been the bloodiest battle ever fought on American soil, but as the phrase echoed around Richmond, Lizzie remembered how it had been applied to previous battles, and she wondered, despairing and heartsick, how many more times it would be employed in the months and years to come as more colossal battles were waged.

Despite their devastating losses, the Union considered the Battle of Antietam, as they called it in the North, to be a victory, for although the perpetually overcautious General McClellan had allowed the battered Confederate army to withdraw to Virginia without pursuit, he had managed to repulse General Lee's advance into the North.

The costly victory must have heartened President Lincoln, for less than a week after the battle, newspapers across the North published a proclamation in which the president declared that "on the first day of January in the year of our Lord one thousand eight hundred and sixty-three, all persons held as slaves within any State or designated part of a State, the people whereof shall then be in rebellion against the United States, shall be then, thenceforward, and forever free."

When the entire preliminary Emancipation Proclamation was reprinted in Southern newspapers, it sparked outrage and alarm throughout the Confederacy—except within the Van Lew household, where it evoked jubilation. The Richmond press condemned the measure, warning that it would incite the four million slaves in the South to rise up and slaughter their masters, whose blood would be on Mr. Lincoln's hands. Other editorials jeered that the proclamation was ridiculous, for the Union president had no jurisdiction over the South and was powerless to enforce any laws there, just as surely as he could not impose his policies upon Great Britain or France.

Even within the Van Lew household and among their Unionist friends, the proclamation was not immune to criticism. In the days that followed the announcement, as they weighed and debated the president's words, their rejoicing was tempered by concerns that the proclamation did not go far enough. It called for the abolition of slavery only in states that were in rebellion as of January 1, 1863, so if a state agreed to return to the Union before that date—an unlikely occurrence—slavery would be permitted to continue there. The proclamation also did nothing to free the enslaved people living within the loyal Union border states of Delaware, Kentucky, Maryland, and Missouri, as well as Tennessee and parts of Louisiana, Confederate territory that had come under Union control.

"What practical good does it do to declare slaves free in regions where the people don't recognize Mr. Lincoln's authority?" William asked one afternoon after bringing Lizzie and her mother the afternoon papers.

"It does seem that Mr. Lincoln has emancipated slaves where the Union cannot free them," Mother acknowledged, "but has kept them enslaved in places where the Union does enjoy the power to give them liberty."

"Most slaves out on the plantations will probably never even know they've been freed," William said, frowning. "Come January first, I don't expect planters and overseers to gather their slaves together and read them the official proclamation, then unlock their chains and let them walk away."

"I have trouble imagining that too," Lizzie admitted. "It's true that Mr. Lincoln's plan is not without its flaws, but think of what else it does, in addition to freeing the slaves—"

"It won't really free all that many slaves," William broke in pointedly.

Lizzie held up her hands in appeasement. "Think of what else it will accomplish. From the earliest days of secession, the South has hoped and prayed for and expected Great Britain to recognize them as a sovereign nation and side with them in the conflict. But Great Britain abhors slavery. They'll **never** establish diplomatic relations with the Confederacy now, and they certainly won't intervene in the war on their behalf, not even if it meant they could fill every English mill from cellar to chimney top with Confederate cotton."

As far as Lizzie was concerned, despite its weaknesses, the proclamation was worth celebrating as proof that the nation was moving toward greater freedom and liberty for all. The old Union was gone forever. When the nation was restored, it would be a new United States.

But she knew the only way Mr. Lincoln could enforce his Emancipation Proclamation where it was needed most was to win the war.

The Confederacy was determined to deny Mr. Lincoln that victory.

To that end, they needed more accoutrements of war—food, arms, horses, and especially men. On September 27, the Confederate Congress voted to amend the conscription act to raise the age limit from thirty-five to forty-five.

With the stroke of a pen, John had become eligible for the draft.

"I cannot take up arms against my country," John said, "nor can I in good conscience hire a substitute to do so on my behalf."

He sat in the library with his elbows on his knees and his head buried in his hands. It was late in the evening, the girls had been sent off to bed, and soon he would have to return to the lonely home he shared with his estranged wife. To Lizzie he seemed as exhausted and strained as it was possible to be without collapsing utterly.

"You should go to the North," said Mother, distressed. "You can stay with Anna until the war is over."

"That could be years, Mother," said John, lifting his head wearily. "I cannot leave the children for so long, nor Mary for any time at all, with her nerves in such a delicate state. I can't leave the store either, not if I want to keep a roof over their heads."

"You forget they have my roof over their heads now," said Mother, "and I would happily share it with you again too."

"With all four of you," Lizzie quickly added, in case anyone thought she might object.

He shook his head. "I won't leave Richmond."

"But you'll be thrown into Castle Thunder for desertion," said Mother, her voice breaking.

"Not so." He managed a wan smile. "I can't desert until I'm drafted, and that hasn't happened yet."

"And might not happen," Lizzie said firmly, hiding her own dismay for her mother's sake. She was afraid for John, but she understood why he could not flee. They all could have chosen to go North when war broke out. With the housing shortage, they easily could have sold the Church Hill mansion to a newly appointed general or member of the Confederate Congress, fled North, and settled in a pleasant residence in Philadelphia near Anna's family, but they were Virginians born and bred, and Richmond was their home. It had changed dramatically, but it was still their home, and they could not relinquish it to the madness of secession and war, not while any hope remained that they could save it.

By early October, with the threat of invasion by the Union army diminished, Jefferson Davis's family returned to Richmond and Mrs. Davis resumed her public duties. She paid calls on important dowagers to bolster support for her husband's administration and hosted dinners for officers and other dignitaries, where she charmed some guests with her intelligence and wit but offended others with her irreverence. In other circumstances, Lizzie mused after reading a description of one such event in the **Enquirer**, she and Varina Davis might have become very good friends.

Varina Davis's return to Richmond meant more official receptions and dinners, which led to a corresponding increase in orders from McNiven's Bakery. One afternoon Lizzie returned home from her customary walk past Libby Prison to discover the bakery's delivery wagon behind the house, and after hurrying inside, she found Mr. McNiven in the kitchen, ostensibly delivering a dozen buttery scones.

"I am so glad you always feel obliged to deliver something to keep up appearances," Lizzie teased.

"Aye, lass," he said. "If a curious neighbor calls and you have nothing from my bakery to serve, they'll wonder why I was here." He settled himself into a chair at the kitchen table, glanced warily at Caroline as if considering whether to ask her to leave the room, and then shrugged and turned back to Lizzie, apparently concluding that the cook could be trusted. "They know me fairly well in the kitchens of the Gray House now. They're looking for an able colored lass to wait at table and help with the cleaning. I said I knew such a lass, even though I don't, because I thought you might."

For a moment Lizzie couldn't draw a breath from excitement, and she grasped the edge of the table to steady herself. If she could place a trusted servant in Jefferson Davis's own household, the secrets she could obtain could be invaluable. "I know of one young woman who would be perfectly suited for the position."

"Is she trustworthy?" asked Mr. Mc-Niven. "Literate?"

"Yes to both, and she also has a prodigious memory." Lizzie inhaled deeply, thinking. "But she is no slave and might not wish to impersonate one, not even to help the Union."

"We must find a worthy lass and quickly, before they hire someone else."

Lizzie nodded. "Yes, of course." They might never have another opportunity to get so close to the Confederate president, and she could not let it slip through her fingers.

As soon as Mr. McNiven departed, Lizzie took the carriage to the Bowser residence. She found Mary Jane bidding her pupils good-bye for the day, sending them out through the doors alone or in pairs to avoid drawing the unwanted attention a single crowd would bring. As soon as they were alone—quickly, eager to finish before Wilson came home from work and interrupted them—Lizzie told Mary Jane what she wanted her to do.

Mary Jane listened to Lizzie's proposal without a word and remained silent for a long time afterward. "I would have to close my school."

"Yes, I feared as much."

"But perhaps that would be a small loss now for a great gain later. If I can learn anything from Mr. Davis that will bring about a Union victory and a swift end to this war, is it not better for my students if I do so?"

Lizzie gave a small, helpless laugh. "Of course I think so, but I'm hardly a disinterested observer."

Mary Jane fixed her with a resolute look. "I must be allowed to live out," she said. "I will not spend my nights in the Gray House, away from my husband."

"That can be arranged, I'm sure."

"And I will keep the wages I earn."

"Of course," said Lizzie, surprised. "You're the one doing the work. Why shouldn't you?"

"Then I suppose I'll do it, but—"

"Oh, Mary Jane, that's—"

"For one month," Mary Jane finished, raising her voice to drown out Lizzie's. "I'll close my school and serve at Jeff Davis's table and dust his office and do whatever else they ask for one month. If I don't discover anything important by then, we'll consider the experiment a failure and I'll leave. If my work there proves more fruitful, I'll stay."

"Thank you, Mary Jane." Lizzie embraced her. "If President Lincoln were here, I'm sure he would shake your hand and thank you himself."

"If President Lincoln were here, that would mean the war was over. Oh." Mary Jane gave a little start. "I suppose I should have talked it over with Wilson before giving you my answer."

"No need," said Lizzie cheerfully, quickly getting to her feet. "You've already said yes, and you can't back out now. I need you. The United States needs you."

"My **people** need me," said Mary Jane emphatically. "That's why I'll pretend to be a slave and risk being thrown into Castle Thunder or worse if I'm caught spying in the president's own home. Slavery will never end until Mr. Lincoln conquers the South. There is no other way. That's why I take this risk. Do you understand?"

Lizzie did.

Over the next few days, she introduced Mary Jane to Mr. McNiven and he instructed her in her role—what to look for as she tidied the president's office, which visitors she should be sure to eavesdrop upon, how to get information to him undetected. Mr. McNiven became nearly giddy from delight when Mary Jane demonstrated her prodigious memory by reading a letter he happened to have in his pocket and reciting it back to him verbatim ten minutes later. As for her husband, Wilson was not pleased that his wife had chosen to put herself in danger, but he could not talk her out of it, nor did he make more than a halfhearted attempt to do so, because he too understood the need.

Within a week of joining the Davis household, Mary Jane learned that the Confederate government faced a significant labor shortage and that the state intended to enact laws to allow for free Negroes to be impressed for months at a time to make up the difference. She discovered factions within Jefferson Davis's cabinet and knew of Secretary of War Randolph's intent to resign days before the president did, as well as the reasons for it—Randolph's frustration with Jefferson Davis's indecisiveness, his inability to discern what was important and what was not, and his refusal to take advice. In December, after the Confederates turned back a Union offensive at Fredericksburg, Mary Jane learned that President Davis wanted to join General Lee at the Rappahannock, where General McClellan was rebuilding his forces and another major battle was expected to begin, but he was instead obliged to travel to Chattanooga on an urgent mission to boost enlistments in the West, to soothe jealous tempers among his generals, and to reassure the citizens and soldiers made anxious by the squabbling.

All of these secrets Mary Jane collected and passed on to Mr. McNiven, who delivered them to Mr. Rowley or to Lizzie. Somewhere in the North, Lizzie trusted that their information was being put to good use.

Mary Jane must have thought so, for one month in the Davis household became six weeks, and then eight, and still she stayed on.

On Christmas Eve, one hundred and eighty Union prisoners arrived in Richmond and were lodged in Libby Prison. They had been captured by General Hampton near Dumfries a few days before while guarding two large wagon trains of supplies that the general's men eagerly confiscated. Lizzie sent the prisoners ginger cakes and spiced cider to mark the holiday, and later, Lieutenant Ross assured her that her gifts had been delivered and gratefully enjoyed. Lizzie was sorely disappointed that she could not give the captives a proper Christmas feast, but General Winder remained impossibly stingy with his passes and often would not agree to see her when she called on him at his office, although he never failed to send thank-you notes for the delicacies she left for him.

A few days after Christmas, Lizzie found herself overcome by indignation so intense tears filled her eyes when she read in the paper of a "handsome and bountiful Christmas feast" provided by the generous ladies of Richmond to patients at Camp Winder, an expansive hospital complex at the western terminus of Cary Street, named in honor of the general. "I beg to see you, to tell all about our Christmas dinner," the matron, Mrs. Mason, happily addressed the gift givers through the pages of the **Enquirer**. "It went off famously—everybody delighted. Think of fifteen turkeys; 130 chickens and ducks, a barrel of corned beef, 240 pies, and a barrel of cider, for the convalescents; rice custard, pudding, oysters, and egg-nogg for the sick!"

Lizzie did not begrudge the wounded Confederates their feast, but she wished she could have provided even half as much to the poor suffering men in Libby Prison. She would have done so if she had been permitted and if it would not have exposed her too much, though the expense would have been considerable and her fortune was dwindling at an alarming rate, gone to bribes, food, cots, blankets, medical supplies, charity to Unionists of the lower classes, payoffs to clerks in the adjutant general's office and the War Department and the Treasury—

She would give every penny to her name if it would speed the Union victory.

The Van Lews celebrated Christmas simply, with church services in the morning, a delicious meal of duck and oysters afterward, gifts and candy for the girls, and the customary raises for the servants. John joined them, but Mary stayed home, although she had enough presence of mind to send gifts for her daughters with him, warm knitted jackets and pretty china dolls.

Mary was getting better, Lizzie thought, her relief interwoven with worry. How much longer until she demanded that Annie and Eliza be returned to her?

On the last day of the year, Lizzie learned from Lieutenant Ross that of the two hundred wounded prisoners brought from

Fredericksburg and placed in the hospital of Libby Prison, at least twenty-five had died. If not for Lizzie's bribe money and Lieutenant Ross's clandestine influence, the number would have been much higher, but she took little comfort from that.

She was all too glad to see 1862 end, but she looked ahead to the New Year with dim hopes that they had passed through the worst of the war.

Still, 1863 began on a glorious note, full of hope and promise, for January 1 was the day President Abraham Lincoln signed the revised Emancipation Proclamation. Soon after he set pen to paper in Washington, the text of the official document was telegraphed far and wide, and two significant changes immediately seized the attention of all who read it. First, the list of territories under Union control had been revised to note the advances the army had made in the interim. Second, but far more significant, were two new paragraphs that had not appeared in the preliminary version released the previous September. In the first of these, President Lincoln enjoined the people newly freed by the proclamation "to abstain from all violence, unless in necessary self-defense."

The words were simple, straightforward, and of great consequence. Never before had slaves been permitted to defend themselves physically, to fight off a vicious beating by a cruel white master or mistress. Now they had been granted the right to stand their ground and fight to preserve their lives, if confronted by such a choice.

The second addition was more astonishing yet.

President Lincoln declared and made known that such persons among the newly emancipated "of suitable condition, will be received into the armed service of the United States to garrison forts, positions, stations, and other places, and to man vessels of all sorts in said service."

Lizzie could scarcely believe it, and she had to read over the proclamation twice to be sure that she had not skipped a critical line or misunderstood the phrasing. But it was the same upon each reading. Unless the typesetter had gotten it wrong, in the rebellious territories, slaves were free and men of color would be allowed to take up arms and fight for the Union.

Across the South, newspapers denounced Mr. Lincoln as a barbarian, a villain, a coward, and in some towns he was
burned in effigy in the streets. That, of
course, reflected the sentiments of the white
population. Lizzie suspected that, like the
people of color in her own household, most
colored residents of Richmond, slave and
free, privately rejoiced—although beyond
the larger cities, she supposed that most
colored folk were utterly unaware that anything had changed, just as William had said.

It was a cold, gray, blustery day, but
within the Van Lew residence, all was
merry and bright, more joyful even than at
Christmas. Mother arranged for them to
enjoy a luncheon feast, where they all sat
down at the table together and toasted Mr.
Lincoln's health and General McClellan's
and their own, and they prayed for the
Union army and for all the people held in
bondage who had no idea that they had
been freed. "You all are free now too,"
Lizzie told the servants, beaming. "What
the law forbade us to do, Mr. Lincoln has
done. You can leave us if you wish, or stay
on as paid employees as before, but either way, you are free."

"In your eyes and in your mother's, we have been for years," William said. "But not so to the rest of the world, not then and not now."

Some of the elation faded around the table, and the servants grew silent and somber, except for Hannah, who could not stop smiling. She was free at last, and her sons were free, and that was all she had ever wanted. The practicalities of the matter could not diminish her joy.

"That is true," said Mother. "If you remain with us, we will have to keep up the pretense. If you wish to be truly free, you should seek your fortunes in the North."

"We can smuggle you out of the city and set you on your way," said Lizzie. "If you go to Philadelphia, my sister will help you get settled."

One by one, they all shook their heads and told her soberly that they would stay, for now. It was not for her, Lizzie knew, or even for her mother, whom they all loved dearly, but for themselves, for the families and friends they could not leave behind, not just yet. After the war they might go, but their new freedom was too tenuously held and the times too uncertain to risk such drastic changes.

The meal was finished, the mess cleared away, and the servants dispersed to enjoy the rest of the day off. Lizzie was in the library indulging in a novel, a Christmas gift from John, when Peter cleared his throat in the doorway. "Miss Lizzie," he said, "can I talk with you?"

"Of course, Peter," she said, marking her place, closing the book, and beckoning him into the room. Then, with a sudden jolt, she said, "You haven't decided to leave us after all, have you?"

"No, Miss Lizzie," he said, shaking his head. "I intend to stay, and since I will be staying, I have a favor to ask of you."

She regarded him, puzzled. He was usually the more lighthearted of the brothers, but at that moment he seemed as serious as William. "Certainly, if it's in my power."

Peter crossed the room and halted a few paces in front of her chair. "You've met my wife, Louisa."

"Yes, I have." Lizzie recalled a bright, slender girl, a head shorter than her husband, with apple cheeks and a beautiful singing voice. She had worked for a family a few blocks away on Church Hill until early in the war, when she had been sold to a Confederate colonel who had moved his wife and children from Mississippi to Richmond to better promote his rise within the administration.

"Louisa's master got himself shot at Fredericksburg, and he passed on a few days ago. Now her mistress wants to move back to their plantation, and she'll take Louisa with her."

"Oh, no, Peter, no," Lizzie exclaimed. "How dreadful! I can't imagine how you must feel, to be separated from your dearest love—"

She stopped short, and her hand involuntarily went to the locket around her neck, and she felt the weight of the watch in her pocket. No, that was not true. She could imagine very well what it felt like.

"Yes," said Peter grimly. "Yes, it's dreadful. It's the cruelest pain I've ever felt. But it doesn't have to be."

"No?"

"Not if you help us." Peter hesitated, a muscle working his jaw, and then he plunged ahead. "I would like you to buy my wife."

She blinked up at him. "I beg your pardon?"

"I want you to buy my wife, please." He took from his pocket a sizable fold of bills, most of them Union notes, with a few Confederate dollars mixed in. "I have this to put toward the cost. I know it won't cover everything, but it's a start, and I can work off the rest. If I have to work the rest of my life I will pay you back, Miss Lizzie, I swear."

Lizzie felt faintly ill. In her heart and in her mind and to the very core of her being, she believed that slavery was the whole and sole cause of the dreadful war. The slave state crushed freedom of labor. It was arrogant, it was jealous and intrusive, it was cruel and despotic, not only over the slave, but over the community, the nation.

"You want me to buy a slave," she said, pained and bewildered. "On the day President Lincoln declares all slaves in the states under rebellion henceforth and forever free, you want me to perpetuate the institution you know I abhor."

"I want you to buy my wife's freedom," Peter said, emphasizing each word. "I'm not asking you to buy her to keep her **in** slavery, but to get her **out** of it. You and your mother have done that before, for other folks."

That was certainly true. Her father's will prevented them from freeing or selling any of the slaves Mother had inherited upon his death, but his decree held no sway over any slaves they might purchase afterward. Before the war, they had on several occasions bought and freed particular slaves, usually elderly relations of their servants. What Peter wanted was essentially no different, but to buy a slave on the very day she had toasted Mr. Lincoln for ending slavery seemed utterly wrong.

But Peter might never see his wife again if she did not.

"Put your money away," she told Peter, smiling fondly, and yet feeling a pang of regret. She should not have to buy Louisa. Louisa was no longer a slave, and she ought to be able to walk away from her mistress's household unimpeded as she wished. "You'll need it when you and Louisa start a family. John tells me children are quite expensive." She rose and smoothed her skirt. "While you get the carriage ready,

I'll tell Mother we're going out. Let's go fetch your wife home."

Louisa's mistress proved a shrewd bargainer. She knew she had the advantage and she pressed it, bemoaning the loss of her favorite maid, who would be extraordinarily difficult to replace. Eventually she named a fee five hundred dollars above the going rate, to which Lizzie agreed, smiling through clenched teeth as they shook hands.

Louisa was summoned, and although Lizzie knew the younger woman recognized her, she accepted the news stoically and went to gather her few possessions. Peter did not embrace her as he helped them into the carriage, nor did she greet him with anything more than a murmur and a nod. Only when the carriage had pulled away and turned the corner did her composure break, and she wept tears of joy. "I thought if the mistress knew how much I wanted to leave, she'd never let me go," she confessed, wiping her eyes.

The Confederate government was less willing than Louisa's mistress to let its slaves go.

In the middle of January, when the Confederate Congress reconvened, Jefferson Davis delivered to them a lengthy address in which he responded with fiery indignation to Mr. Lincoln's Emancipation Proclamation, which he excoriated as "the most execrable measure in the history of guilty man." People of all nations, Mr. Davis declared, following the instincts of their God-given common humanity, were readily able to "pass judgment on a measure by which several millions of human beings of an inferior race—peaceful and contented laborers in their sphere—are doomed to extermination, while at the same time they are encouraged to a general assassination of their masters by the insidious recommendation to abstain from violence unless in necessary defense." In retaliation, he vowed to turn over all Union officers captured in the South to local authorities, who would ensure that they were "dealt with in accordance with the laws of those States providing for the punishment of criminals engaged in exciting servile insurrection."

Lizzie understood that very well to mean that the enlisted men, whom Mr. Davis dismissed as mere pawns following orders, would be treated no better or worse than before, but their officers would be summarily executed. Never could Lizzie have imagined that warfare, already brutal, cruel, and merciless, could become any more barbaric. Now it seemed that every week ushered in a new horror once beyond imagining.

What these new evils were building toward, where it would all end, was too horrific to contemplate.

Chapter Fifteen

The winter dragged on, interminably miserable, dark and wet and cold. The stench of death hung everywhere, seeping from the hospitals and prisons until the odor rather than the steel-gray clouds seemed to blot out the sun. Food had become scarce, and shockingly expensive when it could be found. Lizzie and her mother knew of many true-hearted Unionists of the working classes whose families suffered terribly, and they took to preparing baskets of food and necessities for them, and providing funds so they could buy coal or pay a doctor's bill. Smallpox broke out in Castle Thunder and quickly spread through the poorer neighborhoods, terrifying the citizenry and compelling the authorities to establish separate hospitals where the suffering patients would be nursed, and the affliction, it was hoped, would be contained.

The usual illnesses—dysentery, typhoid, scurvy, jail fever, malnutrition—also continued to torment the prisoners wherever they were held, and in early February, Lizzie took a particular interest in a Lieutenant McMurtries, who had been wounded at Fredericksburg, and soon thereafter had taken ill with a terrible fever. Lizzie provided soups and custards for all of his meals, heartened by Lieutenant Ross's reports that he was showing steady improvement. Then, to her surprise, she learned that the prison commandant, Major Thomas Pratt Turner, had apparently been monitoring the lieutenant's condition as well.

> C. S. Mil. Prison
> Richmond, Va, Feby 15, 1863
> Miss Van Lew

Dear Madam—
Lt. McMurtries being now nearly well I have to request that you will

discontinue furnishing him his meals.

Abundant and palatable food is prepared for the patients in the prison Hospital, and I would prefer that they be not supplied by persons outside, as it has a tendency to subvert the consistency of Prison rules and discipline.

I am, Madam,
Your Obdt. Servt.
Th. P. Turner
Maj. Commanding

Angrily Lizzie crumpled the note in her fist. Adequate food was certainly **not** provided for the patients or any other Union prisoners, as their wasted frames and hollow cheeks made evident. As for its palatability, the men were usually fed little more than a thin, watery, insubstantial soup with a piece of bread so coarse Lizzie could not conceive how it could be eaten, the flour having been supplemented with pieces of corncobs and coarse bran and meal. Major Turner's assessment of the prisoners' rations was a bold untruth, and they both knew it, and Lizzie was shocked at his audacity.

She also understood that the letter was meant to forbid her from providing food and nourishment not only to Lieutenant Mc-Murtries, but to every prisoner henceforth. "Again and again they banish me," Lizzie muttered, alone in the library. She was tired of having her permission granted and revoked, restored and revoked, but it would be a waste of breath to protest to the Major Turner, an odious and utterly depraved man. She would appeal directly to General Winder.

They had no ginger for ginger cakes, nor fruit for a tart, and few preserves to spare, but they did have fresh milk, and butter as well, thanks to the bounty of their farm as well as Mr. Rowley's generosity, so Lizzie had Caroline bake a loaf of her finest bread, simple and wholesome and nourishing, which she packed in a basket with a ball of butter and a bottle of milk. Then Lizzie and Peter set out in the carriage in a freezing drizzle, which turned to snow by the time they arrived at the general's headquarters at Broad and Ninth Streets.

Lizzie was determined not to be put off by the general's secretary this time, not to be delayed or told that the general was out when she knew he was in. "I must see General Winder at once," she announced, setting her basket on the secretary's desk with a thud. She did not need to give her name, so familiar had she become to the staff. The smell of freshly baked bread, quite possibly one of the most enticing aromas ever created, wafted out from beneath the cloth. Whether inspired by the promise of her basket or intimidated by her imperious manner, the secretary hurried off and returned moments later to say the general would see her.

Before he could change his mind, Lizzie assumed her most charming smile and swept into his private chamber. "General Winder, what a pleasure," she purred, hastily concealing her shock at his appearance. Dark circles shadowed his eyes, worry had cut new furrows in his brow, and his haggard look spoke of exhaustion and toil.

"Miss Van Lew." His greeting was curiously flat, although a new interest came into his eye as he spied the basket and caught the delicious aroma. "What delicacies have you brought to tempt me today?"

"Nothing too fancy, just simple bread, butter, and milk." She smiled as she set the basket before him and drew back the cloth. "What evokes fonder memories of home than a good loaf of freshly baked bread?"

"Apples plucked fresh from the tree," he said distantly. "Sweet and ripe, a perfect fit to the hand. The view from my father's hayloft."

Lizzie regarded him with true sympathy as she seated herself. "I'm sure you must be terribly homesick."

"Yes, well, as to that—" He sat up and briskly straightened a few scattered papers on his desk. "I sleep in a comfortable bed at night rather than in a tent in the mud like so many thousands of our brave soldiers, so it would be unconscionable for me to complain overmuch. What do you require of me today, Miss Van Lew?"

She tried to conceal her surprise at his sudden directness. "Major Thomas Pratt Turner has forbidden me to send food to the men suffering in the hospital of Libby Prison. I cannot understand his presumption in countermanding your orders."

"What orders of mine has he counter-manded?"

"Why, you granted me permission to provide food, delicacies, and other necessary items to the prisoners," she said, bewildered, "and he will not allow it."

"I have charged him with maintaining order. If he feels that your gifts subvert his authority and discipline, then he is right to refuse you."

Lizzie studied him, mindful that General Winder's explanation echoed words from Major Turner's letter, as if they had conferred before he wrote it. "Major Turner denies me because he believes the prisoners receive good food in ample quantities. You and I both know that is not so."

"No one in Richmond receives enough good food these days, whether they be prisoners, soldiers, politicians, or civilians." He scowled and added, as if to himself, "Or wretched newspapermen."

"I do what I can to see that **your** pangs of hunger are few and far between," Lizzie reminded him, gesturing to the basket. "But let us speak of the prisoners and what **they** suffer. Perhaps you are unaware that there are more than one hundred men crammed into each of the six rooms on the upper floors of Libby. They endure scarce rations, regardless of Major Turner's protestations to the contrary, and lacking cutlery, they eat with their fingers like savages when permitted to eat at all. Their quarters are poorly ventilated and lit, they have no furniture and few blankets, and they are subject to all manner of cruel abuse from their guards."

"I do not believe it," said the general, affronted. "The Yankees exaggerate to provoke your sympathies."

"Do you truly think so? Are you familiar with the lively phrase 'sporting for Yankees?'"

"No. Should I be?"

"Indeed you should. It's the name the guards have given to their favorite pastime— shooting prisoners who venture too close to the windows, or who otherwise break the rules. 'To lose prisoners' is another charming euphemism they've devised, which we all understand to mean cold-blooded murder. Both phrases can be used in concert, as in, 'When one goes sporting for Yankees, one can expect to lose prisoners.' Nor do the guards restrict their brutality to the prisoners. The colored workers, slave and free alike, are flogged as a matter of routine, and civilians too feel their wrath. Not long ago, six colored women were stripped and beaten for passing bread to the prisoners as they were marched through the streets. Stripped and beaten, sir!"

General Winder's frown deepened as she spoke. "The prisons are no better and the guards no gentler in the North, let me assure you."

"I assure you that they are. They must be."

"How would you know that, Miss Van Lew?" he thundered. "Have you been to any Yankee prisons? Have you carried any delicacies or necessities into the prison where your noble Yankees held my brother for nineteen months without any charges being raised against him?"

Lizzie stared. "Your brother—"

"William. My elder brother William, a prominent resident of Philadelphia. He was arrested in September of the first year of the war because he refused to take an oath of allegiance, and because he publicly denounced Lincoln's actions. They confiscated all his private correspondence and certain personal possessions and locked him away, first in Fort Lafayette in New York and then at Fort Warren in Boston Harbor. My aged mother, a widow utterly dependent upon him, tried in vain to get him released, as did my other brother, who was imprisoned too for a time, as did our minister, all to no avail. A few months later William's jailers offered to release him if he would abandon his principles and swear the oath of allegiance, but this he could not do, so he languished in prison for nearly another year, still protesting his arrest, still not charged with any crime, and no good lady brought him custard or books or medicines or"—he lifted a corner of the cloth covering the basket—"or a loaf of bread and ball of butter and bottle of milk." Contemptuously he let the cloth fall.

"General Winder, I beg your apologies," said Lizzie, her voice trembling. "I had no idea."

"Of course not. Why should you?" He rested his elbows on the desk and fixed her with a steely look. "Although I can't help thinking that if he were a Yankee in Libby, you would have known."

"You're right, I might indeed have

known—not because he was a Yankee, but because he would be here in Richmond. I care for the suffering where I find them."

"You have a ready answer for every challenge, don't you, Miss Van Lew?"

"Has your brother returned to Philadelphia?" asked Lizzie, fighting to steady herself. "My sister lives in that city. If there is anything you would have her do for him—"

"Do you mean, take him ginger cakes and buttermilk?"

She pretended not to detect his sarcasm. "If you think that would please him."

"I think it would please him better to be left alone." Abruptly he stood. "I find myself feeling much the same way."

Wordlessly she rose and unpacked the basket, leaving her gifts on his desk. She inclined her head in farewell and departed, fighting the urge to sob in frustration and break into a run.

Lizzie was desperate to keep her supply and communication lines into the prisons open, with or without General Winder's consent, for she knew that with the coming of spring, furious and constant fighting would resume, and with that, the flood of Union prisoners into the capital.

On the morning of March 13, at not quite half past eleven o'clock, Lizzie was writing letters in the library when a low rumble shook the house, rattling the windows and setting her teacup clattering in its saucer. Instinctively Lizzie seized the armrests of her chair until the temblor subsided, but then, heart pounding, she bolted from the room and into the foyer, where William, Louisa, and Mother immediately appeared, all of them breathless and startled.

"What was that?" Mother asked shakily. "Are we under attack?"

William shook his head, baffled and wary. "That didn't feel like artillery."

From outside they heard exclamations of surprise and fear, but when Lizzie hurried to the window and peered outside, she saw nothing amiss. Gathering up her skirts, she raced upstairs and outside to the rooftop and scanned the horizon, and then she saw it—a thick cloud of black smoke rising to the southwest, down by the river in the vicinity of the Tredegar Iron Works.

Lizzie stood and watched, transfixed by

horror, as the distant pealing of alarm bells drifted on the wind.

She returned downstairs, where Hannah and the children had joined the others. "I think there's been an accident at Tredegar," she said. It would be a tremendous loss to the Confederate war machine if the ironworks had been destroyed—and given the time of day, and the number of workers employed there, the death toll could be staggering. "Judging from the smoke, the damage must be considerable."

Anxiously, Mother asked, "Is this the work of Unionists?"

"I knew nothing of it," said Lizzie, but then she considered the numerous suspicious fires that had broken out in the factory in the past, and added, "That doesn't mean it wasn't sabotage."

"Peter and I will find out," said William, and hurried off.

It wasn't until much later that the women left to worry and wonder at home learned, along with the rest of the frightened populace, the horror and tragedy that had erupted that morning.

The explosion had occurred not at Tredegar but at the Confederate States Laboratory on Brown's Island at the foot of Seventh Street. Within the low, long-framed ordnance factory, at least seventy employees, most of them young girls and women, had been hard at work as usual, loading cartridges with gunpowder, packaging munitions caps, and filling the friction primers used to ignite cannon charges. An eighteen-year-old worker, Mary Ryan, had tapped a board containing primers against her work bench—and the tap set off the primer, exploding the loose powder in the air and detonating the coal stove. The roof blew off, the walls collapsed, and the roof came crashing down again upon the workers. Ten to twenty were immediately killed. Some who survived the initial collapse leapt into the river, clothes and hair aflame. Others were too horribly burned to move, but lay amid the rubble wailing in anguish, skin charred and clothes in tatters and smoldering. Workers from nearby factories ran to help them while ambulances raced to carry the injured to military hospitals and panicked citizens searched for their daughters and sisters amid the chaos of the ruins.

In the days that followed, Richmond

plunged into mourning as funerals were held for the more than forty-five workers killed in the terrible accident. A macabre and unrelenting series of gloomy processions wound their way through the city from the homes of the deceased to the cemeteries. Nearly all of the dead were indigent women and girls, the youngest nine, the eldest sixty-seven. Another twenty-three had been injured, most of them seriously, and as they struggled to recover, authorities vowed to conduct a thorough investigation and Mayor Mayo appealed for donations on behalf of the victims and their surviving friends.

Lizzie and her mother, their sorrow as deep and heartfelt as any other Richmonder's, gave generously, distressed and ashamed that their less fortunate neighbors had been compelled by hunger and need to place their children in such a dangerous occupation.

Heedless of their grief, the work of war continued unabated.

Two weeks after the ordnance lab explosion, Jefferson Davis declared another official day of fasting and prayer. With inflation soaring and goods scarce, the command to fast in the midst of a famine struck Lizzie as either disingenuous or ridiculously ignorant. Beef was selling at a dollar twenty-five a pound, cornmeal twelve dollars a bushel, flour forty dollars a barrel, molasses a dollar fifty a pint, and turkeys fifteen dollars each. Scarcity drove up prices, but so too did the vast amount of Confederate paper money in circulation—some bills printed on behalf of the Confederacy, others for individual Southern states, and still more small bills, valued at anything from two to fifty cents, printed in vast quantities and so nearly worthless that they were derided as "shinplasters." The army was so desperate for food that the commissary general was authorized to commandeer meat, flour, and corn to feed the hungry soldiers, but the prices they were willing to pay were so far below the going rate that farmers stopped bringing produce to the city markets. The army's food shortages became so dire that General Lee ordered regiments to scavenge the countryside for wild onions, garlic, dandelion greens, and sassafras buds, all the while battling the commissary general to requisition more food for his underfed troops. Even so, the general was so devout and dutiful that he ordered his hungry soldiers to observe the March 27 day of fasting and prayer as President Davis had decreed.

Not so the Van Lews. Long ago Lizzie had resolved to enjoy an even better meal than usual on Mr. Davis's official fast days, and when storm clouds rolled in by mid-morning and thunderstorms threatened, she was inspired to invite their Unionist friends for a feast. The windows would be shut tight against the storm, and no one would be out walking in such foul weather, and if the guests staggered their arrivals and departures, the neighbors would be none the wiser.

The Carringtons came from across the street bearing a smoked ham they had intended to save for Easter. Mr. Rowley, his wife Catharine, and their children brought early spring vegetables from their farm near Oakwood, spinach and asparagus and watercress gathered in the wild. Mr. McNiven brought soda bread, hot cross buns, and shortbread in abundance, although he spent a good portion of the evening glaring darkly at the shielded windows and muttering that it was too dangerous for them all to be gathered together in one place and they must never risk it again. Mary Jane and Wilson came, and Lieutenant Ross, looking comfortable in civilian attire, and Mr. Ruth from the RF&P railroad, who revealed that, back in January, General Lee had accused him of operating the railroad "without zeal or energy." Mr. Ruth assured them, and Wilson quickly concurred, that he was not in danger of discovery. He was adept at deception, and he made certain that intervals of poor performance by his railroad were interspersed with periods of efficiency. He also had powerful Confederate friends who were convinced of his ardent devotion to the cause and would intercede for him whenever suspicions arose.

With the shutters closed and the curtains drawn tight, they enjoyed their feast, nourished as much by the company as by the delicious food. When they had eaten their fill, they withdrew to the library, where they spread out a map on Father's desk and traced the progress of the Union armies. Someday soon they would be able to gather in the open, they assured one another heartily, their spirits buoyed by the restful hours spent among sympathetic friends. Someday soon the Union army would capture Richmond, and they would unfurl their illicit star-spangled banners and sing "Hail, Columbia" and "The Battle Hymn of the Republic" to welcome the men in Union blue.

Mr. McNiven was absolutely right—it was dangerous for so many of them to meet in one place, especially when that place was the Van Lew mansion. But Lizzie knew too that their gathering was necessary, a significant act of defiance that would bolster their morale and strengthen their courage for the difficult trials that surely lay ahead.

For many citizens of Richmond, Lizzie knew, a feast such as theirs had become the stuff of dreams and fond memories, and every day was a fast day.

On the first Wednesday of April, after feeding her nieces their breakfast and playing with them in the garden, Lizzie entrusted them to Hannah's tender care and invited Eliza Carrington to walk with her around Capitol Square. It was a soft, tender spring morning, and they were both eager to slough off the melancholy of winter and reflect upon the seasons of peace that they had once known and, God willing, would see again. The miasma of death still clung to the cobblestones, but the bright sunshine and gentle breezes seemed to clear it away, and the grass upon the square was freshly green, with the bright-yellow pop of dandelions scattered here and there, and songbirds darting and trilling in the boughs.

They chatted as they strolled, and surreptitiously observed officers and politicians going about their business, taking note of anything that might be useful to the Union. As they rounded the second corner, Lizzie realized that the crowd of people milling quietly about was not a chance gathering of citizens innocently enjoying the lovely day, but rather a planned assembly of women, most of them young, some of them clutching children, all of them thin and pale. One young woman with limp, honey-blond hair poking out from beneath her bonnet eased herself down upon a nearby bench as they walked past. "I can no longer stand," she said weakly, and as she raised a hand to adjust her bonnet, her sleeve fell back and revealed an arm so frail and bony that both Lizzie and Eliza gasped aloud.

"My goodness, dear," Lizzie said, hurrying to her side. "Are you ill?"

Embarrassed, the girl pulled down her sleeve and gave an apologetic laugh. "No, but this is all that's left of me."

"Would you like something to eat?" said Eliza, rummaging in her basket.

"Of course," said the girl. "Isn't that why we're all here?"

As Eliza handed her a pair of shiny red apples, Lizzie nodded to the milling crowd, several hundred strong and steadily increasing. "Is this a celebration of some sort?"

"I suppose," said the girl, laughing bleakly. "We celebrate our right to live. We are starving."

"Are you planning to storm the Capitol?" Lizzie asked. "Or perhaps march on the Executive Mansion?"

The girl shook her head, devouring the apples down to the cores. "When enough of us have come together, we're going to the city's bakeries and take one loaf each." She nibbled the last bit of sweet, juicy fruit and flung the cores away. "That is little enough for the government to give us after it has taken all our men."

The look Eliza threw Lizzie was full of fear. "Forgive me, but that sounds terribly imprudent," Eliza ventured. "Won't the governor call out the guard to arrest you?"

"At least we'll have some food in our bellies when they throw us into Castle Thunder."

Lizzie knew the women would just as surely starve there. "Have you appealed to the authorities, explained to them your distress?"

"We have, but no one listens." The girl drew herself up. "We sent a delegation of ladies to Governor Letcher's house to ask for food. They should be with him right now, unless he was too scared to let them in. Our leaders thought it was right to give him a chance to help us before we go out to help ourselves."

The crowd was growing, and when Eliza clutched Lizzie's arm, she knew her friend wanted to be away from there as much as she did. "Do be careful," Lizzie urged. "I hope Governor Letcher gives you all something to eat and more to take home to your families, but if he doesn't—"

"If he doesn't, he'll wish he had," the girl said flatly.

With great misgivings, Lizzie bade her farewell and tucked her arm through Eliza's. As they turned quickly toward Church Hill, a towheaded boy about four years old darted in front of them and began to scale a magnolia tree. A colored maid in hot pursuit snatched her wandering charge down before he had climbed more than a few inches off the ground. "Get away from there, Marse Billy," she scolded, her gaze darting over the swelling crowd of women. "You might catch something from those poor white folks."

Lizzie and Eliza hurried on their way, but just as they were leaving the square, a swell of voices brought them to a halt, and they turned in time to see a group of four women, one dressed as gaudily as a brothel keeper, with an elaborately curled white plume sweeping from the brim of her hat, approach the square from the direction of the governor's residence. Lizzie could not make out what the newcomers reported, but from the lamentations and angry shouts that their address provoked, she could only assume that the quartet was the delegation and that Governor Letcher had given them an unsatisfactory response.

"Let's go home," Eliza urged, tugging on Lizzie's arm. "I don't like this. It feels ugly."

Lizzie agreed. A sense of hopeless outrage radiated from the throng, as if they were on the cusp of turning from a gathering of desperate women into an enraged mob.

It was not long after they returned home that Lizzie heard the alarm bell peal from its tower on the corner of the Capitol Square, but it was another day before she learned what had become of the desperate, ravenous women.

Their delegation had interrupted Governor Letcher's breakfast, so he had asked them to come to his office later, where he would assist them. As Lizzie and Eliza had observed, the crowd disliked his reply, and soon thereafter the angry throng left the square and proceeded down Ninth Street to Main. As the governor ordered the alarm sounded, Mr. Mumford of the Young Men's Christian Association tried to turn them back, promising to distribute food to them if they came to his office. Some of the women did as he asked, but most swept

past him down the street to the government commissary, where they forced their
way in and seized provisions from the
shelves. There was not enough for all, so
they descended on the nearby shops,
snatching up bread, flour, hams, and shoes,
which they loaded into whatever carts and
wagons happened to be parked along the
street. When frightened storekeepers
forced the women out and merchants all
along the street quickly barricaded their
doors, the mob turned violent, smashing
windows with hatchets and grabbing whatever they could lay hands upon, not only
food and necessities but luxuries like bon-
nets, silks, clothing, and jewelry. Soon hundreds more appeared—men and women
both, none starving by the look of it—some
merely to watch, others to join in the swiftly
escalating riot. Fireman arrived on the
scene and hosed down the looters, but that
only inflamed their fury. The alarm brought
the Public Guard running, and with them
at his back Governor Letcher confronted
the crowd and ordered Mayor Mayo to read
the Riot Act.

"You will disperse immediately or the
Guard will open fire," the governor shouted.

The mob ceased looting but continued to mill about, grumbling darkly and refusing to go.

At that moment an ailing Jefferson Davis appeared. He climbed atop a wagon that had been overturned sideways in the street and looked out upon the crowd, stern and sickly. "Go home so the bayonets facing you may be turned toward the enemy instead," he ordered. "Disorder in our streets will bring only famine, because farmers will refuse to bring food into the city."

"Some already refuse," a woman shrilled. "Your commissaries take everything and leave nothing for us and our children!"

As the crowd roared agreement, Mr. Davis raised his palms to quiet them. "I will share my last loaf with you, but you must bear your trials with courage. We must stand united against the enemy." He reached into his pockets, took out handfuls of money, and flung it into the crowd, provoking shrieks and scrambling for paper and coins. Then he took out his watch. "The Public Guard does not wish to injure anyone, but this lawlessness must cease," he declared. "I will give you five minutes to disperse, otherwise you will be fired upon."

He held his watch up and waited as the seconds ticked by.

The crowd waited too, murmuring, shifting—and then it began to break apart, like an ice floe in a river, fragmenting slowly at first around the edges and then with increasing speed as larger sections broke off and drifted away. "There is a power behind the throne mightier than the throne, and that power is the people," a man shouted, but his defiant call failed to draw the mob back together.

The next day, small groups of protesters gathered at street corners, again demanding food from the government, but this time the Guard easily scattered them, arresting nine. The City Council issued vouchers for free food to the deserving poor, and other authorities distributed flour and rice from government stores.

The assistant adjutant general had urged the Richmond press not to mention the riot in their pages lest the shameful events embarrass the Confederacy and encourage the enemy, but the editors promptly refused, so Lizzie and the rest of Richmond learned every detail of the bread riot and its aftermath. For days after the upheaval, Mayor Mayo plowed through the trials of the nearly four dozen people arrested on various charges, and listened, unsympathetic, to their testimony. "There is no reason why there should have been any suffering among the poor of this city," he addressed the courtroom. "More money has been appropriated than has been applied for. It should be, and is, well understood that the riot yesterday was not for bread. Boots are not bread, brooms are not bread, men's hats are not bread, and I never heard of anybody's eating them."

Almost without exception, the elite of Richmond society—longtime citizens, military officers, and politicians alike—denounced the lawlessness and declared that the women's complaints were absolutely without merit. There was scarcity in the city, they acknowledged, but little want, and no one was in danger of starving. Even Jefferson Davis concurred, publishing an address to the Confederate nation in which he seemed to intend to shame the rioters and discourage anyone who might follow their selfish and misguided example. "Is it not a bitter and humiliating reflection that those who remain at home, secure from hardship and protected from danger, should be in the enjoyment of abundance," he protested, "and that their slaves also should have a full supply of food, while their sons, brothers, husbands and fathers are stinted?"

Lizzie had no idea where this abundance Mr. Davis and his compatriots referred to was hidden, for she certainly saw no portion of it, not in the markets, not in the prisons, and not even in her own home, where no one had ever gone hungry before.

How could Mr. Davis fail to recognize the ugly consequences of war suffered by the people of his own city—and if he could not see even that far, how could he possibly understand what secession and war had inflicted upon an entire nation?

Chapter Sixteen

Not two weeks later, Lizzie was presented with inarguable proof that Mr. Davis and his administration were not as blind to the troubles plaguing Richmond as they had seemed.

Reports of atrocities in Castle Thunder had become so grave that the Confederate Congress had ordered an investigation. Captain George W. Alexander, the commandant, was accused of excessive violence and cruelty to the prisoners under his supervision, and a steady stream of inmates, detectives, and prison officers testified for and against him. The committee listened to grim descriptions of inmates tied up by their thumbs, flogged up to fifty strokes with broad leather straps, confined to a windowless sweat house, forced into the painful restraints known as the buck, shut outside in the prison yard in all manner of foul weather, denied food as punishment for impudence, and menaced by Captain Alexander's ferocious, one-hundred-eighty-pound Bavarian boarhound, Nero. One detective attested that he had observed prisoners wearing the same clothes for months until they were ready to drop off in rags. The prison hospital steward testified that he once found a deranged prisoner lying behind a door in the quarters, clad in nothing more than a short swallow-tailed coat, mired in his own filth, with his skin completely covered with scabs and vermin. The abhorrent details that emerged from the sworn statements depicted Castle Thunder as a veritable hell on earth, and Captain Alexander and his underling Detective John Caphart as devils in human form.

Poring over the lurid reports in the papers, Lizzie was impressed by the courage of the men who testified against Captain

Alexander and Detective Caphart, employees and prisoners alike, for they risked
much in speaking against the men under
whose authority they served or suffered.
Again and again, one witness's allegations
corroborated another's, until Lizzie was
convinced that the congressional committee would have no choice but to rule against
the commandant. Lizzie prayed that his
conviction would frighten other prison officials and compel them to treat the captives humanely, and she dared hope that
the entire prison system would be subse-
quently reformed.

She hoped and prayed to no avail.

On the first day of May, the committee
released its report on the management of
Castle Thunder—and it left Lizzie first incredulous, and then annoyed with herself
that she had naively believed justice might
be done. The majority of the members had
concluded that considering the desperate
and abandoned characters of the inmates—
"in the main murderers, thieves, deserters, substitutes, forgers and all manner of
villains"—Captain Alexander's tenure was
not marked by such acts of cruelty and inhumanity as to warrant condemnation. On

the contrary, his traits of character, especially his promptness and determination to enforce rigid discipline, eminently fit him for the management of a military prison. In a minority report, one dissenting member of the committee insisted that the evidence sustained the charges of cruelty and injustice against Captain Alexander, and that he and General Winder both had shown "a want of judgment and humanity in the management of that prison deserving not only the censure of Congress but prompt removal from the position they have abused."

Lizzie fervently agreed with that brave, lone congressman, but the opinion of the majority carried greater influence, and so General Winder, Captain Alexander, and Detective Caphart retained their positions without receiving so much as a word of censure. They all carried on as before, and their cruelty persisted unabated.

Not long after Captain Alexander was exonerated, Lizzie was on the front portico playing dolls with her nieces when a rumble of thunder announced an approaching storm. "Come along inside, girls," she said as the rain began to pelt the floor, first a few fat, loud drops, and then a torrent, stirring up a smell of dust and iron. Shrieking and giggling, the girls gathered up their toys, but just as Lizzie was ushering them inside, she heard a sudden, quick splashing sound from behind her and instinctively turned to look.

A young man holding his jacket over his head was dashing up the walk toward her. "Excuse me," he called, breathless. "May I beg the shelter of your portico until the rain stops?"

"Of course," said Lizzie graciously, with a graceful turn of the wrist to invite him to ascend. Putting on a pleasant expression, Lizzie kept her eyes on him and bent low to murmur into Annie's ear. "Take Eliza and find Hannah, will you?"

When Annie nodded and took her little sister's hand, Lizzie ushered them inside, closed the door, and turned to face her visitor, who had hurried up the steps and stood a few paces away shaking the rainwater from his coat and hat. "Are you Miss Van Lew?"

Lizzie hid her surprise. "I am, sir." As far as she could recall, she had never seen the young man before, and his accent had more of South Carolina than Virginia in it. He looked to be in his midtwenties, with a thick shock of sandy-brown hair, brown eyes, and a stubble of a beard. His clothes fit him as poorly as if he had accidentally grabbed his elder brother's in the predawn darkness of a shared room, but his boots looked almost new.

"I have heard you are much admired in Richmond."

Lizzie laughed. "Well, then, sir, you are either trying to flatter me or you have very poor hearing."

"Or we have mutual friends," he suggested, grinning. "For surely your friends have nothing but good to speak of you."

Lizzie regarded him for a moment, not quite sure what to make of him. "Actually, I don't think my friends are in the habit of discussing me with strangers."

"Of course not, Ma'am," he said, removing his hat and looking abashed. "I meant no insult. In fact, I have something to tell you which I think will interest you—and the government also."

Lizzie was tempted to ask him which government he meant, but instead she smiled. "I can't imagine what you would have to say on that subject to interest me, but I confess you've piqued my curiosity. Would you care to come in for a cup of tea until the storm passes?"

He promptly accepted, and when Lizzie called for tea and escorted the visitor to the parlor to introduce him to her mother, he gave his name as Billy Dockery and said he was employed as a courier.

"Not soldiering?" inquired Mother politely.

"No, Ma'am, that's not for me." He grinned again; it seemed his natural expression. "I'm no coward, I just don't like being told what to do. I like to go my own way at my own pace."

"Then it would seem you've found an occupation well suited to your temperament," Lizzie remarked.

"That's mostly true, but even a courier has to go where his clients bid him."

Caroline came in with the tea, and Billy looked on eagerly as she set out little sandwiches and sliced peaches.

"I imagine your occupation is particularly dangerous in wartime," said Mother, looking on as their guest loaded his plate.

"Dangerous, but all the more profitable for it." He devoured a sandwich in two bites. "The people I meet and the things I hear— why, you wouldn't believe half of it."

"Probably not," said Lizzie pleasantly, sipping her tea.

"I come to Richmond often, but I don't stay long enough to justify the expense of taking a room." Billy looked around, and suddenly his eyes widened as if inspiration had struck. "Say, I had a thought. I could board here with you."

Lizzie and her mother exchanged a look. "I'm sorry, but we aren't taking on boarders at present," said Mother.

"Why not?" he protested. "You got enough room, as anyone can see. There's not a closet in a boardinghouse to be found any- where in the city."

"Nor here either, I'm afraid," said Mother regretfully.

He looked from one to the other, per- plexed. "But I know you've taken boarders before."

"Yes, but not anymore," said Lizzie. "My nieces are living with us now, and they're terribly noisy, especially at night and in the very early morning. You would get no sleep at all."

For a moment Billy Dockery said nothing, allowing the silence to refute her claim. "I'll sleep anywhere," he eventually said. "Here, on the sofa. In the library. On the floor."

"Dear me, you are most insistent," said Mother with a little laugh. "I cannot tell you how much it grieves me that we're unable to accommodate you. Do take another sandwich."

Scowling, he obeyed, and Lizzie turned the conversation to the scarcity of food in the capital and how fortunate they were to have early peaches and how exciting and dangerous a courier's life must be. Grumpily at first, but soon with more enthusiasm, he told them enough of his adventures for Lizzie to conclude that he probably truly was a courier, or had been, but for whom, and why he was so determined to board with strangers he had only just met, she could not say.

They were as polite and charming as could be for nearly an hour, but when they finally managed to send him on his way, Lizzie felt as if she had been soaked in hot water and put through the mangle. Mother looked equally wrung out and limp. "What on earth was the meaning of all that?" she asked, smoothing back tendrils of silver-gray hair that had escaped from her bun. "I don't fault him for wanting to live here, but what an odd way to go about finding lodgings."

"Perhaps we should warn the Carringtons. He may be going from house to house until he strikes gold." Lizzie inhaled deeply and pressed the back of her hand to her forehead. "He knew my name. He said he had something to tell me that would be of interest to the government."

Mother's eyebrows rose. "Which government?"

"We'll never know." Lizzie went to the front window and drew back the curtain, but when she peered outside, she saw only puddles and rain and a couple hurrying down the sidewalk beneath a shared umbrella. "He's gone, and I don't think we'll ever see him again."

She was wrong.

The next week, while she and Eliza were marketing for the prisoners at Libby, a regiment of South Carolina volunteers marched by, new recruits from the look of their uniforms. As they approached, Lizzie glanced up from a sparse bin of turnips and spotted Billy Dockery marching among them, clad in the garb of a private.

He did not glance her way and probably never knew she was there, but she knew him, and she stood and watched, seized by a chill so intense she almost dropped her basket, until the regiment marched out of sight.

Spring and summer brought more fighting, more carnage, more prisoners, and more grief to Richmond.

In early May, Union troops again ventured perilously close to Richmond, wreaking havoc in the suburbs, cutting telegraph lines, capturing horses and mules, burning warehouses full of Confederate supplies, and destroying railroad bridges, engines, boxcars, and miles of track. Richmond—and indeed, the entire Confederacy—plunged into mourning when the beloved General Stonewall Jackson, the hero of Manassas, died from injuries received by friendly fire at the Battle of Chancellorsville. When his body was brought back to the capital, bells tolled solemnly for hours in expectation of his arrival at the depot, where thousands had gathered to follow the hearse to Governor Letcher's mansion. The next morning, a solemn and ceremonious funeral procession escorted his coffin to the Capitol, where twenty thousand mourners paid their respects as he lay in state in the House chamber. Although Lizzie would not speak ill of the dead, she could not bring herself to truly grieve for General Jackson, for he had chosen to betray his country and had brought untold grief to countless Northern families. She knew she was nearly alone in this. The rest of Richmond seemed to suffer his death with a sharper pain and greater sense of loss than any other calamity that had yet befallen them in that war.

Union prisoners and Confederate wounded kept coming to Richmond, an unrelenting stream that ebbed and flowed but never ceased entirely as skirmishes broke out and great battles were waged. Chancellorsville was followed by Port Gibson, and then by a second battle at Fredericksburg, and then Salem Church, and then more engagements in Mississippi that culminated in the Sieges of Vicksburg and Port Hudson, and then more fighting in Virginia at Brandy Station and Winchester.

As the Union stranglehold tightened around Vicksburg more than nine hundred miles to the southwest, threatening to wrest control of the Mississippi River from Confederate grasp, General Robert E. Lee led his Army of Northern Virginia once more into Pennsylvania, even as rumors came that Union troops were approaching Richmond from the Peninsula. The public knew only that General Lee was on the move, but while dusting Mr. Davis's study, Mary Jane had fortuitously glimpsed documents outlining their plans. The general intended to take his troops north not only to feed his men and horses on the bounty of fresh territory, but also to win a decisive victory on Union soil, ideally the capture of an important city. General Lee and Mr. Davis agreed that a bold, decisive strike might finally impress France and England enough that they would intervene in the war on the side of the Confederacy—and perhaps frighten Washington into suing for peace.

At the end of June, Governor Letcher

summoned all men liable for duty in the militia and anyone else capable of volunteering in other capacities to organize for the defense of the capital. The next day, as excitement and alarm swept through the city, Mayor Mayo issued broadsides warning that the enemy was approaching and calling the people to arms. "Remember New Orleans!" he exhorted. "Richmond is now in your hands. Let it not fall under the rule of another Butler."

Alarm bells rang out on July 2, and as the militia scrambled to respond, Lizzie and her mother distracted themselves from worry by refreshing the room they had once prepared for General McClellan. He no longer led the Army of the Potomac, and they were not certain whether General Hooker was in charge or if, as rumors claimed, he had been replaced by General Meade, but whoever liberated them, he would find comfortable accommodations awaiting him.

A few days later, a frenzy of fear swept over Richmond as Yankee cavalry destroyed the train depot at Ashland, not twenty miles to the north. Farther afield, no one, not even President Davis, knew exactly what had happened or might still be

happening in Pennsylvania and Mississippi. Rumors reached the capital that
General Lee had taken Harrisburg, but
from the South trickled reports that Vicksburg had fallen, so no one knew whether
to rejoice or to lament. On July 7, the Richmond **Sentinel** reported that General Lee
had routed the Union army at Gettysburg
and had taken forty thousand prisoners,
while the **Dispatch** exulted with the news
that Generals Johnston and Pemberton had
outmaneuvered General Grant at Vicksburg. Later that same afternoon, Mary Jane
discovered the truth in Secretary of War
Seddon's official report to President Davis:
Union general Ulysses S. Grant had taken
Vicksburg. Lizzie shared the joyful news
with Mr. Ford, who shared it with the
Union prisoners in Libby, who broke into
cheers and a rousing chorus of "The Star-
Spangled Banner" and kept their furious
guards awake past midnight singing "John
Brown's Body."

Reeling from the terrible loss of Vicksburg, all of Richmond waited, anxious but
hopeful, for a reliable account of General
Lee's invasion of the North. On July 9 the
news finally came: the Army of Northern

Virginia had been repulsed from Gettysburg with heavy losses and was retreating to Virginia.

Soon thereafter, Mary Jane surreptitiously read letters the general and the president exchanged in the aftermath of the demoralizing defeat. General Lee accepted full responsibility for the outcome of the battle, as he had told his men as they dragged themselves back from Union lines. He asked Davis to replace him with someone younger and stronger who still possessed the confidence of the people. Mr. Davis would have none of this, and immediately wrote back, "To ask me to substitute you by some one in my judgment more fit to command, or who would possess more of the confidence of the army, or of the reflecting men of the country, is to demand an impossibility."

And so General Lee retained his command—which greatly disappointed Lizzie, who had hoped Mr. Davis would hasten a Union victory by appointing a far less capable man.

The war raged on as the blood-soaked summer crested and began its slow, gradual descent into autumn. Every prison in Richmond was packed full of more Union soldiers than it could possibly hold, and the situation worsened as exchanges ground to a halt over procedural disputes, especially the Confederacy's refusal to treat colored Union soldiers as prisoners of war rather than recaptured slaves. As bad as conditions were in Libby Prison, they were far worse on Belle Isle, where on average fifty men perished every day, and the rest languished in their fragile tents or on the sandy plain, cadaverous, hollow-eyed, and despairing. Lizzie trembled from outrage when she learned that boxes of food and clothing that the federal government, the United States Sanitary Commission, and Northern civilians had sent for their relief had been confiscated by their jailers. Prison officers, surgeons, and stewards sipped the rich coffee and dined upon the good beef Union commissaries sent to Richmond, while the prisoners for whom the provisions were intended gnawed on dry gristle and bone and drank ersatz coffee made from chicory and toasted okra seeds. The Confederates attributed the disturbing death toll on Belle

Isle to dysentery, but it was a poorly kept secret that exposure and starvation were equally to blame.

Staggered by demoralizing losses on the battlefield, Confederate officials became more obsessed with the idea that spies lurking in the capital had contributed to their failures, and they resolved to root them out. In mid-July, Mrs. Mary Caroline Allan, a Cincinnati native who had married into one of the most prosperous and respectable families in Richmond, was arrested and charged with treasonable correspondence with the enemy for sending letters to acquaintances in New York in which she identified Confederate sympathizers in the North and offered observations of strategic military developments. In deference to her social status, General Winder arranged for her to be confined to the Saint Francis de Sales Hospital rather than Castle Thunder.

The general showed far less mercy to another accused Union agent, Spencer Kellogg, an abolitionist Kansan who had conducted espionage for General Grant in Tennessee and had helped bring about the fall of New Orleans. He was sentenced to death for presenting himself as a federal deserter, entering Confederate service under false pretenses as a member of the Engineer Corps, and collecting information about Confederate defenses and fortifications to deliver to the enemy. He was hanged at Camp Lee on September 25, but Lizzie did not attend, out of fear that her anguish would betray her true sympathies. She read a lengthy account of his final hours in the **Examiner** the next day in the seclusion of the library, trembling, tears streaming down her cheeks.

She herself had delivered to the Union more valuable information than Mrs. Allen and perhaps almost as much as Mr. Kellogg. If she wanted to preserve her life, she had to make sure she was never caught. That was all, and that was everything.

The Confederate army, desperately short of soldiers and supplies, used the draft to acquire more men and impressment to obtain food and other necessities. By law the military was required to pay a fair price for whatever they confiscated, but their agents usually neglected to compensate civilians adequately. Often too the goods taken were impossible to replace, so even if the market rate had been offered, the loss would still be very keenly felt.

Such was the case with horses. War-horses and beasts of burden were just as vulnerable to shrapnel and bullets as their riders and drivers, and army grooms were often sent through the city to seize every horse in fine fettle they could put into a harness and reins. During raids or panics, Lizzie had seen the army handlers take horses off the street from bread carts and country wagons hauling produce to market, even though officials had vehemently declared that they would not resort to such measures. Often there was not a horse to be seen on the streets except for those in the government employ. Twice Lizzie and her mother had been obliged to pay an enormous sum, enough for the army to purchase a substitute, to exempt their horse from impressment, but healthy horses eventually became so scarce that the government refused to renew their protection papers.

They could not sacrifice their horse to the Confederate cause, not when they were so fond of him and needed him for their service to the Union. A clerk in the quartermaster's office whose friendship Lizzie had bought with precious Union silver dollars gave the Van Lews advance notice whenever a sweep was scheduled, so they first tried hiding their horse in the smokehouse, but his whinnies as he sniffed the air were so loud that it was only a matter of time before he would be overheard and discovered. Lizzie and her mother decided that their horse was more valuable than their floors, so they spread a thick blanket of straw upon the study floor and spirited the stallion inside.

"It is not unlike preparing a room for General McClellan or Meade," Lizzie reflected as she and her mother stood in the doorway inspecting their work.

"No," said her mother. "Not quite."

Lizzie went to the horse, stroked his flank, and patted him on the neck. "Well, old boy," she said, "you may be unaware that Mr. Edgar Allan Poe recited terrifying stories in this room. The 'Swedish Nightingale,' Miss Jenny Lind, sang in this room. I know it's not your comfortable stable, but I hope you will appreciate its storied history and make the best of it."

Their horse seemed to accept his new surroundings at once, either because he was impressed to learn of its illustrious visitors, or, more likely, because he was relieved to be away from the scent of smoked meat. Each time they were obliged to return him to his hiding place, he behaved as though he thoroughly understood matters, never stamping loud enough to be heard, nickering softly but never neighing.

He was in his sanctum, as Lizzie had dubbed it, on a day in late October when a knock sounded on the front door. They were not expecting company, so Lizzie made sure the sanctum door was shut tight before hurrying to the parlor to await the caller. But when William appeared, he was alone, and his expression was guardedly curious. "It's a woman from the country," he said. "She wouldn't give her name, but she says she has a letter for you. I asked her to wait in the foyer."

It was two o'clock in the afternoon, hardly the hour for villains to be skulking, so curiosity compelled Lizzie to follow William back to the front door. There stood a short, round woman with chapped hands and sunburned cheeks despite her deep bonnet, and she squinted as she looked about with great interest.

"Good afternoon," Lizzie greeted her.

The woman peered up at her quizzically. "Are you Miss Van Lew?"

"I am indeed." Lizzie waited for the woman to give her name, but when she merely grinned, revealing a missing front tooth, she prompted, "And who might you be?"

"Oh, I'm nobody. Just a friend."

Lizzie managed a polite smile. "It's impossible to be both. My friends are certainly not nobodies to me."

The woman chuckled. "He said you were clever." She reached into her apron pocket and brought out a piece of paper, folded and sealed. "This is for you."

Evidently it was, for it had her name written upon it. "He?" she echoed as she broke the seal and unfolded the page. The woman merely smiled and shrugged, so Lizzie began to read—and her heart began to thud in her chest as she discovered a scrawled request for information regarding the provender and stores in Richmond and where the sick of the hospitals were being taken. The signature identified the author as a Union general, but Lizzie did not recognize the name.

Lizzie's thoughts flew to Billy Dockery, the young soldier who had turned up at her home claiming to be a courier. "What is the meaning of this?" she cried, feigning horror and surprise as she pressed the incriminating paper into the woman's hands. "Why on earth would any general of any army anywhere believe I could supply him with information of this nature? And even if I could, how dare he believe that I would?"

The woman blinked at her. "I thought you said you was Miss Van Lew."

"I am, which is why I am appalled that anyone would question my allegiance to the Confederacy."

The woman looked at the paper in her hand, read the name, and then squinted quizzically up at Lizzie. "You mean you don't want it?"

Lizzie wanted to fling it in the fire and send the woman away with all speed. The letter could be legitimate, or it could be the tempting bait lying in a trap ready to be sprung. "I don't know the person who wrote this letter, and its content is treasonous, so I want absolutely nothing to do with it or him."

"All right, Ma'am, you don't have to shout." Frowning, the woman folded the letter and began to put it away.

"Wait." Lizzie snatched it from her hand, vigorously tore it up, and tucked the pieces into her pocket. "Now there can be no danger to either of us. Do you know the man who gave that letter to you?"

"No, but the silver he paid me spoke well of him."

Lizzie shook her head, amazed at the woman's bravado. "Do you know what a great risk you took in bringing this to me?"

The woman drew herself up, indignant. "I wouldn't have been found out. I'd like to see any one try to put their hand in my pocket."

"Yes, you're quite intimidating. Who would risk it?" Lizzie nodded to William, who promptly came forward to show the strange little woman out. "If anyone asks you how I received the letter, you be sure to tell them."

Alone again, feeling faint, she returned to the parlor and sank into a chair. Was it a trap as she feared, or a hapless but genuine overture from a Union general who, for some reason, had been unable to find a better messenger?

Lizzie brooded over the strange encounter for several days, wondering if she had narrowly evaded entrapment or had rejected a request from the very men whom she had been risking her life to help for more than two years. She knew that she could not recklessly put her faith in every stranger who appeared at her door—Billy Dockery had taught her that—and yet, if the United States had finally decided to recruit agents from among Richmond's Unionists instead of sending Northerners to infiltrate the South, she wanted to help. With all her heart, she wanted to help.

She could not trust strangers who showed up uninvited at her door claiming to carry letters for Union generals, but she could send a trusted envoy to deliver her message to a Union general—and she knew just the one.

Union major general Benjamin Butler had already become notorious throughout the South long before he was appointed commander of the Department of Virginia and North Carolina. Indeed, from the way

Southerners' lips curled when they snarled his name, it was quite possible that he was the man most despised by the entire Confederacy.

He had given the rebels ample reason to loathe him. In May 1861, as commander of Fort Monroe on the Virginia coast near Washington City, General Butler had declared three runaway slaves who had fled to Union lines to be "contraband of war," and had refused to return them to their masters. His actions prompted the United States Congress to pass the Confiscation Act in August 1861, which authorized the Union Army to take slaves laboring for the Confederacy and put them to work for the Union military instead. Outraged Southerners considered this a repudiation of the rules of civilized warfare and vowed to retaliate.

Then, in April of 1862, General Butler was appointed commander of the Union forces occupying New Orleans. He immediately acted to suppress insurgency, arresting the mayor and his associates, refusing to release paroled prisoners, and ordering the execution of a man who had torn down a United States flag. For the most part, the men of New Orleans sullenly acquiesced to the new order, but the ladies remained ardent Confederates to the end, rallying to the cause of making their occupiers' sojourn in their fair city as miserable as possible. The ladies of New Orleans shrieked and spat at Union soldiers in the streets, avoided them for fear of contamination, and occasionally emptied chamber pots upon them from upstairs balconies as they passed on the sidewalks below. Exasperated by their persistent insolence, in May of 1862 General Butler had issued Order No. 28, his soon-to-be infamous "Woman Order" that proclaimed that any Confederate woman who by word, gesture, or movement insulted Union soldiers would be treated as a woman of the town plying her nefarious avocation. Not even the most defiant secessionist lady wanted to be arrested as a prostitute, and so the torment of Union soldiers had subsided even as the reprehensible insult against the honor of Southern womanhood provoked the wrath of the Southern people. Jefferson Davis had declared that General Butler's actions rendered him an enemy of mankind deserving of capital punishment, and a ten-thousand-dollar reward was offered for his head. So reviled was General Butler that it was deemed a particular insult when he was placed in charge of the extensive portion of eastern Virginia occupied by the Union—and was made responsible for directing the Army of the James in its campaign to capture Richmond.

It was this man, the most loathed Yankee in the Union, to whom Lizzie intended to offer her services.

Chapter Seventeen

At the end of November, the Richmond **Sentinel** reported that there were 16,411 Union prisoners remaining in Richmond. Lizzie and her Unionist friends were determined to free as many as they possibly could before winter set in and travel became too hazardous—although conditions in the prisons and on Belle Isle were so heinous that many men would rather risk frostbite and execution than endure another week as a guest of the Confederacy.

Sometimes prisoners seized a sudden opportunity to flee—a door left ajar, a guard dozing at his post—and found their way to the Van Lew mansion or another friendly haven thanks to whispered instructions from Mr. Ford or Lieutenant Ross. When such opportunities did not present themselves as often as Lizzie desired, she enlisted the help of her friends to move things along.

In early December, an assistant surgeon with the First Wisconsin Infantry named John R. McCullough was sent to the hospital of Libby Prison for a minor affliction. On one of her visits, Lizzie noted that except for his illness, from which he was recovering quickly, Dr. McCullough was otherwise hale and hearty, more able than any other patient on the ward to endure the rigors of hard travel. After discussing his case with her Unionist friends, Lizzie decided to arrange his escape, if he dared risk it.

When Lizzie next returned to the prison hospital, she brought in her basket of delicacies the usual breads and soups and custards, as well as books and paper and pencils for letter writing. She distributed these to the men, but she reserved a small bag of tobacco for Dr. McCullough. "I hope this is to your liking, but there's not enough to share," she said, smiling as she handed him the bag and strolled away. Inside he would find a note: "Would you be free? Then be prepared to act. Meet me in the surgery at ten a.m."

The next day, shortly before ten o'clock, Lizzie departed from her usual rounds and slipped away to the surgery, where she found Dr. McCullough waiting for her, pacing warily. He stopped short at the sound of her footfalls. "Can you help me?" he asked in an urgent whisper.

She nodded and drew closer. "It will not be easy."

"I don't care how difficult it is as long as it's soon. I'm to be transferred back to the officers' quarters the day after tomorrow."

Lizzie had not expected that. "Then it will have to be tomorrow. You may choose a single friend to accompany you, but no more."

He nodded, his brow furrowing as he folded his arms and leaned closer. "What do I have to do?"

"You must pretend to be dead."

"What?" He drew back, uncertain. "How?"

"Close your eyes and lie very, very still

for a long time." Lizzie paused before adding, "Also, I have bribed the orderly who
will confirm your death, and that will go a
long way toward convincing your jailers."

Dr. McCullough inhaled deeply and
raked his long, sturdy fingers through his
hair, receding at the temples but otherwise
thick and tangled. "All right. I can do that."

"Tomorrow, noontime, after the physician
has come and gone, you will expire," Lizzie
said in an undertone, glancing toward
the door, which could open any moment.
"Your friend will tell the orderly, who will
listen to your heartbeat but declare you
dead anyway. Choose a few inmates you
trust to help your friend lay you out as a
corpse, cover you with a blanket, and convey you to the dead house. There your
companion will keep vigil, and you must
lie as still as you can, scarcely breathing,
until dusk."

He nodded. "And then?"

"Some of your friends will distract the
guards with a sham fight. As soon as the
way is clear, you and your companion must
leave the hospital and immediately proceed two blocks to the north and one block
east. There, a young colored woman in a

blue kerchief will be waiting. She will acknowledge you with a nod. Do not approach her, but rather follow her at a
distance and she will lead you to a place
of refuge, where you will be given shelter
and food and instructions. Do you understand?"

"I do," Dr. McCullough replied quietly, and
they both jumped at the sound of a door
slamming elsewhere in the hospital. "Thank
you, Madam. Thank you."

She nodded, gave him a quick smile,
and hurried away.

All the next day her stomach knotted
with anxiety as she imagined what Dr. Mc-
Cullough and his friend were doing at that
precise moment, if they were waiting eagerly in the morgue or if they had been
discovered and beaten and flung into the
worst corner of Libby. As the hours slowly
passed, she organized their supplies—
passes Mr. Ruth had procured for them
that would allow them to exit the city, three
thousand dollars Confederate apiece and
worth every cent; suits fashioned from Confederate blankets, which they had learned
made convincing disguises; and a small
purse of silver dollars to ease their pas-

sage. Finally, just before dusk, Louisa tied on her blue kerchief, kissed Peter, and hurried off to meet the fugitives.

Less than an hour later, Louisa returned, and not two minutes behind her followed Dr. McCullough and a companion, whom Lizzie recognized as a prisoner employed as a steward in the prison hospital. Dr. McCullough seemed surprised to see Lizzie when she stepped out on the front portico to usher them quickly inside, and both men bore the strained, wary, excited expression she had seen on the faces of many fugitive prisoners before them.

As she led them upstairs to the secret chamber, Dr. McCullough introduced his companion as Captain Harry S. Howard of Cameron's Brigade. "Thank you, Miss Van Lew," Captain Howard enthused as she guided them into their hiding place. "From the bottom of my heart, I thank you."

"If this is how you feel now, just wait until you've had a good supper." Leaving them to settle in, Lizzie went downstairs to help Caroline carry up their trays.

Once they had eaten, she explained the rest of the plan. They would remain with her three days to allow the hunt for them to run its course, but on the fourth evening, a Unionist friend would convey them in his wagon to Mr. Rowley's farm on the outskirts of the city, where they would remain until it was safe to proceed. "Mr. Rowley will lead you through Confederate lines to the Potomac," she said, "where you can make your way to Washington City. What do you say to that?"

"I say you are an angel of mercy," Dr. McCullough replied.

"And I heartily concur," Captain Howard chimed in.

She smiled as she gathered up their dishes, which had been cleaned of every last crumb. "Thank you, gentlemen."

She left them to rest, enjoying their happiness, but guardedly. In their exhilarating first hours of freedom, she didn't have the heart to remind them that they had many miles to go before they were safe in Union territory again, and that any mistake could land them back in prison.

All the next day they rested, and ate, and studied maps, and plied Lizzie with questions about the progress of the war and the fortifications around Richmond. Lizzie told them all she knew, which was considerable. Captain Howard promised to pass her information to the Union authorities. "The highest authorities," he emphasized, giving her a knowing look.

"Mr. Lincoln himself?" Lizzie inquired.

"Perhaps not so high as that," he admitted, and Lizzie laughed.

As twilight fell on the fourth day, the men prepared to depart. Mother packed them a haversack full of bread and cheese and assured them that she would pray for their safe deliverance.

Just as Lizzie heard Mr. McNiven's bakery wagon pull up outside and she was preparing to bid her guests good-bye, inspiration struck. First she dashed to the library to retrieve a letter she had written several weeks before but had been unable to deliver. Then she ran outside to the rear gardens, where she quickly cut a lovely bouquet, tied it up with ribbon, and hurried back to the foyer. "Give this to General Butler if you can," she said, handing the bouquet and letter to Dr. McCullough. "Offer him my sincere compliments and tell him I hope to welcome him to Richmond soon."

Both men promised her they would, and

with that, they slipped outside, concealed themselves aboard the wagon, and were gone.

A few days later, Louisa and Peter returned from a drive out to the countryside with a note from Mr. Rowley hidden within the hollow egg. The doctor and the captain had reached the Potomac safely, he reported, and when he saw them last they were waving to him from the deck of a steamer bound for Washington City.

Lizzie felt tears of joy spring into her eyes as she cast the note onto the fire. What glad tidings her loyal friend had given her, and just in time for Christmas! Her spirits soared when she imagined the two men celebrating the holidays within the loving circle of their families.

She only wished she knew for certain whether they had made it safely home.

Lizzie thought of them on that bitterly cold Christmas Day as she counted her own blessings. Though she was surrounded by danger and threatened every hour with betrayal, she had a sturdy roof over her head, enough to eat if only barely, trusted friends, loving family, and two precious nieces to distract her from her troubles with laughter and play. Perhaps this would be the last Christmas of the war, she allowed herself to hope. Perhaps the worst was behind them at last.

On New Year's Eve, she received a sign—for that was how she decided to interpret it—that 1864 would be a year of danger as well as blessings.

Mr. Rowley had sent his son to deliver two unexpected gifts—a sack of potatoes and onions for the Van Lews' New Year's Day feast, and a newspaper, the December 25 edition of the **Boston Daily Advertiser**. He often sent her newspapers smuggled from the North, which she always read thoroughly, for even a few days old they were full of useful information. Intuition told her that Mr. Rowley believed this newspaper contained something of particular interest to her, and after scanning the page, she understood why.

"An Escape from Richmond," the headline sang above an account of "two enterprising soldiers of the U. S. Army," who on the afternoon of December 24 had "reported themselves at the Provost-Marshal's office, dressed in gray clothes made by Union ladies at Richmond from secesh blankets. Their names are H. S. Howard, of Cameron's brigade, and John R. Mc-Cullough, of the 1st Wisconsin infantry." The two men asserted that they never would have escaped without "assistance from the Union people of Richmond (who are more numerous than is generally supposed)."

"Yes, we are," Lizzie said aloud to the empty library as she folded the newspaper and tucked it away in her father's desk drawer for safekeeping. They were more numerous, and together more powerful, than anyone imagined.

She wondered, briefly, if the doctor or the captain had delivered the bouquet and the note offering her services as his Richmond correspondent to General Butler. Probably not, she thought, regretful. Their paths would likely never cross the general's, and the flowers were certainly long dead.

What mattered most was that Dr. Mc-Cullough and Captain Howard had successfully escaped—and that the Union underground had eluded detection another day.

"Standing upon that narrow isthmus of time which connects the two segments of the calendar, the Old and the New Year," the Richmond **Examiner** solemnly wrote on the first day of 1864, "it is natural that we should pause to reflect; should cast a keen retrospective glance upon the troubled tide over which we have passed, and peer intently into the Cimmerian darkness which envelops our future path. . . . What does the impenetrable face of 1864 conceal of good or of evil for us?"

Sometimes Lizzie wished she knew, but although her hopes for a Union victory increased with every successful prisoner escape, with every intelligence dispatch smuggled out of Richmond, she still dared not peer too deeply into the shadows that stretched before her.

The turning of the year brought to light the offenses of Captain Alexander, who had narrowly avoided punishment for the inhumane treatment of prisoners at Castle Thunder earlier that spring. Arrested, charged with malfeasance in office, and confined to his quarters, he stood accused of "extensive trade in greenbacks" and of accepting bribes from prisoners to ensure their release. General Winder agreed to an investigation of his conduct before a court of inquiry, but while the court-martial was pending, he relieved Captain Alexander of duty, his mind on more pressing matters than the tyrant of Castle Thunder.

At the general's orders, construction had begun on a massive new prison compound of twenty-six acres outside the town of Andersonville, Georgia, where the climate was more benign and food more plentiful. Lizzie realized that she ought to be pleased to hear that many, though not most, of the Union captives would soon benefit from new, more spacious quarters and ample provisions, but she had serious misgivings about sending the men deeper into the South, from where it would be far more difficult, if not impossible, for them to escape to Union lines. She also knew that Andersonville might turn out to be far less comfortable and benevolent than General Winder promised, and from so great a distance, she would be powerless to help.

The men trapped within the dismal prisons preferred their own methods for relieving overcrowding.

One snowy evening, Lieutenant Ross appeared unexpectedly at her door, dressed in civilian clothes, feigning a limp, and completing his disguise with a cane. "Something's in the works at Libby," he told her, after she had shown him into the library and called for hot tea to help warm him. "It's my job to count the roll twice a day. Recently, four or five men have been missing each time, although they've gotten away with it so far."

Lizzie couldn't help smiling. "Because you've deliberately miscounted?"

"No, because they've tricked me," he admitted. "As I go down the line, some of the men I've already counted leave the front and sneak around to the end so I count them twice. This morning they decided to have some fun at my expense. The first time I counted, there were ten prisoners too many, so I had to start over. The second time through, there were six too few. The third time, there were twelve extra men. Even though I knew what they were doing, I got so annoyed that I exploded. Oh, they enjoyed that. I've never been laughed at so hard by so many."

"You can't blame the men for wanting to tease their despicable prison clerk."

"No, I can't, and I couldn't then either. I burst out laughing too."

"Oh, no!"

He nodded, rueful. "I immediately caught myself and screamed at them all the more for the rest of the day to make up for it. I think I left everyone at Libby none the wiser."

Lizzie certainly hoped so. She would hate to lose him to Castle Thunder. Lieutenant Ross was a good, brave man, and because of his position, he would be impossible to replace.

Not long thereafter, Mr. Ford, the colored prisoner employed as a hostler for Libby's commandant, confirmed Lieutenant Ross's suspicions that the imprisoned officers were up to something. "There's going to be a breakout," he told her in an undertone, brushing a horse while she paused on the other side of the fence, pretending to shift the items in her heavy basket. "A mass escape, as many as can go. A group's been tunneling for weeks. Colonel Rose of the Seventy-Seventh Pennsylvania is the ringleader."

"How soon?"

"A few more weeks, a month—they won't know until they break through to the surface someplace out of sight of the guards."

Mr. Ford fell silent as another inmate sta-
blehand passed, and waited for him to disappear around the corner before continuing.
"I've told them all the safe houses in the
city. Tell everyone to make ready."

Lizzie nodded her thanks and hurried
on her way.

She spread the word to her Unionist
friends, reminding them to be silent and
watchful. The secret chamber in her attic
would not suffice for a mass escape, so
Lizzie and her mother hastily prepared
more accommodations for whomever might
come, choosing a little-used end room facing the back of the house, drawing the curtains tight, and nailing dark blankets over
them so not a glimpse of light or movement
could be discerned from outside. Nelson
checked to make sure the gas was ready
to be turned on at a moment's notice, and
Louisa helped Lizzie arrange cots and
bedding, enough for ten men to wait out a
search for a week or more in relative comfort. The newly prepared quarters were
not invisibly concealed like the attic chamber, but the room was as secure as they
could make it, and it would be ready to
shelter the fugitives whenever their tunnel

broke through to the surface beyond the prison gates.

A blast of frigid temperatures struck Richmond in the middle of the month, freezing the ice in the canal so hard that men and boys skated upon it even as it drove most of the population indoors. The prisoners on Belle Isle retreated to the feeble shelter of their thin tents, and although her sources had frustratingly little contact with anyone on the island, Lizzie knew the death tolls climbed steadily, shockingly higher as the cold snap stretched on.

The first day after the severe freeze lifted, Lizzie received a startling note from Mr. Rowley, delivered by his eldest son, Merritt. "My Dear Miss Van Lew," he wrote, "you will be pleasantly surprised to hear that our mutual friend Mr. Howard is visiting again. He says he would enjoy nothing better than the pleasure of your company, to which end I invite you to come for supper tomorrow."

Lizzie read the letter over again, dumbfounded. Mr. Rowley had not employed the hollow egg, so his letter was necessarily circumspect in case it was intercepted. Lizzie searched her memory, but the only Mr. Howard that came to mind was Captain Howard, the former fugitive of Libby whom she believed safe in the North or returned to his regiment. "Has this Mr. Howard visited your farm before?" she asked Merritt.

He nodded, but he kept his expression carefully impassive. "Yes, Miss Van Lew. He stayed with us a few days last month."

"And now he has returned."

"Yes, Ma'am." Merritt hesitated before adding, "My father was surprised to see him, but glad."

The youth had clearly been instructed to say as little as possible about their unexpected visitor. "Please tell your parents that I look forward to dining with you tomorrow."

Merritt nodded and turned to go, but Lizzie called him back, laughing, and insisted he stay for lunch before riding home.

The next day, Lizzie had Peter drive her in the carriage out to Rowley's farm, employing General Winder's old pass, now so creased and worn that it was barely legible, to leave the city. Mr. Rowley and his wife, Catharine, greeted her warmly, but Lizzie was so distracted that she could hardly reply to their kind welcome, because there in the middle of the parlor stood Captain Howard, looking remarkably more vigorous than the last time they had last met.

"It **is** you," she said in wonder as she shook his hand. "Dr. McCullough is well also, I hope?"

Captain Howard smiled. "He is, and I'll be sure to let him know you asked about him."

"And my deliveries?" she teased. "Did you give my bouquet and letter to General Butler?"

"The flowers, alas, did not survive the journey, but Dr. McCullough placed your letter into the general's hands himself. I informed General Butler how you and your associates arranged our escape so adroitly, and he was very impressed indeed."

For a moment Lizzie could only blink at him in astonishment. She had expected demurrals and apologies, and perhaps a promise to keep trying to deliver her letter, but not this. "I assume," she managed to say, "he enjoyed the adventurous tale so much that he insisted you return and pay me his compliments."

"In a manner of speaking." Captain Howard beckoned to Mr. Rowley. "Mr. Rowley, Miss Van Lew, I have a matter of grave importance to discuss with you, if you would be seated."

The rest of the Rowley family understood this as their cue to depart. Lizzie's heart pounded from excitement, but she managed an outward appearance of calm as she gracefully seated herself, folded her hands in her lap, and awaited Captain Howard's address.

"Miss Van Lew has generously offered to act as General Butler's correspondent in Richmond," the captain said, looking from her to Mr. Rowley. "The general hopes to enlist your aid too, Mr. Rowley, and he formally requests for you both to become his federal agents in the Confederate capital."

"With all my heart, I accept," said Lizzie promptly, and then she glanced at Mr. Rowley. "Of course, I can speak only for myself."

"I accept as well," said Mr. Rowley somberly.

The captain smiled, his relief readily apparent, but he cautioned, "Make no mistake, this is dangerous work."

"We are well aware of the danger," said Mr. Rowley. "We've been living with it for years."

"Yes, indeed," said Lizzie. "And yet we never let that dissuade us. If we're going to risk our lives and freedom anyway, why not do so under the auspices of General Butler's command?"

"Excellently put, Madam." Captain Howard took a folded paper from his pocket and handed it to Lizzie. "A letter for you, from an admirer."

Lizzie broke the seal and read an innocuous missive from a fellow named James Ap. Jones to his "Dear Aunt"—someone named Mary was recovering from a bad cough, Jennie sent her love, and Mother had given up all hope of seeing the dear aunt again until they met in heaven. "Should I know these people?" she asked, scanning the letter a second time before returning it to the captain.

"No, because they don't exist." Captain Howard draped his handkerchief over his lap, lay the letter flat upon it, produced a small vial of clear liquid from his pocket, and poured the contents over the page. Lizzie smelled vinegar as he rose and held the letter close to the lamp until the paper was in danger of scorching—and watched in amazement as more lines of writing appeared perpendicular to those she had already seen. With a satisfied smile, Captain Howard handed her the transformed letter and gestured for her to read it.

My Dear Miss:
     The doctor who came through and spoke to me said that you would be willing to aid the Union cause by furnishing me with information if I would devise a means. You can write through Flag of Truce, directed to James Ap. Jones, Norfolk, the letter being written as this is, and with the means furnished by the messenger who brings this. I cannot refrain from saying to you, although personally unknown, how much I am rejoiced to hear of the strong feeling for the Union which exists in your breast and among some of the ladies of Richmond. I have the honor to be,
          Very respectfully,
          Your obedient servant.

Lizzie felt a heady rush of excitement that left her momentarily breathless. She handed the letter to Mr. Rowley, who read it, frowning thoughtfully, and as she studied him, she felt her first twinge of doubt. "Captain," she said, "we've always relied upon our own couriers to smuggle intelligence past Confederate lines. Not one has ever been caught. While it's true that it would require less risk to life and limb to send letters through the flag of truce boats, we must assume that the Confederates read and censor our mail."

Mr. Rowley nodded his agreement. "I would in their place."

"If they do, and I've no doubt they will, they will read nothing more than an innocently dull conversation between a dutiful nephew and his doting aunt." Captain Howard reached into his coat pocket and produced two small glass bottles containing a transparent liquid. "This is the same substance General Butler used to write to you. Write with it as you would any ink. The lines will appear with the application of a mild acid and heat." He handed each of them a bottle. "I will also give you a cipher in case you run out of the fluid, or if you wish to doubly secure your message."

The cipher he taught them was a system of converting letters to numbers, a grid of forty-nine squares with numbers along the left column and bottom row and letters filling the rest. Lizzie and Mr. Rowley copied the key over carefully, and when Captain Howard exhorted them to conceal them in the most secure location they knew, Lizzie needed little time to decide. She folded the paper as small as she could and tucked it into the back of the case of her pocket watch, which she carried with her always.

When they parted company, Lizzie promised to send General Butler a report on the state of Richmond's defenses and prisons as soon as she could gather enough credible information. "My code name is Quaker," Mr. Rowley said ruefully as he escorted her to her carriage, where Peter already had the horses ready. "I'm a Dunkard."

Lizzie, whose alias was the straightforward Eliza A. Jones, laughed. "Perhaps that's all a part of the ruse. If you were called Dunkard, it would lead the rebels right to your doorstep."

It was easy to be lighthearted in that moment, when they had at last made contact with the gentlemen most likely to put their hard-won intelligence to good use. But as Lizzie rode home in the gathering twilight, she knew that invisible ink and an impenetrable code provided them with but scant protection. If it fell into the wrong hands, a message written in an indecipherable string of numbers would incriminate them as swiftly as one put down in plain English.

Although the Union army did not threaten the capital directly as that bleak January dragged on, disturbances within the borders of its defenses unsettled the populace. Almost daily the newspapers reported escapes from Castle Thunder, and on a single night, eighteen Yankee deserters believed to be spies fled the provost prison established in the Palmer & Allison tobacco warehouse on Cary Street by cutting through a wall into an adjoining commissary storehouse. Five nights later, on the same evening the president and Mrs. Davis hosted a gala reception at the Executive Mansion, an arsonist attempted to burn down the residence by placing a large quantity of combustible matter in one of the basement rooms and setting it on fire. Smoke billowing up the basement stairs alerted the occupants in time for them to extinguish the fire before much damage was done, but too late to prevent the culprit from helping himself to a quantity of groceries. Two days after that, arson or accident destroyed seven buildings at Camp Winder. Although the fire caused no injuries or deaths, more than fifty thousand dollars' worth of damage was done, including the loss of the commissary's building and most of the contents.

Compounding the pervasive anxiety was the dire scarcity of food. Lizzie's heart ached for the suffering of the very poor. Women who had never had to resort to begging before now stood on the sidewalks pleading for bread with tears in their eyes, often with hungry children clinging to their skirts. One day Lizzie went to the market to buy cornmeal, only to learn there was not a grain to be found. Undaunted, she proceeded to the City Mills, where she was told they had no corn and could procure none.

"But I hear the grinding of the mill," protested Lizzie. The noise of the millstones turning was loud and unmistakable.

"We grind what people bring to us," the miller explained. "If not for the toll we keep, I would have nothing to provide my own family. The people come to me crying for meal and I don't know what to do. I have nothing to give them, so they must starve."

"What shall we do?" said Lizzie faintly, more to herself than to him. She felt her knees grow weak and wished she could sit down. How would the city survive? It was too early in the year to plant a kitchen garden, much less harvest anything from one, and the Van Lews' winter stores of their farm's bounty were almost depleted. Their family was wealthier than most, but no fortune could buy what could not be had.

"I hear they're grinding at a little mill on the dock," the miller told her. "If you go there at once, they might have some left."

Lizzie thanked him and quickly raced off to Rocketts Wharf, where she found crowds swarming near the mill. They were indeed selling cornmeal, but they refused to sell more than a single peck to each family at any price. Although Lizzie would have preferred to acquire more, she supposed the rationing was only fair and promoted the greater good of all. A peck for her family cost her five dollars, astonishingly inexpensive for the times.

A few days later, she managed to obtain one hundred pounds of rice for fifty dollars, and soon thereafter she bought a bushel of cornmeal for seventy. That would keep the household fed for a while, but not forever. A starvation panic had gripped the city, and when she thought back to the Bread Riots of the previous spring, she realized that the fear of starvation could prove as dangerous as starvation itself.

All the while, compelled, perhaps, in part by hunger, Lizzie avidly searched for useful information to send to General Butler, determined to do her part to hasten the liberation of Richmond. At the end of the month, employing the cipher and the mysterious ink, she wrote her first official dispatch, hidden beneath a pleasantly boring letter from an aunt to her nephew about inflation and the weather.

January 30, 1864

Dear Sir:

It is intended to remove to Georgia very soon all the Federal prisoners; butchers and bakers to go at once. They are already notified and selected. Quaker knows this to be true. Are building batteries on the Danville road.

This from Quaker: Beware of new and rash council! Beware! This I send you by direction of all your friends. No attempt should be made with less than 30,000 cavalry, from 10,000 to 15,000 infantry to support them, amounting in all to 40,000 or 45,000 troops. Do not underrate their strength and desperation. Forces could probably be called into action in from five to ten days; 25,000, mostly artillery. Hoke's and Kemper's brigades gone to North Carolina; Pickett's in or about Petersburg. Three regiments of cavalry disbanded by General Lee for want of horses. Morgan is applying for 1,000 choice men for a raid.

Lizzie fervently wanted General Butler to understand that time was of the essence if he wanted to capture Richmond before thousands of prisoners were conveyed south beyond his reach, but he must strike with abundant forces or not at all, or the consequences would be disastrous. Her message was too urgent and too important to trust to the flag of truce ships, despite the protections of aliases and ciphers and invisible writing. To her relief, Merritt Rowley offered to carry the letter to General Butler himself. When his parents consented, Lizzie gratefully accepted, and after Mr. Rowley found Merritt a trustworthy guide, she sent off her dispatch with prayers for the youth's safety.

Lizzie knew she had given General Butler wise council founded upon sound observations and facts, painstakingly gathered and scrupulously interpreted. The course of action he decided to set in response was entirely out of her hands.

Chapter Eighteen

At a time when the Van Lew family was so preoccupied with other grave concerns that they had almost forgotten the danger, the day they had dreaded ever since the age limit for conscription was raised finally came.

John was drafted.

Over the previous year, he had received a series of medical deferments due to an old injury that made it painful for him to raise his left arm higher than his shoulder, but the Confederacy was running too low on vigorous young men to allow the slightly imperfect to be exempt any longer.

"I will not fight for a government I abhor," John said, utterly resolute. "I cannot do it. Nor can I turn my rifle upon a Union soldier knowing that his cause is just, even at the cost of my own life."

"What will you do?" asked Mother.

He spread his hands, a helpless gesture that told them he would resort to the best of the few options remaining to him. "I'll desert."

Lizzie nodded—she had expected as much—but Mother gasped. "Oh, John. Must you?"

"He must, and he will," said Lizzie firmly. They could not waste a moment in debate, not when John had already decided and they had so little time to plan.

John would have to close the hardware store and, with his income sharply curtailed, give up the residence on Canal Street. Annie and little Eliza would stay on at the Church Hill mansion, but when Mother offered to take in Mary too, John flatly refused. Despite his best efforts, Mary had fallen back into her disgraceful habits, and he did not want her anywhere near their daughters. She had a widowed cousin in the city who had offered to take her in before and likely would again if John prevailed upon her. As for John, their network of Unionist friends included several farmers outside the city; he could stay with one of them until it was safe for him to flee to Union lines, and from there, to Anna's home in Philadelphia.

Once resolved, they swiftly made the necessary arrangements, and after a tearful parting with his mother, sister, and daughters, John slipped away in the night to the farm of Jeb and Charlotte Hawkins about a mile northeast of the pickets guarding the road into the city. He carried with him gifts of gratitude for the Hawkins family, letters for Anna and her daughters, and all their hopes and prayers for his safety.

On the first Saturday of February, rumors circulated wildly throughout the city of a Union advance on Raccoon Ford and Morton's Ford on the Rapidan. For the next two days, Lizzie gathered all the information she could, her anticipation mounting as one source after another confirmed the presence of Union brigades in the area. Did this mark the opening sorties of General Butler's response to her dispatch? Was he, even now, mounting a raid upon Richmond to liberate its suffering prisoners?

On Monday morning, the **Examiner** weighed in: "How many of the startling stories circulated on yesterday, were mere Sunday rumors, and how much foundation of truth supported others, are questions not now to be completely answered," the reporter admitted. "It is at least certain that the enemy have advanced up the Peninsula, and their pickets can be seen from the railroad bridge over the Chicka-hominy. So far as is known, this column consists of eight thousand men; but it may be the advance of a more considerable force."

It had to be, Lizzie thought, dismay war-ring with hope in her heart. In her report to General Butler, she had been emphatically clear that Richmond could not be taken with fewer than tens of thousands of troops. Perhaps these eight thousand men the **Examiner** had counted were a diversionary body, and a more substantial force was even then stealing toward the city.

Within days, her suspicions were proven true, and her hopes for the success of the raid utterly dashed.

The Union demonstration along the Rapidan had indeed been a diversion, intended to distract the rebel army away from Bottom's Bridge, twelve miles east of the capital. There, convinced that a powerful and sudden surge would allow him to breach the city's defenses and liberate the prisons, Brigadier General Isaac J. Wistar sent forth a single cavalry brigade to capture and hold the bridge until he could send the infantry through. He did not realize that the excursion was doomed from the beginning. On the night before the attack, a private from New York, accused of murdering his lieutenant, escaped from his Union guards, fled to the rebel lines, and promptly divulged all he knew about the planned raid. Unaware of this betrayal, General Wistar's forces reached Bottom's Bridge only to find the road blocked by felled trees, the bridge destroyed, and Confederate artillery batteries and infantry regiments firmly entrenched within extensive earthworks and rifle pits. Though the Union brigade valiantly charged by the only passable route, the Confederates handily repulsed their assault, and since the element of surprise had obviously been lost, General Wistar broke off the attack and with-drew.

As Lizzie gathered scraps of informa-tion and pieced together the story of what had unfolded, she felt profoundly sorry for the Union prisoners, who might have been liberated that day if not for the betrayal of one of their own. If any good came of the failed raid, perhaps it would be that Gen-eral Butler surely now understood that when Lizzie reported that an attack would require a substantial force, she meant it, and no half measures would suffice.

General Wistar's failed raid added to the urgency of John's predicament, and Lizzie knew he would have to attempt to escape to Union lines soon. After he made it to the North—or God forbid, if he was cap-tured on the way—none of them knew when they might be reunited. Determined to see him one last time before he de-parted and well aware that she might not have another chance, Lizzie decided to visit him at the Hawkins farm. Rather than lead the authorities right to her brother, she donned a disguise she had employed successfully before—a coarse, ill-fitting dress; a heavy shawl; a deep, sun-bleached calico bonnet; and a battered market basket to carry on her arm—and as she walked, she adopted a stooping posture and a shuffling gait. Whether anyone recognized her she could not say, but no one stopped her except the pickets guarding the road at the city limits, and they took one look at her, gave her forged pass a single bored glance, and waved her through.

Jeb and Charlotte Hawkins were poor but industrious, the proud owners of ten rocky acres from which they reliably eked out enough corn and oats each year to feed themselves, their four children, and their livestock—a plow horse, a cow, and Charlotte's pride and joy, a flock of chickens reputed to be the most prolific layers in the county. John remained inside out of sight as Lizzie shuffled up the dirt path to the cottage, but Mrs. Hawkins spied her from the window and hurried outside to greet her, a wool wrap thrown over her faded calico dress, her long blond braid coiled around her head with only a few wisps out of place. She was five years younger than Lizzie but looked ten years older, toil in the sunshine and the cares of poverty having cruelly aged her beyond her years. And yet she had a beautiful smile, Jeb adored her, and her children admired and obeyed her, and she seemed to consider herself blessed.

"How glad I am to see you," she cried, beaming as she hurried to meet Lizzie half-way down the path. Charlotte was clever too, Lizzie noted; she had not called out Lizzie's name in greeting just in case an enemy was lurking nearby.

"And I you," said Lizzie, taking her hands and smiling back.

"My goodness, you're half-frozen," Charlotte exclaimed. She linked her arm through Lizzie's and escorted her to the cottage. "Come warm yourself."

"Oh, I'm fine. The walk kept me warm. How is my brother?"

"He is well." Charlotte hesitated. "You've come just in time. He hopes to set out to-morrow night."

"So soon?"

"We told him he's welcome to stay here as long as he likes, but the rebel patrols pass by too often these days, and he says he can't endanger us any longer. I think it's far riskier for him to take to the road. Maybe you can persuade him to delay."

"I won't even try, because I agree with him. Every day he spends beneath your roof puts you at risk." Lizzie paused at the door of the cottage and lifted the towel she had draped over the basket to keep out the snow flurries. "I brought some bread and cheese and apples, and Caroline made some little cakes for the children. It's not much, but I had to walk since our carriage is well known, and this was all I could fit in the basket." The dress she planned to wear the next day took up room in her basket too, but she'd had to bring it, since couldn't wear her disguise home lest she give herself away.

Charlotte's face lit up as she peered into the basket. "Thank you. What a welcome addition to our supper this will be. You're too generous."

"Me? Nonsense. This little basket can't even begin to repay you and Mr. Hawkins for your bravery and kindness in offering my beloved brother a safe haven." She decided not to mention that Peter would be bringing the wagon in the morning with more supplies; let it be a delightful surprise. "I don't know what we would have done without you."

"We Unionists have to look out for one another," Charlotte said stoutly as she led Lizzie indoors.

They stepped into a front room that ran the length of the cottage, a cookstove and table at one end, a fireplace with two chairs drawn up to it at the other. A braided rag rug lay on the floor, and on the back wall Lizzie spied a doorway leading to a bedroom. The cottage smelled of woodsmoke, wet wool, and frying lard—a humble, homey smell.

As soon as they crossed the threshold, John bounded out of the back room and swooped Lizzie up in a hug. "John, your shoulder," Lizzie exclaimed, laughing as she flung her arms around him.

Charlotte immediately set about preparing dinner, and over her protests Lizzie tied on an apron and joined in. While they worked, John queried Lizzie about Annie and little Eliza, his expression sad and full of longing. "You'll see them again soon," Lizzie promised cheerfully, although she had no way of knowing whether this was true and did not really believe it herself.

Supper was a simple but nourishing affair, and the children were sweet and charming, their parents kind and sympathetic. When the children finished eating and ran off to do their evening chores, the adults lingered at the table and spoke in hushed voices of the progress of the war and the recent activities of the underground, instinctively glancing at the windows for eavesdroppers from time to time, although the dogs would have barked a furious alarm had any strangers trespassed upon their secluded land.

Night fell. Charlotte tucked the children into bed in an upstairs room, while Jeb and John shared the room beside it, and Charlotte and Lizzie settled into the back room below. The sheets were freshly washed and smelled of the winter air, and someone had arranged a pretty bouquet of dried wildflowers in a glass at Lizzie's bedside. The Hawkins' courteous attention touched her deeply, and she felt anew the urgency for John to be on his way. It would go very badly for the family if they were discovered sheltering a deserter.

Lizzie lay down, pulled the pretty patchwork quilt up to her chin, and bade Charlotte good night. She expected Charlotte to climb in beside her, but instead she settled into a rocking chair in the corner. "Do you mind if I read a bit before turning in?" she asked, taking a worn black leather-bound Bible from a little shelf on the wall. "Or will the lamp keep you up?"

"Of course not. Read as long as you like. I'm so tired I won't even notice the light."

Charlotte thanked her and dimmed the lamp slightly. Lizzie rolled over onto her other side to put her back to the light and closed her eyes, wishing she could close her ears too. She was used to the noise of the city—horses' hooves and church bells and carriage wheels on cobblestones—but on the farm the silence was somehow deafening. In any other season, insects would have been raising a terrible racket, but all Lizzie heard as she drifted off to sleep was the wind buffeting the walls, the rattle of a loose shutter, the runners of Charlotte's chair softly creaking on the floorboards, and something else, a strange puffing, and there was an odd odor too, something familiar yet acrid—

Blinking, Lizzie propped herself up on her elbows and glanced about, only to find

Charlotte rocking gently, studying a page in her Bible, and puffing on a long-stemmed pipe. "Charlotte," Lizzie blurted. "Are you smoking?"

Charlotte looked abashed. "Oh, I know. Tobacco's a terrible extravagance if you don't grow it yourself, but in my defense I didn't buy it. A neighbor traded it to me for some eggs."

"Oh," said Lizzie for lack of anything else to say. Her astonishment had nothing to do with the expense.

Charlotte held out the pipe. "Would you like a puff?"

"Absolutely not," Lizzie declared, but then she hesitated. "Are you truly fond of it? It smells so—so dreadful, I beg your pardon but it's true."

Charlotte smiled and settled back into her chair. "You get used to it." She studied her pipe, rueful, before putting the stem between her teeth again. "It's better that you don't try it. You might decide that you like it very much, and tobacco's too hard to come by these days."

"Then I shall endeavor to resist temptation," Lizzie said, lying down again and closing her eyes.

She tried to sleep, but her astonishment as well as the lingering smell of tobacco smoke and the peculiarities of the unfamiliar room kept her awake long after Charlotte finally put away her pipe, doused the lamp, and came to bed. Although Lizzie eventually did drift off, she was startled awake several times by anxious dreams and a strange presentiment of danger. When dawn finally broke, she felt tired and drawn, and her head ached, although at breakfast she smiled and assured her hosts that she had passed the night in peaceful slumber.

Not long after she and Charlotte had tidied the kitchen and she was preparing herself for a sorrowful parting from her brother, she heard a wagon rumbling up the slope to the cottage. "Peter has come," she said, brightening somewhat as she rose from her chair, threw on her shawl, and went to meet him. The Hawkins's enjoyment of their gifts would fend off her sadness for a little while.

She called for the children to follow her outside to help bring in the food and other supplies they had obtained for John's hosts—a peck of rice and another of cornmeal, dried apples, a ham, and a few other delicacies, including silver dollars and good Union greenbacks, which were becoming more valuable day by day as the overprinting of Confederate bills weakened the local currency. In all the bustle of the children jumping up and down and racing into the house with the packages and Charlotte's tearful joy and Jeb's astonished, stammered thanks, Lizzie did not at first notice that Peter had said very little since his arrival, but as the Hawkins family returned inside, the clamor died down and she became aware of his strange reserve.

"Why don't you come inside and warm yourself?" she suggested. "I have to say good-bye to my brother, and then we can depart." She studied his face. "Something's wrong, I can see it. Is Mother ill, or the girls?"

"No, Miss Lizzie." Peter lowered his voice, glanced over his shoulder, and drew nearer. She was struck suddenly by the familiarity of his movements, a wary dance they all performed before confiding secrets. "The mass escape from Libby Prison you and Missus been expecting—it was last night."

Lizzie's heart thumped, and for a moment she couldn't breathe. "Last night?" she echoed. "What—how many? What's happening now?" She took a deep breath and pressed a hand to her heart to steady it, dismayed to think that when she could have been most useful to the prisoners, she had been miles away. "I imagine search parties are scouring every corner of the city."

"Yes, miss, they are." Peter hesitated. "I don't know how many men made it out all told, but it was a lot."

"No, I don't suppose you would know precisely. They were instructed to disperse among numerous safe houses, so they wouldn't all have come to us." Light-headed, she groped for the wagon and leaned back against its sturdy side. "How many are there at home? Did we have cots enough? Food?"

"Well, Miss Lizzie . . ." Peter grimaced, took a deep breath, and quickly plunged ahead. "There aren't any prisoners staying with us."

Lizzie stared at him, uncomprehending. "Why on earth not?"

"You see, Miss Lizzie, there were some

who came to the house, and knocked on the door, but William—well, all of us, not just him—we'd heard about the escape, and we feared that your enemies might see this as a good chance to catch you in the act of helping Yankees, and so they might send their own people to you pretending to be runaway prisoners. . . ."

"Do you mean to say," Lizzie said distinctly, disbelieving, "that last night, desperate prisoners came to our house, and knocked upon our front door, and were turned away?"

Bleakly, Peter nodded, but then he quickly shook his head. "They didn't knock upon the front door. They knocked on the door to the servants' quarters and asked for Colonel Streight."

"I know of him," said Lizzie. Colonel Abel Streight and nearly one hundred of his officers had been captured in May of 1863 during an extended raid through Georgia and Alabama. The rebels feared and reviled him more than any other inmate, for he had been accused of intimidating Confederate civilians and destroying their property. The guards at Libby hated him for his impudence and frank defiance of their threats, but those same qualities had earned him the admiration of every other officer in the prison.

"Colonel Streight escaped through the tunnel too, and I guess they thought he would come to you. They begged us to let them in, but William spotted other men across the street by Saint John's Church watching us from the shadows. It was too suspicious, Miss Lizzie. We had to send them away."

Distressed, Lizzie pressed the back of her hand to her forehead. "I should have been there." Of all the nights for her to go away, of all the nights for the prisoners to make a mass escape— "I should have been there to help." But she had not been, and lamenting and moaning would not change that. She pushed herself away from the wagon, straightened, and looked steadily up at Peter. "You and your brother made the prudent choice. I'm grateful that you thought first of protecting the family. Those men very well could have been rebel agents sent to entrap us. They've tried before."

"Yes, Miss Lizzie. My brother and I were mindful of that."

"Now we must get back to see what assistance we can yet offer. I'll say good-bye to John, and then we'll go." She spun around to hurry back into the cottage, but suddenly she stopped short, her heart plummeting. In the wake of the escape, pickets would be doubled at every bridge and crossroads. Patrols would be out in full force, searching the city and countryside for miles around for the escaped prisoners—or anyone else trying to elude the Confederacy.

Lizzie steeled herself and went inside to tell John.

His expression turned grave as she explained what had transpired in Richmond the night before. "Vigilance will be heightened a hundredfold," he said, dropping heavily into a chair. "They'll double or triple the patrols. I cannot hope to cross to Union lines now."

"No," said Lizzie. "No. It would be far too dangerous. It would be impossible."

Charlotte clutched her husband's arm and they exchanged a look of anxious resolve. "We've said it before, and we'll say it again," said Jeb stoutly. "You can stay here as long as you need. Till the end of the war if need be."

"I think you would grow weary of my company long before that." John stroked his beard absently, and for the first time Lizzie noticed that the black hairs were finely threaded with silver. "Perhaps I should report for duty after all, and resolve to be a very poor soldier."

"No," said Lizzie firmly. "I commend you for your refusal to fire upon Union soldiers, but I assure you, they won't repay the compliment. They'll see only the color of your uniform and turn their guns upon you. And if you don't first get shot by a Yankee, sooner or later your comrades will notice your reluctance to attack. They'll accuse you of cowardice or worse, and you'll end up being executed for treason or desertion."

"I'd prefer to avoid that if I can," said John, sighing.

"We'll think of something else. I will not have you marching off to war against the Union." Lizzie turned to Jeb and Charlotte. "Please accept my apologies, but my brother will need to impose upon your hospitality a little while longer."

Desperate situations sometimes required despicable remedies, so after bidding her brother and the Hawkins family good-bye, Lizzie had Peter drive her straight to General Winder's office without pausing at home to tell her mother how John's escape plans had been thwarted. She wrapped the heavy shawl around herself to ward off the cold as they raced back to Richmond, the wagon bouncing and jostling until her head ached. Along the way they passed Confederate soldiers on horseback and on foot, determinedly searching for the fugitives in even greater numbers than she had feared. When they reached the pickets, Lizzie queried them about the prison break, but the soldiers knew only that more than one hundred Yankees had escaped and about a dozen had already been recaptured. As they continued on their way, Lizzie could not help but wonder whether that count would be lower had she been home to receive the fugitives who had sought refuge there.

When she arrived at General Winder's office, she found his clerks bustling frantically as they dealt with the bureaucratic nightmare of the aftermath of a massive security failure. Although the outer office was full of officers, civilians, and newspapermen demanding an audience with the general, Lizzie was waved right through, perhaps because his secretary realized that of all his visitors, she was the least likely to rail at him.

General Winder received her kindly, but his face was haggard, and he looked as if he had not slept in days. "Well, Miss Van Lew," he said wearily, dropping heavily into his chair after courteously rising when she entered and waiting for her to sit. "Have you come to confess your role in this great humiliation?"

"No, General, certainly not," said Lizzie with genuine shock. "Surely you don't think I had any hand in this. You sound like my dreadful neighbors."

"No, no, of course not." He rested his elbows on the desk, closed his eyes, and rubbed his temples.

"General Winder—" She paused, steeled herself, and continued. "The truth is I was not even in Richmond last night."

"No?" he replied vaguely, his eyes still closed.

"No, but I have returned to throw myself upon the mercy of your office."

For a heartbeat he froze, and then he

lowered his hands and peered at her, bemused. "What have you done, Miss Van Lew?"

"It is not I but my brother who has made a mistake." She inhaled shakily. "A few years ago, he suffered a broken collarbone, which failed to heal properly because of all the lifting of boxes and equipment he is obliged to do every day at our hardware store. He cannot raise his left arm above his shoulder without pain, and for this reason he was entitled to a medical deferment from the draft."

"I see," said the general, expressionless.

"Not long ago, although his condition is in no way improved, his deferment was revoked. He was drafted and ordered to report to duty, but since he knew that to march to battle in his condition, unable to defend himself, would amount to suicide—" Lizzie dropped her gaze and waved a hand helplessly. "He deserted. I know that was wrong of him—"

"Yes, very wrong."

"And he realized that the moment he ran off, but he didn't know what to do. If he turned up at Camp Lee with no explanation for his delay, he could be thrown into Castle Thunder or shot or worse."

"And so your brother sends you, his emissary, to plead his case."

"Yes—well, no. This was entirely my idea." Lizzie clasped her hands in her lap, her fingers like ice. "He doesn't know that I'm here."

"He's fortunate to have such a devoted sister."

Lizzie managed a wan smile. "He didn't think so when we were very young, but through the years I think he has come to appreciate me better."

General Winder sat back in his chair, studying her. "Tell me one thing, Miss Van Lew," he said. "When your brother told you he intended to run off, did you discourage him?"

For a moment Lizzie wavered, but she was too exhausted and worried to invent a plausible lie. "I did not," she admitted. "I was frightened and thought only of his safety."

A grim, satisfied smile appeared on the general's face. "I suspected as much, but since you were brave enough to tell me the truth, I will help you."

Lizzie gasped and clasped her hands to her heart. "Oh, sir, would you?"

"Your brother should not have deserted," General Winder reminded her, tapping his desk with a forefinger for emphasis, "but bring him to me tomorrow morning, and I will do what I can for him."

Lizzie thanked him profusely and hastily departed before he could entertain second thoughts. From there she went immediately to McNiven's Bakery, where she arranged for Mr. McNiven to smuggle John back into the city in the delivery wagon. When John arrived home after nightfall, his daughters greeted him with great delight, smothering him in hugs and kisses while his mother and sister looked on, smiling but apprehensive for what the next day might bring.

In the morning, Lizzie and John reported to General Winder's office, where the general examined him and, thanks to John's convincing performance, concluded that he was indeed unfit for service. "I will see the examining physician personally and do all I can to secure you an exemption," he promised.

"I am in your debt, sir," said John, shaking his hand vigorously.

They arranged to call on the general again in two days' time, and remained hopeful in the interim, certain that General Winder's recommendation would be obeyed. But when the appointed hour arrived, the general told them that the examining physician had flatly denied the request and had demanded that John report for duty immediately.

"Is there anything more we could try?" asked Lizzie, distressed.

"There is something." The general turned to John. "Mr. Van Lew, you must join a company. The Eighteenth Virginia Regiment is mine, and if you choose it, I can protect you." He quickly wrote a letter to Colonel Peyton at Camp Lee, which he sealed and handed to John. "Deliver this to the colonel when you report. I've asked that he grant you a three-day furlough and allow you to select your regiment. I regret that this is all I can do for you."

John and Lizzie thanked him profusely and assured him that he had done a great deal for them and they would not forget it.

When John presented himself at Camp Lee, Colonel Peyton fumed and cursed, but he complied with General Winder's request, although out of spite he reduced the furlough from three days to two. John was issued a Confederate uniform, he reported for duty, and thanks to the liberal dispensation of gifts of whiskey to his fellow soldiers, he soon won the friendly feeling of the company. Because of General Winder's intervention, for the immediate future he would be permitted to reside at home and go about his usual business except in case of emergency, when he would be obliged to shoulder his rifle in defense of the city.

Whether that meant John was safe for months, weeks, or merely days, they did not know.

Chapter Nineteen

In the aftermath of the great Libby Prison break, all of Richmond hung on the astonishing details as they emerged, and thanks to Lieutenant Ross and Mr. Ford, the Van Lews soon knew more about the escape than anyone.

Libby Prison took up an entire city block, with Cary Street and the city to the north and the James River to the south. The basement was exposed on the riverside, and whitewashed so that any prisoners passing in front of it would stand out in stark relief. The eastern section of the basement contained an abandoned kitchen that had once been used by the prisoners, but had been closed off long ago due to persistent flooding and an infestation of rats. The stairway to this area, appropriately dubbed "Rat Hell," had been boarded up, but a group of prisoners led by Colonel Thomas E. Rose had contrived to move a stove and dig their way into an adjoining chimney to gain admittance to the eastern basement. From there they dug a tunnel three feet in diameter and roughly sixty feet long with no tools save a stolen chisel and a few wooden cuspidors, toiling day and night, nearly suffocated by the powerful, fetid stench of the nearby sewers as rats scurried over them and suspicious guards prowled about overhead.

After several thwarted attempts, including a near drowning when a tunnel flooded, Colonel Rose broke through to the surface behind a board fence on the other side of a vacant lot adjacent to the prison. The ringleaders had planned a stealthy, orderly egress on the night of February 9, but as word of the tunnel spread throughout the prison, more men desperately clamored to join the escape party. After Colonel Rose's original group slipped out, a mad stampede for the tunnel ensued and continued through the night until just before dawn, when those who remained behind replaced the stones to disguise the opening of the tunnel and crept back to their quarters.

At roll call on the morning of February 10, the inmates slipped in and out of the counting lines to confound the guards, whose counts kept coming up short by varying amounts. Only when the prisoners were accounted for by name did the baffled and horrified prison officials realize that one hundred and nine men were missing.

Unaware of the tunnel, Major Turner assumed the sentinels on watch that night had been bribed—a misapprehension the remaining prisoners encouraged with false reports—and immediately placed them under arrest and confined them in Castle Thunder. Couriers were sent in all directions to raise the alarm, and as Lizzie and Peter had observed, the number of pickets posted on the roads and bridges leading to the Peninsula had been doubled. In the meantime, a careful inspection of the prison had uncovered the entrance to the tunnel, and when Major Turner sent a small colored boy in to explore, guards, officials, and prisoners craning their necks at the windows looked on in astonishment as he soon popped out of the ground, grinning, in an open patch of land between two buildings on the other side of the fence.

The Confederates acted swiftly to recapture the Union fugitives before they could reach the embraces of Butler the Beast. One officer was spotted within the city by a newsboy, whose shouts alerted rebel soldiers, who promptly apprehended the poor man. Another fugitive was captured crossing a field outside the city by a hoe-wielding slave whose misguided loyalty compelled him to march the unfortunate man to his master's farmhouse, where a Confederate patrol soon collected him. Within a few days, fifty-two prisoners were caught and returned to Libby, including, tragically, Colonel Rose himself, who was captured within sight of Union pickets. These unfortunate men were given heroes' welcomes by their fellow inmates upon their return to prison, which Lizzie hoped would lessen the sting of their disappointment and blunt the pain of Major Turner's wrath. Furious and humiliated, he ordered the men clapped in irons in narrow and loathsome basement cells and placed on bread and water rations.

To Lizzie's horror, Major Turner inflicted the worst of his vengeance upon Mr. Ford, whom he suspected of complicity in the escape although he had no proof. The commandant ordered Mr. Ford whipped nearly to death, five hundred lashes, which he bravely bore without admitting his role or betraying a single member of the Union underground in whose homes the fugitives had sought refuge. As soon as Lizzie heard of Mr. Ford's sufferings, she used General Winder's pass to visit him in the prison hospital, where she offered him what comfort she could, changing his dressings and feeding him soothing broths. "You have earned your own escape," she murmured, tears in her eyes as she tended him. As soon as he regained his strength, and as soon as the means could be found, she would do everything in her power to spirit him away to the North.

In the days that followed, shocked, disbelieving citizens came to Libby in droves to view with their own eyes the tunnel, which was placed on exhibition and titled the "Great Yankee Wonder." Newspaper reporters gloated over the arrests of particular officers, such as Colonel Rose, and lamented the loss of others, especially the notorious Colonel Streight, whose recapture they coveted more avidly than any other prisoner's. Rumors abounded that many of the escapees had not yet fled to the North but were concealed in private homes throughout the city, biding their time until the search for them would be abandoned. Suspected Unionists came under increased scrutiny, and one morning Lizzie stepped out upon her front portico to discover a pair of uniformed guards watching her home. She expected them to demand admittance so they could search the mansion from cellar to attic, but although the Van Lews spent several anxious days waiting, the guards did nothing more obtrusive than watch the house and take note of their visitors.

As Lizzie privately rejoiced for every fugitive who avoided recapture and lamented each one returned to prison, she noted well the effect the mass escape had on the people of Richmond, prison keepers and civilians alike, and concluded that it was wrong to evaluate the success of the breakout solely upon the number of men who managed to reach Union lines. Until the events of early February disabused them of the notion, no one—including Lizzie herself—had believed that an escape from Libby Prison on such a grand scale was even remotely possible. The Confederate capital was greatly upset by the failure of its prison to retain its prisoners, and their confidence was badly shaken, in sharp contrast to the immense satisfaction and soaring morale of the prisoners who remained behind. Their machinations had kept the escape secret until the last possible moment, so that more than twelve hours had elapsed before the Confederates realized that a massive jailbreak had occurred. Lizzie was certain that those precious hours had made all the difference to the men who remained free.

In the weeks after the breakout, the angry and embarrassed guards at Libby Prison lashed out at their Union captives, reducing their rations, pawing through their meager stores, arbitrarily confiscating their few possessions, and subjecting them to constant scrutiny and invective.

On Belle Isle, every day the suffering prisoners slipped closer to death. Tentatively at first, but with increasing boldness, Lizzie asked to be allowed to visit the soldiers there, and to take them a few comforts, food and blankets and clothing. Near the end of February, the authorities finally relented and agreed that she and a single companion could tour the perimeter of the outdoor stockade under strict surveillance.

Lizzie first asked Eliza to accompany her, but her friend blanched and begged off. "I could not bear it," she said. "The rumors of that harrowing place are enough to give me nightmares. Forgive me, but I haven't the courage."

"I understand," Lizzie assured her, smiling sympathetically and patting her hand, although Eliza's refusal dismayed her. "Few of the boldest men at the highest levels of army and government have toured Belle Isle. If they cannot look upon what they themselves have wrought, how could I expect my most tenderhearted friend to do so?"

John volunteered to escort her, though he had never visited Libby or Castle Thunder or any of the hospital wards. Lizzie had observed dreadful scenes of suffering in prisons and hospitals before, but Belle Isle surpassed in wretchedness and squalid filth her most grim and vivid imaginings. Long lines of forsaken, despairing, hopeless-looking beings gazed upon Lizzie, John, and their stone-faced military escort with gaunt hunger staring from their sunken eyes. The wind whipped her shawl into her face as she took in the crowds packed onto the frozen patch of bare earth, the wretched, smoky, tattered tents, the men lying on the ground, some without a scrap of a blanket over or under them, some picking vermin off their legs, some slowly and methodically searching their clothing for more, all within a few steps of the newly made graves of their late companions. Their despair was tangible, and Lizzie had to fight back sobs and resist the urge to cover her eyes and beg her escort to lead them away from that place of horrors. Instead she and John distributed their gifts— hopelessly inadequate to the overwhelming need—and she felt her heart break when the men could barely summon up the strength to accept them. When she had nothing left to offer them, when even words failed her, she clung to John's arm and asked the guard to take them back across the bridge to the city.

As they left the island behind, she felt the prisoners' weary, longing, dying eyes upon her back, and she could no longer hold back her tears. John put his arm around her but could find no words of comfort. She did not care what the guard thought of her grief but rather wondered, angrily, how he could refrain from weeping himself, to witness such suffering day after day and to know he was complicit in it. Soon there would be nothing of Richmond's humanity left to save.

"Oh, day of deliverance," she murmured, "will you never come?"

The Union had to make another raid upon Richmond, and this time, it could not fail.

Word came to Lizzie from her sources in the North of a scheme proposed by Brigadier General H. Judson Kilpatrick and endorsed by President Lincoln himself. The general—who had earned the nickname "Kill-Cavalry" for his bravery and recklessness—would thrust at the north of the Confederate capital with three thousand troops, and Colonel Ulric Dahlgren would split away with nearly five hundred men to cross the James above Richmond. Colonel Dahlgren—twenty-one, handsome, and headstrong—would sweep downstream on the south side to free the prisoners on Belle Isle, while General Kilpatrick would plunge into the city to liberate Libby and the other prisons. With thousands of freed Union men joining their forces, they would set fire to the city and capture Confederate leaders.

When Lizzie, Mr. Rowley, and Mr. Mc-Niven discussed the scant details of the campaign that had been divulged to the Richmond underground, the two men concurred that the attack, expected to come in the first few days of March, was bold but risky, for the two commands would be unable to communicate until they reached the city perimeter. Lizzie had stronger misgivings; she doubted that the weak, emaciated, unarmed prisoners, once freed, would be in any condition to join the attack in the numbers General Kilpatrick expected. Even so, Lizzie took reassurance from the reputations and accomplishments of the two commanders. In May of 1863, General

Kilpatrick had led the most destructive column of Stoneman's raiders during the Battle of Chancellorsville, destroying valuable Confederate depots, bridges, warehouses, and other resources on the outskirts of Richmond, which eminently qualified him to lead a similar, though more audacious, sortie on the city. Colonel Dahlgren, the son of Rear Admiral John A. Dahlgren, cut an even more dashing figure. Despite his youth, he had already earned acclaim for bravery, valor, and strong leadership; although he had lost a leg at Gettysburg, as soon as he could sit a horse, he had donned a prosthetic and resumed his command.

The Union underground did not know precisely when the attack would come or where, but they made ready as best they could. Through Robert Ford, who was still recovering from his terrible beating, Lizzie informed the officers held in Libby that the raid was imminent, and Mr. Ford reported back that they were organizing into companies to fight under the command of whoever liberated them. Lizzie also sent a warning, though she could not identify her source: Lieutenant Ross had learned that

Major Turner had planted kegs of gunpowder in the basement, enough to blow up the prison and all its inhabitants, which he had vowed to do before letting it fall to Yankee invaders.

Their first indication that the raid had begun were rumors that Union cavalry had crossed the Rapidan River beyond the west flank of General Lee's army—a distraction, Lizzie surmised, if indeed it was truly happening—and reports that telegraph lines into the city had been cut. The second sign was unmistakable: Terrified countryfolk sought refuge in the city, with tales of Yankee marauders rampaging close behind. The alarm bell on Capitol Square pealed, summoning the home guard to defend the city—a poorly trained mass of underage boys, aged men, and clerks, as well as officers on furlough. John reluctantly donned his uniform and reported to Camp Lee, sent off with tearful hugs and kisses from his daughters, mother, and sister. But Lizzie's apprehensions were not for John alone. If General Kilpatrick's plan had depended upon the element of surprise, it had already been lost.

On the first day of March, an oppressive,

heavy silence hung over the capital. The home defense brigade was organized into five battalions and sent to the battlefront, while the women and infirm left behind to wait and worry rolled bandages and prepared for another onslaught of wounded and prisoners, if not an invading army. Curiosity compelled Lizzie to drive out in the afternoon, and at Camp Lee she found the militia drilling. Although she did not see John among the men, she spotted others she knew to be Unionists. She wondered if fear of invasion had roused them to join the defenders, or if like John they had used up all their exemptions. She felt the ponderous dread as strongly as any citizen of Richmond, but for different reasons; she passionately wanted the Union troops to sweep into the city, but she knew what General Kilpatrick and Colonel Dahlgren could not—that the rebels were prepared to defend their city fiercely.

Later that day, artillery fire boomed about a mile outside the city. Windows rattled and china clattered in the cupboards, and Lizzie paced and listened and waited. All the sounds of battle came from the north, which suggested that General Kilpatrick's forces were in place, but where was Colonel Dahlgren?

Then the sounds of battle diminished. "No," murmured Lizzie, racing up the stairs and outside to the rooftop. The raid had to succeed. They had endured three years of bitter, bloody war and daily life under a hostile regime. The prisoners on Belle Isle would surely perish if they were not liberated soon. "No, no, no." Shivering in the wind, she shielded her eyes from the whirling snow with her hands and peered off to the north, but she saw nothing—no smoke, no rebel troops hastily retreating back into the city. The view to the south was equally ordinary. "No," she said again, letting her hands fall to her sides. They were not coming. Hours of daylight remained. The fighting would not have stopped unless one side had forced the other into retreat or had utterly vanquished them, and if the Union had triumphed, she would soon glimpse signs of their swift march upon Richmond.

She waited, clutching her arms about herself to ward off the cold, but there was nothing.

Heartsick, she descended into the house, found her mother, Judy, and Louisa in the parlor, and reported what she had seen. "When John returns, he may be able to tell us what happened," she said dully, sinking into a chair. "I'll contact the military clerks on my payroll in a few hours, to give them time to read the dispatches from the field." Suddenly it occurred to her that some of her clerks might have witnessed the battle firsthand as members of the Departmental Battalion, the reserve company composed of deskbound clerks, who ordinarily saw no battle fiercer than jealous squabbling among their superior officers.

Before nightfall, Lizzie's suspicions were confirmed: General Kilpatrick's incursion had indeed been the cause of the artillery fire they had heard earlier that day, but after his cavalry raiders had advanced as far as the inner line of Richmond's defenses, he had withdrawn to the outskirts of the city. She did not yet know why. None of Lizzie's informants in the War Department mentioned Colonel Dahlgren or a second raid from the south. She could only imagine what had become of the dashing young officer.

It was not until the next day that Lizzie learned the disheartening truth. A former slave had been assigned to guide Colonel Dahlgren and his riders to a little-used crossing over the James, but when they arrived, they had discovered that heavy rains had rendered the ford impassible. Furious and convinced that the guide had betrayed him, Colonel Dahlgren had ordered him hanged by the roadside, providing his own reins for the grisly deed.

On March 2, with his original plan foiled and unaware of General Kilpatrick's retreat, rather than abandon his mission, Colonel Dahlgren had decided to ride east above the James and charge into Richmond. His men had broken through the Confederates' outer defenses at Westham Plank Road near Benjamin Green's farm, but had been turned back by strong resistance from the Departmental Battalion. With the surprise attack thwarted, Colonel Dahlgren had withdrawn, splitting his forces to better avoid the Confederate defenses and riding on himself with little more than one hundred men. Late that night, Colonel Dahlgren had ridden into an ambush near Mantapike in King and Queen County, and in a quick exchange of fire, the dashing young officer had been shot and killed.

The Confederates stripped him and dumped his corpse over a fence to protect it from hogs roaming the road, and the next morning, they fashioned a rough pine coffin and buried the slain officer where he had been killed, at a crossroads in a slushy, muddy hole about two feet deep.

Though Colonel Dahlgren was the only man killed in the skirmish, all but twenty-one of his companions were taken prisoner and one hundred horses were captured. The men were marched into Richmond and confined within Libby Prison, where many prominent citizens were allowed to visit them for the sole purpose of disparaging and castigating them in person. Lieutenant Ross later told Lizzie that Mrs. Seddon, the wife of the secretary of war, had screeched insults at the men—"Thieves! Murders! Fiends! Hell monsters! Assassins!"—and had declared that she would use all the influence she possessed to see the men hanged, and if she could not accomplish that, she would have them thrown into dungeons and starved to death.

Over the next few days, the Richmond press and the rumor mill ran rampant with stories of the failed raid, and the death of the handsome young Yankee provoked a particular fascination that Lizzie found disrespectful and gruesome even as she too pored over every painful detail. Three days after his death, a shocking report appeared in the **Enquirer** claiming that a thirteen-year-old member of the home guard had searched Colonel Dahlgren's person for valuables shortly after he was killed, and discovering a cigar case, a memorandum book, and several folded documents, he dutifully passed them on to his teacher, who was also his commander. The papers included a schedule for the raid, a checklist of assignments, special orders for different groups within the party, and an address Colonel Dahlgren had delivered to his men at headquarters before they embarked on their mission. The papers and memoranda, the newspaper trumpeted, contained "the indisputable evidence of the diabolical designs of the enemy," which they revealed in long excerpts from the offensive documents. "We hope to release the prisoners from Belle Island first," Colonel Dahlgren had written in his address, "and having seen them fairly started, we will cross the James River into Richmond, destroying the bridges after us and exhorting the released prisoners to destroy and burn the hateful city; and do not allow the rebel leader Davis and his traitorous crew to escape." In his special orders and instructions, the colonel had exhorted, "The prisoners loose and over the river, the bridges will be secured and the city destroyed. The men must keep together and well in hand, and once in the city it must be destroyed and Jeff Davis and cabinet killed."

Richmond exploded in outrage. Their worst accusations about the inhumanity of President Lincoln and his generals had been confirmed. In plotting the assassination of President Davis and his cabinet, the Yankees had provided irrefutable proof that they were barbarians, too cowardly, unprincipled, and vile to abide by the accepted rules of warfare.

Lizzie could not believe it. If the Dahlgren Papers existed—and she had not seen them, so she had no reason to believe that it was not all a complete fiction—they were surely forgeries, invented to incite and infuriate all of rebeldom and bring shame upon President Lincoln, his cabinet, and his generals. The raiders had been under orders to capture the Confederate leaders, not to kill them, but Colonel Dahlgren's shocking execution of his Negro guide, who had probably acted in all innocence, made the wild claims all the more believable.

Truth or lie, the effects of the revelations were immediate. The day after the shocking orders appeared in the Richmond dailies, Colonel Dahlgren's body was dug up and transported to the York River Railroad Depot, where vast crowds of the curious came to gape at it. Appalled, Lizzie stayed away, and she was sickened by a description of the spectacle that appeared in the **Whig** two days later:

DAHLGREN'S BODY.

—The body of Col. Ulric Dahlgren, killed in the swamps of King and Queen, by the Ninth Virginia Cavalry, was brought to the city Sunday night, and laid at the York River depot during the greater part of the day yesterday, where large numbers of persons went to see it. It was in a pine box, clothed in Confederate shirt and pants, and shrouded in a Confederate blanket. The wooden leg had been removed by one of the soldiers. It was also noticeable that the little finger of the left hand had been cut off. Dahlgren was a small man, thin, pale, and with red hair and a goatee of the same color. His face wore an expression of agony.

About 2 o'clock P.M. the corpse was removed from the depot and buried—no one knows, or is to know, where.

Mother was so appalled by the outrages committed upon the young man's body that she wept. "They took his artificial leg?" she choked out, disbelieving, shoving the newspaper to the far end of the sofa as if distance would erase the ghastly images from her mind's eye. "They cut off his finger? Why?"

"According to the **Examiner**, to claim the precious ring that encircled it," Lizzie said tightly as she paced the length of the parlor. "They say it was something of the curse he came to bestow upon others, visited upon himself. Those forged papers have maddened the people, and they are so used to inflicting wrath upon their slaves that they believe every offense must be answered with violence."

"His poor father," Mother lamented. "His family, his friends. How will they ever cease mourning? They were denied the right to keep vigil by his body. They will never know where he has been laid to rest. They will never be able to visit his grave and see that it is properly tended. It is . . . it is uncivilized and cruel!"

"Their hatred has overpowered their reason." Lizzie was too angry to weep, too offended to lament. She had seen too many good Union men denied a proper burial, refused the rites of their faiths and creeds. The men flung into pits like offal after the Battle of Bethel Church. The hasty and quiet funeral of Mr. Huson. The countless corpses dropped into shallow holes on Belle Isle a mere few yards away from their dying comrades. Colonel Dahlgren's disrespectful treatment and ignominious burial were simply too much.

"We must find the hidden grave," Lizzie declared, "and remove his honored dust to friendly care."

This would be no small task, she knew, but the heart of every loyal Unionist had been stirred to its depths by the heinous mutilation of the young colonel's corpse, and when she contacted her most trustworthy, intrepid agents to enlist their help, every one of them immediately agreed. Although Colonel Dahlgren had been denied a good death, they were resolved to see that he received a good interment, with all the proper rituals observed.

They knew that Colonel Dahlgren had been laid to rest outside Oakwood Cemetery, where all the Union dead were buried so as not to desecrate the hallowed ground where Confederate soldiers were interred, but they did not know which of the unmarked graves belonged to him. Several of Lizzie's deputies volunteered to find out where he lay, a task perilous in no small degree because Mr. Davis himself had warned the public, both in the press and before Congress, that no one was ever to know.

While the Unionists carefully cultivated their sources, the grieving Admiral Dahlgren repeatedly prevailed upon the Confederate agent of exchange to return his son's remains to his bereaved family. At first the officials refused, and then they relented, and at the end of March, the admiral awaited the flag of the truce boat at Fort Monroe, expecting to receive his son's casket only to be bitterly disappointed to discover that the rebels had reneged. A few days later, the Richmond **Examiner** jeered at the failed exchange, mocking both the request and the Confederate officials who had almost granted it.

THE BODY OF DAHLGREN.

—Northern papers hint significantly to the fact that the body of Ulric, the Hun, who lost his dog's life in prosecuting an unholy crusade against Richmond, and who was buried with all the dishonours of war, is to be disinterred from its unknown grave, and delivered over into the embrace of an impious father, who has for months been striving, with all the ingenuity of a devil, to make a bon-fire of the peaceful homes of Charleston, South Carolina. What has become of the gusty pronunciamento of the Confederate Government, that Ulric Dahlgren's body should be disclosed only by the trump of the last judgment? Butler's trumpet call for it has been more potent than Gabriel's, and behold he appeareth!

Not yet, Lizzie thought, stinging with anger from the malicious taunts. Colonel Dahlgren had not yet risen from his ignoble grave, but he would.

Even as rebel patrols were still rounding up Yankee stragglers and the newspapers were calling for the captured raiders to be summarily executed, the grocer F. W. E. Lohmann's discreet inquiries around the city led him at last to an eyewitness. A workman had been out in the burying ground at midnight when the Confederates brought in Colonel Dahlgren's coffin, and concealing himself behind a tree, he watched and waited until the men departed, and then carefully marked the grave.

Lizzie provided the sizable stack of Confederate bills required to persuade the man to divulge the site. In the midst of a fierce and frigid tempest on the night of April 6, more than a month after the colonel had been slain, Mr. Lohmann, his brother, and the workman unearthed the coffin, pried off the lid, and identified the body by its missing limb. Then the two brothers quickly loaded the coffin onto a mule-drawn cart and took it to Mr. Rowley's farm, from whence they summoned certain trustworthy Unionist friends for the funeral.

When Lizzie, John, and their mother arrived at the Rowley farm the next morning, they discovered the coffin lying atop a makeshift catafalque in an outbuilding and Mr. Rowley keeping vigil nearby. "Oh, Mr. Rowley," Lizzie said tearfully, taking his hand. "Such a mournful day."

"But such a triumphant one too," he replied, clasping his other hand over hers and managing a weary, encouraging smile. He had probably sat there all night, paying the slain officer the respect and honor he had been denied since the moment he had fallen.

Soon the Lohmann brothers arrived, bearing a metallic coffin that would provide a far more suitable resting place than the pine box the Confederates had cobbled together out in the field. Lizzie marveled that they had been able to procure one, since it was common knowledge that only one or two such fine caskets existed in Richmond anymore, but the brothers

had proven themselves astonishingly re-
sourceful. "God bless you for your courage,"
she said fervently, shaking their hands in
turn. "When I think of what would have become of you had you been discovered in
the graveyard—" She pressed her lips together and shook her head, unable to continue.

"We weren't observed, so you needn't
be troubled," said the elder of the pair. "It
is Mr. Rowley who needs our prayers now."

Lizzie nodded, inhaling deeply. Mr. Rowley had volunteered to transport Colonel
Dahlgren to his final resting place, the farm
of a loyal Unionist near Hungary Station. It
would be a perilous journey past the Confederate picket posts, which had been
strongly reinforced to protect Richmond
from any forthcoming Union raids.

Before long more Unionists arrived,
among them Charles Palmer and Franklin
Stearns, whom she knew well. When all
were assembled, several of the gentlemen
transferred the body from the pine box into
the coffin, and with sad and sorrowful
hearts, the mourners gathered around. Mr.
Rowley led them in prayer, and a few of the
men offered brief remarks, and as a final

parting ritual, they cut off locks of his hair to be preserved as mementos for his father.

After Mr. Lohmann sealed the casket, the gentlemen solemnly conveyed it to Mr. Rowley's wagon, where they concealed it beneath dozens of young peach trees, packed as neatly and tightly as a nursery would have done. As the Lohmann brothers set out on horseback ahead of the wagon as guides and lookouts, Mr. Rowley took the driver's seat, gave the command to the horses, and drove away.

When they had disappeared around a bend in the road, Mrs. Rowley invited them all inside for something to eat, but none of them had much of an appetite. They spoke quietly of how well the colonel had looked, considering how long his rough, coarse coffin had lain beneath the soil, and how unlike the descriptions in the Richmond press. His face had not borne a look of agony, they all agreed, but one of firm and marvelous energy, which spoke well of his spiritual state at the time of his death.

As the afternoon waned, most of the mourners departed for their homes, but the Van Lews remained behind at Mr. Rowley's request—in case he was prevented from returning, he had told Lizzie privately. She dared not allow herself to think too much of this possibility, although she realized that if the pickets inspected the wagon too carefully, by ordering Mr. Rowley to unpack the trees or simply by poking the load with a bayonet, he would be undone. Death would be his reward, but first torture so he would reveal his accomplices.

They spent the night in restless sleep and the next day in pensive waiting. Then, at last, an hour before dusk, they heard the wagon approaching and raced outside to meet it. Mr. Rowley was alone, for the Lohmann brothers had returned home by another route. He looked even more exhausted than he had the day before, so Lizzie and Mrs. Rowley took him inside while John and Merritt tended to the horses.

"It was the most terrifying ride of my life," Mr. Rowley admitted as he ate a bowl of stew his wife had kept warm for him. "I tried to appear unconcerned as I approached the picket post—letting the reins fall with perfect indifference when a lieutenant ordered a guard to inspect the wagon."

"Oh, dear," Mother said. "What did you do?"

"I nodded to the guard in greeting," Mr. Rowley replied, "but before he could address me, another wagon approached from the opposite direction, driven by a man with a furrowed brow and an anxious frown. The guard hesitated, looked from me to him and back, and seeing me at my leisure, he went to inspect the other driver first."

"Did you charge through the post when his back was turned?" joked Merritt.

Mr. Rowley smiled briefly. "Of course not, son. I wouldn't be sitting here with you if I had. Instead I sat as if I had patience in abundance, and when the guard returned his attention to me, I engaged him in an easy conversation about the cultivation of peach trees. By this time, a cart had come along, and the guard broke off to go examine it. When he returned again to me, I picked up the thread of our discussion and kept him talking until another wagon rolled up. Twice more his duties interrupted our friendly chat, and then, when we had quite exhausted the subject of peach trees, he said, 'It would be a pity to tear those trees all up, when you have packed them there so nicely.'"

"We have the Lohmann brothers to thank for that," said John.

"Indeed we do. The guard went on to say, but not loudly enough for his lieutenant to overhear, 'I don't want to hinder you any longer. I think it all right, anyway your honest face is guarantee enough for me—go on.' And with that he waved me on through without disturbing a single twig of my cargo."

"You do have an honest face," Lizzie remarked.

"Did you find a peaceful spot to lay the poor boy to rest?" Mother asked.

"Yes, Madam, we did. After I reached Mr. Orrick's farm, the brothers and I finished digging the grave he had already begun, and we buried him in the company of Mr. Orrick's wife and two good German women, neighbors and Unionists both. We planted a peach tree over the grave."

"A fitting memorial," said Mrs. Rowley quietly, and they all fell into a reflective silence.

In the days that followed, Lizzie and Mr. Rowley attempted to send word to Admiral

Dahlgren that devoted friends of the Union had taken possession of his son's remains so that proper respect would be shown to them, and so that they could be conveyed to him at the earliest possible date. Evidence that the grieving father had not received their letters appeared at regular intervals in the Richmond papers in the form of updates on his ongoing campaign to convince the Confederate government to return his son's body to him—and in mid-April, they finally agreed. On the appointed day, however, a bemused reporter for the **Examiner** noted, "The late Colonel Dahlgren's body did not go down under the flag for the best of reasons—it could not be produced."

"Oh, dear," Lizzie murmured, alarmed, and then she laughed.

Chapter Twenty

APRIL–OCTOBER 1864

The grave in which the body was buried was opened under the direction of the officials who interred the remains," the **Examiner** testily reported the next day, "but the grave was empty—Dahlgren has risen, or been resurrected, and the corpse was not to be found. If the facts be as stated, an explanation and apology, not the corpse, will go down to City Point by the present flag of truce."

By the time the article appeared, Lizzie had managed to get word to General Butler that Colonel Dahlgren's remains were safely beyond Confederate reach, but the

Richmond press and the Confederate government remained ignorant, mystified, and unsettled. In distinct contrast, the incident had left the Union underground satisfied and invigorated, and they took much secret amusement from the rebels' consternation.

Each glimmer of hope and levity, however small and fleeting, offered them much-needed encouragement in an apprehensive season. Everyone knew that as soon as the spring sunshine dried the muddy roads of Virginia enough to make them passable, the armies would be on the move. For the first time, General Lee would face General Ulysses S. Grant, who had triumphed in Tennessee and at Vicksburg but had provoked harsh criticism, including demands that President Lincoln remove him from command, for the devastating casualties taken at the Battle of Shiloh. At the time, Mr. Lincoln had famously replied, "I can't spare this man; he fights," and in March, the president emphasized his confidence by promoting him to lieutenant general and naming him general-in-chief of the armies of the United States. General Grant made his priorities clear by establishing his headquarters in the field with his army rather than in Washington City, and in April, he halted all prisoner exchanges.

In March, so many hundreds of Union prisoners had been shipped south or exchanged that in the last week of the month, the **Whig** reported that only eighteen hundred remained in Richmond, but Lizzie knew that number would rapidly soar with the prisoner cartel shut down. Although she was dismayed on behalf of the prisoners languishing in Libby and Belle Isle and elsewhere in the capital, she understood General Grant's rationale. Every Confederate prisoner freed was a rebel soldier returned to the battlefield, killing more Union men and prolonging the war.

On a warm, breezy afternoon on the last day of April, Lizzie was playing with Annie and Eliza in the gardens when Mary Jane unexpectedly paid her a visit. Lizzie frequently received encoded notes from Mary Jane as well as messages conveyed by Mr. McNiven, but they had not seen each other in weeks. Delighted, Lizzie embraced her, offered her a cup of tea, and invited her to stay for supper, but Mary Jane pressed her lips together, shook her head, and said, "No, thank you. I haven't any appetite."

Only then did Lizzie notice that Mary Jane looked queasy and drawn. "What's the matter?" she asked, guiding her to a chair on the piazza.

"There was a dreadful accident at the Gray House today."

Lizzie's first thought was that President Davis had been killed. A few scattered attempts on his life had already been made—but no, Mary Jane had called it an accident. "What happened? Is Mr. Davis—"

"Grieving but otherwise unharmed." Mary Jane placed a hand on her abdomen and took a deep breath. "At about one o'clock, I was helping Mrs. Davis carry lunch to Mr. Davis's office on the second floor. Sometimes he's so preoccupied with work that he forgets to eat. Mrs. Davis had just uncovered the basket when the children's nurse came running."

"Oh, dear," Lizzie murmured, sinking into a chair.

"The children had been playing in Mrs. Davis's room, but when she left to arrange her husband's lunch, Joseph—he's the four-year-old—he wandered onto the rear balcony, climbed onto the railing, slipped— and fell to the brick walk below."

"My goodness, the poor child. Is he—"

Mary Jane shook her head, her eyes filling with tears. "His brother Jeff ran down to him, but when Joseph didn't move, he ran to find Catherine." She paused to clear her throat. "He told her, 'Joe wouldn't wake up,' and when she looked and saw him lying so still, she ran for Mrs. Davis."

Lizzie reached out and clasped Mary Jane's hands, unable to speak.

"We all ran down to him together, the Davises, Caroline, and I, but there was nothing we could do. He lived only a few minutes longer, cradled in his father's arms."

"The poor child—and the poor parents!"

"The Davises are devastated—utterly torn apart. Joseph was his father's greatest joy and hope. Mr. Davis kept saying, 'Not mine, oh, Lord, but thine,' over and over again, completely distraught. A messenger brought him a dispatch—"

"He couldn't have waited?" exclaimed Lizzie. "Has he no heart?"

"Mr. Davis held the dispatch for a moment, looking at it but not really seeing it, and then he handed the paper to an aide and said, 'I must have this day with my little child.' And Mrs. Davis—oh, how she screamed and screamed."

Lizzie imagined the scene all too vividly. "Mary Jane, I'm so sorry."

"His poor little body lying broken on the bricks—" Mary Jane shuddered. "I see it afresh every time I close my eyes."

"Try not to think about it," Lizzie urged. "The shock will fade. The vision won't torment you forever."

"No, that unhappy fate belongs to Mr. and Mrs. Davis," said Mary Jane. "You know they've lost a son before, in Washington."

"I had heard that."

"And Mrs. Davis is with child again even now, did you know?"

"You told me," Lizzie reminded her gently. "I do hope she takes care of herself. Such a terrible grief cannot be good for her baby. Is anyone there to look after her?"

"She has her maid, and her friend Mrs. Chesnut was immediately summoned, and other friends are coming tonight—" Mary Jane caught herself. "And Mary, John's Mary, she came too, with Mrs. Chesnut."

Lizzie felt a jolt. "She's well enough to call on friends?" Not only to call, but with enough presence of mind to comfort a grief-stricken mother. Mary must be well recovered, then. Lizzie had heard nothing from her since they had given up the house on Canal Street and Mary went to stay with her widowed cousin and John returned to Church Hill. Lizzie knew she ought to be relieved that Mary had been restored to health, but instead the news filled her with trepidation.

"Apparently so. She didn't recognize me," Mary Jane quickly added, before Lizzie even thought to ask. "She never paid much attention to black faces, and she's never seen me in a maid's garb before. Her gaze slipped right past me as if we had never met." Her tone had turned bitter. "If her visits become too frequent, though, I may have to resign."

"Of course." Lizzie felt a pang of regret at the thought of losing such an essential part of her intelligence network, but if Mary Jane was recognized and exposed, the entire Richmond underground could be ruined.

"But none of this is why I came to see you today." Mary Jane shook her head as if clearing it of shock and horror. "The provost marshal's office and the Signal Bureau are blaming spies for every setback the Confederacy has faced in recent months."

"With good reason," said Lizzie, thinking of the Libby Prison break and Colonel Dahlgren's mysterious resurrection.

"They're demanding that the president and Congress take firm, decisive, and immediate action to discover and eliminate the spies in their midst."

"Eliminate?" Lizzie echoed warily.

Mary Jane nodded.

"So we can expect harsher measures directed toward suspected Unionists."

Mary Jane nodded again. "You should prepare, you and all your friends."

Lizzie thanked her for the warning and again offered her tea or perhaps coffee, and this time, Mary Jane gratefully accepted a cup of coffee. She was probably expecting the ersatz coffee that had become the beverage of last resort in the capital, but Lizzie surprised her with a cup of real, rich, robust coffee, made from freshly roasted and ground beans smuggled in from the North. Lizzie had intended to use the delicacy to win friends in influential places, but Mary Jane had been through quite an ordeal, and a good cup of coffee would brace her. There would still be enough left over for the weak-willed clerks and guards she meant to win over, low-paid staff who could hardly afford their daily bread on their pitiful salaries, what with food stores diminishing and prices inching higher day by day.

As soon as Mary Jane departed, Lizzie sent out a flurry of coded messages, warning her friends to take every precaution and not a single unnecessary risk. Jefferson Davis was distraught and grieving, and in that state of mind, he would show them no mercy.

Less than a week later, excitement surged throughout the city and many were the rumors as the Union and Confederate armies clashed in the Wilderness, north of Richmond. General Grant had conceived a new strategy, making the most of the superior manpower and resources of the North to strike multiple, simultaneous blows at the Confederacy. General Meade and the Army of the Potomac confronted

General Lee, General Butler's forces were moving up the James River to threaten Richmond from the south, and the German-born general Franz Sigel engaged the rebel troops in the Shenandoah Valley so they could not reinforce the Army of Northern Virginia. In the meantime, General Sherman moved to take on his Confederate counterpart in Georgia, and General Nathaniel Banks seemed poised to capture the vital port of Mobile, Alabama.

It was a bold, aggressive strategy, meant to trap the rebels in the grip of a closing vise, but the people of Richmond were more concerned with the battle on their doorstep than the broader scope of the coordinated assaults. Lizzie watched the distant fighting from the rooftop, but she had been disappointed too often to allow herself to hope that liberation was at hand. When she thought back to the exhilaration she had felt racing on horseback with Eliza and her cousin on the road to Mr. Botts's farm, she could scarcely believe she had once found battle thrilling. Now nothing elated her, not the approach of the Union army, not the novel audacity of General Grant's campaign. She felt only a calm hope, but with much sadness in it.

On May 6, the fighting was so close that the smoke of battle hung heavy in the air. All the stores were closed and few people ventured out onto the streets. Before long, word trickled into the capital that in the two days of savage fighting, the Confederacy had lost about eleven thousand men and the Union more than eighteen thousand. Lizzie was sickened to learn that many of the Union fatalities included wounded soldiers who had been unable to flee when fire broke out, and had been consumed alive by the burning woods.

The next day, Lieutenant Ross reported that an uprising at Libby had begun around midnight, when about one thousand officers had been ordered to prepare to be transported to Danville. The prison walls could not keep out the sounds of battle, and the men concluded that their captors believed the city would soon be taken, and were determined to move them to a more secure location where they could not be liberated. The prisoners swore they would not go and refused to have their names registered, but when confronted by several hundred Confederate bayonets, they submitted with bad grace. While most lined up for roll call, some of the officers slipped away and set fire to a lot of boxes on the second floor, intending to destroy the prison, but the blaze was extinguished before any damage was done. Furious, the prisoners spent their last moments in Libby dumping precious sugar and coffee and cutting up blankets and books that had recently been sent to them from the North, refusing to leave them for the benefit of their jailers. "As they were marched out to the depot, they swore they would escape from the train on the way to Danville," Lieutenant Ross told her, "but I haven't heard if they made good on their vow. They left on the Danville train at three o'clock this morning."

"Let us hope they manage to escape," said Lizzie wearily, with little hope that they would find the chance. However many hundreds the Confederates shipped south, she had no doubt that Libby Prison would soon be full again.

From the Wilderness the fighting moved on to Spotsylvania Court House, where the slaughter intensified. Assessing the city's fortifications, Lizzie sent a dispatch by her most trusted courier to inform General Butler that a great number of Richmond's defenders had been sent to reinforce General Lee. "The city is rarely so lightly garrisoned," she emphasized. "Now is the time to strike at the heart of the Confederacy."

General Butler's dogged advances over the next few days seemed a deliberate, methodical, affirmative reply to her summons.

On the night of May 12, Lizzie was awakened by the roar of cannons, and with John, William, and Nelson, she watched from the rooftop, her hopes and fears and prayers intermingling as she strained to glimpse the fighting, which seemed astonishingly close. "Uncle Nelson, can you tell the Yankee guns from the Confederate?" she asked the aged man.

"Yes, Miss Lizzie," he said, squinting off into the distance. "Them deep ones, they're the Yankee cannon."

"Are they coming closer?"

"It seems so."

Lizzie smiled despite her worry and fatigue. She had thought so, but she wanted to be reassured.

She needed more reassurance in the week that followed, as General Butler's advance seemed to grind to a halt. On May 16, Confederate General Beauregard launched a fierce counterattack on the army of Butler the Beast, driving him back to a narrow strip of land between the James and the Appomattox and holding the Union forces there while he dispatched reinforcements to General Lee.

And then the war truly did strike home: John was ordered to report to the field.

The Van Lews had expected the summons, and from the moment the campaign had begun, they had waited with dread for the inevitable. Richmond had never been in greater danger. The federal army coming up the James was much stronger and faster than government officials had anticipated, and Confederate defense forces were sent out to the north, south, and east to meet them. In the city, every man was called to arms, and in the streets none was without his musket and cartridge box. The hospitals braced themselves for another onslaught of wounded, and with the railroad lines to the South destroyed, anxious politicians scrambled to find horses to carry them to safety. Lizzie heard stories of ladies who sat up all night dressed in their best clothes and all their jewelry, ready to flee at a moment's notice, although where they thought they might find refuge and how to travel there, Lizzie could only wonder. At a time of great distress, when even the city's newspapermen had formed a company and prepared to fight off the enemy, John could not have hoped to avoid service.

Nevertheless, Lizzie fought to have his medical deferment extended, but the surgeon in charge refused to speak with her. She tried to arrange to smuggle him out of the city, but the raging battles had rendered her most reliable routes impassable. In desperation, although she knew it was risky, she decided to appeal to General Winder. She reminded him that he himself had confirmed John's disability and had blamed the military's relentless pursuit of him to a particular bias against the Van Lew family.

"I am sorry, Miss Van Lew," the general replied. "The last time we spoke on this matter, I told you I could do nothing more for him."

"But surely there is something else."

"The cause needs every man."

"Perhaps John could serve in another role," she proposed. "As a prison guard, perhaps. A clerk. He is an excellent businessman. He can serve the cause better using his brain rather than his brawn."

The general regarded her wearily. "Many gentlemen in worse physical repair than your brother are fighting and dying while he takes his leisure in your gardens."

Lizzie felt her heart pound heavily in her chest. She had one last card, and she intended to play it—although if it failed, she could never come to him again. "General Winder," she said quietly, "I know what answer I want. Perhaps I have been asking the wrong questions."

She reached into her bag, withdrew a thick wad of Confederate bills, and placed it on the general's desk.

He stared at it for a long moment, silent and still. "What, may I ask, is this?"

"Six thousand dollars," she said. "There was a time when this would buy dozens of substitutes."

"That time has long passed." The general looked up and held her gaze, his face reddening with fury. "Miss Van Lew, I strongly urge you to remove that offensive bribe from my sight before I forget you are a lady."

"General Winder," exclaimed Lizzie, feigning injured innocence. "I think you forget yourself, or you have forgotten who I am. This is no bribe. This is a fee. I am paying for a substitute—for several substitutes. Granted, I did not find them myself, as I believe is the custom, but time is of the essence, and as you said, I am a lady and hardly familiar with how one arranges such transactions."

"Enough," he barked, shoving his chair back from the desk and glowering. "Remove your property from my desk, and remove yourself from my office before I dispatch you to Castle Thunder."

"But, General—"

"Not another word," he said, his voice blistering.

Quickly Lizzie snatched up the money, returned it to her bag, and swept haughtily from the room, her chin lifted in a pose of offended dignity. She quickened her pace as she made her way down the hall to the exit, so that by the time she reached the sidewalk, she was nearly running.

Her error had cost her dearly, she knew. She had not saved her brother, and she had almost certainly destroyed whatever trust yet remained between her and the general.

She had made a terrible mistake, but there was no undoing it.

And so John reunited with his regiment at Camp Lee, and he marched off to battle as the fighting moved to the North Anna River and beyond. Lizzie and her mother had no idea where he might be as skirmishes were reported in all directions and reports became more confusing and contradictory. The only certainty was that casualties were massive on both sides, disproportionately so for the Union, although the rebels suffered the devastating loss of their revered, daring cavalry commander General J. E. B. Stuart, who died at the Richmond home of his brother-in-law after being shot in the abdomen at Yellow Tavern.

General Stuart's death was a great blow to the Confederacy, bringing a feverish anxiety upon the people at a time when nature, indifferent to their suffering, was at its loveliest. While cannon rumbled and long lines of wounded soldiers straggled into the city, green leaves unfurled overheard, songbirds twittered, and flowers bloomed, though their perfume could not mask the stench of death. Nor could it divert the people from a newly stirring sense of apprehension as they weighed rumors and reports from the battlefield. Although some of the battles had proven tactically inconclusive, they revealed something significant about General Grant each time he failed to destroy General Lee's army: In circumstances where his predecessors had always chosen to retreat, General Grant invariably regrouped and moved his army forward, again and again, keeping General Lee on the defensive and inching ever closer to the Confederate capital. The citizens of Richmond realized then that General Grant possessed a very different military mind from what they had yet witnessed from any Yankee leader.

Mary Jane sent word from the Gray House that President Davis and General Lee were determined to destroy the Army of the Potomac before it could reach the James River. If they failed, General Grant could lay siege to Petersburg, the most important supply base and railway depot for the entire region. General Lee requested reinforcements, but when General Beauregard scathingly refused to provide one of his divisions, General Lee had appealed to President Davis, who immediately ordered the transfer. Lizzie prayed that the generals' squabbling would buy the Union precious time to prepare.

When the forces finally met at Cold Harbor, everywhere there was a sense that this would be the final struggle. On June 1, General Lee's forces halted a Union attack that had nearly turned the Confederate flank. The next day the armies positioned themselves on opposite sides of a six-mile-long front stretching from the northwest to the southeast, and early in the morning on June 3, General Grant drove his forces into General Lee's well-entrenched divisions. The attack failed utterly. Shortly after midday, as thousands of Union troops lay dead or wounded between the lines, General Grant broke off the assault.

In mid-June, in the last major battle of the bloody campaign, General Grant surprised General Lee—and everyone else, for that matter—by directing his engineers to construct a pontoon bridge twenty-one hundred feet across the James, and then stealthily crossing the river and threatening Petersburg, a mere twenty-five miles south of the Confederate capital. If General Grant could capture Petersburg, Richmond would inevitably fall.

The Union troops settled in for the siege.

Shortly after the Battle of Cold Harbor, General Winder was ordered to report to Americus, Georgia, to assume command of the forces in the city and the prison post at Andersonville. It was a prestigious post, for Andersonville had become known as the "grand depot" of all the prisoners taken in the war. Just as she had when Captain Gibbs replaced Lieutenant Todd, Lizzie felt a curious mixture of triumph that she had outlasted his reign and trepidation that she would have to learn the ways of a new adversary. She considered delivering General Winder a farewell ginger cake for old time's sake, but by the time she learned of his transfer, he had already gone.

Later in June, Lizzie received word from her Northern contacts that Colonel George

H. Sharpe, the intelligence chief for the Army of the Potomac, would be taking over for General Butler as the primary patron of her network. Soon thereafter, she was overjoyed to receive, tucked carefully in with one of the colonel's dispatches, a letter from John.

Shortly after the Battle of Cold Harbor, her brother had managed to slip into Union lines, where he presented himself at General Grant's headquarters. "They tried to recruit me as a scout," John wrote, "but I demurred, and explained that I was en route to Philadelphia. I did reassure them that you are in a position to furnish them with valuable information, a claim they can verify with General Butler." He sent his love to Mother, Annie, and Eliza, and promised to kiss Anna for them.

It took several weeks for word of John's desertion to reach the Richmond press, but when it did, the response was withering:

GONE TO THE YANKEES.

—J. Newton Van Lew, for many years a hardware merchant of this city, has gone to the Yankees, and is said to have been taken by Beast Butler as a special detective. Van Lew, notwithstanding an incurable disease, which rendered him unfit for anything, we should think, being conscribed about the time Grant made his flank movement to the Southside, one evening rode out in his buggy in the direction of Malvern Hill, and has not been seen since. If he displays any brains in his new character of detective, it will be for the first time in his life.

Lizzie would have expected nothing less than an **ad hominem** attack from the **Whig**, but John's many friends would not let it stand. They promptly wrote to the editor protesting that John had not deserted at all but had been captured by a Yankee raiding party. The editor grudgingly printed several of their letters, but could not resist adding a remark from the chief of the Confederate police, who flatly stated, "Van Lew rode out with a colored man in a buggy. The man and the buggy came back, but Van Lew didn't. It is d—d strange if the Yankee raiders took Van Lew that they didn't take the colored man and buggy, too."

Lizzie was immeasurably relieved and elated that John was safe in the North, but she wished that somehow his desertion could have escaped the notice of the press. Their contemptuous remarks would bring more unwanted attention to the family at the very moment when, as Mary Jane had warned, Unionists needed to be at their most circumspect.

But when the next arrest came, the knock sounded not upon her door but Mr. Rowley's.

In a frenzy of alarm, Lizzie scrambled to gather information and to retain a lawyer for her dear, loyal, courageous friend. As best she could determine, his neighbors had reported him to the authorities, accusing him of being a Union man who was shirking out of the Confederate service. He was arrested and taken to Castle Thunder, where, after giving him a few days to consider his position, the authorities forced him to join an ambulance crew. Several hot, miserable, frightening weeks later, Mr. Rowley finally was allowed to make his case that as a

Dunkard, he was a conscientious objector, and so they released him—after he paid the five-hundred-dollar exemption fee.

The Richmond underground was shaken by Mr. Rowley's arrest, but rather than cease, they intensified their activities. They helped the valiant Robert Ford, who had finally recovered from his terrible beating but would probably suffer from its effects for the rest of his life, escape from Libby Prison and away to the North. Throughout the summer and the fall, they provided a wealth of crucial information to the Army of the Potomac via Colonel Sharpe, not the least of which concerned Richmond's defenses—the locations of picket posts, the strength of the fortifications that encircled the city. They provided insight into the condition of the rebel troops—how they had protested when their coffee and sugar rations were eliminated, how the fire brigade had been sent through the city to round up able-bodied men, how the conscripts had been examined so quickly and carelessly that a blind man had been sent to the front. They reported on severe shortages of soft iron for the manufacture of ammunition, and raw iron for making nails and spikes. Most significantly, they kept General Grant well informed on the location and status of General Jubal A. Early's Army of the Valley, taking careful note of the shifting of reinforcements between General Early's army and General Lee's, and evaluating the rumors circulating in the capital about General Early's plans.

In September, thanks to Mary Jane, Lizzie had also been able to convey what had transpired at a council of general officers at the Gray House. All the prominent generals in Richmond and from General Lee's army had attended, unaware that the colored woman serving them would remember every detail—General Early's insistence that he could not hold the Shenandoah Valley without more men, General Lee's assertion that without reinforcements he would be unable to hold his lines, the officers' acknowledgment that their lines were stretched so thin that in some places it amounted to nothing more that a skeleton force.

Lizzie's network of informants never failed to alert General Grant when the time had come to strike.

· · ·

One morning in late September, an unexpected visitor called at the Van Lew mansion, a childhood friend whom Lizzie had not seen in years, though they lived scarcely a mile from each other. "Why, Miss King," Lizzie cried, embracing her. "What a delightful surprise! What brings you back to Church Hill?"

"Dreadful news, I'm afraid," she said shakily, taking Lizzie's hand. "Is there somewhere we can talk alone?"

"Of course." Lizzie called for tea to be brought to the library, where she settled Miss King into a chair. "Please tell me what's wrong, and I will do everything in my power to help you."

"I come not to ask for help but, I hope, to give it." Two deep creases of worry appeared between Miss King's brows as she took a letter from her pocket and held it out to Lizzie. "This came for me yesterday afternoon."

With some trepidation, Lizzie unfolded the letter and read it. A Detective W. W. New had written to Miss King to inform her that Assistant Provost Marshal T. W. Doswell requested her presence at Commissioner John H. Sands's office to give testimony against Mrs. Eliza Van Lew. "You need not see anyone but Commissioner Sands, if you feel a delicacy in going," the detective had assured her. "They wish to have your testimony to conclude the case and would like to have you come as soon as you can. You will not see Mrs. Van Lew, nor will your name be mentioned to her."

"Give testimony against my mother?" Lizzie exclaimed, appalled.

"I don't understand it either," said Miss King. "We haven't been neighbors in ages. I can't imagine why they would want to question me, unless they're questioning everyone your mother has ever known."

"But why Mother?" said Lizzie, sinking into a chair, reading the letter a second time. "My mother is the very embodiment of goodness and honesty. Why would they investigate her—" Instead of me, she almost added, but she stopped herself just in time.

"I cannot imagine why, unless you have a secret enemy bent on revenge. A disgruntled servant, perhaps. A jealous neighbor who envies your mother's touch in the garden. Anyone can inform on anyone else these days and make trouble for everyone they dislike." Miss King cradled her tea-cup in her hands and shivered. "Of course there's no grounds for it, but they must investigate, and I thought you should know."

Lizzie thanked her profusely and begged her to tell no one lest rumors heighten the detective's suspicions. "I won't breathe a word," Miss King promised. "As for what I shall say when I give testimony, I will tell them the absolute truth: Your mother is the epitome of goodness and piety, and I have absolutely no reason to suspect her of any ill will or wrongdoing."

Lizzie thanked her again, tears spring-ing into her eyes. Miss King would defend Mother staunchly, but what of others, less scrupulous and faithful than she?

The very next day, the reverend Philip B. Price, a longtime family friend, called on the Van Lews to warn them that he too had been summoned by Provost Marshal Doswell to offer evidence against Mother. "When I told them I could think of nothing to betray the mistress of the house, they told me to 'refresh my memory,'" he said indignantly. "How they can badger a mature woman whose character and standing in

the community are absolutely unimpeachable, I cannot understand."

Mother thanked him for defending her
so courageously, and he declared he
could do no less, for every word he had
spoken was true, and she could count on
him to defend her before the highest court
in any land if need be. "I am greatly comforted to know that I have such a friend as
you," Mother told him, but she looked pale
and frightened.

Lizzie was furious. There were but two
reasons the authorities would fix their
sights on the irreproachable mother rather
than the eccentric spinster daughter: Either some enemy had specifically named
Mother, which was highly unlikely because
she was beloved by all who knew her, or
the rebel government wanted an excuse
to confiscate her property. The house and
all that was in it, the outbuildings, the farm,
the livestock—and those of their servants
whom the rebel government considered
slaves—all were in Mother's name. If Lizzie
was convicted of treason, they would claim
only her personal wealth, of which only a
sad, small fraction remained due to her
wartime expenditures. If Mother were found

guilty, the rebels could commandeer a fortune.

But the worst shock was yet to come.

In October, one of her paid informants in the adjutant general's office smuggled out a sheaf of hastily scribbled copies of documents relating to the investigation. The first startling disclosure was a memo between Provost Marshal Isaac Carrington and Charles M. Blackford of the adjutant general's office that revealed that the focus of the investigation had shifted from her mother to herself.

The second revelation came as such a shock, such a terrible, profound betrayal, that she felt its force like a staggering blow, and she stumbled back, dizzy, and let the pages slip through her fingers and drift to the library floor.

Mary Carter West Van Lew, John's estranged wife, had condemned her before the provost marshal.

Chapter Twenty-one

Mary's accusations went on and on.

The clerk had copied the official deposition so hurriedly that his handwriting was difficult to decipher, but it was clear that Mary's indictments were condemning. She had sworn before Commissioner Sands that she was well acquainted with Mrs. Eliza L. Van Lew and Miss Elizabeth L. Van Lew because she had resided with them from 1854 to 1857 and again from before secession until recently. She swore that she had frequently visited them since the war commenced and that she often heard them express ardent desire for the success of federal arms and the failure of the Confederate States of America to establish its independence. She swore that they were strongly abolitionist and offered as evidence that, years before, they had freed one of their Negro slaves and had sent her North to be educated. She swore that John Newton Van Lew, her own husband, had absconded to the North on account of his preference for that government, and that if Miss Van Lew and her mother were exiled to the North she did not want her children to accompany them. She concluded by emphasizing that she had no interest whatsoever in their estate.

Lizzie felt anger and remorse wash over her in equal measure. How she wished she had never spoken a word against the Confederacy in Mary's presence—but how much more fervently she regretted every mocking smile, every arch retort, every unkind word she had offered her sister-in-law. If Lizzie had been kinder, more tolerant, as gentle and forgiving as Mother, Mary would not have been so maliciously eager to denounce her.

"Perhaps if you made peace with Mary, she'd renounce her testimony," Mother said, struggling to keep her composure. "There must be something we can do."

Lizzie had considered that before, and she was about to agree when a flash of insight struck. Mary had disavowed any interest in the Van Lew estate too emphatically for someone who truly did not care. Instead her words were a message to the Confederate government, letting them know that if they wished to claim the Van Lews' wealth, she would not interfere, as long as they exiled Lizzie and her mother to the North with her traitorous husband— and restored her children to her custody.

That was the impetus for her betrayal. She wanted Lizzie punished, and she wanted her daughters.

"I would crawl to her on my knees and beg forgiveness if I thought it would make any difference," said Lizzie, going to the library window and gazing outside at the garden. Its autumnal colors glowed with an unearthly vividness, lit by the last shafts of sunlight that had followed a day of rain. "It won't. Even if she agreed to retract her testimony, the provost marshal would still believe every word of it. And why not? It's true. Everything she accuses me of, I've done."

Mother placed her hands on Lizzie's shoulders and turned her around. "Lizzie, my darling, you cannot wait here for them to come and arrest you. You must follow John into the North."

Lizzie was so astonished she laughed, but it came out as a sob. "I can't, Mother. I'm needed. I've never been more necessary to anyone or anything in my life. If it means spending the rest of my years languishing in Castle Thunder, I won't run. I'll gather information and send dispatches to the Union until the rebels come for me. Then I will stop. Then and not a moment before."

Her mother trembled. "It may not end in Castle Thunder for you," she choked out, her eyes overflowing with tears. "It may end at Camp Lee, upon the gibbet."

Wordlessly, Lizzie embraced her. She knew that too, but she would not run.

When Mother prevailed upon her, Lizzie agreed to go to Mary and apologize, even though she doubted it would make any difference. Reluctant to face her sister-in-law alone—not because she was afraid, but because she wanted a witness to the exchange, as well as a friend who could silently warn her if her tone became sardonic or insulting—she asked Eliza to accompany her. Just as they were getting ready to set out in the carriage, a young messenger furtively came to the kitchen door bearing new messages from Lizzie's informant in the provost marshal's office. "I'm afraid to read them at the moment," Lizzie confessed to Eliza, smiling halfheartedly at her foolishness. "What if the news they contain robs me of my courage? I can't face Mary without it."

Eliza held out her hand. "I'll read them for you."

Lizzie gave her the letters and they sat down at the kitchen table while she read. "The first is a note the provost marshal included with the copy of Mary's deposition that he delivered to the adjutant and inspector generals' offices," said Eliza. "He asks whether any additional evidence should be taken, with the intent to remove the parties—you and your mother, I assume—from the Confederacy."

"That's some good news, I suppose," said Lizzie shakily. "Exile would be preferable to imprisonment or death."

"He seems somewhat reluctant to act."

Eliza frowned thoughtfully as she studied the page. "He points out that you are ladies of wealth and position."

"We have less of both now than we have ever had, but if his belief constrains his hand, I will not enlighten him."

Eliza turned her attention to the second document. "This appears to be the reply from the adjutant general's office. 'Miss Elizabeth Van Lew of this city is very unfriendly in her sentiments toward the government,' he writes."

The accusation, though milder than she had feared, was still unsettling. "He isn't wrong."

"He goes on to say, 'It does not appear that she has ever done anything to infirm the cause. Like most of her sex, she seems to have talked freely—and in the presence of female friends, who have informed on her. The question is whether she shall be sent beyond the lines because of her opinion?'"

"Then it would seem that they are aware of my opinions but not of my actions."

"And of course, as a woman," added Eliza archly, "you can hardly be blamed for your foolishness and your predilection to chatter nonsense."

"The Confederate government has punished people for their opinions before, even if their actions have been above reproach," Lizzie reminded her. "Not only men. Women too."

Eliza sighed and nodded, acknowledging her point, but then she gave a little start, and her brow furrowed as she examined the heading of the second letter more closely, and then quickly confirmed the signature on the first. "Lizzie," she said, "did you see the names of the gentlemen involved in this exchange?"

"No," replied Lizzie, puzzled. "I couldn't even bring myself to unfold the pages. I left that to you."

Eliza lay the documents upon the table and pointed at the lines that had captured her attention. "The provost marshal who sent this letter and received that one is Isaac Carrington. **Carrington**, Lizzie."

Lizzie peered closely at the signature, hardly daring to hope. "Is he a relation?"

"Yes," Eliza said, her face lighting up with joy. "Distant, but nevertheless, yes, we are related."

Lizzie pressed a hand to her heart. "Do you think he would help me?"

"I don't know. We haven't spoken in ages, but that won't prevent me from appealing to him." Eliza bounded to her feet. "I will go to him at once and beg a favor on behalf of the good Carrington name."

"Oh, Eliza," Lizzie exclaimed, rising and embracing her. "I have never doubted your friendship, but today you have proven yourself the truest, most loyal friend I've ever known."

Eliza hugged her, but then she quickly cautioned, "Don't shower me in too much praise too soon. I haven't done anything yet."

"Oh, but you have," Lizzie insisted. "Your kindness has lifted me from the depths of despair. Take the carriage. Peter has it ready and waiting, and I would much rather send it on this errand than the one we had intended."

Eliza agreed, urged her not to worry, and hurried on her way.

Lizzie spent the day in anxious, hopeful waiting, and when Eliza returned late that afternoon, her proud, satisfied smile told Lizzie that she had met with success. "Don't waste another moment worrying about this investigation," she said, taking Lizzie's hands in hers and beaming. "It's going to quietly fade away."

"But—how?" Lizzie felt dizzy and weak from relief and thought she might burst into tears. "What did you say? How did you persuade him?"

"I told him that you are my dearest friend and that I have accompanied you on most of your missions of mercy to care for the Union soldiers, which is what inspired the cruel gossip about your loyalty," she said. "I told him that if he prosecutes you, he must do the same to me, and whatever punishment you receive, I must share."

"You didn't," gasped Lizzie, horrified. "What a risk you took! What if he had called your bluff?"

"It was no bluff. It's true. This investigation cannot bring shame to the Van Lew family without also disgracing the Carringtons." Eliza smiled. "As you might expect, Provost Marshal Isaac Carrington is not eager to do that."

"I should think not," said Lizzie, laughter and hope bubbling up within her. She was safe—from this threat, at least, if none other. She would not be sent to Castle Thunder, or exiled to the North, and her

nieces—her precious, beloved nieces—
would not be taken from the home they
loved best.

What a blessing was the courage of a
true and loyal friend!

Tensions grew and tempers flared in Richmond as news from the disparate battlefields grew ever more demoralizing for the
Confederacy. Mere survival was celebrated
with forced good cheer as if it were a victory. The papers celebrated the recapture
of six hundred slaves from the Yankees
while disparaging the Union's increasingly
more visible use of colored soldiers. They
noted with satisfaction that countless
households across the North were engulfed in mourning thanks to the butcher
Grant's heavy losses, and they took heart
from reports of Old Abe's political troubles
as he faced re-election, noting that unlike
their President Davis, he contended with
significant opposition. Northern Peace
Democrats had nominated General George
McClellan as their candidate to replace Mr.
Lincoln, and thanks to Mary Jane's delicate touch in Mr. Davis's study, the Richmond underground had learned that the

Confederacy fervently wanted General McClellan to triumph at the polls. They all knew that if Mr. Lincoln lost, the Confederacy's chances for victory would increase a thousandfold.

No strained cheer in the papers or forced frivolity at ladies' parties could conceal the truth that the rebel armies were struggling, worn down by the enemy's superior numbers and resources. In September, Union general Sherman had defeated General Hood and captured Atlanta, despite the anguished, fervent prayers of the devout throughout the Confederacy. In October, General Sheridan dealt General Jubal Early his most significant defeat and seized control of the Shenandoah Valley, confiscating or slaughtering livestock and provisions, burning crops and barns, and thereby laying waste to the most important source of food for Richmond and the Army of Northern Virginia.

On November 8, Abraham Lincoln won re-election handily, crushing General McClellan's political ambitions and destroying any hope of a negotiated peace that included the preservation of slavery. Behind closed doors and drawn curtains, the

Van Lew household celebrated, splurging on a chicken dinner with all the trimmings and an applesauce cake for dessert.

Surely, they told one another, they had come at last to the final months of the war.

The day after the election, the mood in Richmond was sour and angry everywhere but in the Van Lew residence, and, she surmised, the homes of other secret Unionists throughout the South. Since Lizzie doubted she would be able to conceal her merriment, she spent most of the day contentedly at home, writing dispatches and perusing the newspapers for information that might interest Colonel Sharpe. Shortly after evening fell, she was on her way from the library to the kitchen when she passed through the foyer and noticed a folded piece of paper that had been slipped beneath the front door.

Quickly she snatched it up. None of her messengers ever delivered messages so carelessly, but perhaps some unknown danger had demanded haste. Her eye immediately went to the crude skull and crossbones drawn at the top of the page, and then to the harsh scrawl that followed:

Miss Van Lough.

Old Maid: Look out for your fig bushes. There ain't much left of them now. Do you have insurance? White Caps are around town. They are coming at night. Look out! Look out! Look out! Your house is going at last. FIRE. White Caps. Please give me some of your blood to write letters with.

Without thinking, Lizzie crumpled the paper in her fist, tore open the front door, and dashed out onto the portico, where she glanced wildly up the street and down—but she saw no one, not even the smallest glimpse of a telltale white hood the members of the new vigilante group donned whenever they committed their acts of intimidation and violence. Whoever had left the malicious note was long gone.

"Cowards," she muttered to the empty street. Glaring defiantly into the darkness, she turned stiffly and strode back inside, where with trembling hands she shut the door and locked it firmly.

. . .

A week after President Lincoln was re-elected, General Sherman set out from Atlanta with roughly sixty-two thousand troops and marched toward Savannah on the Atlantic coast. As the army moved inexorably to the sea, they laid waste to plantation and farms; destroyed rail lines; confiscated cattle, horses, and provisions; and utterly demoralized and infuriated civilians across Georgia and throughout the Confederacy. When Savannah fell to General Sherman's forces on December 21, a wide swath of devastation seared his route into the earth behind him. Richmond's newspapers bitterly reprinted a story that their Northern counterparts had reported with unrestrained jubilation: On Sunday, December 25, General Sherman had sent President Lincoln a telegram declaring, "I beg to present to you, as a Christmas gift, the city of Savannah, with 150 heavy guns and plenty of ammunition, and also about 25,000 bales of cotton."

Morale in the Confederate capital had plummeted as Christmas approached, but on that holy day, the citizens tried to make merry. In the streets, boys fired pistols into the air and set off firecrackers, and tipsy carolers sang boisterously in hopes of gifts of food or drink. Jefferson Davis had been ill so often throughout the autumn that occasionally rumors had sped through the city that he was dead, but on Christmas Day, he attended morning services at Saint Paul's and returned in the afternoon to play Santa Claus for the city's orphans. Later that evening, when Mary Jane stopped by the Church Hill mansion bearing holiday greetings and gifts of preserves, her voice was wistful as she described the Davis family's Christmas tree, a Virginia holly decorated with candles and clever little dolls made of flannel and hickory nuts. Their guests had enjoyed cakes, gingersnaps, real coffee, and eggnog, and after Mrs. Davis had passed out gifts, the children had played hide-and-seek in the mansion. "Mrs. Davis was a gracious and pleasant hostess," Mary Jane reported, "but when Mr. Davis came down from his office to put in an appearance, he looked tall and thin and sickly and sad. I've never see such a contrast between husband and wife."

Lizzie's mouth watered at Mary Jane's description of the feast—turkey, beef, mince pie, and plum pudding, delicacies the servants had hoarded for days. Later that night, Mr. and Mrs. Davis planned to attend a neighbor's "starvation party," where there would be dancing and singing but nothing to eat. Such parties had become quite the fashion in the Confederate capital, for spirits needed lifting in direct proportion to the scarcity of food.

Richmond's farm markets were nearly bare, and with the Shenandoah Valley laid to waste, railroad lines severed, the Union army dug in on three sides, and winter setting in, no family escaped the gnawing pangs of hunger. Some Church Hill ladies realized that if their families had scarcely enough to eat, the soldiers huddled in the vast arc of trenches spanning more than thirty miles from Richmond to Petersburg surely struggled to survive on even less. The compassionate women vowed to provide a New Year's feast for the soldiers, and they appealed to merchants, farmers, and ordinary citizens for donations. Mother contributed several loaves of bread that Lizzie was sorry to see given for that purpose, as she had hoped to distribute them at Libby Prison, but Provost Marshal Doswell's investigation had reminded her anew that they must perform a role for a critical public.

Nor, truly, did she want anyone to starve, whether rebel or Union.

Later Lizzie heard that the weary, ravenous soldiers had risen early and eagerly on New Year's morning, and while the Van Lews and their servants dined on ham and black-eyed peas and coarse bread and made wishes and spoke prayers for better days to come in 1865, the rebel soldiers waited expectantly for the promised feast. They waited with dwindling hopes all day and into the night, and shortly before dawn on the morning of January 2, the long-anticipated feast arrived—each man received a sandwich with a thin slice of ham. The soldiers were sorely disappointed, but one corporal from Georgia reportedly said aloud what all were thinking: "God bless our noble women! It was all they could do. It was all that they had."

Whether the incident had indeed occurred or was but a sentimental, apocryphal tale, it rang true every time Lizzie heard it repeated, in the streets and in the churches, and in the nearly empty markets.

As the New Year commenced, the mood in Richmond was utterly bleak and wretched. Food was scarce. Confederate money was all but worthless. Frigid rains had turned the streets to mud, which froze overnight into hard ruts that made for teeth-rattling carriage rides and turned more than a few ankles. Beggars in rags had become so commonplace that neither merchants nor police officers bothered to drive them away anymore. The oppressive, unrelenting anxiety kindled worrisome rumors, which circled about and provoked more anxiety. The rumor that stirred the most fear in the hearts of the rebel citizens also seemed the most likely to be true: Now that he had subdued Savannah, General Sherman intended to march north and join his forces to General Grant's. There were also rumors of clandestine peace negotiations going on at the highest levels of government, but Lizzie suspected these were probably nothing more than wishful thinking to a populace weary of war. Other murmurs on the street claimed that the government knew the end was near and was already drafting plans to evacuate Richmond, schemes that included measures to destroy the city's warehouses full of tobacco, alcohol, and provisions before the government took flight rather than allow them to fall into Yankee hands.

The most preposterous tale of all said that Mr. Davis and the Congress were seriously considering the creation of colored regiments composed of slaves who would be granted their freedom in exchange for military service. Lizzie could not imagine the Confederates allowing such a thing, for once colored men fought in the trenches side by side with white soldiers, it would be nearly impossible to ignore their humanity, their inherent equality, and that was a philosophical point she was convinced the rebels would never concede. She also could not fathom how any colored man could take up arms to support a regime that had kept him, his family, and all his race enslaved. If colored men wanted to fight for freedom, they could cross over to Union lines and enlist in the United States Colored Troops, and a great many slaves had done exactly that.

But even though she personally found the rumor about colored Confederate regiments dubious, enough people in important places had mentioned it for her to decide it warranted inclusion in her dispatches to City Point, where General Grant had established his headquarters. Lizzie diligently reported verified facts and only the most plausible rumors to Colonel Sharpe, who in turn informed General Grant, who was undoubtedly satisfied to know that his siege was working, even if it meant that innocents suffered alongside his enemies.

As if fearing that the Confederacy's weakened state would inspire Richmond's Unionists to mount a killing blow, the rebel authorities struck first. On January 20, Lizzie was badly shaken by the news that Mr. F. W. E. Lohmann, who had so valiantly helped with the exhumation and burial of Colonel Dahlgren, had been arrested at his home, although his brother had eluded capture. Soon thereafter, she learned that several other members of the loyalist underground had also been snatched up in a scattering of swift, simultaneous arrests, like traps springing all over the city. The next day more accused Union men were taken into custody, and later that week, detectives arrested Samuel Ruth at the RF&P Railroad office on Eighth and Broad

Street. Mary Jane's husband had witnessed his arrest, but the detectives apparently had not suspected Wilson of any wrongdoing, for they questioned him briefly at the station about Mr. Ruth and then told him he was free to go. Wilson brought the devastating news straight to Lizzie, who soon confirmed that the men had been taken to Castle Thunder.

Lizzie was not permitted to visit them, but she bribed the guards to deliver food, blankets, and warm clothing to them in their cells. Those who possessed wealth and influence immediately hired lawyers and appealed to their powerful friends to intercede on their behalf. Quietly, Lizzie retained counsel for the accused loyalists who could not afford it and sent gifts of money and food to their families to sustain them until their menfolk could return home. Not expectedly, before any of the accused faced a judge or jury, they were tried in the press. Mr. Lohmann was presumed guilty, due to rumors that incriminating documents had been found in his coat pockets, while Mr. Ruth was presumed innocent, thanks to his reputation for exemplary service on the railroad and the assertions of his staunchly faithful friends among the Richmond political and social elite, who apparently had no idea how profoundly his loyalties and beliefs differed from their own. In February, Mr. Ruth managed to secure an honorable discharge and returned to his post, but Mr. Lohmann and many others languished in prison, where Lizzie was continuously frustrated in her attempts to see them.

The Richmond underground had been dealt a staggering blow, but Lizzie was too angry, too determined, too hungry, too frightened, too weary of war to quit. As circumspectly as she could, she called on her Unionist acquaintances whose courage might be faltering and shored them up with encouraging speeches and with gifts of money and food. The war had taught Lizzie that it was far too easy to succumb to fear and intimidation when one's belly was empty.

Her network had taken a beating, but even before the bruises healed, and despite their diminished numbers, Lizzie and the Richmond underground continued their work for the Union with newly inspired vengeance. If legal maneuvers and bribes could not free Mr. Lohmann and the other loyalists from Castle Thunder, the fall of Richmond certainly would.

In early February, the rumors of tentative peace negotiations suddenly became vividly real when Mr. Jefferson and Mr. Lincoln agreed to name commissioners to meet and discuss their options. Mary Jane learned well before most of Mr. Davis's cabinet did that Mr. Davis had first rejected suggestions that he appoint Vice-President Stephens to lead the Confederate delegation, but had eventually acquiesced because Mr. Stephens and Mr. Lincoln had been friends when they had served in the House of Representatives together.

Even as General Sherman's army marched from Georgia into South Carolina and ominously closer to Richmond, talk of peace filled the Confederate capital. Mr. Lincoln had sent his secretary of state, William H. Seward, to meet Mr. Stephens's party at Fort Monroe, but astonishingly, three days later President Lincoln himself joined the parties at Hampton Roads. On February 3, aboard the steamboat **River Queen**, Union and Confederate representatives began talks that all present hoped would end the long struggle before another drop of blood was shed. Unfortunately, they never broached the finer points of the matter because the Confederates insisted the goal was to achieve peace between two sovereign nations, while Mr. Lincoln emphasized that he sought peace within their one common country. Mr. Lincoln insisted upon the end of slavery, Mr. Stephens was bound to the idea of Southern independence, and neither would yield, and nothing was agreed, and all returned home with little to show for the excursion. When the Richmond press published the delegation's report and denounced the Union for demanding the total subjugation of the South, talk of hope and peace vanished, superseded by anger and the defiant certainty that Southern independence would be established not at the negotiating table but on the battlefield, once and for all, and soon.

Lizzie wondered how even the most ardent rebel could believe that anymore. The Confederate army was starving. Sickness, death, and desertions had reduced General Lee's army to some fifty-seven thousand malnourished soldiers, including troops from the Home Guard and reservists, in stunning contrast to General Grant's force, one hundred twenty-four thousand strong. General Sherman had captured Columbia, Charleston had been evacuated, and Wilmington, the last major port in rebeldom, had also fallen. It was only a matter of time until the Union army overpowered the rebels entirely, Lizzie thought, time that meant more bloodshed and hunger and needless suffering.

Lizzie's disappointment with the failed peace conference had begun to fade by the time news of a very different sort appeared in the February 10 edition of the Richmond **Whig**.

GEN. WINDER DEAD

We regret to learn that Brigadier General John H. Winder, who, for a considerable time, it will be remembered, commanded the Department of Henrico, died at Florence, S. C., on the 6th.

Stunned, Lizzie quickly turned to the **Enquirer**, searching each column of newsprint for his name. Why had they given no cause of death? Had he been shot on the battlefield? Strangled by one of his own prisoners? She had to know. She had been entangled with him too long not to wonder.

Then she found it, another announcement: "He died in an apoplectic fit, and was, up to the moment of his illness, apparently in excellent health."

She sank back into her chair, staring into space.

Her longtime nemesis was truly gone, struck down without warning as if by a bolt from above. It was impossible not to sense divine judgment in his demise.

On March 4, one hundred miles north of Richmond in Washington City, Abraham Lincoln took his oath of office inside the Capitol. Soon thereafter, he emerged upon the East Portico, the newly completed dome high above him, to deliver his second inaugural address. Lizzie wished with all her heart to be there to hear what was surely a stirring speech, full of noble ideas and simple eloquence, but she settled for a celebratory glass of sherry and a tiny slice of ginger cake with her mother and Eliza and a few other dear Unionist friends, who regarded the day with the same joyful reverence as she. Someday, she vowed, someday when peace again reigned from North to South, she would go to Washington City. She would see Mr. Lincoln—the Great Emancipator, the savior of the Union—see him with her own eyes, and if she had the chance she would introduce herself and perhaps, modestly, tell him all she had done for him. Or perhaps, she thought mirthfully, amused by her own silly pride, perhaps he would have already heard of her. Perhaps his eyes would light up at the mention of her name, and he would shake her hand, and bow, and offer her his thanks.

And then, if she were very lucky, Mr. Lincoln would introduce her to General Grant, whom she admired and greatly desired to meet.

That would indeed be a perfect day. That was a fond wish to keep her heart warm in the midst of a seemingly endless winter.

Confederate troops had been ordered down the Danville road, Lizzie wrote to General

Grant one bitter winter day less than a fortnight later. Warehouses of cotton, tobacco, and other valuable goods had been turned over to the provost marshal. Mrs. Davis was packing some household goods, selling others, and giving away still more to trusted, loyal friends, and Mr. Davis had taught her how to fire a pistol. Citizens were ordered to "be organized," although what that meant in practical terms had not been explained.

Taken together, the curious, unsettling incidents convinced Lizzie that the ephemeral rumors of an impending evacuation that had drifted through the capital since the turning of the year were now apparently coalescing, solidifying into a form yet unknown.

"May God bless and bring you soon to deliver us," Lizzie concluded the dispatch, her hand shaking from fatigue, her stomach cramping painfully from hunger too long ignored. "We are all in an awful situation here. There is great want of food."

And then, only a few days later, long after Lizzie had assumed that the events of the war had lost their power to astonish her, the truly unexpected happened.

The Confederate Congress passed a bill authorizing the War Department to raise companies of Negro soldiers, free and slave alike, not to labor but to take up arms in defense of the homes in which they had been born and raised, and in which they had found contentment and happiness—or so the recruitment handbills enjoined them.

Lizzie could hardly believe her ears when she learned the bill had passed, and she could scarcely believe her eyes when, only nine days later, the first three companies of colored soldiers paraded in the streets of the capital. Thousands of citizens packed Capitol Square to watch the new recruits march proudly to the strains of fife and drum, their uniforms spotless and new, their motives unfathomable, their judgment impaired—or so Lizzie concluded. She had joined the throngs of spectators because she had hoped that watching the colored Confederates would help her to understand them better, but the insight she gained from the parade had less to do with those poor, bewildering, misguided men than the politicians who had granted them the right to bear arms for the Confederacy. As she wrote in a dispatch to Colonel Sharpe and General Grant immediately upon returning home from the spectacle, the rebel government must be desperate indeed to do now that which they had vehemently sworn could never be done.

On the first day of April, Lizzie discovered that her suspicions that the beginning of the end was upon them were shared by the most prominent rebel of all.

She had just sat down to a meager breakfast of cornmeal gruel with her mother and nieces when Mary Jane burst into the dining room, breathless and wide-eyed from astonishment, her shawl and bonnet glistening with raindrops.

"Miss Lizzie, Mrs. Van Lew," she gasped, clutching her side and panting as if she had run all the way from the Gray House. "Mrs. Davis has fled Richmond."

Chapter Twenty-two

Mrs. Davis and the children departed in the small hours of the night," Mary Jane told them, sinking into a chair at the foot of the table. "When I arrived for work this morning, I found them gone and the household in a state of great distress."

"And Mr. Davis?" Lizzie prompted eagerly. "Is he soon to follow?"

"He remains in Richmond to direct the affairs of state, but for how much longer is anyone's guess."

Across the table from Lizzie, to Mother's left, Annie and little Eliza watched Mary Jane wide-eyed, their breakfasts forgotten.

Suddenly Lizzie realized that at nine and seven years of age, her nieces could not remember a time before the war, and her heart ached for them.

Soon, perhaps, they would discover peace.

"Where did Mrs. Davis go?" Mother asked.

"Mr. Davis's valet told me that she, the children, and her sister Margaret boarded the train to Charlotte escorted by his private secretary," Mary Jane replied. "She begged to be allowed to stay—Mrs. Lee has no intention of fleeing—but Mr. Davis insisted."

"Well, of course. He wants his family out of harm's way," said Mother. "Mr. Lee would probably insist that his wife go too, if she were not in such poor health."

"Mr. Davis told her that if they stayed in Richmond, their presence would only worry and grieve him, and offer him no comfort," said Mary Jane. "So at last she agreed. He gave her his pistol and all of his Confederate money and gold except for one five-dollar piece, and told her to make her way to the coast of Florida, where she could take a boat abroad if necessary."

"She would flee not only Richmond but the entire continent?" Lizzie asked, astonished. "Surely this means Mr. Davis believes the Confederacy is finished."

"Not so," Mary Jane cautioned. "His valet told me that Mr. Davis intends to go to Texas and continue governing from there. General Lee has given him reason to hope that the fall of Richmond would not necessarily mean the end of the struggle. If his army no longer needs to protect the capital, General Lee would be able to direct his forces as he sees fit for the first time since he took command. He believes he can prolong the war for another two years."

"God help us, no," gasped Mother. "We cannot have two more years of this. We cannot endure it!"

Lizzie reached across the table and clasped her hand. "We won't have to. When Richmond falls, the Confederacy will crumble, and it will happen sooner than Mr. Davis and Mr. Lee think."

If it happened tomorrow, or even that very day, it would not be too soon.

The previous day, ten thousand rebels under the command of General Pickett had fought off five times that many Union troops at Dinwiddie Court House. Lizzie had expected the fighting to resume in the morning, but when it did not, she sent Peter out into the rain-soaked morning to collect the latest rumors. He soon returned to report that General Pickett, cut off from the rest of the Army of Northern Virginia, had pulled back to Five Forks, a vital crossroads General Lee had exhorted them to hold at all hazards.

At about a quarter past four o'clock in the afternoon, the battle resumed more fiercely than before. The Van Lews soon became so accustomed to the relentless hammering that it was the silence between barrages that caught their attention, bringing their work or play to an abrupt halt as they stood perfectly still wherever they were, straining their ears to listen. The interludes of hushed expectation never lasted, and on that day the cacophony persisted long after Lizzie put her nieces to bed. Somehow the girls slept through the battle, though the ground trembled and flashing guns and exploding shells turned the night into intermittent day.

Lizzie managed to seize a few hours o

sleep, but a huge explosion shook her awake at dawn, and after she threw on a dressing gown and raced upstairs to the rooftop, she glimpsed lurid flashes lighting up the morning sky in the direction of Petersburg. Spellbound, she lost track of time as she watched the red shells bursting in the distance, but she returned inside when she heard stirring from within. It was a Sunday, and whatever else might be going on in the outskirts of the city, she had to get the girls up and dressed and fed and ready for church.

It was a beautiful day, warm and gentle and sunny, with daffodils blooming and trees unfurling a fresh, green canopy of leaves overhead. As they crossed the street to Saint John's church, Lizzie took it all in gratefully, glimpsing God's benevolence in the natural beauty of her beleaguered city, but as she escorted her mother and nieces into the family pew, her attention was riveted by the hushed, worried murmurs all around her. General Pickett had met a fearful loss near Petersburg, some said. Veteran troops manning Richmond's defenses had been hurriedly marched away to reinforce divisions elsewhere, and barely trained reserves had taken their places. The battle was still ongoing, but some trick of the wind carried the sounds of warfare away from Richmond so it was impossible to tell whether the armies clashed nearby or far away, whether they were approaching or retreating.

Lizzie tried to forget her earthly cares in the familiar, soothing rhythms of worship. The minister was reading from Zechariah when Lizzie heard footsteps coming up the center aisle behind her. When the footsteps suddenly halted and a flurry of murmurs and shifting began, Lizzie glanced over her shoulder and discovered a messenger standing at the end of a pew five rows back, handing a folded paper to— Lizzie gave a start—to Colonel Trinidad Martinez, whom she had not seen in ages. She had not known he was back in Richmond, but when he read the note, supported himself with a cane as he rose, and followed the messenger from the church, she realized that he must have been recently wounded, and was recovering in one of the many hospitals scattered throughout the city. If she had known, she would have invited him to move into the

Van Lew mansion while he recuperated— but, of course, that would have put her clandestine activities in jeopardy, so it was just as well he had not sent word.

The disruption over, the minister resumed his homily, and Lizzie struggled to return her attention to his words of faith and redemption. He had nearly finished when another messenger hurried up the side aisle and bent to whisper in the ear of a gray-bearded man Lizzie recognized as a member of President Davis's cabinet. The secretary strode from the church, mouth set in a grim line, and the door had scarcely closed behind him when yet another messenger entered, middle-aged and portly and huffing from exertion. The distracted worshipers' murmurs swelled with curiosity and alarm as he hurried past the pews and halted at the pulpit. There he stood at attention and held out a folded piece of paper to the minister, who stared at him a moment before accepting the note. As the minister read in silence, the furrows in his brow deepened and his shoulders slumped. He bowed his head on the lectern for a long moment, then straightened, looked out upon the congregation gravely, and said, "Brethren, trying times are before us. General Lee has been defeated, but remember that God is with us in the storm as well as in the calm."

A woman moaned with such unearthly despair that Lizzie felt chills prickle up and down her spine from her neck to the small of her back.

"We may never meet again," the minister intoned. "Go quietly to your homes, and whatever may be in store for us, let us not forget that we are Christian men and women, and may the protection and blessing of the Father, the Son, and the Holy Ghost be with you all."

Lizzie seized little Eliza's hand, Mother took Annie's, and they joined the flow of worshipers as they swiftly fled the church, some weeping openly, others grimacing in anguish. Outside, songbirds chirped merrily in the sunshine beneath a blue, cloudless sky, but the residents of Church Hill were insensible to their song as they rushed to and fro seeking information, reassurance, the comfort of a friend's embrace As Lizzie quickly ushered her little family across the street, she observed men striding off toward Capitol Square and black clad women gathering up their skirts and fleeing for home. So many women were dressed in mourning, Lizzie thought as she gazed back upon the scene from the safety of her own front portico. In the grayness of winter, it had been easier not to notice how nearly every woman of her acquaintance was mourning a husband, a son, a brother, a father, but against the pastel hues of springtime, their black attire stood out in contrast as stark as their grief.

While she stood watching, a dowager making her way stiffly down Grace Street waved frantically to a pair of younger women passing on the opposite side. "Oh, Alice, Martha, have you heard the dreadful news?" she called out, her voice shrill with terror. "The city is to be evacuated immediately, and the Yankees will be here before morning! What can it all mean? And what is to become of us poor defenseless women? God only knows!"

"Don't despair," the younger of the two ladies called back. "I don't believe they're going to evacuate. That has been the false report so often, it can be nothing more than another of the usual Sunday rumors."

But her voice quavered as she spoke,

and after bowing her head in farewell, she linked her arm through her companion's and they hurried off together at a much brisker pace.

Lizzie followed her family inside, and when she summoned Peter she was relieved when Louisa reported that he had anticipated her request—or had wanted to satisfy his own burning curiosity—and had already gone to Capitol Square for the news. Impatiently she waited, wondering whether her time would be better spent sending General Grant information or asking for it.

She had her answer when Peter came back with observations and rumors in abundance. Apparently a messenger had come to Mr. Davis as he attended services at Saint Paul's earlier that morning, and his face had gone gray as he read the note. Without a word, he had risen with singular gravity and determination and had quietly left the church, his hat in his hand. Colored folks whose ministers had announced the news from the pulpit had emerged from their African churches beaming and glancing with great anticipation toward the James and down the road to the east as i they expected Yankees to storm the city at any moment. Citizens spotting officials on the street had watched them as if trying to determine from their behavior what they themselves ought to be doing—packing their belongings, hiding their valuables, destroying incriminating wartime journals, or grabbing their loved ones and fleeing for their lives. Increasingly frantic crowds had gathered at the Spotswood Hotel and clustered around the bulletin boards outside the telegraph and newspaper offices, desperate for news from Petersburg and the battlefields. Government clerks loaded boxes of documents and kegs full of gold onto wagons, carts, and any other wheeled conveyance they could lay their hands upon. Peter happened to run into Mr. Ruth, who told him that the quartermaster had been organizing trains to carry officials, documents, and treasure south into exile on the Richmond & Danville Railroad, and Mr. Ruth was doing his very best to keep the RF&P train cars out of his desperate grasp.

The evacuation of the government, though not yet formally announced, was clearly well under way.

At two o'clock, though it was a Sunday, the banks unlocked their doors and instructed customers to claim their deposits. Two hours later, Mayor Mayo confirmed to the City Council that the Confederate government was leaving the city. The City Council, fearful of what triumphant Yankee invaders might do if alcohol were poured upon the flames of their vengeance, appointed men to destroy all liquor supplies in Richmond. When Peter heard that the mayor had authorized a citizens' committee to meet the federal army and arrange the peaceful surrender of the city, he decided he had learned enough. He had hurried home, pushing his way through crowds of people rushing toward the city's bridges on foot, carriages and wagons rumbling away stuffed full of trunks and luggage, scrawny horses and mules carrying lone riders into the countryside to the west, and weary and wary servants hauling parcels and bundles to the train station, their eyes burning with expectation in their dark, carefully expressionless faces.

Lizzie had summoned her most reliable young messenger hours ago, and while Caroline kept the lad occupied in the kitchen with biscuits and simple chores, Lizzie swiftly compiled Peter's observations into a dispatch. Sealing it, she sat back in her chair, light-headed and overcome with emotion.

This could very well be her last dispatch. General Grant might enter the city before he could receive it.

She sent it off immediately anyway, just in case it contained even a single neces-sary detail that would hasten the liberation of Richmond.

Soon after her messenger raced off to carry her dispatch to a Unionist compatriot who would convey it to General Grant's camp, a knock sounded on the front door. It was a neighbor, a quiet silver-haired wid-ower who resided with his three widowed daughters on the next block, carrying what looked to be a large box of silverware. "Will you hide this for us?" he asked urgently, glancing nervously over his shoulder. "The Yankee soldiers will not molest you, but my daughters' husbands fought them, and they will tear our place apart."

Speechless with astonishment, Lizzie could only nod and hold out her arms for the box. William quickly carried it off to a safe hiding place in a closet, but he had not yet returned from the errand when another neighbor called, pushing a wheelbarrow full of valuables—silver candlesticks, a portrait of a venerable ancestor on horseback in Revolutionary War costume, hatboxes stuffed with papers, and jewelry cases tied shut with twine. He too begged her to keep his family's treasure safe from the Yankees, and this time she found her voice and promised him she would.

As the frantic day drew to a close, Lizzie observed young soldiers on horseback and on foot bidding hasty farewells to their friends and loved ones before they raced off to what could be their final battle. Some looked resolute, others pale and terrified, and one, a lad Lizzie had known since he was Annie's age, confessed that he dreaded to report but must obey his orders.

Lizzie walked with him back to his parents' home, hoping to persuade him to desert now that all seemed lost, but he said he would rather be shot by the Yankees for fulfilling his duty than by the Confederates for abandoning it. Lizzie would rather he not be shot at all, a sentiment she imagine he shared, but he was resolute, so she bade him a sad farewell and turned toward home.

Church Hill was in a frenzy, and from the sound of it the downtown was in an even more frantic state, so Lizzie was almost too distracted to notice the woman in the worn brown dress sitting on her front porch steps within a fenced yard, a plaid wool shawl wrapped tightly around her shoulders. Her gaze was fixed upon the west, her expression so fiercely melancholy that for a moment in the deepening twilight, Lizzie did not recognize her and almost passed by with nothing more than a polite nod. Then, suddenly, the mousy, pinched face and the brown hair thinning along the center part and pulled back tightly into a broad bun evoked a flash of memory, and she stopped short. "Why, Mrs. Lodge," she gasped. "You're still here."

Mrs. Lodge eyed her distastefully. "Of course I am. Where would I go?"

"I certainly wouldn't know," Lizzie managed to reply. "It seems that half the city has taken flight."

"Well, not us, and apparently not you either. How is your sister-in-law?"

"Mary?" Lizzie was again taken aback, and she wished she had not lingered. "She is as fine as she can be, I suppose, given the circumstances." She would leave it to Mrs. Lodge to puzzle out what that meant.

"She stopped coming to our sewing circle."

"Well—" Lizzie was struck by the utter ridiculousness of the exchange, chatting banalities as if the city weren't going mad with panic all around them. "You know how difficult it can be to keep up acquaintances after one moves away."

"They moved across town, not across the sea," Mrs. Lodge retorted, but then a disconsolate shadow came into her eyes. "I wonder how many friends I will never hear from again after this night."

Somehow, the irritating woman's melancholy touched Lizzie's heart. "They'll return," she said. "When the panic is over, they'll see there's nothing to fear and they'll come home."

"Nothing to fear?" Mrs. Lodge echoed.

"Of course not," said Lizzie. "It might not seem so at the moment, but this is a good day. The war will end now. The young men's lives will be saved."

"I have a son in the army outside Petersburg," she said flatly.

Something in her tone made Lizzie hesitate before she replied. "You must be very proud of him—and very worried for him. I am sorry, and I hope you see him soon. You must hope for his life. All that talk about fighting to the last man—it is simply that, just talk."

Mrs. Lodge fixed her with a cryptic stare. "Death would be better, anything would be better, than to fall under the tyrannical power of the United States government."

It was useless to talk to her. "Good night, Mrs. Lodge," Lizzie said gently, and turned away.

She was almost home when she heard swift footfalls and glanced up to see Louisa hurrying toward her. "Miss Lizzie, come quick," she cried. "They're going to set fire to the house!"

Lizzie went cold, but she froze only for the length of a heartbeat. As she gathered up her skirts and broke into a run, vivid memories flashed in her mind's eye: the threatening note from the White Caps, and the red-faced, irate man who had shaken his fist at her the night Union troops had been attacked in Baltimore. That fine house of yours can burn! he had shouted. She had almost forgotten him until the note had been slipped beneath her front door, with the scrawled skull and crossbones and the gleefully malicious warning, Your house is going at last. FIRE.

When they reached home, they slipped through the garden gate and entered the mansion unseen from the rear piazza. "Where are Mother and the girls?" Lizzie asked Louisa as they hurried from room to hall to foyer.

"In the library with Judy and Hannah and the others."

But not all the servants were hiding inside, Lizzie realized when she tore open the front door and strode out onto the portico. William, Peter, and even the aged Nelson stood there, feet planted firmly, hefting shovels and axes and her father's ancient flintlock, which was usually displayed on the mantel above the library fireplace. They glared with firm resolve and defiance at a small cluster of men milling about on the sidewalk on the other side of the fence. Lizzie had expected a mob hundreds strong brandishing torches and pitchforks, not a handful of disgruntled fools, and relief sent courage surging through her.

"We don't want any trouble," Lizzie called to them sharply. "Leave now and I'll forget you were here."

A chorus of boos and hisses greeted her words. "If Richmond falls, you're going down with it," a man in a rumpled, threadbare suit snarled, his face distorted by rage.

"You're a goddamn abolitionist Yankee," another shouted, balancing on crutches, his trouser cuffed at the knee where his right leg had been amputated.

"How dare you?" Lizzie exclaimed. "I'm a proud Virginian. I was born in this city. How many of you can say the same?"

"Light up the place, boys," cried another, and a match flared, and a torch was kindled.

"Don't be fools," Lizzie snapped. "If my house burns, yours will follow. I know who you are," she declared, thrusting a finger toward a man on the right. "Mr. McKinney, the shoemaker. And you, Mr. Fannin, you live above your grocery on Main Street." Defiant, glaring, she leveled her gaze upon each man in turn. "You are all known to me. If I am what you think I am, do you really believe you could destroy my home and not suffer the consequences, with General Grant about to take the city? And if I am **not** what you say, may God strike you down for burning innocent women and children out of their home. Shame on you!"

The man with the torch halted, and a few of his companions exchanged wary glances.

"Leave now," Lizzie ordered firmly. "Go home. Protect your families and your property. Leave the judgment of my actions to history and to God."

After a long moment that crackled with tension, one by one, the men drifted away. When the last of them had disappeared into the traffic of frantic, frightened citizens hurrying to and fro, Lizzie's knees weakened beneath her and she would have crumpled had not Louisa steadied her. "Thank you, all of you," she breathed, forcing herself to stand.

"This is our home too, Miss Lizzie," said William. "You've said so enough. No one's

burning us out, not after all we've suffered, not when we've almost reached the
end."

Had they? Lizzie wondered. They had
struggled so long it was almost unfathomable that deliverance could finally be at
hand. It was almost impossible to believe
that there would ever come a time when
they could lay down their burdens and
rest.

While the men arranged to stand watch
from the rooftops in shifts throughout the
night, the women anxiously packed valuables and food, only what they could carry,
and left them in bundles by the front door
to snatch up quickly were they obliged to
flee. Then Lizzie put her nieces to bed,
heard their prayers while artillery rumbled
in the distance, and kissed them good
night. Mother and most of the servants
went off to bed soon thereafter, including
William, who planned to relieve Peter on
the rooftop at two o'clock, but the bursting
shells rending the night air and lighting
up the darkness kept Lizzie and Louisa
awake, pensive and watchful lest the
vengeful men or an even worse threat return.

They were sitting in the library chatting wistfully about their plans after the war— Louisa dreamed of opening a dressmaker's shop, while Lizzie longed to visit Anna and her family in Philadelphia, followed by a sojourn in Washington City—when not long after midnight, the front bell rang. Wondering why William had not raised the alarm, the women steeled themselves and hurried to the foyer. When Lizzie opened the door, she was shocked when three thin, filthy, shabbily clad men tumbled inside.

Dumbfounded, Lizzie recognized the tallest of the three. "Why, Mr. Lohmann," she exclaimed.

"Miss Van Lew," he greeted her, winded and weak but drawing himself up proudly. "Allow me to introduce my companions, Mr. John Hancock and Mr. William White, late of Castle Thunder."

"Oh, my goodness. Come in, come in," Lizzie urged as Louisa shut the door behind them. While Louisa raced off to the kitchen to find them something to eat, Lizzie led them to the back room she and her mother had prepared more than a year before in expectation of the mass breakout from Libby Prison. After seeing to their comfort and confirming with William at his lookout post that the men had not been followed, she attended them while they ate and explained how they had made their escape. As the government was evacuating, the authorities had rounded up the Union prisoners and marched them across Mayo's Bridge to the southern shore, determined to keep them out of reach of the advancing Union army. In the chaos, some of the men had managed to slip away from their captors, and under the cover of darkness Mr. Lohmann had led his companions to Lizzie's front door.

An hour later, just as the men had settled down to sleep, exhausted but well fed for the first time in months, a soft rapping came upon the front door—another fugitive from Castle Thunder, this time a woman of Isle of Wight County in West Virginia named Mary Pitt, who had been imprisoned for spying since late October. Lizzie sent Louisa on to bed and tended to the woman herself, who was emaciated and covered in bruises and wept silently from relief as Lizzie, angered and horrified by her condition, fed her and washed her face and hands and helped her into a clean nightgown and bed. She could not think of Mary Pitt without imagining the fate that she herself had perhaps only narrowly escaped.

Lizzie could not sleep from anger and worry and excitement, so she went to the library and hastily wrote an account of all that had transpired that day, but whether it was the beginning of a dispatch or an entry for her occasional journal, only time would reveal.

She must have dozed off in her chair, for hours later, she was startled awake by an enormous explosion that shook the house. The smell of smoke permeated the room.

It was not yet dawn. That much she understood through the thick fog of fatigue and fright muddling her thoughts as she pulled herself to her feet and stumbled into the hall. The odor of burning hung faintly in the air, but in the foyer she saw no smoke, and as her disorientation faded, she realized that the smell dissipated as she moved away from the open windows.

She heard footsteps behind her and

whirled about. "William," she gasped. "Is it fire?"

"Yes, Miss Lizzie," he said, "but it's not the house. It's the city."

"The Yankees have done this?"

"No, the rebels. Mr. Davis left by train at about eleven o'clock last night, but he gave orders to set fire to the railroad bridges to cut off pursuit, and to the warehouses full of cotton and tobacco so the Yankees couldn't have them." William shook his head, his expression drawn and apprehensive. "The wind from the south has been picking up, and the fire's spreading."

Lizzie gathered up her skirts and raced upstairs and out to the roof, where she discovered Annie and little Eliza staring at the churning black smoke and red flames in the distance below, Eliza with her mouth agape in stunned horror. "Girls," Lizzie cried. "What are you doing up here alone? It's dangerous."

"I'm holding Sister's hand," Annie pointed out. "I wouldn't let her fall."

"Will the fire burn our house too?" Eliza asked plaintively.

"No," came Lizzie's firm, immediate reply, but then she looked again and was relieved to see that her instinctive reassurances appeared to be true. The wind seemed to be carrying the flames toward the Capitol, away from Church Hill. But it was a dreadful sight to behold nonetheless— black smoke billowing, tongues of fire devouring, ruins of once-proud structures crumbling. A huge explosion sent a fireball curling into the sky and shook the house; instinctively she gasped and clutched the girls to herself—the fire had engulfed an armory, setting off all the ordnance within. In the early morning light, the railroad bridges over the James were clearly visible as outlines of red flame against the black water below. Strangely, Mayo's Bridge seemed undamaged, but as Lizzie strained her eyes to see, she thought she saw wagons and men on foot racing to Manchester on the opposite shore, and flickering lights at the terminus that could have been torches, ready to set it ablaze after the last fleeing rebel crossed.

Suddenly she realized that aside from the distant roar of the flames and the occasional explosion as heat and fire set off stored ammunition, all was silent. Richmond was burning, but the alarm had not been sounded. Why had the authorities not rung the tocsin?

Lizzie stood motionless and scarcely breathing, her gaze locked in horror upon the conflagration, which threatened to engulf the entire business district. Her heart ached for anyone in the path of the dreadful, hungry flames. She thought she glimpsed small figures darting about, but only a few seemed to be fighting the fire, while the others—looters, she realized with a chill. Law and order had apparently fled with the Confederate government.

"Annie, take your sister inside," Lizzie instructed. "Hannah must wonder what's become of you. She's probably searching everywhere. Find her, then wash up, get dressed, and go down to breakfast—and don't come up here again without an adult."

"Yes, Aunt Lizzie," Annie replied obediently, and with Lizzie's help the girls climbed back into the house. Lizzie meant to follow immediately after, but she could not tear herself away from the nightmare scene unfolding in the distance below. Suddenly she heard a shout, and when she spun to face it, she spotted a man clad in a prison officer's uniform sprinting for the Van Lew mansion as if death pursued him.

Lizzie knew at once who the frantic runner was. "Lieutenant Ross," she breathed, and whirled about, and scrambled back in through the window. By the time she reached the foyer, William had let him in, and he stood with his back to the door bent over and gasping, his hands on his knees.

"Miss Van Lew," he said in a strangled voice. "I beg you to hide me. The prisoners—they're free, and they all want my head. They don't understand." He coughed, fighting for breath. "I'm a dead man."

"No, indeed you're not," she vowed, hurrying to his side. "You're safe with us. You'll live to hear their thanks once they know all you've done."

His fear of reprisals was so great that she led him upstairs to the secret attic chamber rather than to the back room, where the other men still lay abed. There he told her what he knew of the chaos outside. The explosion that had woken her before daybreak was the CSS **Virginia**, the Confederate flagship, destroyed along with the rest of the ironclads while their crews escaped upstream in wooden gun-boats. The fire had begun at dawn when the provost marshal, reluctantly obeying orders, set the torch to Shockoe and Van Gronin's warehouses, and then to the rail-road bridges. No one had thought that the wind might rise, or that the liquor the Con-federate government had ordered dumped into the gutters would fuel the flames. The looting had gone on all night, ignited when the officials opened the commissary ware-houses rather than leave the provisions to the Yankees. When the starving citizens pushed their way in and discovered how much flour and bacon had been locked away, their fury erupted, and after plun-dering the commissary the crowd turned upon private shops, snatching up shoes, clothes, hats, candy, whatever they could lay hands upon.

Lieutenant Ross asked for paper, pen, and ink so he could write letters to his fam-ily, and after fetching them for him, Lizzie returned downstairs to find her nieces chatting happily with Mr. Lohmann and his companions in the back room. Miss Pitt had walked thirty-two miles the previous day, first in the forced march from Castle

Thunder and then as she followed a circuitous route to her sanctuary, so Lizzie did not wake her for breakfast but set a tray outside her chamber door instead. The rest of the household she called to the table, but they had just sat down when they heard a familiar tune piping merrily outside.

"'Yankee Doodle,'" Annie cried, bounding out of her chair and racing to the window. She glanced outside but, dissatisfied with the view, she ran from the room, little Eliza on her heels. Lizzie and her mother rose to follow them outside, and when they caught up with the girls at the bottom of the garden, in the distance below they saw soldiers in Union blue marching up Main Street.

Overjoyed, they cried out and embraced one another, and tears of happiness filled Lizzie's eyes, and the children danced and twirled and cheered. Then Lizzie realized that the streets of Church Hill were empty, and that the smell of smoke hung thickly in the air from fires burning out of control not far away, and that any neighbors observing them from their windows were likely seething with anger and hatred. Richmond had fallen, but the war was not over.

"Let's go inside," she said, taking Mother's arm and herding the girls back to the piazza.

They returned to the dining room to share the good news with their guests. Lizzie ate quickly, finishing well before the others, and then she begged their pardon and excused herself. Her work was not yet finished.

The presence of Union soldiers in the city streets reassured her that it was safe to go out, probably, so she tied on a bonnet, snatched up a basket, and set off on foot toward the War Department. Most Confederate offices had packed up their important files before the evacuation, but in their haste, they couldn't have taken everything of value. Lizzie was determined to gather whatever useful information or evidence she could from what had been left behind before fire or frantic Confederate clerks destroyed the documents.

Lizzie strode as quickly as she could, a handkerchief to her nose and mouth to ward off the thick, drifting smoke. The streets were quiet and empty compared to the frantic, frightened mayhem of the night before, but as she drew closer to the Capitol, she saw more riders in Union blue. She wanted to clap her hands and cheer, and run to them and thank them and offer them bouquets of daffodils from her garden, but she had no time.

Then she came upon Capitol Square and stopped short in amazement: Union soldiers were marching on Governor Street, cheered on by throngs of joyful, cheering, elated civilians, most of them people of color, who waved handkerchiefs and sang and offered the soldiers fruit and flowers as they passed, celebrating as if the day of Jubilee had come. Lizzie nearly sobbed with relief and happiness when she looked up and beheld the Stars and Stripes flying in the smoky air above the Capitol once more. As she made her way through the crowded streets and sidewalks, she observed Union officers organizing every able-bodied man regardless of color to go and fight the fire. Then, through a break in the milling crowd, Lizzie spotted hundreds of people—men, women, and children, rich and poor—huddled on the fresh spring grass of the Capitol Square, some with nothing but the clothes on their backs, others with hastily packed bundles on the ground beside them, their soot-streaked faces turned dully toward the marching Yankees or deliberately turned away. With a pang of sympathy, Lizzie hurried on.

When she reached the War Department, she expected to encounter resistance, but there were no guards, no scrambling clerks, no Union soldiers seeking stray Confederate officials to arrest. The offices were in a state of disarray that spoke of fear and haste—lamps broken, desk drawers open, papers scattered, chairs overturned as if their last occupants had fled in alarm. Ankle deep in documents, Lizzie gathered her skirts in one hand and began sorting through the pages, discarding most but placing a few pieces of particular interest into her basket.

She had been rummaging through the detritus of the fallen government for nearly an hour when she heard the quick strike of boot heels in the hall outside, the sound of several men approaching at a quick, deliberate pace. Her heart jumped, but she kept at her work, not even glancing up when the footsteps fell silent just outside the open doorway.

"Pardon me, Miss?" a baritone voice spoke.

She looked up and discovered a Union major with a blond Vandyke and flowing mustaches watching her expectantly, flanked by two lieutenants. "Yes?" she replied, straightening.

"Are you Miss Elizabeth Van Lew?"

"Why, yes," she replied, surprised. "I am Miss Van Lew."

The major smiled. "General Grant sends his compliments and his sincere thanks."

The military guard had looked for her at home first, but Mother had told them where she had gone, and after leaving two of their party to guard the residence, they had hurried off to find her. Although General Grant had not entered the city, he had been so concerned for her safety that he had sent an aide with a guard detachment to protect her, her family, and her property. They were under strict orders to make certain that she wanted for nothing.

When Lizzie finished searching the abandoned files in the War Department, the officers escorted her home, where she found an armed guard posted around the mansion. By two o'clock, the valiant Union soldiers and civilian volunteers had subdued the fire, although the ruins still smoldered and patrols remained alert for new outbreaks.

The destruction was staggering—more than fifty-five blocks of homes and businesses. Gone were all the banks; the Columbian and the American hotels; the offices of the **Dispatch**, the **Enquirer**, and the **Examiner**; the Henrico County Court House, the General Court of Virginia, and the irreplaceable records they had contained; the arsenal and the laboratory; the Gallego and Shockoe mills, once the largest flour mills in the world and the pride of Richmond; bridges and depots; pharmacies and groceries; shops and warehouses and countless saloons. More than nine hundred in all had burned, and the count rose while the rubble smoked and flames flared up amid the stark brick shells of what once had been. Wreckage clogged the streets, and when she toured the scorched downtown later, Lizzie became disoriented, unable to distinguish one block from another without familiar landmarks to guide her. But the fire had destroyed something else, something intangible and far more precious to the Confederacy—the goodwill of the people. Everywhere Lizzie heard dark mutterings and curses for Mr. Davis and his government, who had fled and left his loyal citizens to the mercy of the Yankee invaders and had nearly brought down the entire city upon them. General Lee was as admired, respected, and fervently prayed for as ever, but not so for the fugitive president.

The acrid, smoky stench of the conflagration still hung heavily in the air the next morning when Lizzie woke to discover new guards at their posts around her home. Lizzie asked Caroline to send out breakfast to them, and although their larder was nearly empty, they set out the best of what remained for their guests, four erstwhile prisoners and one nervous prison guard. Miss Pitt and Lieutenant Ross had emerged from their chambers, and everyone was in good spirits, recovering their strength and making eager plans for their first days of liberty.

All that morning and into the afternoon,

prominent Union officers called at the Church Hill mansion to thank Lizzie for her loyalty and service. She had toiled so long under suspicion and animosity that it was strange to hear her labors praised, and unsettling to discover that her name was known to important men unknown to herself. "Will General Grant enter the city soon?" she inquired of each visitor, but all replied that they did not know but thought it unlikely. The war had ended for Richmond, but General Grant was still pursuing General Lee, and it was General Godfrey Weitzel who commanded the occupying forces. Several of the officers gallantly offered to introduce her to General Weitzel, but she politely demurred, making the excuse that she wouldn't dream of imposing upon him when he was busy subduing the rebels. In truth, she wanted to meet General Grant, and nothing and no one else would do.

Her conviction lasted until early afternoon, when William came to her in the foyer where she was graciously bidding farewell to a captain. As soon as the door closed behind the departing visitor, William blurted, "The president is in Richmond."

"He came back?" Lizzie exclaimed. "Is he mad? He'd better be careful. Mr. Davis is not so popular with the people as he once was, and General Weitzel has turned his home into his headquarters."

"Not Mr. Davis," said William excitedly, his usual reserve falling away. "President Lincoln."

For a moment Lizzie could only stare at him. "President Lincoln is in Richmond?"

William nodded eagerly. "Peter saw him step off a barge at Rocketts Wharf."

"It cannot be true," she said, but nevertheless, she snatched up her shawl and pulled open the door. "Mother, I'm going to see the president," she shouted over her shoulder in a very unladylike fashion. As she stepped out onto the portico, she turned back to William. "Well? Aren't you coming?"

He nodded and begged a moment to fetch his brother and whoever else might want to accompany them. A few moments later, Lizzie, William, Peter, Louisa, and Caroline were hurrying off toward the Capitol, where they were certain Mr. Lincoln would go. The sounds of cheering drew them toward Cary Street, where they managed to intercept the president's procession at Twenty-Third Street. The tall, gaunt man in the stovepipe hat could not be mistaken for anyone but President Abraham Lincoln, not only because he stood head and shoulders above his escorts, but because the humility, kindness, and wisdom in a face marked by hard toil and care set him apart from other men. At his side was a proud boy of about twelve years of age who surely was his young son, Tad.

All around them, elated men and women of color, and a good number of whites too, cheered and wept for joy and flung their hats in the air. As she and her companions hurried closer, Lizzie heard shouts of "Thank you, Jesus," and "God bless you, Mr. President!" from the rapidly swelling throng. Suddenly she felt a surge of uneasiness as she glimpsed a few white faces in the crowd that were glaring and twisted and ugly with hatred, but her fear was forgotten a moment later when an elderly colored man standing quietly on the sidewalk doffed his hat to the president and solemnly bowed. Mr. Lincoln paused and silently returned the gesture—and the crowd roared its approval. As the impromptu procession moved on, a young girl, her hair in two black braids, darted from the crowd, kissed his hand and said, "God bless you, only friend of the South!" Looking quite overcome, the president smiled and thanked her kindly, and watched after her as she hurried back to her mother, beaming.

He strode onward, surrounded by his anxious and wary escort of Union sailors who tried to prevent the jubilant people from crowding too close. They had almost reached Fifteenth Street when a group of colored workmen digging with spades in the wreckage shouted, "Glory, hallelujah!" at his approach and fell to their knees to kiss his feet.

"Please don't kneel to me," President Lincoln urged them, looking pained and embarrassed, and his face seemed to bear all the grief of the nation. "You must kneel only to God and thank Him for your freedom."

The crowd cheered and pressed forward, but at that moment, a cavalry squad galloped up, encircled the president and his entourage, and escorted them the rest of the way to the Executive Mansion.

Following along behind, Lizzie and her companions joined their voices to the rest of the crowd, cheering and singing and laughing for joy. She glimpsed some pale faces glaring sullenly down upon the scene from their windows, and other pale hands yanking curtains shut rather than glimpse a single joyful former slave welcoming the Great Emancipator to Richmond. Even so, Lizzie was certain that other rebels whose ardor had cooled after the Confederates had set fire to the city were observing Mr. Lincoln, hearing his words of benevolence and reconciliation, and thinking that this man could not possibly be the Yankee villain who had been represented to them as a monster for so many years.

When the slow procession reached the former residence of the Confederate president, tears flowed freely down Lizzie's cheeks as she watched President Lincoln remove his hat, bow respectfully to the people as if to acknowledge his debt to the loyal Unionists of Richmond, and disappear within the Gray House.

She should have preferred to see the president of the United States entering the subjugated capital of rebeldom with an escort and fanfare more befitting his high station—but no, for that was the way of a conqueror who had come to exult over a brave but fallen enemy. It was far better that he had come instead as a peace-maker, his hand extended in kindness and brotherhood to all who desired to take it.

Chapter Twenty-three

 APRIL 1875

TEN YEARS have passed since the evacuation of Richmond, and in that decade what mighty changes have taken place in this city! Look around you, citizens of Richmond, and contemplate the results of your own energy and industry, and then consider what your city will be, if you continue to push it ahead at the same rapid rate, in ten years more. If you will reflect upon it, this brief text is as good as a sermon.

"How typically self-congratulatory and unhelpful," said Lizzie, sighing as she folded the **Enquirer** and slid it across the breakfast table to her nineteen-year-old niece, Annie. "Not a word of honest reflection about the problems confronting this city—this entire nation, for that matter—and the vast amount of work remaining until true justice is achieved for all men and women of all races."

"Talking to the newspaper again, dear?" Mother inquired, sipping her coffee.

Lizzie smiled, but she felt a pang of worry and a sense of impending loss. Mother's health and vigor had declined precipitously in recent months, but thankfully, her sense of humor was as deft as ever. "No, indeed. I was addressing you and Annie and little Eliza. The newspaper never replies."

"I'll always be 'little Eliza' at home," lamented the seventeen-year-old.

"Probably," agreed Mother, "unless someday you have a daughter of your own and name **her** Eliza."

"They mention the fall of Richmond here too," said Annie, touching a page of the newspaper. "In the 'Briefs' section. 'Yesterday was the anniversary of the evacuation of Richmond by the Confederate troops.'"

"Aptly named," remarked Mother. "That was brief indeed. I wonder, do two short mentions of the occasion equal one lengthy, thoughtful discussion?"

"Absolutely not," said Lizzie. "The papers do us all a disservice. Tell me, Eliza, what do you remember of that day?"

Eliza smiled. "I remember watching the flames from the rooftop until you scolded us and sent us inside, and I remember that Annie and I begged you to take us out to meet the Yankees, and that you refused."

"The city was on fire and we were still at war," protested Lizzie. "What responsible auntie would have dragged two young children out into the streets in such circumstances? Anyway, you met plenty of Union soldiers in the days that followed."

Laughing, Eliza agreed that she had, that indeed, they all had.

The passing of the years had not faded Lizzie's vivid recollections of that tumultuous era. The burning of Richmond, the arrival of Union troops, the astonishing visit by Mr. Lincoln while the ruins yet smoldered—and then, not five days later,

General Lee's surrender at Appomattox and his quiet, weary, subdued return to his residence at 707 East Franklin Street. The stunned and demoralized populace had welcomed him respectfully, as did many men in Union blue who counted themselves among his admirers although they had been mortal enemies only days before.

The surrender at Appomattox had fallen on Palm Sunday. On Good Friday, John Wilkes Booth, once a favorite performer on the Richmond stage, had crept into the State Box at Ford's Theatre in Washington City, where President Abraham Lincoln was enjoying a performance of **Our American Cousin** with his wife and a younger couple, and shot him in the head behind his left ear. While Mrs. Lincoln screamed, Mr. Booth leapt over the railing of the box to the stage below, raised the bloody knife above his head, and shouted, "**Sic semper tyrannis!**" Thus always to tyrants—the motto of the Commonwealth of Virginia.

That night, Union regiments rushed from the city's outskirts into Richmond, doubling patrols and street guards. In the morning, Lizzie did not have long to wonder why: The front page of the **Whig**, bordered in black, announced the terrible news that Mr. Lincoln had been assassinated.

In the erstwhile Confederate capital, Union troops, who had revered President Lincoln, lashed out in grief and wrath upon every former rebel soldier they could find, pouncing upon them with the ferocity of wild beasts, beating them, driving them from the streets. They were certain the assassination was the work of a vast conspiracy and that a rebel uprising was at hand. General Grant too suspected a wider conspiracy, and from Washington City he ordered the arrests of Mayor Mayo, the entire Richmond City Council, every paroled Confederate officer in the city, and several other officials. In Richmond, Union general Ord was reluctant to obey, pointing out to his commander that if the revered General Lee were thrown into Libby Prison, the rebellion might erupt anew. General Grant relented, and before long the anguished Union soldiers' violent outburst too subsided. But the grief of the fragile nation newly plunged into mourning had only just begun.

Shaking off her mournful reverie, Lizzie sighed, rose from the table, and bade her nieces and mother good-bye. She had lingered over breakfast too long, and she would have to walk briskly if she did not want to be late for work.

As she made her way down Church Hill toward Capitol Square, her thoughts returned to the aftermath of the war—her brother John's return home from exile in April, Jefferson Davis's capture near Irwinville, Georgia, in May. Later that summer, when General Grant had toured Richmond for the first time since the end of the war, she had been honored when the general and his wife called on her at home. "My husband was most eager to meet you, as was I," Mrs. Grant had confided over tea in the parlor. "He insists that you provided him and his generals with the most valuable intelligence ever to come out of Richmond during the war."

Flattered, Lizzie had thanked her for her kind words, to which General Grant had added his own. "You rendered valuable service to the Union, and to me, at no small risk to yourself," he had told her somberly. "I will never forget that. You will always find a friend in me."

Deeply moved, Lizzie had thanked him and said it had been her great honor and duty, and as a loyal Union woman, she could not have done otherwise.

Soon after that visit, life had become increasingly difficult for Unionists in Richmond. Although many former members of Lizzie's intelligence network had been appointed to important federal, state, and municipal offices, resentment against loyalists flourished in the corners and shadows of the city. Indeed, throughout the South, Confederate defiance had soared as Mr. Lincoln's successor, President Andrew Johnson, had demonstrated leniency toward former rebels, indifference for Southern Unionists, and absolute contempt for freedmen. In Richmond, harsh Black Codes were enacted, requiring people of color to carry passes or be arrested for vagrancy, despite protests that such laws hearkened back to slavery. In October, conservatives had swept local elections and had immediately passed several compulsory labor laws giving white former slaveowners control over colored workers. Lizzie had joined Mr. Botts, Mr. Palmer, and other like-minded allies in denouncing the measures and condemning the persecution of Richmond's loyalists. Although she could not vote, Lizzie could make her opinions known, and she had joined in a vigorous letter-writing campaign to demand federal intervention.

Eventually Lizzie and her allies were heard. Their persistent complaints had shifted the mood in the United States Congress by casting doubt upon President Johnson's claim that the former Confederate states could be trusted to manage their affairs justly without federal involvement. In April and July of 1866, over Mr. Johnson's vetoes, the Congress had passed the Civil Rights Bill and the Freedmen's Bureau Bill, extending the protection of the law and the courts to former slaves.

It had been a remarkable triumph, but it had not improved daily life in Richmond for Lizzie and her compatriots, as their neighbors' unwavering hostility took its toll upon their peace of mind and their livelihoods. John's hardware store faltered, and since Lizzie and her mother had severely depleted their fortunes during the war, Lizzie searched with increasing desperation for some other means of support for her family.

The months of struggle stretched into years, but just as she reached the limits of her resources and endurance, Lizzie learned that General Grant had not forgotten her, and that he indeed was her friend.

Remembering his faithful generosity, Lizzie paused outside the old Custom House, the stately edifice facing Main Street between Tenth and Eleventh. It was thanks to Mr. Grant's patronage that she had come there that day, and almost every day for the past six years. She marveled to think that ten years before, in the midst of war, Mr. Davis had kept his presidential offices on the third floor of the historic building—and now, in peacetime, Lizzie kept her offices on the first.

She entered the post office to find the morning shift of employees already busily engaged in their tasks. "Good morning, Postmaster," one of her newest clerks greeted her.

"Good morning, George," she replied, and smiling all around, added, "Good morning, everyone. Beautiful day, isn't it?" Without interrupting their work, they returned her smile and agreed that it was, indeed, a lovely spring day in Richmond.

After the war, Lizzie had needed employment, and like many other loyalists and veterans, she had petitioned the federal government to help her obtain a position in acknowledgment of the sacrifices she had made on behalf of the Union. Only a trickle of reimbursement for her expenses had followed, and the Van Lews' circumstances had become alarmingly straitened leading up to the presidential elections of 1868. Lizzie was elated when Ulysses S. Grant won the presidency, her only regret being that she had not been permitted to vote for him.

She soon had more reason to rejoice: Fifteen days after his inauguration, President Grant appointed Miss Elizabeth Van Lew the new postmaster of Richmond.

A postmastership was without question one of the most coveted appointments in the federal government. Not only did it provide an excellent salary, but it also bestowed considerable political clout upon the fortunate appointee. Postmasters hired clerks and carriers, controlled the distribution of political information, and possessed the same franking privileges congressmen enjoyed—and therefore could dispense patronage generously to one's own benefit.

And when it came to her, Lizzie had dispensed it—firmly, often, and unapologetically—to right grievous wrongs in her beloved city.

She had begun by hiring loyalists and men of color as carriers and clerks, and women too as clerks. She counted her dear friend Eliza Carrington and her former butler William Roane as two of her most productive employees, and her brother John had worked at the post office until he and Augusta, whom he had married after his troubled wife Mary passed away, had moved to a pretty farm in Louisa Court House. Compelled by her usual tireless determination, Lizzie had expanded and modernized the Richmond post office— implementing citywide letter deliveries, enlarging the facilities for money orders and registered letters, and installing convenient public mailboxes on the city's main thoroughfares. In 1871, she published a post office manual that soon became known as the best and most comprehensive in print. In the first two years of her tenure alone, she had increased the number of letters delivered in the city from about fourteen thousand to eighty-three thousand each month.

She was enormously proud of her accomplishments, not only because a more efficient, productive postal service benefited the entire community, but also because her hiring practices had shattered traditional restrictions of race and sex. Throughout her tenure, she had been an excellent postmaster, and she was proud to know that no one could honestly claim that a man would have done better.

Along the way, and not surprisingly, she had made enemies among those who coveted her power and position. They tried to discredit her, and they argued that as a woman and a radical she could not be trusted with such authority, but although they obliged Lizzie to spend far too much time and energy defending herself, they did not triumph. When President Grant won a second term in office, he extended her term as well.

President Grant was her most powerful friend, but she found support in other quarters too. Even as many white citizens of Richmond shunned or openly despised her, the people of the North who knew of her wartime activities became her champions, rallying to her cause when her political enemies in the South tried to tear her down, and soliciting funds for her support when her financial circumstances were at their most desperate. She also found strength and consolation in knowing that the colored community regarded her as a champion for equal rights, and she was proud that they considered her a friend in need, which she vowed she would be until the end of her days.

For while the war to abolish slavery had ended ten years before, the struggle for freedom and equality continued. Although the triumph of the Union had wrought wonderful deliverance for a people held in bondage, Lizzie realized that the nation would know no lasting peace until it truly did enjoy a new birth of freedom, and became at last a government of **all** the people, by **all** the people, and for **all** the people—men and women, black and white, all of them as equal before the law as they were in the sight of God.

To see that dream fulfilled, in the words of the martyred president she had helped to save the Union, she would gladly give the last full measure of her devotion.

AUTHOR'S NOTE

The Spymistress is a work of fiction inspired by history. Some events and people from Elizabeth Van Lew's wartime years, though noted in the historical record, have been omitted from this book for the sake of the narrative. While many characters appearing in this novel are based upon historical figures, in some cases two or more individuals have been combined to form a single composite character.

Readers familiar with Elizabeth Van Lew may wonder why I do not refer to her as "Crazy Bet," as the vast majority of authors who have written about her have done, or why I have not portrayed her feigning mental impairment to divert suspicion. I made this choice because nothing in the historical record during the

Civil War and its aftermath supports this characterization—not her wartime "occasional journal," nor the memoirs of the Union soldiers she assisted, nor even the writings of her numerous critics. The concept that Elizabeth Van Lew succeeded in her espionage work because of her ability to disarm her enemies by acting daft first appeared in a **Harper's Monthly Magazine** article published in 1911, written eleven years after her death by someone who had never met her. The author was heavily influenced by a man who had met Elizabeth Van Lew after Reconstruction, when she was in her late sixties and age, poverty, political troubles, personal heartbreak, and isolation had taken their toll. For an excellent analysis of this matter, please see "The Myth of 'Crazy Bet'" in Elizabeth R. Varon's book **Southern Lady, Yankee Spy: The True Story of Elizabeth Van Lew, a Union Agent in the Heart of the Confederacy** (New York: Oxford University Press, 2003).

In the years that followed the final scene of **The Spymistress**, Elizabeth Van Lew successfully fought off local attempts to replace her and continued as postmaster of Richmond throughout President Grant's administration. In 1877, Grant's successor, Rutherford B. Hayes, bowed to pressure from conservative Republicans and Democrats and appointed a man considered more politically moderate in her place, making Van Lew one of the hundreds of progressive Southern Republicans who lost their appointments during Hayes's first five months in office. A writer for the Richmond **Whig** could barely contain his glee when he reported that the news of "the downfall of the masculine VAN LEW [had] spread like wild-fire from one end of the city to the other" and had put the citizens in an "unusual good humor," but even the **Whig** soon conceded that "Miss Van Lew accepts her removal with quiet and becoming dignity."

For years thereafter, Van Lew petitioned the government to reinstate her, but although she was eventually given a clerkship in Washington, DC, when the working conditions proved demoralizing, she resigned and returned to Richmond.

Though she never again held the influence she had possessed as postmaster, she continued to work diligently on behalf of progressive Republican causes, women's suffrage, and civil rights for African-Americans, driving a wedge ever more deeply between herself and most of Richmond society.

In the early morning hours of September 25, 1900, Elizabeth Van Lew died at home in the Church Hill mansion, impoverished and ostracized at the age of eighty-one. She was laid to rest in Richmond's Shockoe Cemetery near the graves of her mother and father, her casket interred vertically rather than horizontally because the family plot lacked sufficient room.

Determined that Van Lew's grave would be marked by a memorial worthy of her courage, loyalty, and wartime contributions to the Union, her longtime admirers in Boston arranged for a boulder from the grounds of the Massachusetts State House to be shipped to Richmond to serve as her headstone. Upon it, a bronze tablet is inscribed:

ELIZABETH L. VAN LEW

1818–1900

SHE RISKED EVERYTHING THAT IS DEAR TO MAN—FRIENDS—FORTUNE—COMFORT—HEALTH—LIFE ITSELF—ALL FOR THE ONE ABSORBING DESIRE OF HER HEART—THAT SLAVERY MIGHT BE ABOLISHED AND THE UNION PRESERVED. THIS BOULDER FROM THE CAPITOL HILL IN BOSTON IS A TRIBUTE FROM MASSACHUSETTS FRIENDS

In 1993, in recognition of her daring espionage work on behalf of the United States, Elizabeth Van Lew was inducted into the Military Intelligence Hall of Fame, established by the Military Intelligence Corps of the United States Army to honor soldiers and civilians who made exceptional contributions to the profession of military intelligence.

ACKNOWLEDGMENTS

I offer my sincere thanks to Denise Roy, Maria Massie, Liza Cassity, Christine Ball, Brian Tart, Kate Napolitano, and the outstanding sales teams at Dutton and Plume for their support of my work and their contributions to **The Spymistress**.

I am very grateful for the people who generously assisted me during the research and writing of this novel. Geraldine Neidenbach, Marty Chiaverini, and Brian Grover were my first readers, and their comments and questions were, as always, insightful and helpful. I appreciate the support and encouragement of Heather Neidenbach, Nic Neidenbach, and Marlene and Len Chiaverini. Christina Hillgrove of the Museum of the Confederacy and Doug Crenshaw of the American Civil War Center at Historic Tredegar provided me with tours and graciously responded to my many questions, and Mike D. Gorman's outstanding website on Civil War Richmond proved invaluable throughout. Many thanks to you all.

I am fortunate indeed to live near the Wisconsin Historical Society, whose librarians, staff, and excellent archives I have come to rely upon in my work. Of the many resources I consulted, the following proved especially instructive: George W. Bagby, **Selections from the Miscellaneous Writings of Dr. George W. Bagby**, Volume 1 (Richmond, VA: Whittet & Shepperson, 1884); John Minor Botts, **The Great Rebellion: Its Secret History, Rise, Progress, and Disastrous Failure** (New York: Harper & Brothers, 1866); Sallie A. Brock, **Richmond During the War: Four Years of Personal Observation** (New York: G. W. Carleton & Co., 1867); Benjamin F. Butler, **Private and Official Correspondence of General Benjamin F. Butler** (Norwood, MA: The Plimpton Press, 1917); Joan E. Cashin, **First Lady of the Confederacy: Varina Davis's Civil War** (Cambridge, MA: Belknap Press of Harvard

University Press, 2006); Federico Fernandez Cavada, **Libby Life: Experiences of a Prisoner of War in Richmond, Va., 1863-64** (Philadelphia: King & Baird, 1864); Ruth Ann Coski, **The White House of the Confederacy: A Pictorial Tour** (Richmond, VA: The Museum of the Confederacy, 2012); Alfred Ely, **Journal of Alfred Ely, a Prisoner of War in Richmond** (New York: D. Appleton and Company, 1862); Ernest B. Furgurson, **Ashes of Glory: Richmond at War** (New York: Alfred A. Knopf, 1996); Nelson Lankford, **Richmond Burning: The Last Days of the Confederate Capital** (New York: Viking, 2002); David B. Parker, **A Chautauqua Boy in '61 and Afterward: Reminiscences by David B. Parker, Second Lieutenant, Seventy-Second New York, Detailed Superintendent of the Mails of the Army of the Potomac, United States Marshal, District of Virginia Chief Post Office Inspector** (Boston: Small, Maynard and Company, 1912); Allan Pinkerton, **The Spy of the Rebellion: Being a True History of the Spy System of the United States Army During the Late Rebellion** (New York: G. W. Carleton & Co., 1883); David

D. Ryan, ed., **A Yankee Spy in Richmond: The Civil War Diary of "Crazy Bet" Van Lew** (Mechanicsburg, PA: Stackpole Books, 1996); United States Sanitary Commission, **Narrative of Privations and Sufferings of United States Officers and Soldiers While Prisoners of War in the Hands of the Rebel Authorities** (Philadelphia: King & Baird, 1864); Elizabeth R. Varon, **Southern Lady, Yankee Spy: The True Story of Elizabeth Van Lew, a Union Agent in the Heart of the Confederacy** (New York: Oxford University Press, 2003); H. Donald Winkler, **Stealing Secrets: How a Few Daring Women Deceived Generals, Impacted Battles, and Altered the Course of the Civil War** (Naperville, IL: Cumberland House, 2010); and C. Vann Woodward, ed., **Mary Chesnut's Civil War** (New Haven and London: Yale University Press, 1981).

Most of all, I thank my husband, Marty, and my sons, Nicholas and Michael, for their enduring love, tireless support, and inspiring faith in me. You make everything worthwhile, and I could not have written this book without you.

ABOUT THE AUTHOR

Jennifer Chiaverini is the **New York Times** bestselling author of **Mrs. Lincoln's Dressmaker** and the Elm Creek Quilts series. A graduate of the University of Notre Dame and the University of Chicago, she lives with her husband and two sons in Madison, Wisconsin.